P
Safe in My Arms

"A smart and insightful page-turner, *Safe in My Arms* is a twisty mystery filled with keen observations about the impossibly high standards of motherhood and the critical importance of finding friends willing to accept you as the forgivably flawed person and parent you really are."
—Kimberly McCreight, *New York Times* bestselling author of *Reconstructing Amelia* and *A Good Marriage*

"We've read stories about the cutthroat world of high school and colleges, but in *Safe in My Arms*, Sara Shepard reminds us that things can get dark in academia way before that. This sharp, smart, and oh-so-twisty look at the sinister side of a privileged preschool is the kind of book that will have you staying up way too late—even if it's a school night."
—Rachel Hawkins, *New York Times* bestselling author of *The Wife Upstairs*

"Sara Shepard returns to the domestic suspense scene with a deep dive into the lives of three mothers at a fancy private preschool, all of them harboring dark secrets. Taut, smart, and twisted, *Safe in My Arms* is everything I love in a suspense novel, a whip-smart tale of just how far a mother will go to protect her child. All the stars!"
—Kimberly Belle, internationally bestselling author of *Stranger in the Lake*

"Set against an intriguing backdrop of ambition, privilege, and entitlement, *Safe in My Arms* explores how friendship, family, and loyalty help us persevere. Sara Shepard has crafted a twisty, compelling meditation on the long-buried secrets that haunt us, and the ways in which embracing those dark aspects of our pasts can ultimately set us free."
—E. G. Scott, internationally bestselling author of *In Case of Emergency*

"No one writes about secrets like Sara Shepard! *Safe in My Arms* is a whopping page-turner of a book, packed with lies, betrayals, and head-spinning twists. I'll never think about preschools the same way again."
—Samantha Downing, *USA Today* bestselling author of *My Lovely Wife* and *He Started It*

Praise for *Reputation*

"*Reputation* follows the goings-on in a university community after a hack lands everyone's private business squarely in the public eye. Like all of Shepard's work, it is an inarguable page-turner filled with murder, intrigue, and female characters who are somehow simultaneously easy to adore and loathe."
—Fortune.com

"*Reputation* has everything you've been waiting for: university gossip, Internet hackers, scandals, affairs, murder."
—Literary Hub

"An Agatha Christie for the twenty-first century, Shepard masterfully crafts a prestigious town rife with hidden temptation and sin. . . . From chapter to chapter, Shepard's plotting breathlessly careens between characters, with each cliff-hanger swiftly answered by another, ratcheting up the stakes until the killer is finally unmasked. A fast-paced, twisty-turny mystery perfect for a cozy weekend read."
—*Kirkus Reviews*

"Sara Shepard reaches delicious, vicious heights with *Reputation.* I felt like I was sucked into a video game, slipping into different skins in every chapter. It's the love child of *Dead to Me* and *Scream*, a creepy tale about modern technology and good old-fashioned human flaws. We're so lucky that Shepard is out there watching the way we live, seeing the best in us, and, oh yes, the cringe-inducing, often laugh-out-loud worst as well."
—Caroline Kepnes, author of *You, Hidden Bodies,* and *Providence*

"[Shepard is] a master at keeping you on your toes—and this novel is no exception. If you're looking for a new novel that draws you in and just won't let go, you've found it."

—*Marie Claire*, "The 27 Best Fiction Books by Women This Year"

"Shepard throws every cliché imaginable at the reader and then artfully massages them into a brilliant narrative told in the voices of the many women involved in the story who, having managed to make victims of one sort or another of themselves, all emerge victorious, each in her own fashion. . . . Everyone is hiding a closetful of secrets, which, when finally revealed, provide some excellent misdirection and a few OMG moments, until one final and shocking truth emerges. Fans of domestic suspense will devour this one."

—*Booklist* (starred review)

Also by Sara Shepard

YA

Pretty Little Liars Series

The Lying Game Series

The Perfectionists Series

The Amateurs Series

ADULT

The Visibles

Everything We Ever Wanted

The Heiresses

The Elizas

Reputation

Safe in My Arms

A NOVEL

Sara Shepard

DUTTON

DUTTON
An imprint of Penguin Random House LLC
penguinrandomhouse.com

LIBRARY OF CONGRESS CATALOGING-IN-PUBLICATION DATA
has been applied for.

ISBN 9781524746780 (paperback)
ISBN 9781524746797 (ebook)

Printed in the United States of America
1st Printing

BOOK DESIGN BY KATY RIEGEL

For Mothers

PART ONE

You lie on the hard, cold floor. You can't scream. Your head throbs in pain, and you think you might be bleeding. You can hear kids laughing not so far away, on the playground. You want to call out to them, but there's something wrong with your voice. You can't open your eyes. The pain is in your back, your jaw, your chest. Pain that doesn't make sense. This might be the end. It might be coming soon.

Why had you done it—any of it? Why hadn't you been happy to leave well enough alone? If only you could go back to the beginning. If only you could start over, change things, change yourself. This is what you think about as you lie there, helpless: your regrets.

But also that maybe, just maybe, you deserve this.

One

When they walked into the loft that first day, they were full of hope. It was fall again. The autumn after a tough year, the economic downturn sweeping through even the toniest of communities, including theirs. But now, things were starting to look up. It was the start of a new school year. New beginnings. Everyone was eager to connect, eager to be part of something bigger.

Even those who had things to hide.

The Silver Swans Nursery Academy was new to Lauren Smith, Andrea Vaughan, and Ronnie Stuckey, but they'd heard it was the best place to send one's young children in all of Raisin Beach, California, and they felt fortunate that there was a spot for their children this term. They were excited to attend the school's Welcome Breakfast, an event held every September on the very first day the kids were sent into the classrooms. The breakfast used to be a lavish affair, with a pyramid of donuts, piles of every fruit imaginable, and an ice sculpture of the school's mascot, an erudite, bespectacled owl sitting on a branch, ostensibly ready to teach the young Silver Swans students all he knew.

But this year was more tempered. There were bagels and a variety of spreads; there were grapes and pineapple and an assortment of juices; there was coffee, the tureens lined up, the paper cups ready, though also accompanied by a sign of a smiling cartoon Planet Earth declaring, *Love me! Travel mugs preferred!* There was not, however, a man in a chef's hat cooking omelets to order. Nor were there caterers circulating with bacon-Gruyère bites. It felt excessive to shower everyone with a gluttonous spread after so many had lost their jobs and so many businesses had gone bust.

After Lauren Smith shook sugar packets into her coffee, she came face-to-face with Piper Jovan, the school's director, who was making a point of greeting each parent. It was hard not to gape at even a dressed-down Piper. The woman's dark, thick hair spilled down her shoulders. Her eyes were ethereal blue, and her lips were plump, and she had a Marilyn Monroe beauty mark next to her mouth. And that body!

"Wow, the Grand Recession didn't hurt *you* any," Lauren blurted.

Piper blushed mock-bashfully, then looked Lauren up and down. "I don't think we know each other yet."

"Lauren. My son is Matthew? Seven months? My husband should be up in a minute. Well, I hope. He works on a TV show? *Ketchup*? We moved here last year." Lauren was babbling. She always did when she was nervous.

Then a young man standing just behind Piper tapped her arm and murmured. Lauren studied him closer. "Is this your son?" she asked Piper.

The guy—chubby-cheeked, dark hair neatly combed, wearing a fastidious black oxford buttoned up to his collar—barked with laughter. "I'm her *assistant*!"

"Oh. Sorry." Lauren's gaze bounced from him to Piper. "I'd heard you had a son, Piper, and I just thought . . . anyway, it's nice to meet you!" She smiled dumbly at the man. "What's your name?"

"Carson Dillard." He was still snickering. "And I'm twenty-*five*. Piper's son is thirteen. No amount of moisturizer is *that* good."

Lauren's guffaw came out like a honk. Piper just stared like Lauren had three heads. Lauren slunk off, her face blazing. They all would talk about this later, how Piper had the tendency to make you *slink away.*

"Oh, Lane!" Piper said loudly, turning to the next parent who'd arrived. Lane Wilder looked like the human version of a Labrador retriever. "Thanks for stopping by!"

Lane smiled sheepishly. "Oh. Yeah, thanks. I put Patricia on the kids." He was the kindergarten teacher downstairs. This was his first foray to the loft as a parent, and his girlfriend, Ronnie Stuckey, beamed at him with pride.

But Piper's smile flattened when she noticed Ronnie. Ronnie was taller than Piper, and thinner, and her face had perfect golden-ratio proportions. This made other women jealous, even women like Piper.

"Hi, I'm Ronnie!" Ronnie said brightly. Her accent was from . . . *somewhere.* Not Raisin Beach, that was for sure. "My daughter, Esme, she's in the fours? Lane and I are—"

"Partners." Lane reached for Ronnie's hand. "Piper, I'm so excited you're going to finally meet Esme's brave, wonderful mom."

Piper's gaze swept up Ronnie's body. While other mothers were going for the natural look this morning, Ronnie unapologetically had a smoky eye and glossy lips, and her face looked airbrushed. Piper also seemed utterly confounded by Ronnie's bag, which looked like an old-style western jacket with its long leather tassels and grommets and was emblazoned with a large *G* for *Gucci.* A trained eye might say it was a fake.

A pink tinge crept up Ronnie's neck. "I hope it's okay Esme is enrolled. Lane and I aren't married, I mean. But I saw on your website that partners' children can enjoy the staff benefits, and we filled out the application and were accepted—"

"Of course it's fine," Piper interrupted. "Our inclusion policy extends to all sorts of families. Parenthood doesn't fit into just one box."

"Oh." Ronnie looked relieved. "Okay, good."

"I like your earrings." Piper's assistant poked his head around Piper's frame. He pointed at the jagged metal sculptures that hung so low from Ronnie's earlobes that they nearly grazed her shoulders.

Ronnie grinned, touching her left lobe. "Thanks!" But as she walked away, her smile faded. "Did I do something wrong?" she whispered to her boyfriend. "That seemed weird."

"What? No!" Lane patted her hand. "Piper can be brisk sometimes, but seriously, she's great. You're going to love her."

Lauren, meanwhile, was still loitering by the coffee, listening to a pack of mothers nearby talking about how their ten-month-olds were talking in full sentences. Another mother in the group said she'd brought her toddler daughter to volunteer at the local food bank with her. "It's really enriching her spirit." A toddler *volunteering*?

When someone touched Lauren's arm, she jumped guiltily. "Sorry!" a voice said. "I just— What you said to the director's assistant back there, about being her son? I asked her the same thing."

Lauren turned to the blond woman speaking. She had a delicate nose, high cheekbones, and kind eyes that were a bright, shimmering blue.

"I'm Andrea," the woman said. She offered a hand with pink nails squared off at the ends.

Lauren introduced herself, too. Then she added, "Now, what were you saying about the assistant?"

They both eyed Carson Dillard. He was still standing subtly behind Piper with his hands folded at his waist like he was some kind of consigliere.

"I asked if he was her son, too," Andrea whispered. "Sometimes, my son stands behind me in just the same way. Like he's waiting to see what move I'm going to make before doing anything himself."

"And when you asked it, did they look at you like you were from another planet?"

"Well, they were looking at me like that *anyway*." Andrea gestured to her body with a shrug. "It's my first time out. I mean, not *out*, not out as *this*"—again she pointed to her chest, which had a hint of a bosom. "I mean out in this community, as a mom. I'm new. God, sorry, I'm so nervous. Don't mind me."

"Ah," Lauren said. "It's okay. We're new, too. Moved here this past winter, right when my baby was due."

Andrea took a big drink of her coffee, then cast Lauren a guilty look. "Do I smell like Baileys? I shouldn't be telling you this, but I had to spike my drink."

"Do you have any more?" Lauren blurted, her eyes sparkling.

Andrea paused a moment as though shocked, but then whipped out an airplane bottle and glugged some into Lauren's coffee cup. Both of them sipped and smiled conspiratorially.

"So how old's your son?" Lauren asked, after mentioning that her seven-month-old was in the nursery.

"Four. In pre-K. With Miss Barnes."

"Miss Barnes?" Ronnie Stuckey, overhearing, came toward Lauren and Andrea tentatively. "The fours? My daughter has her, too."

"Oh!" Andrea said, and more introductions were made between her, Ronnie, and Lauren. "So what do you think of her?"

"Miss Barnes? She seems great." Then Ronnie looked around the loft in the same way Audrey Hepburn's character did the first time she walked into Tiffany's in that movie. "This is *all* great, you know? Like, *insanely* great. Although . . ." She glanced at Andrea with trepidation. "Does your son know how to read yet?" she whispered. "Because I just ran into another mom who has a kid in Miss Barnes's class, too, and she said that her kid breezed through every unit on the Hooked on Phonics app, and now she reads at the third-grade level."

Andrea's eyes bulged. "Were we *all* supposed to be doing that?"

"I don't know! Was there a handbook we missed?"

"*Psst*," Lauren said, moving closer to Ronnie. "She's got Baileys for your coffee." She pointed at Andrea. "Just in case all *this*"—she gestured around at the other mothers, who were clustered and talking in high-pitched voices—"is too much." Then she quickly added, "I'm just saying, it's a little . . ."

". . . Overwhelming?" Andrea finished.

The three women shared a look of understanding. Ronnie's eyes widened at their coffee mugs, but after thinking it over, she said, "What the hell?" Then she glanced toward her boyfriend, who was now speaking in one of those gaggles of eager mothers. "But pour it in quick. My boyfriend over there? He teaches kindergarten here. I don't want to get him in trouble."

Andrea dumped the rest of the bottle into Ronnie's cup with impressive sleight of hand. After she finished, she did a double take at something on Ronnie's left wrist. It was a yellow rubber bracelet not unlike the Livestrong bracelets people were wearing in the early 2000s. "Where'd you get that?"

Ronnie inspected the bracelet and shrugged. "Some guy gave it to me—my boyfriend and I did a meal-delivery service for him and his wife over the summer, after those wildfires? It's like a cancer bracelet or something?"

"Does the guy have Willy Wonka hair?" Andrea's voice had an edge. "Bulgy eyes?"

"Yeah, that sounds right. His name was . . . Jerome?"

"Jerry." Andrea looked more and more uneasy. "Do you . . . *know* him?"

"Only in passing." Ronnie sipped. "He seemed nice, though."

"Ah." Andrea's shoulders relaxed a little. "He is nice. His wife has cancer. The bracelets, look"—here she showed her own wrist; she was wearing a similar yellow bracelet—"his daughter made them. Flora. She launched a sportswear brand last year, and I guess this was part of the line."

"Impressive." Ronnie smiled, and then added, to Andrea, "I bet you have a lot of cool friends like that. Designers and whatnot. You have that look."

"Me? Oh, not really." Andrea blushed. "And Flora moved up the coast, actually—we weren't even friends. I actually don't know another soul in Raisin Beach."

"Me neither," Ronnie admitted. "I mean, not *really*." She mentioned that she, like Andrea and Lauren, hadn't moved there that long ago.

Lauren took a sip and looked at Ronnie. "Do you work?"

"Me?" Ronnie froze. "Um, yeah. At this . . . nonprofit. It's really boring."

"Your looks are wasted on a nonprofit!" Lauren chided, then pointed to herself. "*My* looks, however, are not wasted on being a stay-at-home mom." Then she looked at Andrea. "How about you?"

Andrea took another big swig of her coffee. "I run this blog/support group thing. For people transitioning." Again, she gestured to herself, shrugging. "Or anyone dealing with micro-aggressions, actually. It's not limited to just one group of people."

Lauren looked intrigued. "Does mom-shaming about how I should *love* breastfeeding even though my nipples still feel like they're going to fall off count as a micro-aggression?"

"Absolutely. You're welcome to chat anytime."

Lauren smiled. Then Ronnie raised her cup. "Well, cheers! Nice to meet some normal people."

They toasted and smiled at one another. From across the room, they noticed Carson, the assistant, looking their way. "*Think he knows what we're drinking?*" Lauren whispered, stifling a giggle.

"Maybe *he* needs some," Andrea said. "The kid needs to lighten up."

Then Piper clapped her hands. "Everyone? Can we gather around?" She stood in front of the loft's massive stone fireplace. Everyone dutifully quieted down and turned to her.

"I just want to say, welcome—or welcome back—to Silver Swans Academy." Piper's voice was honeyed and regal. "I'm glad we're all back on track and here together." She laced her hands together like she was doing a cat's cradle. "For those of you who are new, I want to give you our origin story. Our *birth story*, if you will. Though don't worry, it doesn't involve eating the placenta."

A few men chuckled uncomfortably.

"So. Once upon a time, I had recently moved to Raisin Beach after a very difficult relationship. And I was walking with my son down this very block, and I passed this very building." Piper waved her arms about the space. "Back then, it was called Glory Be Nursery School. Maybe some of you knew it?"

Most faces were blank. Five years ago, when Piper had started as director, was a long time in the parent world. Most of those who had preschool children at Glory Be were long gone. And even though many parents had grown up in this town, it wasn't like they kept tabs on the preschools until it was a necessity to do so.

"And it . . . well, it was beautiful . . . but it needed TLC. And I just felt . . . *called*. I wanted to teach, but I didn't want to teach just anywhere. I wanted to make a difference. I thought about working where my son went to school—he was in elementary school by then—but I thought, *Oh, North, he'll be okay*. But I remembered him as a younger child. He *wasn't* fine then—the separation from his father was hard on him. And I thought, *That's the age group that needs me*. Such formative years, you know? So much can go wrong."

Everyone murmured appreciatively. When Piper became director at Glory Be, she'd inherited an already thriving preschool. Maybe it wasn't the choicest preschool in town, the one with the miles-long waiting list that required an entrance exam, but the parents who brought their children there were fashionable and professional and educated. Yet after Piper started, she rebranded it into Silver Swans and turned it into the only school that mattered.

"Now, if it had been last year, this would be the part of the speech where I'd talk about our programs," Piper went on. "Our art installations. Our playground renovation. Our impressive list of famous guests who will teach and inspire your kids, everything from cooking to botany. And while all of that is still in place, the world is a little different, isn't it? In the past year, a lot of us have had a wake-up call. A lot of us have learned valuable lessons about what matters . . . and what's superficial." She cleared her throat. "And maybe some of you—more than some—felt so uncertain that things would bounce back. I just want to say we hear you. We *see* you. It's been hard for us at Silver Swans, too. And I just want to say, thank you for making the investment in us again this year. I know that for some, it might be more of a hardship, and maybe it doesn't seem as important. But education *is* important, and we will try our hardest and do our best and always be a place of support and caring."

A few people murmured. The economic disaster—or Grand Recession, as it was called, a market bubble that burst for a variety of reasons and set off a chain reaction of sell-offs and layoffs—was still on everyone's minds. And Silver Swans cost upwards of $16,000 a year for baby care, $20,000 for full-day preschool services, and even more for kindergarten. This year, the school had instated some new ways to pay—through credit cards, or through monthly withdrawals from a bank account—but to some, it was more of a struggle. Most knew they were still privileged—first-world problems and all that, to worry about a pricey preschool instead of putting food on the table. But for some parents who thought of where their children went to school as a status symbol, the struggle represented something much bigger.

"Anyway, I just want to say thank you for being part of the tribe. You mean so much to me, and I hope that this year will be a bright spot after a bit of clouds." There was a smattering of applause, but she held up a finger. "Before we go back to the donuts—some of them are vegan, by the way, so look for the placards—I also want to talk about an exciting opportunity that's come up." She stood straighter. "I've been approached to work on a . . . *project.* A documentary television series, actually, produced by and broadcast on Hulu. They're hoping to shoot a story about parenting. Mothering. Children. Education, especially in changing times. I have to admit, I pitched them hard. I talked about how I'm a single parent, and I talked about Silver Swans, and I talked about all of you, hardworking people who only want the best for your kids. And . . . I just found out they went for it. Silver Swans is going to be a featured school."

Carson let out a whoop. "I *knew* they'd choose you!"

Others started to murmur. Andrea spluttered up a sip of coffee, sending Lauren, who was standing next to her, jerking away from the spray. "Sorry, sorry!" Andrea cried, grabbing napkins. The air smelled slightly like crème liqueur. "Wrong pipe!"

"This won't take any time away from my commitment to your children," Piper said, her voice raising. "However, I wanted to give you a heads-up that there may be a few cameras around. Your children might be recorded, as this is partly a documentary about kids. Unless, of course, you don't want that, and you can sign a waiver, and they'll pixelate out your children's faces in postproduction. Absolutely up to you—*however*, please consider the merits of participating. Your child, if you choose to be involved, will be interviewed carefully and sensitively. You may find out insights about them. You also might treasure the professionally shot footage once they get older. And, of course, if there are any budding actors, this might be a way to find representation!" She laughed mirthfully. "Kidding! Kind of!"

Hands shot up. "How many episodes?" This from a very blond, very tiny woman at the fireplace.

"I'm not sure," Piper said. "Ten, to start. For the first season, anyway."

"If we'd like to be interviewed, do we have to apply?" asked another mother.

"Check in with me, and I'll connect you with Kelsey, the producer who's handling all of that."

"Is this like a reality show?" That was from a balding, bearded father at the front.

Piper looked mortified. "Oh *no*. Far from it. It's a *documentary*."

Ronnie now looked faint. Lane, who'd reappeared by her side, took her arm. "You okay?"

"I . . ." Ronnie ran her hand across the back of her neck, then nodded. "Uh-huh. Sure. Whatever."

"Anyway, enough of me. Thank you for coming to our breakfast." Piper did that prayer-hands thing again. "Thank you for being part of our tribe. And enjoy the breakfast! Please, stay as long as you like! Mingle and meet—I always say that Silver Swans parents are the *best* this town has to offer."

Everyone smiled and clapped as Piper waved and exited the building—quickly, like she had somewhere important to be. Ronnie, Lauren, and Andrea applauded: they still felt full of hope, like they were accepted members of this shiny group.

Little did they know that what was going to happen next had already been put into motion. Someone watching had already made up their mind. The notes came so soon afterward, after all.

Someone in the room was already preparing a plan.

Two

A half hour later, after the breakfast ended, Lauren went to pick up her son from the nursery. This morning was just a trial run at Silver Swans, only an hour of time for the teachers and kids to meet one another.

Piper had vanished, but her assistant, Carson, stood at the big red door that led to the classroom building, trafficking families along. Bizarre that this dude would want to work at a preschool, Lauren thought as she stood in line at the door. But then, maybe he just wanted to work with Piper. That woman sure did have a fan club.

Ahead of Lauren, moms were chatting like old friends, which made her feel lonely. She looked around for the drinking buddies she'd made inside, but they'd gotten lost in the throng. And . . . were some of the moms looking at her strangely? She glanced down and mentally compared her wrinkled skirt to the polished outfits on everyone around her. She hadn't known this was going to be such a fashion show. You'd think after so many people lost their life savings and jobs, people wouldn't care about fashion as much.

She also couldn't help but notice how many couples there were—moms *and* dads. She glanced over her shoulder for her husband, Graham, and could just make out his head through the windows of her car. *Still* on the phone! He was going to miss out on picking up his son for the first time. Graham was missing out on everything. Even Matthew's birth, for God's sake: Lauren's water broke while Graham was out of town for work, and her labor progressed so quickly that he couldn't get back in time. As the contractions came on stronger, sad-eyed nurses hovered over Lauren, their pity palpable.

"Dad's going to regret not seeing this," one of them said, and Lauren wanted to punch her. She'd imagined her birth going wrong in a lot of ways—accidentally having the baby at home, the need for an episiotomy, an emergency C-section—but she'd never imagined she'd have to do it without the baby's father.

Even after Matthew slid out relatively easily, a perfectly formed child, Lauren still throbbed with the wrongness of having to go through it alone. There was no doubt she had a touch of PTSD from the whole ordeal. Maybe, in fact, the birth was what led to what Lauren was going through now. This . . . *darkness.* The growing feeling inside her she couldn't quite describe or control. And the sleeping, all the sleeping, just to escape.

Her phone bleeped. It was her mother. *How are things?*

Lauren felt a confusing rush. On the one hand, she wanted to tell her mother the truth. On the other, she was too proud. And there was yet another part of her that was annoyed because her mother had barely reached out. Didn't she remember how hard a newborn was? Shouldn't a mother know her daughter was struggling? It was a bizarre tug-of-war.

She slid the phone back in her pocket without responding.

It was finally her turn at the door, but still no Graham. Lauren put aside her annoyance when she saw her baby, who gave her a big, gummy smile. "Your first day!" she cried at him. "Aren't you a big boy!"

She gathered Matthew from the caretaker, a kind woman named Rose, and scooped up his raccoon-shaped backpack that stored his bottles, diapers, wipes, and other necessities. The parking lot was crowded with people; a different crossing guard waved vehicles through onto one of Raisin Beach's busiest streets.

Lauren pulled open the door just as Graham was jumping out to help get Matthew in the baby seat. He looked cowed. "I'm so sorry, babe. The call ended, but then all these texts started, and I knew that if I went inside, I'd look rude. I figured it was better for you to meet Piper anyway, since you'll be seeing her more."

"It's a shame you missed it," Lauren said airily. "Cool loft, the director reminds me of a dark-haired Gwyneth Paltrow, there's going to be some sort of documentary, oh, and also, it was adorable seeing Matthew in the classroom." She opened the passenger door and slid into the seat. "You mind driving?"

Graham looked put out. "Actually, I have a few more texts to send."

"I had some Baileys inside. I don't feel right being behind the wheel."

Graham's eyes widened. "You were *drinking*? What about your milk?"

"It was only a few sips."

Begrudgingly, Graham sat down behind the wheel. As he backed out, Lauren glanced once more at the Silver Swans building, then at Matthew's reflection in the little baby mirror affixed to the back seat. "How was it?" she cooed to him. "Did you like your teachers?"

Matthew answered by waggling a Mickey Mouse rattle. The kid was Mickey obsessed—when he was upset, no other blanket, stuffed animal, or song would do.

Then Lauren looked at Graham, realizing something. "How did you know the director's name was Piper?"

Graham kept his eyes on the road. "Because we've had whole conversations about her. You read me her biography. You don't remember?"

Lauren felt a swoop in her chest. "Did I?"

"Just yesterday, hun." Graham tapped her temple good-naturedly. "Mom brain!"

Lauren hated the term *mom brain*, but maybe it was accurate. Things were slipping past her far more often since she'd given birth. This particular memory, the deep dive into Piper Jovan—it felt ephemeral, like it had only happened in a dream. But how else did she know Piper had been at Silver Swans for five years, that she'd won awards, and that she had a son?

As he was taking the turnoff to a busier road, Graham's phone pinged, and he glanced quickly at the screen. "Oh, shit. Gracie wants me to come in today after all."

Lauren felt her stomach dip. "Ugh. Are you serious?"

Gracie Lord was Graham's quasi-new boss, the female show runner of the hit network comedy *Ketchup,* which shot in Los Angeles. When Lauren and Graham met two years ago, when they were both living in Silver Lake, Graham was an aspiring screenwriter with a degree in the craft from UCLA, picking up bartending shifts to make ends meet. He'd charmed Lauren from behind the bar at her regular dinner haunt up the street. He was witty and confident and good-looking with his height and deep-set eyes and scruffy beard, the kind of guy she figured would go for a young, blond, dime-a-dozen LA stereotype, and Lauren had been flattered that he'd chosen her: four inches too short, about fifteen pounds heavier than the city's median, and thirty-eight years old.

Graham always said she was beautiful. And that he loved her because she was smart, and honest, and made bold decisions. He loved her always-laughing family from Massachusetts, how her childhood was all about homemade granola bars and a tangle of shoes in the front foyer and her mother penning a chore schedule Sunday night. "It's like a seventies sitcom," he said wistfully. Graham had grown up with a single mother in a little town in central California; his extended family were bone-dry, serious Evangelical Christians whose interests and values were alien to him.

And maybe Lauren's family was seventies-sitcom perfect. All five Lowry kids set up homework stations at the dining room table, and Lauren never had a room of her own, and yet her mother always managed to find the perfect Christmas present for each of them. There were summers on the Cape, cheering on her brothers at soccer games, sitting through her sister's school plays. While her older sisters were "the pretty one" and the "theatrical one" and her brothers were both athletes, Lauren was "the brainy one," which wasn't exactly a compliment. She went to science camps every summer, and she was part of a nerdy band of kids who played a lot of D&D and fantasy video games. She always felt a little out of step with her siblings, who had an easy knowledge of pop culture and how to act in social situations and who, in adulthood, settled into lives not unlike their parents'. Her sister Gwen lived not ten miles from where they grew up and was a stay-at-home mom, her husband a prestigious doctor. Her sister Mel lived in New Jersey with her two kids, now almost teenagers, and dabbled with a bunch of careers as hobbies, not because she needed the money. Her brothers had blond, pretty-enough wives who faded into the background and fell into their typical gender roles. It *was* like the seventies, including how they all looked at Lauren a little pityingly because she hadn't made the same choices.

But Lauren's braininess had served her well: after college at UC Santa Cruz, she got into tech, finding coding languages easier to master than German or French. She put her love of gaming to use and developed a game app called Huzzah!, a Candy Crush–like color-matching puzzle that featured elves and sprites. The game garnered a following, and then she helped make Huzzah! 2, and then both games were set to be purchased by a big developer in Silicon Valley for wide distribution. Thanks to a business-minded friend, she'd lawyered up and secured rights to both properties. The sale of the games would earn her a decent nest egg, enough so that she didn't have to figure out her next steps for a while. Right around that time, she'd met Graham.

Also around that time, she'd started to entertain the idea of having a baby—maybe even being a single parent by choice, though she didn't share that notion with her family. When she broached the subject with Graham after just one month of dating, she was sure she'd just ruined the relationship, but Graham was into it, which she found incredibly romantic. They started trying only a few months later. Lauren figured that it would take a long time for them to conceive, but then she got a positive pregnancy test the first month. Things happened quickly after that: wedding plans, and then a move down the coast to a town that was more "family friendly" than LA—Raisin Beach's public schools were some of the best in the state. Suddenly, they were going to be married *and* parents. Lauren was even secretly happy that one of Graham's scripts hadn't hit it big yet. They could be stay-at-home parents together.

But then, last winter, not long before Lauren's due date, Gracie Lord chose Graham's spec script from a pool of thousands of hungry screenwriters to join her writing room for the show's fourth season. Graham was over the moon—Lauren, too, although, if she were being honest, the few times she'd watched the show, she thought it was kind of sophomoric and didn't have believable plotlines. Regardless, not long after, the economy started to tank. Graham's job was safe, but the sale of Lauren's game, which had been a sure thing, was postponed. And postponed again. The money she'd hoped to flood in didn't come. At this point, she wasn't sure if it would *ever* come. It was probably good Graham got a job, and suddenly, their roles had flip-flopped. All at once, Graham was the achiever, and she was the one who wasn't sure of her worth or her identity.

Graham had worked nonstop since he started at *Ketchup*,

commuting two hours daily back up to Culver City. After the first week of working in the office, Graham floated the idea of renting an apartment in LA. But Lauren had had some . . . *trouble*, postpartum. And that idea was dropped.

"Can you text Clarissa?" Graham asked. "See if she can come in?"

Lauren squeezed her kneecaps. "I think I could handle Matthew alone for a few hours without the nanny." But Graham cut her a sideways glance that was a mix between concern, sadness, and—maybe—warning. "Okay, okay," she said, backtracking. "I'll get her."

She started texting. When she looked up, Graham had taken the road that would eventually parallel the ocean. It was the nicest route home.

"So did you say there's going to be a documentary?" Graham murmured.

"I don't know. She didn't get into details. But it could be cool?"

"I don't know if we should have Matthew involved. Privacy issues and all that."

"I doubt they'd want to feature Matthew anyway. He's just a baby." Her cell phone pinged. *Happy to!* Clarissa wrote. "You know, this weird thing happened. I asked the director this totally innocent question, and she looked at me like I was from another planet."

"What did you say? Did you . . . you didn't get angry, did you?"

Lauren stiffened. "Excuse me?"

"No, I mean . . . *you* know." Graham tried to sound jokey, nudge-nudge. "I'm just making sure! This school's costing us enough money—we want to get off on the right foot!"

Just like that, Lauren could feel it coming on. The low simmer with rising bubbles. Silver Swans had been a point of contention with them. Back when Lauren thought she'd be flush from Huzzah!, they put down a deposit to send Matthew—Silver Swans was running an incentive that if they enrolled a child in the six-month-old class, they'd be charged a slightly lower rate going forward. When the game sale didn't go through, Graham argued that they should retract the down payment, but Lauren didn't want to. She wanted Matthew at this school, and who knew if there would be spots for him in the future? (Ironically, there probably *would* be spots for him, considering how many people had pulled their kids out, but Lauren hadn't known that then. And then the deadline to cancel Matthew's spot in the school passed, and she couldn't get their money back, so now they were just . . . going for it.)

"I didn't get *angry*," she said. "I mistook some man for Piper's teenage son, a simple mistake, and *she* got really strange about it." Graham opened his mouth to speak, but she held up a finger. "But the conclusion you automatically jump to is that I'm a hot mess? That I'm going to be inappropriate in public? Do you realize how that makes me feel?"

"Honey." Graham licked his lips. He was nervous, she could tell. He knew her signs by then. "It's also . . ." But then he stopped, changing his mind. "Forget it. Let's talk about this later. When we're not in traffic."

"What were you going to say?"

They were on the ocean road at that point; only a few feet away was a running path full of joggers and bikers. Graham had to slow down to obey the speed limit. He pushed his wedding ring around his finger. "It's just that . . . am I really so out of line for being concerned? Excuse me if I get sort of jumpy about you potentially making a scene."

And there it was: the rolling boil. Lauren had no idea where the fury came from—she'd tried to break it down to Dr. Landry, but it was futile. The fury coursed and snapped inside her, a black, bulbous shape that rose from some other dimension and yanked her by the collar, threw her out of her body, and took the helm. Even now, her waist tensed against the seat belt. A scream burst from within her, making Graham jump and Matthew start crying.

"Do you not respect me at *all* anymore?" It wasn't even Lauren's voice. It was something keening, primal, and bloody. "Do you even *see* me as a person these days—or just some unhinged woman who makes scenes?"

"Lauren . . ." Graham quickly rolled up the window, glancing out at the people on the running path. Regardless, a few passersby looked their way.

But Lauren didn't care. Or, rather, the beast inside her didn't care. "I was just trying to tell you a story about something I perceived as strange. I wanted to have a normal discussion where you took my side and we dissected it together—even laughed about it. But you always write me off!"

"Do you blame me?" Graham pointed at her. "Do you blame me, when this is how you respond?"

"*You* brought this on! And also, if you were so fucking worried, why didn't you come in with me? Why did you stay on your stupid call?"

"Because I have a job," Graham said, defeated now.

Lauren squeezed her eyes shut. "Pull over, please."

"What?"

"Pull over. I don't want to sit next to you."

Graham did as she asked. When the car was in park, Lauren flung the door open and stepped into the murky air. It was scorching outside—how could people run in this? There wasn't even a sea breeze, despite the ocean being so close by. Her long skirt stuck to her legs, and she felt fat and pale next to all the lithe, healthy bodies that were jogging past. Still more people glanced at her. People passing didn't see a diagnosis, probably, a very real postpartum thing Lauren had discussed with a therapist who cost them $400 an hour. They just saw a bitch.

Shoulders hunched, she yanked open the door to the back seat and slid in next to Matthew. Once she was belted, Graham pulled away from the shoulder. He kept his eyes on the road and his hands on the wheel, but he was too still, too watchful. He was afraid of her. Afraid of what she was going to do next. He had good reason to. Look at what happened in the kitchen. Look at how *awful* she was.

"I'm sorry," she said, suddenly feeling drained. "I'm such an asshole."

"No, you're not," Graham said, sounding defeated. "It's okay."

But Lauren didn't feel okay. She was sick of this happening. She was sick of being the hurricane that ravaged her family. She just wanted to be normal again. A good wife. A good mother.

She looked around for something to use to wipe her sweaty face, then noticed Matthew's raccoon backpack on the floor beneath the car seat. Inside was a package of wipes; she pulled out a handful and pressed them to her forehead, savoring their coolness. Again, Graham eyed her in the rearview, but Lauren didn't meet his gaze.

She almost missed the note when she returned the wipes to the backpack. It was just a small square of paper, folded in half. She pulled it out and read the unfamiliar handwriting. And then she felt confused.

And then embarrassed.

And then ashamed.

And then paranoid.

And then angry.

You, the note read, *are not wanted here.*

Three

That same afternoon, Ronnie Stuckey squatted on the wood floor and swiped a pink, fluffy feather duster across a media console. Her nose tickled. Her legs ached from the pose, though she knew this particular stance made her butt look amazing. There was a draft going up her bare ass from her short skirt. And her breasts swung loose and free—*literally* free. That was how Charlie Lowes—and every other client who called upon Ronnie to "clean" for them—liked it.

Charlie watched Ronnie from the other side of the room, his eyes at half-mast. He was twenty-five, three years younger than Ronnie, and had dark, tangled hair that came to his shoulders. From what Ronnie gathered, Charlie was a printmaker—though what he printed *on* was a mystery. He must have inherited money, because he lived alone in a huge house on the ocean, about forty-five minutes away from where she lived in Raisin Beach. His place had a negative-edge pool that overlooked the beach and an updated kitchen. It was also cluttered with shedding plants, hairball-riddled cats, art supplies, old magazines, and empty yogurt containers. What the house needed was a *real* clean—not the sort of ersatz version Ronnie did. Oh, she dusted a little, and sometimes she pushed a vacuum in a sexy way. But mostly she just scooted around the rooms, twirling, twerking, jiggling her butt, and making her naked breasts bounce. That was what Topless Maids, with whom she was employed—her *true* employer, not the job she told everyone she did—was all about.

"How's that little girl of yours?" Charlie asked suddenly.

Ronnie looked up. Sometimes she shared a personal detail with her clients, but questions about Esme were always jarring.

Perhaps Charlie understood this, because he then added, "You told me about her last time you were here. I saw a pic of her on your lock screen?"

Ronnie flicked dust into the trash can. "She's . . . great." She did a little twirl as she kicked the trash can closed. And then, even though Charlie probably wasn't the best person to unload upon, she couldn't help herself. "Her first day at a new preschool was today, actually."

"Oh yeah? Which school's she going to?"

For a moment Ronnie considered not telling—it felt like a privacy infringement, and what if Charlie was some sort of pervert and ended up loitering outside Silver Swans? But she felt she knew Charlie well enough—he had been one of her first clients when she moved there. She was pretty sure he wasn't that sort of guy. And anyway, after she named Silver Swans, he shrugged and said, "I'm not going to even pretend I know anything about preschools. Everything go okay?"

"I think so. She said she had a lot of fun. They had a get-together for the parents while the kids were in there, too. It's funny to be out in the world after being shut in for so long, but it was nice to see people."

She glanced at Charlie, then looked away fast. His erection poked through his jogger pants. Ronnie locked eyes with Bethany, the dancer she'd come with. Bethany was tracking the erection, too. The guys were allowed to masturbate in front of them, but they weren't allowed to get undressed.

Ronnie busied herself by dusting a credenza so she wouldn't

have to look at Charlie for a little bit. At Kittens, the adult establishment in Pennsylvania where she'd gotten her start in this industry and worked until two years ago, dim lighting obscured men's faces. She'd liked that better. Ronnie would rather men look at her and talk among themselves than try to include her in the conversation. She also liked the camaraderie with the other dancers. With Topless Maids, they always had to go in pairs, but Ronnie was always grouped with different girls, often not the same person twice. She hadn't gotten to know anybody.

When Ronnie had to leave Pennsylvania, she'd reached out to Dahlia, one of her friends at Kittens, asking if Dahlia knew of any leads for work far, far away that paid decent money. Topless Maids was what Dahlia came up with. It paid way better than the job Ronnie *told* everyone she was doing—working at the nonprofit group home, caring for patients with mental disabilities. And though she probably could have found work at a strip club elsewhere—she'd even considered Vegas—there was something aspirational about this part of California. Its clean streets. Its quaint, Disneyland-like main thoroughfare. The fantasy-themed playground in the center square where the slides were cheerful, pink-fire-breathing dragons. It was a far cry from dreary Cobalt, which was what she wanted for Esme.

All told, Ronnie didn't mind Topless Maids *that* much; she was used to men looking. Since she was thirteen, men had gone to pieces around her—especially men of an older generation. How many times, growing up, when she was wearing something even remotely revealing, had someone whispered, "*Look at those titties*" or "*Playboy model*" or even just "*slut*" as she passed? Ronnie's dad, Jimmy, was always down on his luck, perpetually getting laid off from jobs, and that instilled in him a certain ineffectualness. He tried to protect Ronnie from the male population, though instead of lashing out at the people who ogled, he told Ronnie to stay inside and not invite the comments at all.

Ronnie's mother, Brenda, agreed. She sent Ronnie upstairs half the mornings before school, saying she looked "too sexy." Ronnie's older sister, Vanessa, wore clothes that were far more revealing . . . but no one looked at Vanessa. Vanessa treated Ronnie's looks as an inconvenience, annoyed that so many boys in her grade came up to ask her if Ronnie was old enough to date. "You're not *that* pretty," she always told Ronnie—right in front of their parents, who made no efforts to correct her. "Don't be stupid enough to believe what those guys say."

When Ronnie was seventeen, her dad died of a heart attack. Ronnie's mother fell apart shortly after that and passed away a year later. Going to college wasn't in the cards for Vanessa, but Ronnie still thought it was a possibility for her. She'd major in business, she thought, or maybe accounting. She was good at managing things and crunching numbers. Though she had no idea how she'd even pay the application fees. Then, when a friend of a friend at a party jokingly told her she should work at Kittens, the county's only strip club, Ronnie took it to heart. She'd heard through the grapevine how much money you could make, so she called to see if they were hiring. For someone like Ronnie, of course they were.

Ronnie kept her new job a secret for a while, but then she blurted it out to Vanessa, who was scandalized but probably, deep down, quite jealous. "How can you do that for strangers?" she asked.

"It's okay," Ronnie said. "And anyway, it's just to raise money for college."

A girl at Kittens got sick; the boss asked Ronnie to come in for extra shifts. The money was so good, but it made her miss the school application deadlines. She had to put it off for another six months. But then Vanessa was out of work, and Ronnie felt obligated to help her out—she took on more shifts and missed the deadline again. Then Jerrod came along, and then Esme, and the prospect of leaving for college was out of the question. It just all . . . *happened,* a snowball growing larger and larger as it rolled down the hill. And now, there she was, all the way in California, still taking off her clothes for money. But if these guys were dumb enough to shell out cash to stare at her naked, what did she care? And she kept it from her boyfriend, Lane, not because she was ashamed—it just wasn't his business.

At least that was what she was telling herself, anyway. But now things had become a little more complicated. Ronnie and Lane had been living together for over a year now. Esme was now going to the school where Lane taught, and because Ronnie and Lane were considered "domestic partners," Ronnie got a huge discount on Silver Swans' tuition. Every day, the hole of lies Ronnie had dug for herself was a little deeper, and her roots to Raisin Beach were a little more . . . *rooted.* Every day, she had more to lose.

After a few more minutes of dancing, Ronnie put down the duster. "Hour's up, babe."

Charlie sucked on a weed pen, then lazily cast his gaze around the room. "Looks great." Laughable: the house was no cleaner. He stretched out his arms. "C'mere, ladies."

She and Bethany walked toward him. Charlie reached into his pocket and pulled out several crisp twenties, doling them out to the girls in *eeny meeny miney moe.* "*Gracias*, mamas." He slapped the bills into Ronnie's palm, but before she could pull away, his fingers curled around hers. Ronnie's feet had been so planted that she tripped forward, almost into his lap.

She caught herself on the arm of the couch. His breath smelled like weed and barbecue potato chips. There was grease at the roots of his hair. He wasn't terrible-looking, though. What did he get out of this? What sort of power did it give him, watching topless women clean?

"You're pinching," Ronnie said, looking down at his hand, which was still clamped in hers. She could sense Bethany hesitating behind her.

Charlie let go slightly. "Take your pants off?"

"Hah." Ronnie pulled her hand away, trying not to appear unnerved. "Not funny."

Charlie stuck out his lip in a pout. "Aw, c'mon."

She stepped back, adopting a powerful stance. Out of the corner of her eye, she could see Bethany's eyebrows rise. Ronnie knew how to stand her ground—or at least fake it, anyway. It helped that she knew she was capable of hurting someone, if it came to that.

She knew *that* all too well.

She changed clothes in the powder room. Threw her hair in a ponytail. Slid on a pair of rubber flip-flops. Once she buttoned the top button of her blouse, she didn't look like the same woman she'd been five minutes before. "See ya," she said to Bethany in the hallway, lobbing her a kind but indifferent smile.

She left through a side door and stepped into the bright sun. The street was empty, yet Ronnie glanced right and left, feeling a strange alertness. The last few weeks, she couldn't shake the sense that someone was tailing her. She made it a point not to take clients anywhere near Raisin Beach—she ran too much of a risk of someone spotting her around town. But maybe someone she knew was nearby? Or, worse, maybe it was Jerrod. Maybe he'd found her.

The adjacent yards were empty; not a single car rolled down the road. Ronnie looked this way and that, her heart lurching and bucking. *Jerrod's not here*, she told herself. *He hasn't found you.*

She had to hold on to that.

⁂

Ronnie navigated her car—the very same one she'd driven cross-country more than two years before, the bumpers starting to rust, the muffler making a worrisome rattle—to the apartment she and Lane now shared. The complex was made up of about ten low-to-the-ground pink stucco buildings. At its center was a playground, a small patch of lawn, and a medium-size swimming pool, which Esme adored.

Lane's car wasn't in his designated spot, which meant he still wasn't home from Silver Swans—the teachers had to remain behind for some staff meetings after the kids went home. Ronnie pulled into her own space and darted up the stairs to her door, suddenly seized by the familiar nervousness she always felt when she left Esme with a babysitter. It had been a while since she'd had to use someone, but now awful scenarios rushed through her mind: *Esme is gone. Mrs. Lombardo stole her. I won't even be able to go to the police.*

When she threw open the door, there was Mrs. Lombardo, the downstairs neighbor, sitting on the blue floral couch watching *Dr. Oz.* And there was Esme on her knees in front of the coffee table, scribbling in a My Little Pony coloring book.

"Mommy!" Esme cried, leaping to her feet, running over, and throwing her arms around Esme's neck. Ronnie felt the panic drain from her.

"Thank you." She handed Mrs. Lombardo some bills. The old lady gave Ronnie a wan smile, gathered her industrial-size handbag from the kitchen table, and excused herself with only a few murmurs of conversation. It was one of the reasons Ronnie liked the lady—Mrs. Lombardo never looked at Ronnie's overly made-up face with skeptical curiosity, nor did she ask what sort of job Ronnie worked at that only required her to be gone for a few hours at a time. Ronnie felt silly for being nervous. Mrs. Lombardo just wanted pocket change for more lottery tickets.

She sat down at the counter barstool and pulled Esme on her lap. "What do you want me to make you for dinner in honor of your first day of school, baby? Anything you want."

"Anything?" Esme's eyes, which were sometimes chocolate brown but today were more of a honey gold, widened. "How about candy?"

"Not candy for *dinner*." Ronnie poked her leg. "I know! What about pink pancakes?"

"You can make pancakes pink?" Esme frowned. "No, Mommy. I don't think you can."

Ronnie loved when Esme's know-it-all attitude shone through. If they'd stayed in Cobalt, would Esme be so spunky, so happy, so smart? Ronnie sincerely doubted it.

"There *is* a way we can make pink pancakes," she said, and then slid Esme off her lap and walked to the cupboard. Several boxes of food coloring were stashed behind the salt and pepper shakers—Ronnie had gone through a baking phase a while back but dropped it when most of her cakes fell flat. She opened one of the boxes and extracted a tiny vial with a red cap. "You can help me."

Ronnie reached for a mixing bowl and a spoon and the instant pancake batter, then started dumping in the mixture. "So tell me about school. Are you excited to go back?"

"Uh-huh." Esme was concentrating hard on squeezing a drop from the food coloring vial.

"Are all the kids nice? Did you make any special friends?"

"They're nice. Well, except for this— Oh, so *pretty*!" The batter was now turning pink. "Oh, Mommy, I love it!"

"What were you going to say?" Ronnie asked. "Except for this— Was there a kid who wasn't so nice?"

But Esme wasn't on that train of thought anymore. "Do you think Daddy Lane will eat them? Boys don't eat *pink* things, Mommy."

"Daddy Lane eats things that are pink," said a voice behind them, and there was Lane, bursting through the door, his ruddy face stretched wide with a smile.

"You *will*?" Esme said, looking delighted. "Pink pancakes?"

"Pink pancakes?" Lane smiled in question at Ronnie. "That's what we're having for dinner?"

"I told her she could choose." Ronnie glanced at Esme again.

The conversation about friends felt unfinished. What had Esme been about to say? Then again, Esme started sentences that felt like they'd be revelatory, but they often ended up being about nothing.

Lane moved across the room to kiss them; Ronnie was paranoid that she smelled like Charlie's weed pen. "I'm going to take a quick shower, and then we'll make these pancakes," she declared, hurrying off to the bathroom.

Ronnie stepped into the shower before the water was properly hot. Halfway through lathering up, she heard the door open and noticed Lane's blurry figure through the shower door's mottled glass. "Just grabbing something!" he called, but then opened the door with a saucy smile. "Unless I can come in?"

Ronnie considered it. She was so drawn to Lane—his big, warm body, his floppy hair, his muscled arms. Just pressing herself into him made her feel safer than she'd felt with any man. But then the notion of Esme walking in on them flitted through her brain. *Nightmare.* She flicked him with water. She didn't mind Esme seeing them being affectionate, but she liked to leave the actual sex until after the little girl was asleep. "I'm almost done," she said.

But as Lane's gaze traveled longingly down Ronnie's frame, she felt a thrill. She leaned out of the shower and gave him a long kiss. "Mmm," he said, closing his eyes. That was one of the things Ronnie loved about Lane—how he seemed to lap up affection, savoring every drop. He experienced the world in that way, one of the few people she knew who was actually *in the moment*, so aware of the world around him.

They'd met in line at Trader Joe's. Before moving to Raisin Beach, Ronnie hadn't realized Trader Joe's was a thing; all Cobalt had was the Kuhn's market, which smelled like old bread and bologna. Esme had been only two and a half at the time, and Ronnie was holding her because the Trader Joe's cart seats were oddly narrow. She couldn't find any of the normal items from other stores—Kellogg's Frosted Flakes, Breyers ice cream. And Esme was on the verge of a tantrum. Ronnie was trying to add up the cost of everything in the cart in her head, worrying if she had enough cash to cover it all.

When she'd gotten to the checkout line, she hadn't known what to do with her groceries. There wasn't a belt, per se—just a little desk where the checker stood. She was suddenly overwhelmed, which brought her right back to what had happened only a few short months before. It amazed her that her hands had done such things.

"Ma'am?" the checker said in a bored voice. He had a long beard, Ronnie remembered, and little John Lennon sunglasses. "Ma'am, can you pull forward?"

But Ronnie couldn't move. And then a man's voice said, from behind her: "He'll take your items from you. It's okay. You don't have to unload them yourself."

What had Lane seen in Ronnie that day? A pretty woman, for sure. But he'd also come to her rescue . . . *and* pegged that she was raising Esme on her own. When she told him her story—well, *most* of her story—later, that she'd had to escape from abuse, how she and Esme were winging it here in Raisin Beach, Lane didn't seem surprised.

The shower suddenly made a whining sound, and the water temperature changed from hot to lukewarm. Ronnie rinsed her hair quickly, and her mind drifted to the Welcome Breakfast. She still wasn't sure if it had gone well or not.

She'd been worried about meeting other mothers in Raisin Beach. Mothers here were . . . *different.* Back in Cobalt, mothers were just *moms*, just doing their best to get by. They didn't wear high heels or go to brunch. They never had time to work out—unless it was to a workout video in front of the TV while the baby napped, but Ronnie didn't know any mothers who actually bothered. They certainly didn't have Instagram pages showing off their beautifully arranged cheese plates or mommy-and-baby matching outfits.

In conversations she overheard at the playground, Raisin Beach mothers talked about things like "Yes spaces" and how their houses were no-screen-time zones, and the benefits of co-sleeping and how they'd die if their kids' sheets weren't made of fragrance-free, conflict-free organic cotton. Half the time, Ronnie couldn't understand the words they were saying. They all felt so *above* her, and she wasn't sure if she'd have anything to contribute to the conversation, *ever.* And though her hipster boyfriend was a plus—the kindergarten teacher, at Silver Swans!—she still worried that she'd stand out among the Silver Swans parents. Making friends wasn't at the top of her priority list—staying safe was, staying *hidden*—but it would be a nice bonus.

But a few mothers *were* nice at the breakfast. Ronnie liked how Lauren cut through the bullshit, and Andrea was hilarious. She—Andrea would want people to refer to her as *she*, right?—seemed lovely. Ronnie had already texted Andrea, in fact—they'd all exchanged numbers before leaving—to thank her for the Baileys hit and to compare notes with their kids' first days.

Maybe Esme and Andrea's son could play together sometime. Ronnie could only imagine what Jerrod would think about that—he wasn't accepting in the slightest—but she'd had some experience with transgender women at Kittens, and as they put it, they'd been women their whole lives; they just didn't know it at first. *Fuck Jerrod*, she thought. Jerrod didn't matter. For all she knew, Jerrod was . . . well, she didn't want to think about that. She considered Vanessa, too. Sometimes her sister popped into her thoughts, unbidden, but she was even more awful to think about, so she pushed both thoughts from her mind.

When she stepped out of the shower, Esme was sitting on the counter, her little legs swinging. "Can we play Lava Floor?"

"Uh, sure. A quick game before dinner." Lava Floor was a

game Esme and Ronnie and Lane made up that involved scattering a bunch of pillows around the room and jumping from one to the next. Probably every kid generation played the game—Ronnie remembered playing it with Vanessa when they were little, too.

After Ronnie was dried and dressed, they walked to the living room and started scattering the pillows. Lane, who was looking at something on his phone, grinned at them. "Lava Floor?" He smiled. "I'll play." He set down the phone and pulled up a couch cushion.

"I want Mr. Nibbles to play, too," Esme decided. Mr. Nibbles was her stuffed bear; Ronnie had bought him for her a few days after they'd first moved to the apartment, and she carried him around everywhere. Though when Ronnie looked around, she didn't see the toy in plain view.

"Oh!" Esme said, remembering. "I took him to school today. He's in my backpack."

"I'll grab him," Ronnie said, spying the backpack on the kitchen table. It was in the shape of Rainbow Dash, the My Little Pony Pegasus with the colorful mane. Ronnie slowly unzipped the main compartment and plunged her hand inside, finding Mr. Nibbles right away. "Here you go," she said, tossing the stuffed animal to Esme, who was already jumping from pillow to pillow.

She was about to put the backpack down when she noticed something else in the bottom, an iPad-like device. She'd heard about these. Each child was given the device, free of charge; on it were preloaded educational games as well as video and art apps so the kids could record their artwork and observations. She thought of the conversation she'd overheard at the breakfast between the moms of kids Esme's age who were already reading.

Ronnie pulled out the device, wanting to take a closer look. When she turned it on, there was a "1" next to an app called Student Work. Had Esme already uploaded a drawing? Perhaps Miss Barnes had already realized what a great artist Esme was. But when Ronnie clicked on the icon and the image came up, she couldn't make sense of the words. She stared into the living room, stunned. Then she felt her knees go boneless.

"Mommy?" Esme whined. "Are we going to play?"

"Hang on," Ronnie said shakily. What on *earth*? There, in the center of the device's screen, was an uploaded image of a few crayon-printed words. The letters were crooked and unsure, but the message loud and clear.

Mommy. Everyone knows. Everyone hates you.

Four

"Mom. *Mom!*"

Andrea Vaughan dreamed she was skydiving. Not that she'd ever done such a thing, but there she was, falling from an airplane, the wind whipping against her face. As she looked down, there was a figure lower in the sky, falling faster. The figure turned onto his back to face her. His features sharpened before her eyes. Andrea saw the familiar round chin and rosebud lips. His long neck and sinewy arms. He was reaching out for her, his eyes full of fear and regret.

She drew in a breath. A name formed in her mind. *Roger.* She needed to help him. She needed to catch him in time.

"Mom!"

Andrea's eyes snapped open. It was Tuesday morning. Her four-year-old son sat on the bed, his face inches from hers, his tiny fingers grabbing fistfuls of sheets.

"Arthur," she said, blinking hard, sitting up. "What is it?"

"You'll never believe it." Her son's grin was huge. "There's a *Power Rangers* episode on *right now*!"

Andrea rubbed her eyes. She was still stuck in that dream. That nightmare.

"Come on, come on!" Arthur was already running out of the room. "You have to see!"

Andrea slid out of the bed. Feet on the floor. Reality again. "Hang on."

She hurried into the bathroom. At the mirror, she leaned in close and inspected the lines on her face and the nakedness of her features. A swipe of lipstick here, a blot of concealer there. *Hang on, let me put on my face for the day*, her mother, Cynthia, used to say. Cynthia's boudoir was teenage Andrea's favorite guilty pleasure: beholding her mom's giant vanity of colors, labels, scents. All those private hours of slathering and puffing and brushing . . . and then hastily wiping it all off when she heard her mother's key in the door down the long, long hall. Because back then, Andrea wasn't a *her* in her mother's eyes. Andrea was her mother's son.

But that was then. That was New York, and this was California, and she was free. Sort of.

And yet her reflection still surprised her, more than twelve months into transition. She'd been on hormones for more than a year, and after all the years of resembling her father, with his thick neck and square shoulders, she now looked more like her mother—crazy how the simple introduction of chemicals could do that. Her breasts weren't as big as her mom's—the endocrinologist said they'd never be quite as bountiful as the female members' of her family from estrogen alone—but still, they were breasts, *real* breasts. And they were attached to her, grown from her body.

Andrea put on clothes she'd chosen for today—a polka-dotted blouse, skinny jeans that accentuated her narrow hips and butt. She pressed her lips together with a mix of relief and satisfaction. Every single cell in her body had always been *Andrea*. Now that she could be Andrea every day, it was like she finally got to exhale that gulp of breath she'd been holding for thirty-four years. Not once had she switched back and presented as male. And yesterday—yesterday!—she and Arthur set forth in this new community with her as a *mother*, presenting herself to all those mothers and letting them get used to it.

Well, with the help of Baileys.

Andrea wasn't even a drinker most of the time, but she'd been so worked up she'd shoved the liqueur in her purse at the last minute. When she'd gotten to the loft, she'd felt such an intense panic at the other women in the room that she'd almost run out of there. As much as she liked Raisin Beach's landscape and amenities and climate, the parents she'd come upon were so dedicated and slick and focused and . . . *conservative*. She'd spied a few cross necklaces. Amid all their bragging about their kids, she'd overheard a group talking about church. A woman with gorgeous blond extensions prattling on about some lifestyle Instagram she ran wore a WWJD bracelet. Andrea didn't universally condemn religion, per se, but there were lots of times where Jesus and the trans community didn't mix.

But Ronnie and Lauren had been different—cool, accepting. Thank *God* they'd been accepting, because she'd put herself out there so fast, her confessions just burbling out of her like lava. But now—well, she couldn't say she *knew* them yet, but at least she had allies.

Weird that Ronnie had crossed paths with Jerry Haines, though. Jerry Haines was the reason Andrea chose Raisin Beach over another Southern California town. He had been her family's lawyer back in New York for a while, though he'd moved out here about ten years before for the better weather. Or perhaps because he was tired of Andrea's father, Robert Vandermeer, one of the biggest sonuvabitches to walk the earth.

After the trouble with Roger, after Andrea's family said it was probably best for Andrea to leave for a while, Jerry called her directly. "Come to Raisin Beach," he'd said. "Bring the kid. Susan and I would love to see you—and Flora's still here." Flora was his daughter; she was a few years older than Andrea, and they'd never really interacted, but she had a child around Arthur's age. "And hey, maybe I can even give you a little legal advice, for old time's sake," Jerry had added meaningfully.

Of course, there was a lot Jerry hadn't planned for. She could still see the surprise on Jerry's face when she showed up not as the young man he'd known but as Andrea. But Jerry had rolled with it. He'd helped her legally change her name and made sure all the paperwork was in order. His wife, Susan, doted on Arthur. Flora, the daughter, ended up moving her family up the coast shortly after the economy tanked, so Andrea never really got to know her or her daughter, but it was nice to have Jerry and Susan around.

Still, it worried her slightly that a Silver Swans mom also knew Jerry. Then again, he was good at keeping secrets.

She rounded out of the bedroom, past the big kitchen with the large, splashy chandelier, past the small office where she worked on her blog, and past the full wall of windows that looked out to a view of the cliffs and the ocean. The sky was gray this morning, and the ocean was a subdued navy, but they had a good chance of spotting dolphins at this time of day.

The TV was on in the living room. A 1990s children's program played; superhero characters in brightly colored unitards zoomed through the air. Arthur stood in front of the screen, waving his skinny arms in ninja poses. Andrea smiled groggily. It was incredible how energetic he could be at such an early hour.

There was a flash at the window, and she looked up as the Blue Iguana Landscaping truck pulled to the curb. "Arthur," she murmured. "Reginald's here!"

Arthur brightened. He ran to the window, watching as Reginald Tucker, the landscaper, unpacked his leaf blower and tricked-out mower. "Can I tell him about my new friends at school?" he exclaimed. "Johnny and King?"

"You can say hi," Andrea permitted. "Ask him if he wants some coffee."

Arthur whooped and threw open the door. Reginald—never *Reggie*, he'd made that clear when they met—set down his rake and beamed. Arthur was filling him in on his new adventures. He'd glommed to the landscaper the moment they met. "King?" she could hear Reginald say. "Whoa, you have a friend named *King*?"

Andrea had had the same reaction. Who named their kid King?

Then her phone rang, and she turned. *Mom*, read the screen. Andrea ran her tongue over her teeth, then checked the clock. No polite East Coaster would ever call the West Coast at 6:30 a.m. Pacific Time, but her mother seemed to have an uncanny knack of knowing Andrea's circadian rhythms. She took a deep breath before answering.

"Hi," she said, tucking the phone between her ear and shoulder. "Everything okay?"

"Oh. Hello." Cynthia Vandermeer, tight and sour. This was a knee-jerk response to the way Andrea's voice had modulated into something more feminine now that she was living as a woman. *I don't like your new* lady *voice*, Cynthia had said once. *You sound like a cartoon character.*

"What's that awful sound in the background?" Cynthia asked. "Are you in a pool hall?"

Like her silver-spoon mother had ever been to a pool hall. Andrea gazed across the room. The Power Rangers were in a heated battle. "It's just a kid's show. We're at home."

"Why are you awake at such an ungodly hour? Don't tell me you've found a job."

"Well, I *have* a job, thanks." Andrea fiddled with a loose thread on a tea towel hanging over the oven handle. Ten seconds in, and Cynthia had already managed to get in so many digs. "I'm trying to get Arthur on a schedule. He officially starts school tomorrow, and they start early."

"Oh. Right. How's that going?"

"Good! I mean, we only had a getting-to-know-you day so far, but he really liked it."

"And *you* aren't attracting any attention?"

Andrea stared out at the horizon for a moment's peace. When she was young, she occasionally caught Cynthia watching her, one eyebrow raised, an unasked question on her lips . . . but she'd never ask it. Then again, Andrea's family wasn't an introspective bunch. Were any wealthy, WASPy families? Of course, Andrea's family was wealthier and WASPier than most—her father was a New York real estate scion, in the leagues with Robert Durst or a man he postured to know better than he actually did, Donald Trump. Andrea had grown up with anything a boy could want: lessons of all kinds, camps of one's dreams, vacation homes, ski trips, a rotating cast of nannies. Her older brother, Max, soaked it up—even now, in the tabloids, he'd developed the reputation as a sort of a rich-boy James Bond, always heli-skiing and flying prop planes and dating supermodels.

But Andrea had always felt so bumbling in her boyness, like it was a pair of pajamas that just didn't fit. When she was eight years old, Andrea tried to tell Cynthia about a dream she'd had the night before. (She'd known by then that this would never be something she could tell her father, who made jokes about people who were different—jokes that everyone in his company laughed along to because they were all afraid of him. He was the kind of man who smacked his boys if he caught them crying, and who called them sissies when they wouldn't step on a bug, and who spoke to Andrea in a girl's voice for an hour one afternoon at their home in East Hampton because Andrea had been too afraid to go in the ocean. "These boys need toughening up," he said to Cynthia more than once, in a voice that made her cower. "You baby them, especially Eric.")

Anyway, Andrea was sitting with her mother in the back of a

Town Car, whizzing through the city. "In my dream," Andrea said, "I woke up, and I got out of bed, and I'd become a princess." Then she looked cautiously at her mother. "It was great."

Cynthia, who perhaps hadn't been paying full attention, snapped up at this last part. "*Pardon*, Eric?" The look of disgust on her face said it all. "A princess?"

The door inside Andrea slammed closed. "Kidding," she said. "Just seeing if you were listening."

A few years later, she confided in one of the many nannies who passed through the house that she felt "girlish," and the nanny misinterpreted this as Andrea telling her she might be gay. At least she was enlightened and brought her books about homosexuality and offered to read them; she introduced her to her gay best friend from high school—*See, look! It's okay!* Andrea didn't have the heart to tell her that she was so wrong. The nanny never repeated Andrea's confession to Cynthia. Sometimes, Andrea wished she had—if only so that someone else could break the ice and it wouldn't be left to her.

But the task had been left to Andrea, in the end. She'd broken the news to Cynthia—and *only* Cynthia, not her brother, and, God forbid, not her father—after she'd divorced Christine, after everything happened with Roger, after her family had banished her to California because of Roger, and after she'd already gotten Arthur used to the idea and started herself on the hormones. It had been horribly messy—Cynthia even threatened to take Arthur from her, because how could Andrea possibly be mentally stable enough to raise a child?

They didn't talk for three months. And then, out of the blue, Cynthia had called again. She missed Arthur, she said. She couldn't stand not having the little boy in her life. Which—of course Andrea was grateful that her son mattered. But then Cynthia had added that she was terrified Andrea would out herself and it would get out to the press. Like *Andrea* wanted that either? She liked living a private life without the tabloid interviews or the photographers or the stupid society events she'd always hated. Nor did she want the whole Roger thing rehashed and reevaluated. So she'd made a deal with her mother not to tell anyone she was a Vandermeer. If she did, no more house. No more supporting Arthur. The end.

"I'm not attracting attention," she said, trying not to sound petulant. She reached for a box of coffee pods from the cupboard. "Not any more than anyone else would be in my situation." The school director's announcement about the documentary film popped into her mind, but she pushed it away. What were the chances it was even going to happen? And anyway, hopefully she could just opt out of having her or Arthur on camera.

Cynthia muttered something under her breath Andrea couldn't hear, then said, "Anyway, can I at least talk to my little star for a minute? I miss him so much."

Out the window, Reginald kicked on the leaf blower, sending a spurt of air Arthur's way. The little boy giggled and covered his eyes. "He's playing outside," she decided. "I'll send some pictures, okay?"

Cynthia groaned. "I feel like I haven't spoken to him in weeks! How do I know he's okay?"

Just because I'm a woman now doesn't mean I'm suddenly a terrible parent, Andrea wanted to snap.

After Andrea hung up, she sat on a kitchen barstool and stared blankly at the junk mail on the counter. Her heart hurt. There was so much condemnation in Cynthia's voice. She worried, too, that maybe separating Arthur from the family, making him live through all her changes, was the wrong choice. A split second later, though, she knew it was the *only* option. What was she supposed to do, stay trapped in her old self, miserable? Live as a trans woman in the city where her father *also* lived and risk enduring his wrath? For all she knew, he'd take out his fury and disgust on Arthur, too.

"I heard there was coffee?"

Andrea whirled around. Reginald was striding toward the kitchen. "Oh." She slid off the stool and tried to assemble a smile. "Yeah. Of course."

She hurried to the coffeemaker. Her cheeks felt hot, like she'd said her thoughts out loud. Reginald came in for coffee most times he serviced their lawn. She'd come to know that he had graduated from UC Santa Barbara with a degree in Russian literature but had no idea what to do with that. His real passion was plants, and hey! At least he was able to work. Andrea, in turn, spoke of how, despite a fancy education, she did "this and that" on the Internet. *You must be doing pretty well with that*, Reginald had commented, appraising her comfortable home. Andrea hadn't had an answer for how she afforded her house. Getting into the details of her family tree was far too complicated and fraught—*should* she be taking their money, considering what sort of man her father was?

It was nice to have someone to talk to. That was something Andrea lacked in this new community. When she'd moved here, desperate for some sort of connection, Andrea had started a blog about her journey transitioning. She never included pictures of herself, but she documented the hormones she took, the doctor visits, the changes to her body and mind . . . and the fear. Through research, she'd figured out how to make the blog pop up on Google algorithms; it began receiving attention from others going through the same situation. So she started a message board. Then some companies wanted to advertise. She offered counseling services—stating specifically that she was *not licensed*, more like a gender-transitioning Sherpa to help someone from one cliff to the next. It was nice to have a community to talk with, even if they didn't know who she really was. They were good sounding boards.

But there was a difference between dashing off an email and speaking to a real-life person. Hence Reginald. Funny thing, though, about Reginald: she suspected he was flirting with her, which made her feel . . . good? And if that wasn't a remarkable experience in itself, not once had he broached the topic that she was trans. Surely he knew, right?

Arthur was running circles in the living room. Andrea caught his arm. "Rein it in there! Where's your *slow down* button?"

"No slowing down!" Arthur giggled. "Can I have two waffles today? Three?"

"Three waffles?" She was amused. "You're quite the growing boy!"

She leaned down and wrapped him in her arms, nuzzling his freshly buzzed head with her chin. Reginald looked on with a pleasant smile. Everything felt so . . . *good*, suddenly. She felt lighter than she had in years. Which was why, when she unzipped her son's schoolbag and saw the folded-up piece of paper at the bottom, it hurt that much worse. She pulled the paper from the messenger-style pack, thinking at first it was something Arthur had drawn. But then she knew it couldn't be.

"Everything okay?" Reginald asked, cocking his head.

Andrea hurriedly refolded the note and stuffed it into her back pocket. "Yep. Totally."

But the drawing flashed in her mind, off and on, off and on, a neon sign. It was of a stick figure woman—tall, with long blond hair and two big blue dots for eyes, big feet and broad shoulders. It looked—well, it looked like Andrea.

But there was a big black *X* through the middle of the figure, too. And a word, in big block letters: *NO.*

Five

Lauren stood at the counter at Sarina Spa & Ranch, a sprawling resort on the ocean cliffs—there was no *ranch* in sight. Rumor had it that a fair number of celebrities visited this place for quick detoxes.

Graham had his hand cupped protectively over her forearm, then looked at the receptionist. "Thank you for taking her. I know you guys are usually really booked."

The receptionist beamed. "Anything for Gracie Lord! We just love her!"

Lauren offered a clenched-teeth smile. Apparently, just by dropping Gracie's name, she was able to bypass the line and receive a 120-minute deep-tissue massage. Because, you know, that was what all women get after almost wrecking the car on the freeway.

Last night, after work, Graham had walked through the bedroom door. Lauren had been in there, sulkily leaving Clarissa the nanny to deal with the baby by herself. She'd sat up, confused. "You're home early."

"Gracie said it was okay. Actually, here." He held the phone outstretched. "She wants to talk to you."

Lauren was racked with guilt, rehearsing all the ways she needed to apologize to her husband for being so irrational again. She was also spinning with paranoia because of the note in

Matthew's backpack. It was almost comical, like something out of a ghost story: *You are not wanted here.* What could someone have against her? The night in the kitchen crossed her mind—their screaming, the blankness, the police showing up.

No. No one knew. That was impossible.

"Um, hello?" she'd said into the receiver. ". . . Gracie?"

"Hey, Mama," Gracie cooed in a low, sympathetic voice. "How's it going?"

Gracie Lord was ten years older than Lauren, with an angular face and dark hair and a dry, masculine, unapologetic self-confidence. She reminded Lauren of Joan Jett. She'd probably been a cool girl in high school. And she had no filter: the first time Lauren met her, Gracie looped an arm around Lauren and asked her intimate questions about Matthew's birth story. But before Lauren could answer, Gracie started in on the birth story of her *own* child—she was a single mother by choice—which included a third-degree tear that forced her to sit on a hemorrhoid pillow for months. Only cool girls in high school could talk about hemorrhoid pillows without shame.

Lauren also noticed how Graham looked at Gracie—his admiration was palpable. She didn't want to think there was something going on between them . . . but, well, that was where her head went, like it or not.

"I'm okay," Lauren had answered on the phone.

The truth? She was beat. From crying. From being angry and worried and freaked. Matthew had been fussy and grumbly, and nothing had soothed him: not a bath, not songs, not food, not drink, not baby massage, not colic drops, not even Clarissa vigorously swinging him back and forth, her arms nearly buckling. Lauren hadn't even had the heart to step in and tell Clarissa not to swing him.

"Listen," Gracie went on, "I can only imagine what you're going through—the new mother thing is a bitch. And now daycare! What a scary transition. So I booked you at Sarina Ranch tomorrow morning. My favorite masseuse is going to treat you right."

"You don't have to do that." She wasn't used to being babied after behaving badly—Lauren's mother had been more of the tough-love type, following through with the threats she issued when her kids were in the middle of tantrums. One time, she'd even canceled Lauren's sister's birthday party because Mel had mouthed off one too many times. She was the definition of someone who *followed through*.

And as Lauren looked around the ranch, she guessed the massage was going to cost a fortune. Did Gracie pamper other writers' wives? Was there a deeper implication here, maybe even guilt? Once again, the thought that Graham might be too cozy with Gracie crept into Lauren's mind. He'd seemed a little cagier in the past few weeks, like he was keeping something from her. And Gracie's relationship status was a constant question mark. At a party, Lauren had heard her referencing a past male partner, and a gossip site once paired her with a semi-famous actor. Would she really sleep with a lower-level writer on her team? That seemed kind of . . . tacky.

Now, all checked in, Graham turned to a shelf of products, grabbed a box of bath bombs, and placed them on the counter. "Put these on my card," he told the receptionist.

"Don't buy me things." It felt even worse when he was so nice after her episodes.

"Oh, stop."

Graham dropped a kiss on Lauren's cheek. He was always forgiving, but what he said yesterday in the car stuck with her. She knew how she could get—her explosive anger, post-baby, wasn't limited to just him. It reared its head with customer service reps, the UPS man, and even Matthew's pediatrician.

Lauren was embarrassed by her outbursts, always, but she hadn't known that Graham was *just* as embarrassed. When they met, he'd struck her as the kind of guy who didn't give a shit what people thought of him. But maybe Graham had developed some self-awareness since *Ketchup*. Maybe it had something to do with Gracie's opinions. Or maybe it had always been there and Lauren was just now seeing his true colors. They'd only been together two years. She often worried they hadn't had enough time together as just a couple before the baby came. She'd asked him about that lately: Did he regret having kids so quickly with her? What about his past girlfriends? Graham had mentioned a few long-term relationships, but he said they were nothing much. A woman who now lived in Florida came up. A trip to Italy with another girlfriend to take pasta-making classes was mentioned, then dropped. Did he fantasize about these women now? Did he think about how much fun he used to have with these women, all the outings, all the sex, none of the baby, none of the crazy?

The note in the backpack clearly wasn't helping her mental state. If only Lauren had someone to bounce theories off of. Her first instinct was to call her mother . . . but say *what*? Her mother's lack of phone calls felt pointed, though Lauren wasn't sure why. *Oh, that one, she doesn't need* our *help*, maybe. She wondered, sometimes, if Joanne judged her for waiting so long, or moving to California, or having a career—who the hell knew? She was in a little cabal with Lauren's sisters—they traded recipes and baby clothes and holiday schedules, and Lauren always thought they were gossiping about her. She wanted to think her mom would keep something like this to herself, but honestly, she really wasn't sure.

After Graham left the spa, Lauren let the receptionist guide her into the dressing area. "Lockers are here." She handed Lauren a terry robe. "And feel free to use our eucalyptus room."

"Thanks." Lauren whipped open a locker, shoved in the box of bath bombs Graham insisted she accept, and kicked off her clogs. Her resentment felt childish. She should be grateful to have time to herself. She knotted the robe around her waist and padded into the waiting area, which offered lemon-and-cucumber-infused tea and mixed nuts in contained little cups. A few women were already lounging on chairs spaced widely apart. Lauren avoided making eye contact. She didn't quite feel like she deserved to be here.

"Mrs. Smith?"

A tall, bald man stood in the doorway. He wore maroon medical scrubs and had a smile so kind that Lauren felt her body unclench. That her massage therapist was a man surprised her—she'd pegged Gracie as an I-only-like-women-to-massage-me kind of gal. She looked at the man's hands again. They were big and looked strong.

"Clancy," he said. He gestured for her to follow. At the end of the hallway, he opened the door to a treatment room and ushered her in. "Undress, and then lie facedown under the sheet." He bowed and exited.

Lauren untied the robe, staring down at her nakedness in the dimly lit mirror. Besides the fact that her belly button had changed shape, her body had bounced back after childbirth—not that she'd been spectacular beforehand, but she hadn't gotten any *worse.* Still, those other mothers from the breakfast popped into her head. How slender most of them were. How they looked like they all did sixty minutes of cardio every day. She wouldn't be getting a note for her appearance, would she? That would be some real internalized-misogyny bullshit.

So why would someone stick that note in her child's backpack, then?

"Lauren?" There was a knock on the door as she was settling under the sheet. "You ready?"

"Yep!" Lauren tried to sound chipper. "Thank you!"

The door opened. She could hear Clancy bustling around, turning on the tap. Then came the slurping sound of the man rubbing oil between his hands. Lauren wriggled on the mattress, trying to get comfortable.

Clancy took a breath, then pressed his hands to her shoulders. Lauren shut her eyes, waiting for that gooey, unraveling feeling to spread through her body—she always wanted that to happen when she got a massage, but it never did. Clancy's touch felt good, but she could feel her body resist whenever his fingers dug in.

"You're very muscular," he said after a minute of rubbing.

"Oh." Lauren felt a thrill. "I can't really credit that to working out."

". . . But you're also really, really tense."

The sides of the face cradle pressed against Lauren's cheeks. She opened her eyes but could only see the tiled floor. "Yeah, well. It's been a tough year."

"Don't I know it." He sighed. "Do you know I never even got a stimulus check? Somehow the government skipped me."

"I'm so sorry," Lauren murmured. She and Graham *had* received a stimulus check, accidentally. They earned too much money to technically qualify. For weeks she'd tried to figure out how to give it back but then eventually gave up.

Then she said, "It's also because I . . . had a baby. Seven months ago. It's been stressful."

"Ah."

"The birth was sort of intense. My husband didn't make it there in time."

"Ooh. Rough."

She could have ended it there. She *should* have, if it were up to Graham. But she couldn't stop. "And I have this thing that happens to mothers sometimes. Postpartum rage."

". . . Postpartum depression?"

"No, *rage*." Lauren tried to laugh, but it came out more like a hiccup. "They're sort of linked. But rage is . . . you know, ragier."

"Oh."

For a while, she listened to the pan flute playing softly through the speakers. Clancy was probably judging her now. There was nothing less appealing than an angry woman. Depression was submissive. But rage made people think of Courtney Love. Frances Farmer. Lorena Bobbitt. *Lock that crazy bitch up before she hurts someone.*

"It's surprisingly common," Dr. Landry had said during that first therapy visit she and Graham attended together. "It's a postpartum condition, but not that many people talk about it. Everyone expects a mom to feel sad, anxious, grumpy, overwhelmed—the anger is a surprise."

"I'm just so *worried*," Graham said. "There was even this time when . . ." He cleared his throat sheepishly, surely thinking of that night in the kitchen, then started over. ". . . We've hired a nanny so that Lauren is never alone with the baby."

"I would never intend to hurt him," Lauren had jumped in.

"Of course not," Graham said quickly, but then looked away. "Still, it's good to have someone else around, just in case you feel . . . overwhelmed." Then he'd looked at Dr. Landry expectantly. "Don't you think?"

When Dr. Landry said that seemed prudent, Graham looked vindicated. "A lot of things are expected of mothers," Dr. Landry then added. "And often, these feelings of rage—they're actually masking other, scarier feelings."

"There are *scarier* feelings inside me?" Lauren cried. The fury she felt—and the way it came on, sneaking up on her like an orgasm—wasn't that terrifying enough?

"Anger is often a mask for feeling overwhelmed, or scared, or sad," Dr. Landry said. "Even feeling guilty that you aren't doing things right as a new mom."

Lauren thought she'd rock motherhood. She'd read all the right books, gone to the right classes. Granted, she didn't intend on the game not selling, nor did she intend on Graham getting a job that kept him away from the house eighteen hours a day. And of course she didn't count on birthing a baby without her husband in the fucking room. But those were the only glitches. The only complications. Where had this anger been hiding the other thirty-nine years of her life? What if she never went back to her old self? And the thing she'd done this summer in the kitchen—the thing she'd *almost* done, the thing Graham had *reeled her in from*, the thing she hated to think about—what if she did that again?

"There's nothing wrong with rage."

"What?" she asked groggily. Lauren hadn't forgotten she was in the dark room, but she'd kind of zoned away from the *now*.

"There's nothing wrong with rage," Clancy repeated. "It's primal."

Lauren sniffed. "My doctor says it's not even a real emotion."

"Of course it's real." He scoffed. "People just say that stuff to keep you down."

He was drumming on her back with the sides of his hands now. "Like, because women aren't supposed to be angry?" Lauren asked experimentally.

"Because people don't want *anyone* to be angry. Anger is hate! Anger is guns! But anger is also real and therapeutic and sometimes feels good—sometimes, it gets to the root. You know?"

"I think so," Lauren said in a small voice.

"Well." Clancy slid the sheet over her back so she could turn over. "Personally, I feel like people should be talking about rage *more*, not less. It's all this bottling up that's making the whole country go nuts. Of course, as long as you aren't hurting anybody, you know? Then I say be as mad as you want."

"Yeah," Lauren said softly.

A butterfly stretched its wings inside her chest. *This* was the kind of permission she was looking for—not Gracie Lord's self-aggrandizing self-care bullshit. Something else Clancy said made her feel better, too. Say this note she'd received in Matthew's backpack *did* have something to do with her rage. Say someone had seen her lash out in public and took things the wrong way. Or say Lauren had had an outburst in a Silver Swans interview and then *forgot* about it, as Graham pointed out she was prone to doing lately. It was possible she'd dug her own grave and didn't even know it! Hell, maybe that was what Piper's lapdog assistant, Carson, had even been whispering to Piper about at the breakfast.

Of course Piper was concerned. Of course they wouldn't want an irrationally furious person in their midst. But that wasn't what was going on with Lauren. Maybe if she just explained herself, if she came forward with her diagnosis, Piper would sympathize. Piper was a parent, too. She had hormones. And Lauren was trying *really fucking hard.*

In fact, *in fact!* Maybe if Lauren wrote the email just right, Piper would be inspired . . . and she'd feature Lauren in the documentary. Think of all the people she could reach. The suffering mothers, angry and frustrated.

After another hour, she was sliding her robe back on feeling just as motivated. Her fingers curled around her phone. On her lock screen was a picture of baby Matthew with a gleeful, gummy smile. Lauren's fingers were a little oily, so it took a few tries to dial the Silver Swans main number. After a prompt, Lauren reached Piper Jovan's office.

"She's in meetings," Carson declared primly when he answered Piper's line. "Who's calling? Would you like to leave a voicemail?"

Lauren took a deep breath. She was standing naked under a robe in a tiny, dark room. She was trembling with nerves and excitement and anxiety over whether this was the right choice.

But then she relaxed. This was getting to the root of it. She had to dive in. "Yes," she told the assistant. "Yes, I would."

Six

Hummus, babe?" Lane's hand caressed Ronnie's bare shoulder, and she jumped. He pulled away, surprised. "You okay?"

"Um, uh-huh." Ronnie's voice was high-pitched and strained. She glanced at the tub of hummus. This was a ritual of theirs: sitting on the balcony, watching the sunset, and eating healthy snacks Lane prepared. "I'm not really in a hummus mood, though."

"Wait till you've tried this, though. It's organic. *And* the company is doing great things with vaccine funding in emerging-market countries."

"Okay, fine." Ronnie reached for the bag of accompanying pita chips. "If it's good for the vaccines."

Lane was political about every decision he made, whether it was which candidate to vote for or which types of biodegradable sandwich bags to buy. He wanted to leave the world a better place, he always said, and actions spoke louder than words. Ronnie tried to keep current with all his rules and choices and positions, but she hadn't been raised with the luxury of options, so sometimes his rationale seemed frivolous. In Cobalt, everyone bought one brand of milk: the cheapest brand. No one gave a shit if the cows were mistreated. No one cared if the blueberries were organic. Actually, no one she knew from home ate blueberries because they were too expensive.

Her phone beeped. Lauren had sent a text. It was a screenshot of Kiddo!, a message board for neighborhood moms; a parent was railing about the state of the baby slide at the local playground—someone had had the audacity to take a marker to the underside of the thing, marring its perfect appearance, and one of the scribbles kind of looked like a curse word. *Don't these people have better things to worry about?* read Lauren's text. *God forbid our babies start swearing!*

Ronnie responded with an eye-roll emoji. This had become their thing in the past day—Ronnie, Lauren, and Andrea copying and pasting notes of ridiculous hysteria within the Raisin Beach mom community. Like the argument that exploded over the mom who'd posted on Nextdoor that she was charging cash for her extra breast milk. Or the fight that had broken out on a local mom Facebook group about who has it harder, working moms or stay-at-home moms? And then there was the constant one-upmanship—whose baby had already learned to walk, whose three-year-old could already ride a two-wheeler, whose five-year-old knew all his multiplication tables. If you believed everything you read, Raisin Beach was chock-full of baby savants.

Ronnie enjoyed the banter. Lauren and Andrea made her feel more normal, especially knowing that they found some of the things people worried about around here ridiculous, too. They were on their way to becoming friends, maybe.

If she didn't pull her kid out of Silver Swans first. It was very possible it was these very moms on the sites who *wanted* Ronnie out.

Lane placed the hummus on the side table and settled into a chair, propping his long legs on the iron railing that circled the balcony and staring at the paltry strip of starry sky. Still, the view was a huge step up from the view of the dumpster she'd had in the shitbox she had lived in when she and Esme first arrived in Raisin Beach. That apartment had been attached to a mechanic's shop—so it always smelled like diesel fuel—and had a two-burner stove, a minifridge, and only enough space for a double bed and a couch. After dating for a little while, Lane had visited Ronnie's just once, when he'd said, "You know, I think you guys should just come stay with me. We've got a pool!" That was a year ago.

What sort of man offered to find housing for a woman and her child after only a few weeks of dating? Well, maybe a man who came from a comfortable background and had two benevolent parents. Lane's mother and father, Sarah and Martin, were always housing exchange students when Lane was young. There was one girl from Liberia, Lucia, who they'd put up for a whole year in high school—and then she came back to the US years later and had no one to turn to, and Lane's parents took her in *again*, and not just her but her brand-new husband and their baby daughter. For almost a year!

They had big hearts, and they'd passed that on to their son. Lane showed his generosity in other ways, too—he volunteered for a handful of organizations, including delivering meals to people going through chemo. Ronnie had gone with him on a few of the delivery runs, and she'd noticed that Lane didn't just drop and go—he wanted to spend time with the people. Brighten their days. Like with Jerry whatever-his-name-was, the man who'd given Ronnie the cancer bracelet Andrea had also been wearing. Lane had stood on his porch and chatted with the old man and his wife about the Yankees for almost twenty minutes. Ronnie was pretty sure Lane didn't even like baseball, yet he listened with rapt interest.

In fact, at first, Ronnie worried that he only saw her and Esme as a kindness crusade, too. They were a mother and child fleeing from abuse, and Lane always called Ronnie *brave*, like she'd overcome some major adversity. Little did he know it was more complicated than that. But as time went on, Lane did seem to love her for *her*. She taught him to bird-watch, which she'd done with her father when she was young. They enjoyed the same British mystery programs. They started a book club where they'd read the same novels and then discuss—Lane had better insights than Ronnie's senior English teacher. They had joyful outings with Esme, who bonded with Lane easily. After a while, Ronnie began to relax into the relationship and enjoy loving Lane. Maybe she would actually get her happily ever after.

And yet, there was so much unsaid. So much Lane didn't know. Topless Maids was the tip of the iceberg. And now, that *fucking note* on Esme's device.

"Day two is in the books," Lane said now, lacing his hands behind his head and looking out on the horizon. It was Tuesday evening. Most of the preschoolers started the following day, on an abbreviated "easing-in" schedule, but Lane's kindergartners were pros, so they'd started today. Esme would have to go back Thursday, though, and it filled her with dread. "Feels like the year is getting off to a good start. Nobody's melted down. Nobody's been left out. Everyone loved the book I read about the superhero potato." He grinned.

"Well, that's good," Ronnie tried to sound cheerful as she crunched on a pita chip. "I'm so happy for you."

"And Esme, too. She's excited to go again on Thursday, right?"

"I think so."

She couldn't look at him. She felt so ashamed about the upload on Esme's device. She'd figured out how to delete it. The message had to be the work of some *other* child. Some smartass kid who could already write and spell and was doing her mother's bidding—*and* who'd known to upload the artwork to Esme's device. Had some self-righteous mother murmured to her child something about Ronnie before they'd even gotten into the classroom?

Could people tell, somehow, how small of a house she'd grown up in, and that she knew a lot of people who'd never learned to read, and that no one where she was from amounted to anything? Maybe they could see the sort of people she'd had to endure just by looking at her face: The men at Kittens. Her sister. Jerrod.

Or maybe someone's husband had employed Topless Maids in the past. One of those mothers had a nanny-cam or something, and up popped Ronnie and her bare tits. Maybe this was the mom's way of subtly shoving Ronnie out, saying they didn't want *her kind* at Silver Swans.

She glanced at Lane, who was flicking the automatic lighter to reignite one of the votive candles. She was dying to tell him about the note, but how could she? It would beg the question of *why?*

"By the way," Lane said, "I called you this afternoon, but your cell went straight to voicemail. Stuck with a client?" He widened his eyes. "You didn't get vomited on again, did you?"

"Oh. Um . . ." Ronnie kept her gaze fixed on the enormous palm across the street, which, at this hour, was a midnight-blue silhouette. It was so much effort to keep up the lie about her fake job. Half the time, she feared she got the details wrong, or that Lane would call the fake number she'd provided instead of her cell. She kept telling herself too much time had passed by now, or that she'd come clean *later*. She should have just told Lane at the start, gotten it over with. If he would have dropped her, then so be it. The problem was that Ronnie loved Lane. *Adored* Lane. Also, telling him now was so wrapped up in telling him so many other things that she couldn't. She hadn't even told him she was from a tiny town in Pennsylvania—she'd said it was a tiny town in West Virginia. And for all she knew, her story was all over the news—a stripper disappears with a little girl in tow. Just do a Google search with the real facts, and there it might be. Even if Ronnie could have told Lane *some* of the truth . . . well, she hadn't, and now too much time had passed, and there was no way.

Ronnie looked up at Lane, realizing she hadn't answered his question about work. "I was just running around," she said. "Work's been crazy."

"Yeah, mine, too," Lane agreed.

Ronnie glanced at him quizzically. What could be crazy about teaching kindergarten at Silver Swans? And then, almost involuntarily, she blurted, "Do people roam the school hallways? Is that allowed?"

"Huh?" Lane paused, spoon halfway to his mouth. "What, at Silver Swans?"

"Yeah. During the day. Are there lots of people . . . mothers, maybe . . . moving about?" Her heart was suddenly pounding.

"Well, parents aren't allowed in after a certain time. You have to check in through the office." Lane looked confused. "Why?"

"No reason." Ronnie pretended to be really interested in the shape of a pita chip. "Have there been a lot of incidents of . . . oh, I don't know, families being bullied at the school?"

Lane looked startled. "Bullied?" Ronnie shrugged. "Honey, Silver Swans would never, *ever* tolerate that. You really think I'd send Esme to a place where bullying was allowed?"

Ronnie shook her head. Of course Lane wouldn't.

"And you heard Piper," Lane said. "She strives for equality and acceptance. We're all in this together. That's what she pitched to that documentary! Which is amazing, huh?" Seemingly noticing some change in Ronnie's posture, he added, "What's wrong?"

"It's just . . . Piper," Ronnie said. "I'm not sure about her." Piper had seemed like every other mom in the group—sort of like the queen bee of the moms, in fact. Ronnie also hadn't liked how nervous Lane seemed around her. If she were being honest, she'd always felt slightly annoyed by his hero worship of Piper—she'd heard Lane speak about her plenty over the past year. And now that she'd met Piper properly, she wasn't impressed.

And oh God, that documentary series. The last thing Ronnie needed was to be on *camera*. It wasn't just about someone spotting her as a Topless Maids girl, either. It was about *Jerrod* spotting her. About her truth going public.

Lane sat back. "What do you mean, you aren't sure about Piper?"

"I . . . I got this vibe at that breakfast. The way she looked at me. She seemed condescending."

There were two vertical creases between Lane's eyes. "I think you're overreacting."

He sounded defensive. Maybe this was the wrong road to go down. "I felt"—how to put this without putting it all out there?—"I felt like she could maybe tell I was from somewhere not as nice as here. Maybe *all* the parents could tell."

Lane's eyes softened. "Oh, *honey*." He shifted closer to her, clapping his hand over hers. "*No*. That's not true."

"But . . ." Ronnie felt like a fraud for twisting sympathy out of Lane, but there was no turning back now.

"Look, I can't speak for all the parents, but Piper's a good person. She does *not* judge. I promise you. Last year—I shouldn't be saying this—but there was this kid in my class, and his dad had just been arrested for some kind of white-collar crime, but Piper was as kind to that kid as she was to the daughter of that A-list actor who's now at the private school up north. She has a heart of gold—and she has great politics." Lane raised a finger. "I mean, honey. I quit my other job in *order* to work for her."

"I know." Ronnie nodded. "And you're a good judge of character."

"And her son? Raised him with no help. I'm sorry if you got off on the wrong foot. But you're welcome there. I promise."

Ronnie rolled her jaw. She couldn't bring up the note. It drew a circle around her. Someone was shaming her, and what if Lane then started digging into *why*? She rubbed her eyes with the heels of her hands. "I'm probably just tired."

"You're a good person," he said quietly. "The *best* person. I wished you believed that as much as I do." Ronnie let out a sniff and turned toward the hillside. "I love you, Ronnie. I want us to be more than *partners*."

Ronnie looked at him, her heart breaking a little. "I know. I love you, too."

"I know you still need time—and I'll wait. But you should know how I feel. And how badly I want to be with you."

She couldn't speak. The pressure in her chest felt like a heart attack. All she could do was nod. Finally, the sliding glass door scraped, and Lane stepped into the quiet living room to put away their food. Ronnie listened to the crickets. She shut her eyes, envisioning the diamond engagement ring he'd presented her with a few months before that now sat tucked away in her top drawer. *I want to say yes*, she'd told him. *But not yet.*

Lane had nodded, his eyes full of sadness. *Because of him?* he'd asked. *Esme's dad?*

Ronnie looked away. They'd never spoken of Jerrod by name. Ronnie had given Lane the impression that Jerrod's name traumatized her. That was true, considering what he'd done on that last day. When she'd come back into the house. Found the baby screaming. Decided that it was the last straw.

Jerrod grabbing her shoulders.

Pressing her against the wall.

Hissing in her ear, *You aren't going anywhere until I say so.*

The toddler's screams in the background.

Her screams in the foreground.

And those hands, all over her body, doing whatever they wanted—until something broke loose inside her, and she made them stop.

But that wasn't the only reason she couldn't say yes to Lane's proposal, despite the fact that she really wanted to. Some of what she'd told Lane was a lie out of self-preservation. If Lane knew the truth, he might change his mind about her.

But now she worried someone *did* know something.

She had to figure out who'd written that note.

Seven

On Wednesday morning, when Andrea stepped into the lower level where the Silver Swans offices were, there was a big video camera sitting in the hallway almost blocking her way. It was the size of a small dinosaur and had all sorts of technical buttons. *Property of Raisinette Productions*, it read. She gazed at it warily, remembering the documentary Piper had announced at the breakfast.

"Cool, right?" said a voice, and Andrea wheeled around to see Carson, Piper's assistant, standing in the doorway, his hands jauntily on his hips. "It's really happening!"

"So they're going to film here?" Andrea asked.

"They're just doing some tests first. They'll film me, maybe Piper, a few of the kids . . ."

Andrea stiffened. "I don't want *my* son filmed." That was the last thing she needed—after a lifetime of cameras following her, she wanted a different life for Arthur.

Carson shrugged. "Your loss. This documentary is going to be great. A real portrait of the community. But if you don't want to be a part . . ." He opened the door to Piper's office. "Make yourself at home. Want some tea? We have a really good chaga."

"I'm fine," Andrea said, trying to keep the sharpness out of her voice. This was not, she thought, going to be a meeting over tea.

She had something to say, and she didn't want any pretense or friendliness.

"Piper will be here in a sec," Carson said, and then walked back into his own office.

The interior of Piper's office was all white like an Apple store. There were several shaggy rugs, and textured, monochromatic art hung on the walls, likely by famous artists, though Andrea had no idea who. Art hadn't been her thing in college, when everyone else seemed to embrace it. Actually, all Andrea had wanted to do in her college days was either hide in her dorm and watch *Melrose Place* or go to dark, seedy clubs where no one recognized her. Those were really miserable times. Even after she and Christine, the part-time model/fashion student, became a couple, she felt drained and empty.

Oh, Christine. Sexy, slinky, seductive, and utterly unsuitable. "Dude, she's the most bangable woman I've ever seen," Andrea's brother told her. Max's approval had meant the world. If she, back then, could land a chick her brother wanted to fuck, then no one would guess what she was secretly feeling inside.

For a while, Andrea was able to be what Christine wanted her to be, but it proved to be too difficult. About a year after they started dating, and only months after they'd married—their courtship had been a whirlwind, as Andrea had thought that marriage would fix something inside her, prove to the world she was okay—things started to fall apart. After Christine came home from fashion shows and they were actually in the same city for long enough, Christine grew jaded. She was baffled by how miserable Andrea seemed—"like a freaking washrag," she said. She also didn't like that her new husband would disappear for hours at a time or sit in the bathroom with the door locked—Andrea would be in there either experimenting with makeup or crying in the bathtub, which Christine could probably hear.

Andrea tried to be a husband, she really did, but all too soon she knew it was a mistake, maybe *she* was a mistake. And they had arguments about sex; Christine was baffled as to why Andrea didn't seem to want her like other men did. Which, of course, had made Andrea feel ashamed, and so she overcompensated, and then Christine wound up pregnant.

Andrea had always wanted a child, and for a while she thought, *Yes. This will save me. This will save us.* But Christine had other ideas. After all, kids weren't something they discussed before marrying. She had a meltdown when she got the positive test, her reaction so vehement that Andrea had had torturous dreams that Christine was going to sneak off and have an abortion. Keeping the baby safe was all Andrea could think about for a while, even putting her own unhappiness aside. She bargained with the universe, saying that if only Christine kept the baby, Andrea would walk the straight and narrow. No more nonsense, as her mother might say.

Best laid plans, though. Christine did have the baby, and Arthur was wonderful, but after some time, Andrea was who she was, and Christine was who *she* was—a woman who still didn't want a child. Christine resented the lack of freedom, the responsibility; she didn't look at Arthur with the same sort of wonderment that Andrea did, which broke her heart. Christine was capable of love, Andrea thought, but she let her resentment and disappointment eclipse any maternal instinct.

An even bigger chasm formed between them, with Andrea doing most of the childcare duties and Christine . . . well, who knew where Christine went. Tabloids sometimes spotted her at various clubs and parties. There were whispers in gossip columns that she was fooling around with some ambassador from Egypt, and then a semi-famous artist, and then a punk musician. Andrea didn't care. She was knee-deep in her own issues again, everything raging back. She'd decided to enter therapy. Dr. Westin was a specialist in gender issues, and she needed clarity.

And then came Roger. Roger, who Andrea could talk to. Roger, the first person who *got* her. All at once, in Piper's office, she could *smell* Roger—bananas, ChapStick, and the musty old apartment building where he lived with his family. They'd met outside Dr. Westin's office. Actually, she'd noticed Roger in the waiting room, occasionally, though he hadn't looked like himself back then. It was only on the sidewalk outside the office that they spoke, and that was because a man had been walking past with a llama on a leash. A llama, in Midtown!

Roger stepped forward with only the excitement that someone so young could have. "Can I take a selfie?" he asked the llama's handler. The man nodded and grinned; he seemed to expect this. Then Roger turned, looked straight at Andrea, and said, "Wanna be in it, too?"

Andrea still had that photo in a drawer. In a parallel world, there were supposed to be more pictures of them to follow: Snapshots from dinners out. Pictures of their trip upstate. Jaunts around the city. A long-standing friendship.

But she only had three pictures of him, in the end. The other was one they'd snapped during their dinner out; Andrea had liked it so much she'd had it printed at CVS. And the third picture, well. The third picture wasn't really Roger at all. It was a school portrait from his senior year that had been printed in the newspaper when the story broke. Roger wore a uniform blazer and had a bright smile, but there was something bruised behind his eyes.

And the caption gave Roger's dead name: *Jeanette McCafferty, 18.*

There was a *click*, and Andrea sat up. Carson poked his head in swiftly, his brow furrowed. "Everything okay?" he asked, his eyes darting to her, then to Piper's desk, which was irritatingly free of clutter.

"Yeah," Andrea said. Had she given some indication she *wasn't* okay?

Carson looked like he didn't believe her. "I just need to grab . . ." He walked over to Piper's desk, brushing invisible crumbs off the surface and then, so subtly that Andrea almost didn't catch it, pulling at one of the drawer handles. It didn't open. "Well. Piper's on her way."

The door shut halfway again. Andrea sat back, rolling her jaw. Was Carson acting paranoid? Or was *she* paranoid? The drawing in Arthur's bag had turned her world upside down. She'd been so worked up she almost mentioned it to Reginald—but she was glad she didn't. She'd also briefly considered showing it to Arthur—*who put this in your schoolbag?*—but she was afraid it would upset him.

She'd also been so worked up she'd called Jerry. "Andrea," he'd said stiltedly, still getting used to her new name. "How are you? How's your little guy? Has he started school?"

She hadn't known what to say. Even though Jerry was a trusted confidant, the note made her feel so vulnerable and terrible. It felt like a reflection on *her*, as a mother, as a person. And so she'd just said, "Yeah, he did start. It's going great. How's Susan?" And a perfectly pleasant call unfolded from there.

She worried about Arthur. She didn't want anyone to pick on him, ever—and especially not because of her. The optimist in her said it wouldn't happen, but look. Now, maybe, it had begun. Was someone watching her, maybe someone from inside the school? And what was the next step, the next threat? She feared that the note was just the tip of the iceberg.

Suddenly, a voice floated through the windows from the parking lot. "I can't believe this," someone said. It sounded like Piper's voice.

Andrea stood and peeked through the window blinds. Piper was standing in the parking lot, one hand on her hip, her back to the window. She held her cell phone to her ear. Andrea couldn't make out the next few sentences, but then she heard "Fuck you!"

After, Piper stood there for a beat, her fist clenched, jaw tight. A full minute passed. She seemed to be in a trance. Andrea blinked, wondering if it was wrong to be witnessing what seemed to be an intimate moment. Finally, Piper lifted her phone again. Tapped the screen once more. And pivoted toward the office entrance.

Andrea ran back to her seat and arranged herself. By the time the door flew open, Piper was a breezy cloud of white silk and linen pants. "Hello!" she said brightly. "Andrea, right?"

"Uh, yes." Andrea leaped to her feet so zealously, her knee bumped the coffee table. She tried not to wince.

Piper was still looking at something on her phone. "Sorry," she said to Andrea. "Just FaceTiming with my son quickly. It's his free period right now—I thought I could catch him."

"Oh." Andrea tried not to give anything away of what she'd witnessed in the parking lot. Was it her son she'd had that argument with?

"Want to say hello, North?" Piper asked in a syrupy voice. So maybe it *had* been someone else on the phone before.

There was static on the other end. Andrea tipped her head to see the screen, but then Piper frowned and tilted it toward herself, tapping the button at the bottom of the device. "Shoot. Dropped."

"Where is he?" Andrea asked. "What school?"

"He goes to private," Piper answered breezily, placing the phone facedown on her desk. "St. Sebastian. It's a few towns over. And let me tell you, I'm thrilled school has started again." When she looked back up at Andrea, her eyebrows knit together. "Has anyone told you that you bear a *striking* resemblance to Robert Vandermeer? He's this major real estate magnate in New York City. My ex-husband used to admire him, though actually, I've heard he's a real bigoted prick."

"Yes, I've heard that, too," Andrea mumbled quietly. Was this some sort of gambit to knock her off guard? Did Piper *know*? She needed to change the subject, *now*. "So, um, look, I wanted to ask you—"

"I can't thank *you* enough for being part of our family," Piper interrupted. "We are going to set the foundation for your child's life!"

"Great." Andrea tried to smile. "I'm so glad."

"And . . . Arthur." Piper had picked up a clipboard of notes now and seemed to spy Arthur's details. "He seems to be fitting right in! His teacher says that on his first day, he really connected with Johnny Fineberg and King Russell." She looked up. "Do you know Jane Russell? King's mom?"

Andrea shook her head. "I haven't really met—"

"You should connect with her. She and her husband live in that gorgeous house at the top of the cliffs—you know the one. It looks like something Frank Lloyd Wright designed."

"I love that house," Andrea mused, knowing exactly which one Piper meant. The house was the jewel in the crown of Raisin Beach.

"The Russells have *tons* of beautiful houses all around the world," Piper said, sounding envious. "You should absolutely say hi to Jane—she's a good person to know. And very, *you* know . . ." She waved her hand to think of the word. "Accepting."

"Okay." Andrea felt off-balance. She just needed to say what she came here for. "But . . . actually, that brings something up. Does anyone at this school have an issue with . . . with me? Being . . . trans, I mean. Are some people *less* accepting?"

Piper looked affronted. "We celebrate everyone here. It's practically our school motto."

"Okay, philosophically, yes. But what about the teachers? The children? Other parents? I understand some of this community is religious. Is it worth maybe having a meeting about . . . inclusion?" Andrea tucked a lock of hair behind her ear. Staging a meeting certainly wouldn't be keeping a low profile, but maybe they could do it in such a way that she wouldn't be front and center. And also—and this suddenly irked her—wasn't it the *school's* job to nurture this? "If people can't deal, well, I can handle that on a case-by-case basis. But I don't want this trickling down to my son."

"Has your son *said* people have treated him poorly?" Piper looked confused.

Andrea considered her words, then just plunged her hand into her bag. "Here." She thrust the drawing across the table. "My son came home with this. I found it yesterday in his bag."

Piper pursed her lips as she stared at the paper. When she didn't say anything for a few moments, Andrea added, "It's me."

"Okay," Piper said. "Well. This is very concerning."

"I *know*," Andrea said. "Thank you."

"We have a psychologist on staff. Well—she rotates schools, but I could call her up. This should be addressed."

"That would be great," Andrea said, relieved Piper was taking this seriously.

"I also think a family therapist might be useful, too." Piper crossed and uncrossed her long legs. "There's no shame. North and I went to a family therapist a while back. It was so hard for him, the divorce, this move. Not all kids are great with change. A therapist can really help a child talk through that. Get to the root of his anger."

"Absolutely," Andrea said, but suddenly she felt a prickly sensation on the back of her neck. "Wait. *Arthur* didn't draw this. Someone else did."

Piper blinked at her benignly. "With all due respect, I'm not sure that makes sense. Why would someone else put a drawing of you in your son's bag? We teach our children to respect people's property."

"Someone else would do it because . . ." Andrea's voice cracked. "I'm not an idiot!"

"Yes, but that doesn't happen here. This is a safe place." It was so Pollyannaish that Andrea wanted to laugh, but Piper didn't give her the time—she kept going. "Look, sometimes kids express what they're afraid to say through artwork. It's very common."

Andrea started to tremble. "Arthur. Didn't. Draw. This. There's no way. He's aware of who I am and why I changed and that I'm happier now, and he supports me."

"But, I mean, he's a four-year-old boy." Piper almost sounded like she was going to laugh. "Four-year-olds aren't really capable of support, in my experience."

But Arthur is, Andrea wanted to say. *Arthur's special.* "I-It doesn't even look like his artwork," she tried, realizing how shrill she sounded.

Piper paused to think. "You found this yesterday? Your files say you're new to the community. Who's even had time to form opinions in those few hours the children were in school?"

Andrea's mouth felt gummy. *A teacher saw me*, she wanted to say. *The parents saw me.* But all at once, she felt the same way she had when she and Roger got caught in that hotel room upstate. It felt like everyone was staring at her, realizing who she was—who she'd been. Everyone made assumptions then, too.

Could Arthur have drawn this? The notion terrified her, but maybe this upheaval was more traumatic than he'd let on.

Piper was looking at the drawing again. "This sort of anger is concerning for us as well. We don't approve of bullying of any kind, and a child with emotional issues like these—well, it may be worth considering if this place is the right fit for him."

"*What?*" Andrea shot up. "You're kicking Arthur out? He didn't even do anything!"

"Of *course* not." Piper's voice was honeyed again. "But I do think it's worth laying the groundwork to make sure Arthur's on a good psychological path. A kernel of anger like this"—she held up the photo, which now scandalized Andrea so badly she couldn't look at it—"can lead to bigger things, against other children. We need to properly address it."

"So wait a minute," Andrea said, backtracking. "Hold on. If I went to Miss Barnes right now, she'd back up that Arthur drew this? She'd say she *saw* him?" It seemed like such an oversight. "Why wouldn't she have brought it to my attention already?"

Piper placed the drawing facedown on the coffee table. "Teachers encourage children to draw and create throughout the day, but they can't supervise everyone all the time. Most likely, Miss Barnes told Arthur that he could put his artwork in his messenger bag so he could bring it home. Arthur might have drawn the picture and put it away before Miss Barnes saw it."

"But . . ." Andrea trailed off. *Could* that have happened?

"Would you like to see a picture of my son?" Piper suddenly blurted.

Andrea blinked. "I'm sorry?"

"I mean, maybe seeing a picture of him will help you normalize family therapy." She grabbed her phone again and pulled up an image. "This is from a few years ago, but he looks about the same."

It was a school picture of a boy of about ten. He sat straight and stared slightly away from the camera with a serious expression on his face. Andrea thought he looked familiar. "This is North," Piper said vehemently. "This is my baby. All I wanted was the best for him. He was angry, too. Confused. And *lost.* But we got help. Which didn't just help him—it helped every child he was around after that. Isn't that what you want? We do what we can, we make the sacrifices where we can, for the good of *everyone*? For the community?"

Andrea opened her mouth, then shut it again. This felt like guerilla warfare, deflecting and obfuscating and twisting the conversation. "I . . . do believe that," she said slowly. "Of course I do."

Piper clasped her hands at her throat. "Good. So I can get you a few therapist names, then? Really, there are some wonderful ones around here."

A prism hanging in the window spilled rainbows across Piper's desk. Andrea's palms were so itchy she wondered if she was having an allergy attack, which used to happen sometimes in school when she was young. Her gaze slid to the picture of the boy on the phone again. North had a shock of slick, dark hair cut in a trendy style. It was the haircut Arthur wanted before starting Silver Swans. The problem was, his hair was curly and didn't lay flat in that surfer style; it had ended up kind of puffy. In the end, they'd just buzzed it all off. But Arthur had liked that, too, though. He was an easy kid.

Except maybe he wasn't easy. Maybe she had it all wrong.

"To use a line from the medical community," Piper added, "when we hear hoofbeats, we look for horses, not zebras. The person who's most attuned with your identity, your *difference*, is your own child. Most children that age are so self-involved they rarely notice people around them, especially not adults. The kids probably looked at you, in a dress, and thought *lady*. They don't know to think anything else. They take things at face value. But your son understands this at a deeper level." She laced her fingers together. "You haven't done anything wrong. No one has. We're going to get through this."

Horses, not zebras, Andrea thought miserably. Every mother wanted to think their child was unusual, that he defied the odds. There wasn't necessarily shame in a therapist. Hell, if it weren't for Dr. Westin, Andrea wouldn't be living her life now.

"You can count on me," Andrea said. She leaned across the table and shook Piper's hand. "Thanks for all your help."

Eight

The sun streamed through the windows like liquid gold as Lauren poured herself her third cup of coffee. It was Thursday morning. She was trying to calculate the amount of sleep she'd gotten last night—an hour snatched here, forty-five minutes there, a big chunk of time blearily watching a *Law & Order* rerun—but her brain refused to do the math. When she finally dozed off, it was blissful, but she'd slept in far too late. Now she felt hungover.

She swiveled around when she heard keys in the lock. The door swung open. First the stroller appeared, then Graham. Though when he saw her, a flare of surprise registered on his face. Then he smiled.

"Hey," he whispered. "You're finally up!"

"Where were *you*?" There was something sweaty about Graham, like he'd been exercising. Her gaze drifted to the stroller. It wasn't their jogging stroller.

Graham stretched one muscled arm to the sky. "I couldn't sleep, so me and buddy went for a drive to the trail. I'm just so excited." He grinned sheepishly. It was his big day, the first day of an episode shoot that was on location and would take him out of town for one night. *Don't look too thrilled*, Lauren thought bitterly. Was this going to be a love nest with him and Gracie? She thought of the one time she'd asked him if they'd hooked up . . . and what had happened because of it.

Graham cocked his head at her. "You okay? You look tired."

Lauren tamped down her annoyance. "I'm fine."

Unbidden, her gaze drifted to the pink, U-shaped scar over Graham's eye. It hurt to look at it. Perhaps on instinct, Graham's fingers flew there, too. Then he turned away to lift Matthew from the stroller. "Anyway," he said. "We need to head out in less than an hour."

Lauren shut her eyes. Her insomnia wasn't even due to Matthew—just garden-variety anxiety. Aside from some fussiness at around 2:00 a.m., the kid had slept the whole night through. Hell, Graham had been the one to get up with him this morning. And—this made her feel even worse—Lauren hadn't even *checked* for Matthew when she woke up. She'd just assumed he was in his crib. Was she ever going to get it together?

But she was so tired. She'd lain awake last night, tortured by her thoughts. Tuesday, Lauren had left Piper a very detailed, very passionate voicemail about postpartum rage. An hour later, she'd followed it up with an email saying more or less the same thing, adding in her phone number. Later, she'd considered calling *again*, apologizing for giving her phone number because of course Piper already had her phone number in Matthew's records. She'd restrained. Piper might think that overbearing and weird once she heard all the messages.

But Piper hadn't called back yesterday. Or emailed. So then her thoughts had returned to the note in Matthew's backpack. Was Piper linked to it? But if she was, wouldn't she have written back, apologizing for her error? Maybe Lauren should have mentioned the note in her messages to Piper—only, it was just so embarrassing.

And she hadn't told Graham, either. Again, she worried he'd . . . blame her, somehow.

The house phone rang. Lauren moved to answer it, but she heard Graham get it first, likely cradling the phone between his shoulder and ear as he changed the baby. "Mm-hmm," he said. "Mm-hmm." His voice dropped then, and was swallowed up altogether as the baby started to squawk.

Graham reappeared with a changed, freshly clothed, smiling baby in his arms. "This guy's all ready for Mommy!"

"Who was on the phone?" Lauren asked.

"Oh, your mom, actually." Graham handed Matthew over. "But she had to run. She's doing fine, though. Said something about Mel's older kid making honor roll."

"Oh." Lauren felt a pinch of despair. Her mother called to brag about her sister? She didn't even want to talk to her?

She tried to smile as she unsnapped her nursing top but here was another flare of resentment. Her kid was seven months old. She was *tired* of breastfeeding, tired of being wedded to the pump and rock-hard boobs and clogs and leaky nipples. But somehow, it had become this unspoken thing that she nurse until Matthew was a year.

As she took Matthew into her arms and tried to push him toward her nipple, he arched away with a grunt. "Come on, buddy," she crooned.

Matthew didn't want to be held. He squirmed away from her so strongly, it was like she was trying to pin down an adult cat. She could feel her milk letting down.

"Matthew," she said sternly, grabbing the upper half of his torso and shoving his head hard into her cleavage. "Come on. Just eat."

Matthew arched away again. Lauren let out a beleaguered sigh. *Calm. Calm. Calm*, she tried to mantra—a lactation consultant had told her to repeat that for better milk production. She was just frustrated because Piper blew her off. Maybe there was a good reason. Maybe she was busy. Maybe she hadn't gotten the messages.

Nursing just wasn't working. Lauren's boobs were sticky with leaked milk, and none of it was getting in Matthew's mouth. "Maybe I'll pump," she announced to the baby—and also to Graham, who was standing in the doorway, watching. "I'll make a bottle with frozen stuff," she announced, then stood, still holding the baby. "C'mon, buddy."

"I'll take him," Graham volunteered. "You're holding him kind of tight."

"No, I'm not," Lauren said.

"When you held him that tightly the other day, he started crying."

Lauren stared at him. She didn't remember that. Still, she pressed the baby into his arms. "I'll be just a sec."

Graham's petulant expression transformed when Matthew was against his chest. "Hey, buddy," he whispered adoringly.

Lauren strode to the fridge to fetch frozen breast milk and a bottle. Finding the breast milk was easy—she had a lot stocked away. But there wasn't a single clean bottle. Nor were there clean pump parts.

"Damn it," she whispered. She yanked the pump parts and a bottle from the dishwasher racks—they'd forgotten to actually run it last night—and ran them under the tap.

She hated spending any time in the kitchen—the awful thing had happened just there, in the far corner. The back door had been open, a fragrant breeze blowing in, Lauren was in bare feet and a maternity sundress. Why could she remember *those* things but not what she did next? She'd held the baby in her arms, his head propped on her shoulder. But the next moment—well, the next moment was blurry. She remembered Graham lunging, grabbing Matthew, shrieking, "*Lauren!*"

"Honey?" Graham called now, snapping Lauren back.

"Coming!" Lauren hurried into the living room to find that

Graham had laid the baby on his back on the floor. He glanced at Lauren over his shoulder, his eyes dark.

"Any idea how Matthew got this bruise?"

Lauren dropped to her knees. Graham was pointing to a purplish splotch on Matthew's thigh. It was shaped like a thumbprint.

"I-I don't know."

A tiny, pointed silence ensued. Graham's gaze flicked to her, then flicked away. She swore she heard the tiniest of scoffs. "What? I don't!"

"Okay. But, like, Clarissa's always been here, right?"

The air felt colder, devoid of oxygen. "*Yes*, Graham."

Graham's throat bobbed. "Sorry. I'm sorry." He rubbed his head. "I'm already so nervous about leaving you guys. I don't like to be away. I'm sorry."

She sat back on her haunches. *Are you ever going to trust me again?* And yet, the night in the kitchen said it all. He shouldn't trust her. Maybe she shouldn't trust herself.

And then something occurred to her. "Could this have happened at school?"

Graham looked appalled. "I hope not. We're paying tens of thousands of dollars to that place. The least they can do is make sure our kid isn't mishandled."

"Maybe it was an accident, though." But as she said this, she wasn't so sure. First a creepy note in his backpack, now a bruise?

Graham's phone rang. As he rose to get it, Matthew started crying in earnest. "Come on, come on," Lauren said, scooping him from the floor. She settled him onto the couch with the bottle, and after a few moments, Matthew was drinking peacefully. Lauren felt the opposite. She stared at Graham's broad, straight back as he moved to the corner, his phone tucked by his ear, his eye on Lauren and the baby the whole time. He wasn't even going to go into his office to take the call.

She checked her email again. Still nothing. But then, she had a thought. She tapped the "Junk" tab; sometimes, messages got stuck there. Sure enough, there was a response from Piper Jovan from early the day before. Her heart did a flip.

She opened it quickly, the one hand she was using to operate the phone suddenly trembling with excitement. But as she read, her smile faded. The email was a reply to her original message, but Lauren wasn't supposed to be the recipient.

Carson—

Get a load of this. I swear, these bitches get crazier every year.

—P

Nine

That same Thursday morning, Ronnie pulled into the Silver Swans lot right next to Lane's silver Honda. Morning drop-off was in full swing. Parents stood on the blacktop unloading their kids. Mothers chatted, sipping Starbucks, making sure hair bows were straight and shoes were tied. They drove vehicles like Volvo wagons and Subaru SUVs and sleek little BMWs; there wasn't a single rust spot in the parking lot save for Ronnie's rotting Toyota with the taped-on side mirror.

"Guess what happened on *Ponies* today? You missed it 'cause you were in the shower." Esme was still in a five-point harness car seat, and the straps cut across her shiny pink raincoat. "It was *awesome*."

"Oh yeah?" Ronnie murmured absently, her gaze still darting across the parking lot. "What happened?"

Then her phone chimed. It was Andrea: *We're running late*, she said. *Won't see you at drop-off. Sorry!*

Ronnie gritted her teeth. She'd hoped to walk in with Andrea so she wouldn't have to go in alone.

Her phone alerted her again—this time a ring. *Bill*, read the caller ID. On instinct, Ronnie hit *Ignore*, then felt guilty. She'd never ignored her boss before. Moments later, a text pinged. Now Bill was texting her, though at least the number didn't come up with the business's name.

Brett Ackerman asked for you again this afternoon, it read. *He's over on Elmore. You remember the address?*

Yes, Ronnie typed quickly. *On it.*

But her cheeks were red as though Bill had been on speakerphone with the volume cranked to ten. It wasn't as if any of the passing parents could see the text. It wasn't like any of them knew.

After she deleted Bill's texts—making a mental note of the time Brett Ackerman wanted her to arrive—she sat in the car for a beat, trying to figure out what to do. Her hands were trembling. Her gaze fell to Esme's My Little Pony backpack on the seat. It felt like a ticking bomb. What if another note showed up today? This morning, as they'd had breakfast, she'd casually asked Esme a few questions. Was she excited about going back to school? *Yep.* Nobody had been mean to her, right? *No.* And how about her ABCs? Maybe you could show Mommy how you might spell a few words. Of course Esme didn't have a clue. When she printed the letter *E*, it looked more like a garden rake. She had no concept of the letter *Y* whatsoever.

Ronnie was 99 percent sure Esme hadn't written that note that was uploaded on the device. But how *did* it get there?

". . . And so then *all of their* cutie marks got scrumbled," Esme was saying. *Scrumbled* was her way of saying *scrambled*. "And Rainbow Dash was trying to talk to the animals and Fluttershy wasn't funny and Applejack couldn't make apples! Isn't that *crazy*, Mommy?"

"Uh-huh." Ronnie watched all the moms approach school. Every woman who passed could have been the culprit.

"Do you know how they got all their cutie marks back?" Esme chattered.

Except Ronnie really didn't want this to be the work of a mother. She wanted to be friends with the parents. Let Esme go on playdates and to birthday parties and frolic with kids in the park. Esme *deserved* as much. And also, how could a mother have executed such a complicated technological plan? Unless she'd hacked into Esme's device? And all the moms had been at the breakfast—who'd had the time?

So what did that mean, then? According to Lane, all the teachers were saints.

"Mommy!"

Ronnie peered at the little girl in the car seat. Both her pony toys lay on their sides now, and Esme was showing her what Ronnie called her "bossypants face."

"Firstly, you didn't answer me," Esme said. She did this when she was angry: talk even more like an adult. Since she'd learned to talk, people had marveled at how her verbal skills were years beyond her age. "And also, why aren't we going into school?"

Ronnie took a breath. "Sorry, ladybug. I was just thinking about something."

She had a choice. She could peel away from this parking lot and never look back, not unlike what she had done in Cobalt. Except that would be to Esme's detriment. Also, what would Lane say when he didn't see Esme on the playground later? And how would Ronnie explain that she'd pulled Esme from school on her second day?

Another option, then: she would walk Esme in with her head held high. What had the girls at Kittens told her? *You're as good as anyone else. Don't let those assholes make you think you're nothing.*

"Let's go," Ronnie said, and grabbed Esme's backpack from the passenger seat.

She didn't make eye contact with a single person as they crossed the blacktop to the red door. Inside, parents and kids crammed the school hallway. No one was looking at Ronnie, per se, but if whoever wrote that note was there, they'd see she hadn't backed down.

Esme pulled Ronnie to her cubby in the hallway and helped the little girl out of her coat. "Excuse me, Miss Stuckey?" came a polite voice behind her. Piper's assistant, Carson, approached. He wore a fluorescent crossing-guard vest and a petulant expression. "Um, we stress that Silver Swans is a *walking-only* zone, except on the playground. Can you try to remember that next time, in the parking lot?"

"Oh. Sorry," Ronnie muttered, feeling her cheeks flare. She *had* been running.

"No problem!" Carson chirped.

Ronnie's hands shook as she hung Esme's coat on a hook. Now a few moms were looking at her.

At Esme's classroom door, her teacher, Miss Barnes, grinned at Esme's approach. Her smile was so guileless that Ronnie was pretty sure she could cross the woman off her suspect list. "So nice to see you! We're going to have a great day today!"

Ronnie pressed her hands to her heart. Then she turned to Esme, who was already pulling away. "Hickory dickory dock," she murmured into Esme's little ear.

"The mouse ran up the clock," Esme answered back, serious if a little rushed. It was their little shorthand, the way they always said goodbye.

Esme ran off. Miss Barnes gave Ronnie a smile and was about to move on to the next mom, but Ronnie cleared her throat. "Um, sorry, this might be a weird question, but is it possible I could sit in with Esme today?"

Miss Barnes looked apologetic. "I'm afraid we don't allow parents to be in the classroom except for birthdays. We find the kids are a little freer to express themselves without their parents around."

Ronnie felt a pinch of annoyance. "Okay, it's just, if you noticed Esme was unhappy during the day, or if anyone was being mean, you'd let me know, right?"

"Has she said someone was mean?" Miss Barnes's mouth made an *O*.

"No! Of course not. I just get nervous . . ." She decided to change tacks. "Also, her device. That iPad thing?"

"Oh, yes!" The teacher beamed. "Esme's so excited about it. All the kids are."

"Do the kids share them? Like, does Esme play on another kid's, while they play on hers?"

A crease formed between Miss Barnes's brow. "If you're worrying about germs, absolutely not. Only Esme is in possession of her device. That's a rule we have in class."

More kids pushed through the doorway. Ronnie moved away slightly to let them pass. Once a fresh batch of kids was settled, Miss Barnes looked back at Ronnie with a tiny expression of not exactly exasperation, but certainly the pull that she needed to be somewhere else. "Can I help you with anything more?"

Ronnie glanced across the room at Esme. She was already settled on the floor with a group of little girls; they were playing with a plastic tea set. There was no way she could sell the idea that she needed to hang around the classroom because Esme was having a hard time.

"Never mind," she decided. "I'll see you later!"

The hall was emptying out, mothers walking toward the door in pairs, others giving last-minute kisses and reassurance to reluctant kids. At the door to the three-year-olds class, a mother stepped away from her sobbing child, exchanging a helpless glance with the teacher. "I'm not sure I should leave her."

"She'll be fine," the teacher assured her. "Really, go."

The mom looked like she was going to burst into tears, and she caught Ronnie's eye before she could rearrange her features. Ronnie quickly smiled reassuringly. "I get it," she said. "I really do."

The tip of the mother's nose was red now. "Thanks. It's so hard, you know?"

This could still be her community. Maybe these parents weren't bad people—when it came down to it, they were all the same: worried mothers. Whoever had written that note, then, was *not* like the rest of them. Whoever had written that note needed to be exposed for who he or she was.

She started toward the door, shoving her hands deep into her pockets, frustrated that she'd come away empty-handed. Then, she spied a little alcove down the hall. She figured it led to a bathroom, but when she reached it, she realized it was a supply closet. The door was ajar. Glancing back and forth, she pushed it open with her toe. Inside were extra picture books, art supplies, and bins of stuffed animals and toys. A dangling string was attached to a switched-off lightbulb in the ceiling.

Ronnie slipped inside, then huddled behind the door, avoiding stepping on some big reams of drawing paper on the linoleum. Doors slammed. Down the hall, she heard a teacher say in a singsong voice, "All right, boys and girls!" Floating from another direction were the first few bars of a song from *Frozen*. Ronnie shifted her feet, feeling a deep sense of shame. She could just imagine one of the teachers flitting out to this closet to grab a stack of books or some modeling clay and—what? How would she explain this?

She immediately thought of the last time she'd been caught somewhere she wasn't supposed to be. That last night in Cobalt fled back to her. Things had been building for a while; Ronnie had an innate sense a crescendo would be soon. Even as she'd turned onto the street, she had a tickly sense something was really wrong.

She skidded into the driveway and entered the house through the garage. The den smelled like stale booze. A chair had been turned over. A lamp without a shade blazed an ugly yellow. *Another fight*, Ronnie had thought with terror. Then she noticed all the beer bottles. The little vials. Her heart sank.

"Vanessa?" she called out.

An appliance dinged in the kitchen, unattended. Then Ronnie heard whimpering sounds from the back bedroom. *Esme.*

Esme, who was just about two, was clutching the bars of her crib, crying, *Mommy, Mommy, Mommy*. By the looks of her sagging diaper, it seemed she hadn't been changed in a while. And when Ronnie touched her forehead, it was warm. Was she sick? She cursed her long hours at Kittens. She should have never left Esme alone.

"Come on," she whispered, reaching in to pick up Esme. "We'll get you changed. And some Tylenol."

Then she heard a *click*. She swiveled around, catching sight of the cold, silver tip of a rifle at her back. Jerrod stank of alcohol, the toxins seeping from his pores.

"What're you doing here?" he slurred.

"Please," Ronnie whispered. "Put that down."

Jerrod pushed the rifle forward. It was an old hunting rifle, heavy and stained, crusty with dirt and animal blood. Ronnie swiveled and set Esme back down, which just sent the baby whimpering again. "Please," she repeated. "Jerrod. *Esme*."

Jerrod lowered the gun and set it on the bureau. A strange smile tugged at the corners of his lips, showing off his grayish teeth. When he came toward her, she knew what he wanted. She'd seen the look on his face plenty of times. She felt trapped. He placed his big, rough hands on her shoulders. Ronnie froze. Slowly, his hands moved from Ronnie's shoulders to around her breasts. She wanted to scream, but she was worried about the gun.

"Yeah," Jerrod said, a smile in his voice. "You're up for it, aren't you? Pretty slut like you, shaking your ass for everyone in town."

He pushed her so that she was facing the wall, a movement so fast and powerful Ronnie had no chance to get away. He held her there with one strong arm at her shoulder blade as his other hand fumbled for the button at his jeans. Ronnie must have made a strange sound Jerrod decided was a moan. "You like that, bitch?" He chuckled. "Course you do."

Something inside her snapped then. She couldn't let him do

this. Ronnie whirled around and brought her knee up hard. It landed square. Jerrod jolted back with a howl, which gave Ronnie just enough time to grab the rifle and whip the butt end into his jaw. She had no idea if it was loaded or how to cock the thing, but it was heavy and solid, and when it cracked against his bone, it made an impact.

Jerrod sank to the ground. Blood spurted at his lip. He clutched his face, writhing, and Ronnie knew he'd be up again if she didn't act fast. She raised the butt of the gun high in the air and brought it down at his temple. The *crack* was deafening.

Ronnie didn't wait around to see what he'd do next. She grabbed Esme and ran, this time circling to the front door. It wasn't until she was nearly tripping over the figure in the front hallway that she realized someone was lying there. Ronnie looked down and screamed. Her sister, Vanessa, was in a battered heap on the ground. Her bruised eyes were crusted shut.

No, Ronnie gasped. How had she missed Vanessa? She cursed herself for not being here when things went wrong. This was why she'd quasi-moved in with the couple, after all. To watch over her sister. To watch over the baby. To make sure Jerrod didn't get too drunk and beat her sister to a pulp. To make sure Vanessa didn't use so much that she couldn't care for her kid. To try to . . . *save* her and Esme somehow. *You have to leave him*, she'd said to her sister, when Jerrod had broken her arm, two months before. *Before he hurts you or Esme. We can leave together.* And Vanessa had nodded, her eyes big and sad, nails digging into the skin around her knees. *I know*, she said. *Okay, I'll think about it.*

But Vanessa never made any moves. Excuses piled up—she shouldn't be so moody around Jerrod. She did this or that the wrong way. Jerrod worked long, hard hours; he was tired; he was hungover; he was hungry; he wanted sex but she was too tired; he was frustrated by how the baby kept them both up; *he'd never do it again.*

But now here Vanessa was, not responding. Ronnie held her

sister's baby in her arms, trying to figure out what to do next. Whatever decision she made would change her life.

A *click* broke her from her thoughts. Ronnie straightened up, pressing her fingers against the wood grain of the supply closet's door. How long had she been crouched here? It felt like hours. She was being ridiculous. What did she think she would discover, hiding out here? And then she considered something else—what if the drawing wasn't even *meant* for her? What if there had been some sort of technical glitch and it had been uploaded to Esme's device when it was really meant for another child's? Ronnie hated the idea of *any* kid saying they hated their mother . . . but it *was* possible it was a mistake.

But when she poked her head out the door, there was someone there. A slip of a figure kept close to the wall, creeping by one of the far doors that led to the rooms for the under-two toddlers and babies. Like Esme's class, these children also kept their coats and backpacks and other items in cubbies in the hallway. The figure scanned each cubby as though looking for something, then hunched over one in particular.

Ronnie heard the *scritch* of a zipper, then the rustle of fabric. A tiny raccoon-shaped backpack came into view. Then came the crinkle of paper, and then she *saw* it—a folded piece of paper sliding into the backpack's front pouch. She clapped a hand over her mouth to keep from calling out. And then, as the figure turned, the light hit things in just the right way, and Ronnie's heart just about stopped.

She couldn't believe who it was.

Ten

After Andrea dropped off Arthur a few minutes late—they'd both overslept—she walked a few blocks away to Raisin Beach's main street, which had a variety of upscale shops. Shopping still felt like a luxury after so many months of not being allowed; she didn't need anything, but she was too antsy to stay at home.

At the crosswalk were a group of women. They were all her age, and they all seemed to know one another. They wore shiny diamond engagement rings, and their lips were glossy, and while a few of them were very dressed up—heels, silk, a Chanel bag on a chain—one in the bunch wore Lululemon leggings and a soft, cream-colored cowl-neck sweater. Their chatter was about a book they were reading, and something about kids' club lacrosse, and if they were going to order a glass of chardonnay or rosé at brunch.

One glanced at Andrea pleasantly. "Cute purse." She pointed to the patent-leather number Andrea carried under her arm.

Andrea nodded coolly but couldn't find anything to say. Even now, she felt she saw Roger everywhere. One of the women had Roger's haunting gray eyes. Another one had Roger's turned-up-at-the-corners mouth.

She thought of the only time she and Roger went out for dinner together. It was taboo. Their age difference was one issue—Roger not even eighteen, Andrea almost thirty. But it had been his idea.

Let's go out, he'd said. *Let's just see what it feels like, you as Andrea, me as Roger.*

They went to a new, trendy restaurant in Tribeca. Neither had been before, yet all night, Andrea sat stiffly, terrified someone from her Vandermeer life might spot her. But the gods smiled on them; she saw no familiar faces in the crowd. Roger enjoyed the night thoroughly, savoring the food, rubbing his hand over his newly cropped hair, peeking at himself in the dark window reflection. *Isn't this something?* he whispered across the table. *I feel so alive. I feel like . . . me.*

Andrea had been thrilled, too. The waiter called her *ma'am*; Roger, *sir.* They'd been able to talk about their hopes and dreams. After graduation, Roger said, he was getting the hell away from his strict parents. Moving to California, maybe. People were cool there. Maybe meet the person he'd spend his life with.

Andrea talked about her own situation. Roger knew she was a Vandermeer; he understood the pressures she felt, the media scrutiny, her tyrannical, unaccepting father. She talked about how much she adored her baby son and how, in a perfect world, she could take Arthur away somewhere and transition, too.

"Maybe I'll come to California with you," Andrea had said, her eyes twinkling. "We'd have each other."

"I have an idea," Roger then said. "Let's go somewhere overnight. Try to be . . . *us* . . . for a whole day." He grinned. "There's this hotel upstate that's right on the water. We could go by train?"

Now, the memory made her feel melancholy. She walked into Pages, the little bookshop on the corner. Bookstores, especially indie ones, had always calmed her. When she was young, she used to hide out in a tiny bookshop around the corner from her family's town house, reading Tolkien, escaping the things normal teenagers did—getting burgers after school, having sex in the park, doing drugs, whatever. The proprietor let her stay all hours, never said anything when she didn't spend a dime.

"Andrea?"

She whirled around. Reginald the landscaper stood at a table by the register. He held a paperback but placed it back on the table and walked toward her, all smiles.

"Hey!" Andrea said, still flustered. "What's up? How are you? What are you doing here?" She was babbling. "I mean, buying books, obviously."

"I'm looking for a new thriller." He pushed his hands into his pockets. "One of those junk-food paperback sorts. I'm an addict."

"I won't tell." Andrea winked. Was it weird to wink? Did people wink anymore? She felt so discombobulated. "Have you noticed how much other stuff they sell in bookstores these days?" She waved her arm around. "Board games, collectibles, Belgian chocolate . . ."

"The toy section is impressive, too." He shifted his weight. "Then again, maybe you aren't looking for toys . . ."

"I'd love to see the toys!" she said, her voice too loud.

"I'll show you. There are some Hot Wheels sets that seem right up Arthur's alley."

He walked toward the back of the store. Andrea followed, taking in his straight spine. Reginald was still wearing his Blue Iguana Landscaping T-shirt. His strong, tanned legs strode with purpose.

He said something she didn't catch. "What's that?" she asked.

"I was just saying that Arthur is a great kid. He seems so happy."

"I hope so." Andrea's smile wobbled. But all at once, she could feel herself cracking. Her knees buckled. She stopped and leaned against a table of calendar journals.

Reginald whirled around. "You okay?"

Andrea stared at the swirls in the carpet. "I don't know if he is, actually. Happy, I mean."

"Why would you say that?"

It just spilled out of her: she hedged what Arthur's drawing was of, exactly, but she did give details of the terrible meeting with Piper the day before, and the way that somehow, by the end of it, she'd agreed to finding a therapist for her kid. She'd accepted that

Arthur was the artist, and she'd acknowledged that he was a bully in training and probably a detriment to the school and should perhaps consider other schools to attend. When she was finished, Reginald looked appalled. "And you *believed* her?"

The question surprised her. "She's the director of a school, so . . ."

"Yeah, but you're the parent. You know him best. Have you asked him his side of things?"

Andrea shook her head. "I don't want to know. It would break my heart."

Reginald slapped his sides. She'd never seen him so worked up. "My sister had this happen once, with her son. She puts him in preschool at two years old, a tiny thing, and suddenly the preschool teacher's calling her up and saying that she needs to have him tested for developmental problems because he wasn't quite like the other kids. Said that if she *didn't* get him tested, they wouldn't be able to take him at the school the following year. But he was two! The teacher had only known him for a month!"

Andrea blinked. "Did she get her kid tested?"

"Nope. He grew out of all his idiosyncrasies, like most kids do. The point is that that teacher jumped to conclusions and made my sister feel bad for weeks."

"I'm really sorry to hear that," Andrea said quietly.

Above them, drawn on the wall, was a peculiar caricature of Oscar Wilde. He'd been one of Andrea's favorite writers in high school, but the drawing didn't look much like him. Maybe Reginald was right. Was she really letting Piper override her instincts? She and Arthur had talked about her transition ad nauseam. He was brutally honest about other things that bothered him—even things about her, like when her breath smelled like bologna, and how it was weird to cuddle with her now because of her boobs. And yes, okay, he was a four-year-old, and obviously four-year-olds didn't understand the world like adults did, but it just didn't fit, Arthur making that drawing.

"Look, I know I'm only seeing this from ten thousand feet, but he's one of the most well-adjusted kids I've ever known," Reginald said. "Way more mature than most kids his age."

"So you think I shouldn't worry about it, then?"

"Dude, if it were me, I'd file a lawsuit. That's what I said to my sister, too. These preschool people, they think they know everything just because they have an early childhood education degree or whatever, but so often they do more harm than good."

"Should I worry about who actually drew the picture?"

Reginald thought a moment. "I mean, I already told you that you should sue. So if you don't want to do that, I don't know, maybe blow up the building? When Arthur's home, of course."

"Right. I'll get on that." Andrea sighed. "But that director. She seems to, I don't know, *expect* something of me."

"Honestly?" Reginald leaned forward then, his face so close to hers that Andrea almost wanted to giggle. "*Fuck her.*"

He smelled like woodsmoke. Andrea could feel heat radiating from his skin. Something unexpected rose up in her, and then she *did* start laughing. "Well," she said, pulling away slightly, ducking her head so he couldn't see how red her cheeks were. "Thanks. Thanks for listening. You certainly know a lot about kids. Do you want them?" It just popped out of her mouth. The question felt so personal.

Reginald looked wistful. "Sure. That would be great."

"Well, you still have time."

They stopped by a table of stuffed animals, and Reginald touched a plush panda's black nose. "I'm not sure. I just turned thirty-five. Do men have biological clocks? Because mine seems to have kicked into high gear." He pointed at a shelf marked *Vehicles*; just as he predicted, there were boxes of Hot Wheels sets. "Anyway, Arthur's a blast. You guys are my favorite clients."

Andrea didn't dare look at his face, but inside, her chest swooped. He hadn't just said *Arthur* was his favorite client—he'd said *you guys*. Or was she reading into that? Really, she shouldn't be going down this road at all.

The Hot Wheels items were comprised of miniature cars and sets of tracks and obstacles. Andrea marveled at them; she'd never played with this kind of stuff as a kid. She touched a large plastic shark toy; apparently, the car would fly across the track, trying to avoid the shark's biting jaws. Arthur *would* love it, and she wanted to get something for him, suddenly, as if he'd been the one to endure this emotional crisis, not her. Andrea rapped overenthusiastically on the top of the Hot Wheels box. "I'm going to get this."

Reginald followed her to the register, snaking around tables of travel mugs and warm socks and magnetic poetry sets. "Do you want to get dinner sometime?" he blurted.

"You want to go out with me?" Andrea felt heat rise to her cheeks, but the question truly surprised her . . . and pleased her, too. "Well . . . sure. Yeah." She dared to smile. "That would be nice."

Reginald beamed. "Does this Saturday work?"

"This Saturday is great."

They looked at each other a long beat, and Andrea felt a thrill. She took in Reginald—his big ears, his lopsided smile, the T-shirt and long shorts and the threadbare Nike messenger bag he carried over one shoulder.

"Hey," she said, pointing to it. "Arthur's got the same bag. He begged for it. Didn't want a backpack like every other kid, no way. I wonder if it's because he saw yours fir—"

Something caught in her brain like a coin dropping into a jukebox. *Messenger bag.* Someone had recently described Arthur's schoolbag to her that same way. It had struck her as odd then, and she hadn't known why. Now she did.

She placed the Hot Wheels set on a random table and stepped out of line. "I-I have to go," she told Reginald. "Sorry."

She ran out of the store without saying another word.

Eleven

Lauren didn't remember the drive to Silver Swans, only skidding into a far-off space in the lot and slamming the car door so hard she was afraid she broke it. Her nails dug into her palms as she marched toward the entrance to the school's offices. The sounds of squeals could be heard from the playground, but that didn't lift her spirits. She hated that her son was inside that building. She hated that she'd said nothing when Graham had dropped him off an hour before, gurgling about how much fun Matthew was going to have and how much he was going to miss him while he was away doing his big episode shoot with Gracie.

And yet, she had to keep her mouth shut. First off, Graham didn't need the additional hassle right before a big opportunity. Second, she *couldn't* tell Graham—that would mean admitting she'd spilled her postpartum-rage story to the school's director in the first place, which she suspected he wouldn't approve of.

She had to handle this on her own.

That bitch Piper thought she was crazy, and Lauren needed to make Piper aware that this was not how you treated parents who were paying you good money. And the way that woman postured at the breakfast! The way she said that she respected all families, that everyone was doing their best, that we were all in this together! What a joke.

But halfway across the parking lot, she came to a halt. She stared down at her hands. They were knotted into fists. She could already feel herself slipping, the edges of her consciousness going blurry. She needed to breathe. She needed to get a hold of herself. It couldn't be like that night this past summer. That time in the kitchen. When everything had gone so wrong.

They'd been arguing about Gracie Lord in a roundabout way: since Lauren met Graham, he hadn't so much as tried the rosé wine she sometimes brought home. It was too girly, he complained. Too sweet. But then, all of a sudden, he *loved* rosé. Couldn't get enough of it. That night, it came out that that was because Gracie drank it, too. "So her opinion matters more than mine, then," Lauren said. She thought she'd said it jokingly, but Graham stiffened and rolled his eyes.

"Have you two hooked up?" Lauren dared to ask, surprising herself.

Graham got a weird look on his face. "No," he said quickly. But he was lying. She thought she could tell.

Lauren had felt herself getting worked up. She'd felt all the fear, the helplessness, the hopelessness, the inadequacy—all those things rolling and twisting and metastasizing into fury. And then, just like that, the rage boiled over. She recalled Graham's placid expression as he tried to talk her down, but that just made it worse.

In a finger snap, she was across the kitchen, next to the fridge instead of by the island. More lights were on, different ones. The faucet was running when it hadn't been before. And Graham was staring at her with a horrified, *damning* expression, and now he was holding the baby. But hadn't *she* been holding the baby? When had she passed him over?

It was so disorienting that she started to panic. It felt like she'd blinked and it had become the next day. She watched as Graham held the baby to his chest. There were tears running down his cheeks.

"What?" she'd said to him. "*What?*"

Graham looked at her with pity. Matthew was crying that terrible, silent baby cry, when they didn't breathe for long, agonizing seconds. "Lauren," he'd said. It was a doomed sort of tone. "You don't know what you just did?"

She knew Graham hadn't meant for the police to come. A neighbor had called, someone across the street who heard them screaming. When they'd shown up, she'd seen, scribbled on his pad, *Woman shouting. Abuse?*

When the cops knocked, she and Graham downplayed it. It had struck them sober, snapped them out of their moods. One of the officers glanced cautiously at Graham's bleeding skin near his eye, but Graham had shrugged it off, claiming it was an accident. The cops had looked at the baby, too, who was still crying hysterically, but both parents made a mealymouthed excuse that he was teething and this was just his "witching hour."

"So no one wants to file a complaint, then?" one of the officers asked, looking more at Lauren than at Graham.

Lauren shook her head. Graham did, too, though no one had been paying much attention. She was shocked that Graham was covering this up. She'd hurt their baby. Graham had had to wrest Matthew from her grasp. She almost wanted to surrender herself to the police then and there. *I think I did a terrible thing. I don't deserve to live*, she wanted to say.

Someone appeared on the other side of a Range Rover that seemed to always be parked in the same spot. After a beat, Lauren realized it was Andrea. Her face was gray, and her hair was mussed, and she was walking with purpose toward the loft.

"Andrea?" Lauren called out. If there was one mom she was okay with seeing, it was her. "You okay?"

Andrea jumped and gave Lauren a distracted wave. "Hey," she said gruffly. She approached the large locked door that led to the staff's offices. She stopped and looked at the intercom system, which had no buttons.

"Jesus Christ," Andrea said through gritted teeth. "I was *just here* yesterday, and I can't remember how you buzz in."

"You've had meetings today *and* yesterday?" Lauren shifted uncomfortably. "Why?"

At first, Andrea's face was shuttered, but then she slowly licked her lips. "Today's meeting isn't exactly arranged. I don't want to make assumptions, but . . . but I think someone on staff doesn't want Arthur at Silver Swans."

Lauren's mouth dropped open. "W-What makes you say that?"

"Because . . ." Andrea looked cowed. "I found this . . . *note* in his bag. This drawing, of me. It was cruel. *Angry.* I swear Arthur didn't draw it, but the school is insisting he did. Except there's something fishy. Something they're hiding . . ." She trailed off and then pressed the lower part of the intercom's plastic covering. A buzzer rang. "*Finally.*"

Lauren couldn't believe what she was hearing. "You got a drawing? In your kid's backpack? And you're sure your son didn't draw it?"

"Positive. I know my son. I know him better than anyone. But that director lady, Piper? She tried to convince me that I was wrong."

"Then I need to tell you something," Lauren said.

Andrea pressed the buzzer again. "What?"

"The note you got? I—"

"Did I hear something?" Andrea interrupted. She pressed her ear closer to the intercom's speaker. "For how much money they charge us, this thing is a piece of crap." She hit the buzzer one more time. A long silence passed. No answer.

Andrea turned back to Lauren then, a strange look on her face. "What were you going to say?"

"I-I got one, too," Lauren admitted, and then watched as Andrea's face fell. "I mean—sort of. It was more of a note. But it said I wasn't wanted here."

"So did I," a voice came from behind them.

Ronnie was walking across the lot from the classroom building, her steps slow, her eyes wide and haunted. She walked up to Lauren and Andrea and blinked at them hard. "I didn't mean to overhear. You both got notes? Do either of your kids have a backpack shaped like a raccoon?"

Lauren gasped. "My son does. Matthew. *Why?*"

Ronnie's eyes were wet now. But they weren't filled with sadness, more like disbelief and anger. "I think you're getting another one. And I just saw who put it there." Her gaze drifted to the office door, still shut tight. "Piper herself."

Twelve

Ronnie wasn't sure how she'd gotten out of the classroom building or how long she'd been standing in the parking lot, reeling from the shock of what she'd just seen. Piper in a black jumpsuit that probably cost hundreds of dollars, leaning down and shoving a folded-up piece of paper into a darling backpack shaped like a raccoon. And then walking out of there like she'd done nothing wrong.

Lauren and Andrea were moving closer to Ronnie now, asking her to repeat what she'd just said. Ronnie tried to explain. When she was finished, Andrea was nodding vehemently. "Oh my God. Same here, more or less."

"Yeah." Lauren's face was ashen. "Me too."

"Mine was in child's printing. I worried my kid did it, though I didn't see how that was possible. And just now, I was in the hall," Ronnie went on, "and there Piper was, putting something in your kid's backpack. I just wonder if it's connected."

Lauren stared angrily at the red door to the classrooms. "What did I *do* to this woman?"

"Piper?" Andrea was clutching her head like she thought it might pop off. "Jesus. You should have seen the way she was twisting things yesterday morning! Making me think my kid was a bully in training and had repressed anger issues. I nearly called a therapist today!"

"Maybe that's why she made it look like kid's writing," Ronnie said. "So we'd second-guess ourselves. We'd figure it was our kids doing it—and that they're unhappy, so we'd leave."

"My note wasn't in kid's printing," Lauren pointed out. "But then again, my kid's too young to hold a pencil, so . . ."

"But why force us out?" Andrea asked. "Me, I understand. But why you?" She was looking at Ronnie. "What would they have against you? If you don't want to say, that's fine, but I just don't understand what's at play here."

It was the kind of day where the sun kept shifting behind clouds, causing sudden temperature drops and changes in the shadows. "I'm not sure," Ronnie admitted, and that was kind of the truth. "But I think it's because of my job. I dance. For men. I'm one of those, um, Topless Maids."

Lauren and Andrea blinked. Ronnie kept talking, her face flaming hot. This was the first time she'd explained this to anyone in Raisin Beach. "My partner doesn't know. The kindergarten teacher. And obviously my daughter doesn't. And I'm careful—I don't take any clients in town. But maybe someone saw me and said something."

"So what?" Lauren finally said. "It's a legal profession, isn't it? You have a right to do whatever you want."

Ronnie shrugged. It did seem petty. Then again, maybe that *wasn't* all Piper knew. Jerrod. Vanessa. What she'd done. That scared her even more.

Ronnie looked at Lauren. "Why would you be getting notes?"

Lauren shrugged. "Something's been happening to me. Ever since I had my baby, I've . . . I don't know, I've had a hard time controlling my anger." She looked wrecked. "The doctor calls it postpartum rage. I get so worked up, and it's not even *me* in my body . . . and then sometimes, I . . ." She swallowed hard. Her eyes were suddenly wet with tears. "Sorry. I haven't really told many people this. I haven't even told my *mom*."

"Oh my God," Ronnie whispered.

"I'm so sorry," Andrea said.

"I've got it under control, sort of, but I'm thinking someone saw me, maybe, in the middle of an episode. And reported it to the school, I don't know." She looked back at the loft building, which had an imposing, fortress-like quality to it. "Piper gave me the oddest look at the breakfast. Like she already knew."

"She's trying to run you out of the school because of a postpartum condition?" Andrea looked appalled.

"I wrote to her, explaining myself," Lauren said. "About the rage, but also that I wanted to be part of the documentary. And you know what happened? She sent a reply to her assistant—you know, the one we thought was her kid?" She looked at Andrea, and Andrea nodded. "She didn't mean to forward the email to me, but I got it anyway. She basically said I was nuts."

"*What?*" Andrea said.

"I wonder if this has to do with the documentary?" Ronnie suggested. "Like, maybe Silver Swans doesn't want us representing the school. It would be easier if we left."

"Like, you mean," Lauren started, "if one of your . . . clients, or whatever, saw you as a parent on the Silver Swans documentary, they would tell the press, and that might reflect poorly on the school?"

"Maybe," Ronnie said.

"It *shouldn't*, but maybe in Piper's warped logic it would. And maybe that's the case with me, too?" Lauren paced. "I'm angry, I'm a loose cannon. They want us all weeded out so when the filmmakers come, they'll be documenting the school Piper wants to reflect, maybe the *community* she wants to reflect."

"That isn't fair," Ronnie said. "This is the best thing for my daughter. There's nowhere else I could afford to send her that's half as good."

"Arthur loves it, too," Andrea admitted.

"It's a good school, with caring staff," Lauren said. "But this thing with Piper is madness." She put her hands on her hips and looked toward the office door, which was locked. "Maybe we stage a coup."

"A what?" Andrea asked.

"There's got to be proof that Piper's executing some cleansing initiatives on some of us. Maybe there's some sort of evidence in her office. A list. We could grab it, make it public."

Ronnie took a few steps back. "I'm not breaking in. What if she's there?"

"You just said she was in the classroom hall. For all we know, she's roaming around the rest of the school, dropping more notes into more backpacks. What if other parents are getting notes? We'd be doing this for the good of the community!"

Ronnie glanced warily at the closed door. "I can't do anything that'll get me in trouble."

"Because of your job?"

Ronnie ran her tongue over her teeth. It was probably better to leave it at that.

Lauren looked like she wanted to say something but then seemed cowed. "Of course. I get it. It is nuts."

But then, behind them, they heard a jingle of keys. A man in a janitorial jumpsuit ambled to the office door, barely sending them a glance. He tapped in a code on the keypad, and the bolt released. When he pulled on the door, it opened. Ronnie and the others stared as he disappeared inside and then, only a few seconds later, reappeared carrying what looked to be a wet vac. "The thing is," he was saying, speaking to someone over the phone through a pair of AirPods. ". . . Jesus, Marie, can you give me a break?" He passed by without noticing them again.

Lauren's gaze darted to the heavy office door; it was swinging closed. With lightning reflexes, she shot forward before the bolt caught.

"*Lauren!*" Ronnie hissed. "What the hell?"

Lauren glanced over her shoulder, held the door open, and gestured inside. "It's a sign. It'll only take a second."

"What?" Ronnie cried. "*No!*"

Lauren didn't seem to hear. She disappeared through the door and into the dark hallway. Ronnie glanced at Andrea in alarm. They had only a few seconds to react before the door swung shut again, and later, after it was all over, Ronnie would ask herself why she went in at all. She barely knew Lauren, and yet she was the closest thing Ronnie had to a friend.

Ronnie leaned forward and caught the door but then turned back to Andrea, feeling a tremble in her throat. "I've . . . done something. Something really bad. If I get caught . . . it won't be good."

Andrea held her gaze, her expression just as terrified. "Same."

They stared at each other before slipping past the heavy door.

⁜

The hallway was dark and cool and smelled like a rose candle. Ronnie and Andrea were at a crossroads—they could go straight, but there was a hallway that ran perpendicular to them as well.

Andrea had pushed in front and was walking straight. "Her office is this way. C'mon." She took a few more steps. "*Lauren?*" she called out in a whisper. "*Lauren?*"

There was no answer. Andrea and Ronnie exchanged an uneasy look.

They passed several rooms. One held books and boxes. The next, a small kitchen. The third was an office with three computer monitors set up like some sort of surveillance station. It *was* a surveillance station, Ronnie realized—one camera showed a view of the playground, children playing. Another was a shot of the red door that led to the classrooms. A third watched a central indoor space that was used for ride-on vehicle play when the weather was bad.

There were books on the shelves and stacks of printer paper in a corner. A green crossing-guard vest hung from a coat stand, and Ronnie thought of Carson accosting her about Silver Swans being a *walking-only* zone. This must be his domain.

"*Over here*," Andrea whispered.

Andrea was farther down the hall, staring at an open door. Ronnie rushed to her and peeked inside. Piper's office was decorated with white furniture; a white rug; a giant, bean-shaped desk; and a sleek Apple computer. Lauren was hunched over the desk, furiously typing on the slim white keyboard.

"Lauren," Ronnie begged. "What on earth . . . ?"

"I used to be in tech," Lauren mumbled. "I bet I can crack her password." She gestured around the room. "See if you can find some physical evidence. A list of names. Maybe there are a whole bunch of us she wants gone."

Andrea didn't move. "I'm not setting foot in there."

Lauren hit the *enter* button several times, then glanced cursorily at Ronnie. "Will you? *Please?*"

Ronnie glanced down the hall again. Who was to say Piper wasn't on her way back? Where was Carson?

Then she looked back at the big filing cabinets in the corner. Against her better judgment, she *did* want to search. It wasn't a list she wanted to find, though. She needed to know what Piper knew about her.

Her mind again snapped back to the memory of Vanessa on the ground in her dirty house. Ronnie's sister wasn't moving. "*Nessie*," Ronnie whispered, jostling Esme in her arms. She knelt down. Put her face to her sister's mouth and felt shallow breath on her cheek. Vanessa was alive, anyway. For now. "*Nessie*," she whispered again. Vanessa didn't stir. "*Vanessa*," Ronnie repeated, tears blurring her vision. "Wake up. *Please*."

A *thud* came from the back room. Ronnie straightened. Jerrod had come to. In moments, he would find them. "I'm sorry," she told her sister.

On her drive out of town, she'd wept hysterically, certain that her sister had died and that Jerrod was alive and furious. At a rest stop, Esme was fussy—she didn't want to be changed, she refused the cut-up apple Ronnie offered. As they sat in a booth around truckers and traveling families, Esme started wailing, and Ronnie was stricken with terror, certain people would know that this wasn't her child. Esme was wailing *because* she'd been taken away from her parents, surely, even though that house was a deathtrap, a slowly boiling pot of water and Esme a frog.

Ronnie had waited for the police to swarm, but they didn't. Instead, families glanced at her exhaustedly but sometimes commiseratively. When she carried Esme back to the car, the little girl cheered up. They played a two-year-old's version of I Spy. Esme smiled.

As time passed, and when no one came searching for her, when lightning didn't strike her down, when the sun rose every morning and Esme started to speak in full sentences and reach for her and call her *Mama*, it all felt divined. Ronnie hadn't meant to take Esme away from Vanessa. Jesus, of course not. But she couldn't deny things were better because she had.

But Piper can't know any of that, she told herself now. *It's impossible.*

Still, Ronnie stepped into the office. Everything was so white and clean that Ronnie feared her shoe treads would leave incriminating marks. She beelined for a filing cabinet along the wall. It looked like it might hold important information. Pulling her sleeve over her hand, she carefully pulled open the top drawer, but she found only tax forms and other paperwork.

"Ronnie!"

She turned. Andrea, still hovering in the hallway, pointed to a drawer in Piper's desk. "That drawer was locked. Maybe you can find a key."

Ronnie moved to the desk Andrea had indicated. The drawer was locked, but the drawer under Piper's keyboard wasn't. Ronnie pulled it out and stared at the carefully organized paper clips, Post-its, and pens. She plunged her hand deep inside the desk, feeling the underside of the work surface. She couldn't say how she knew she'd find a key taped there, but there it was.

A noise sounded from down the long hall. Footsteps. A murmur. Ronnie shot up. "We should leave," she told Lauren.

"I just need another minute." Lauren's fingers flew. "I'm almost there." She glanced at the key in Ronnie's palm. "What's that to?"

The key was small and silver and had an unusual square head. With shaking hands, Ronnie plunged it into the locked drawer's keyhole. It opened easily. Inside were a few unmarked file folders. Ronnie lifted the top of the first one and found an Excel spreadsheet full of numbers. No names, just numbers. She inspected it closer. Were these social security numbers? She searched for her own but couldn't find it.

An engine roared outside. A door slammed. *Parents already?* Ronnie wondered. But then she remembered hearing something about how the two- and three-year-olds were on an abbreviated schedule to get them used to being in school. She'd completely forgotten about this little complication.

Merry voices rose, mothers traipsing off to retrieve their kids. She thought of Piper, standing in the hallway, greeting all of them. Or maybe Piper was on her way back here to grab something . . .

"Lauren," she warned.

Andrea had heard the parents, too. "I'm just going to . . ." Then she disappeared down the hall. Ronnie paused over the open drawer. She wanted to go with her.

"I'm in!" Lauren whispered suddenly. "I'm in her email!"

"Holy shit," Ronnie said, staring at the emails on the screen. This felt too real suddenly. *Dangerous.*

Lauren clicked the mouse. "Weird. I can only see her drafts, but this one is to Carson. Not sent yet. 'We need to figure out what to do about Jean,'" she read. She looked at Ronnie. "Who's Jean? Another mom?" Gritting her teeth, she looked into the hall. "So there *are* others."

And then, abruptly, she exited out of the email and stormed from the office.

"Lauren?" Ronnie straightened from what she was doing, startled. "Lauren, what are you . . . ?"

But then she heard the scream.

Ronnie's breath froze in her chest. She fumbled with the paper she'd found, trying to shove it back into the drawer, but the paper stuck to her fingers, so she folded the thing up and jammed it into her jacket pocket. She rammed the drawer shut again, hurriedly locking it and throwing the key back into the drawer under Piper's keyboard. She was sweating now. Her palms were slippery. Another *thump*. The patter of footsteps.

When Ronnie stepped into the hall, it was empty. But she heard more footsteps. The clatter of someone running. The hair on her forearms rose. She could sense someone was close. Watching? *Waiting?*

"Andrea?" she whispered. "Lauren?"

Nothing. Ronnie stepped down the hall. And then, another sound: an intake of breath. *Forced* breath. Choking. "Andrea?" she whispered again, feeling her whole body tense up. "Lauren?"

When she passed the second open door, she realized something was lying on the ground only a few feet away. Ronnie suppressed a gasp. Andrea had fallen, her legs curled under. She wasn't moving.

"Oh my God!" Ronnie cried, dropping to her knees, pressing her hand to Andrea's cheek. She was warm. "Andrea!" she cried. Andrea didn't respond. Ronnie looked around—at the other offices, at the big, bolted door, down the dark hallways. "Lauren? *Lauren!*"

The words froze in her throat, then, and she shot to her feet. There was something—*someone*—lying on the other side of Andrea that she hadn't seen. Disjointed images flashed before her eyes. A graceful patent-leather heel. A mound of hip, a swath of dark hair. *No*, Ronnie heard a voice in her mind scream. She was just about to put the thought together of who this was, just about to understand what was happening, when she felt something sharp jab the soft spot of her throat. And she whirled around again, seeing faces—Lauren's, Andrea's, *Jerrod's*, his eyes blazing with fury.

And then everything went black.

Thirteen

Andrea opened her eyes. She was lying on her side on the ground. Her head ached. It was hard to breathe. Somewhere nearby came a ragged sucking sound. Above her, a fluorescent light flickered. Far off, she could hear sounds of more car doors slamming, and high, cheerful female voices. She curled and uncurled her fingers. They were clasped around the handle of her handbag. Why was she holding her *handbag*?

She sat up in horror, realizing. She was on the floor of the Silver Swans offices. There was Piper's office door at the end of the hall, still ajar. What had happened?

She turned her head. A body lay next to her—their fingers were nearly touching. Andrea recoiled, but the figure didn't react. This person was on her back, her chest rising and falling unevenly. She was the source of that sucking, snorting sound.

Andrea's brain kicked into gear; she realized who it was. *Piper.*

"Jesus fucking Christ," she whispered, scuttling away.

Two hands clamped on her shoulders and she shrieked. There was Lauren, her skin ashen, beads of sweat on her brow. "I'm sorry, I'm sorry," she said, her eyes darting to Piper. "Oh my God, Andrea, we have to get out of here. *Now.*"

"But . . ." Andrea glanced back at Piper. Was she conscious? Why was she breathing like that? And what was that splotch on the floor next to her head? *Blood?* Then she noticed more blood on the wall. A spatter of it, head-height. There was more blood on the floor and scattered around Piper's body. Andrea looked at her hands in dismay. They were clean.

"What's going on?" she whispered. She turned to Lauren, the panic rising. "What the hell happened?"

"I-I'm not sure. I ran and hid back there." Lauren pointed to a little alcove down one of the offshoot halls. "I heard thuds—I don't know who it was."

"You didn't see anything?" Andrea cried. Lauren shook her head.

"What the *fuck*?" called another voice. Ronnie sat up on the other side of Piper. She looked at Piper like she was going to be sick. "Why is she here? Did one of you do this?"

"No!" Andrea cried, inspecting Ronnie as she stood. She, too, had no blood on her. "What happened? Why are you on the ground?"

Ronnie rubbed the back of her head. "Someone ran into me. Elbowed my head."

"Who?"

But Ronnie didn't answer. Her gaze flicked to Piper again, and then she made a gagging sound. She twisted to her right, steadied her body with her palms, and dry-heaved.

"I'm so sorry, guys." Lauren was backing away from the scene, farther toward the door they'd come through—which, by now, was shut tight. "I should have never brought us in here. I should have told you to stay outside. This is all my fault."

Andrea tried to think. How did she not have answers to what had happened? She remembered standing in the hallway outside Piper's office while Ronnie searched the drawers and Lauren hacked the computer. Her heart had been hammering. Then there had been a noise. *Yes*, that was right—a noise in the hallway, a sort of *thud*. Piper, falling? Her head hitting the wall? Whatever it was, it freaked Andrea out. She'd hurried down the hall, needing to see what had happened. The next thing Andrea knew, she was waking up on the ground. She wasn't immune to fainting; as a child, it happened a few times when she felt stressed or overwhelmed. Perhaps the sight of Piper triggered it? But that didn't explain why Piper was lying on the ground, unable to breathe. And with so much *blood* around her.

"We need to call 911," Andrea said, reaching for her phone. "And I need to get to Arthur." Something terrible struck her—if they hadn't hurt Piper, someone else had. And that someone might still be on school premises, intending to hurt someone else.

"Wait," Ronnie said. Her eyes shone in the near darkness. "We will—but wait. How are we going to explain why we were in here?"

Outside were the grumbles of engines. More cars were pulling into the parking lot. Doors slammed. Parents of the littler kids, here for early pickup, called hello.

"If we leave now, all the parents will see us," Ronnie whispered. "And if we call 911, we'll have to explain how we know Piper was attacked. Behind a *locked door*."

"W-We can't just leave her!" Andrea cried.

"We could say the door was ajar?" Lauren suggested. "And we went inside after we heard the scream, maybe?"

"Do we bring up the notes?" Andrea asked.

"Of course we don't bring up the notes!" Ronnie shook her head vehemently. "That gives us motive!"

They stared at one another. It was insane they were talking about motive and evidence and guilt. Didn't only guilty people do that?

And Andrea knew how people could twist things, depending on what they wanted. People saw only what they wanted to see. Take what had happened with her and Roger on that trip they'd planned upstate. Roger had been so excited about it; he'd wanted everything to be perfect. He'd descended into near despair when he found out that his top-choice hotel was all booked, but then Andrea had suggested an even nicer place a few towns over, right on the water, and his spirits had buoyed.

Andrea headed upstate early, but Roger had to finish the school day. She had been excited when she got off the train. They had plans to eat out, to go on hikes, hit the antique stores. She walked around the little town for a while, soaking it in and thinking—foolishly—that she was flying under the radar.

Roger arrived just as she was giving her name to the front desk of the hotel. In youthful exuberance, he ran across the lobby, threw his arms around Andrea, and said, loudly, how happy he was to be there.

A few heads popped up. The desk clerk looked at both of them carefully. It was only later that she realized that the woman saw Andrea as how she'd looked on her train trip: in a suit jacket, her hair longish but still masculine. A *man*. A semi-*famous* man. The clerk saw Roger as someone else, too.

Still, Andrea didn't think much of it at the time. She and Roger had a fun night together at an out-of-the-way restaurant in the woods. Back in the room, they watched movies on separate double beds and fell asleep halfway through room service dessert. The next morning, they woke to someone banging on the door. When Andrea opened it, a balding man about ten years older than she was stormed inside.

"Hey!" she started. "This isn't—"

But then she'd turned to Roger, who'd scooched back on the bed. He was staring at the man in horror. "*Dad?*"

There was no explaining. Roger's father assumed what he wanted to assume. Hotel security was right behind him, and they called the police because, apparently, Roger's family had reported him missing. Roger was pulled away, but Andrea still remembered the imploring, deeply repentant look he shot her over his shoulder.

But Andrea didn't blame him. How could she? He was just a kid. Just trying to figure out his life.

Now, on the floor, Piper let out another gurgle. Andrea pressed the green phone button on her device's screen. "We have to help her. We can't just stand here."

"Andrea," Ronnie said meekly. "I can't be part of any sort of investigation. I can't have my name released."

"But we haven't done anything. Okay, we're in this hallway, but we found her like this. Someone else must have come through that door after we did."

"You don't understand." Ronnie's throat bobbed as she swallowed. "I've hurt someone, in the past. Esme's father. It . . ." She paused, then shook her head as if casting off the thought. ". . . I fled before I could explain it was self-defense. But if the police figure out that I'm that person, if they connect me to that—"

"It's okay," Andrea interrupted, touching Ronnie's arm. Ronnie was in a sort of C-shape, her head bent toward her legs. "I don't want them to know who I am, either. My dad's this guy named Robert Vandermeer, he's all over the press. I kind of moved to get away from him, away from that life."

Ronnie was staring at her, her tears suddenly dried up. "So what do we do, then?"

"I could call the police."

Lauren was now more than twenty feet from Piper's body, her small frame pivoted sideways almost like she was poised to make a quick escape. "I could call 911. And admit I found her. If it means protecting you two."

"No way," Andrea said, though she was touched that Lauren had offered. "There's got to be another way out of this building. A back door. We could find it, and then we could call 911 together. And even if for some reason they find out we were there, we say we were *all* in here, and we give them a benign reason. We were going to approach Piper about a . . . a special guest program at the school. We wanted to form a committee."

"A committee," Ronnie repeated.

"Of parents," Andrea went on. She was winging it. "Silver Swans seems like an open-door-policy kind of place, and the door was literally open. And we walked in . . . and there was Piper. We had nothing to do with it. It was just terrible luck."

Lauren unpeeled herself from the wall. Ronnie nodded tentatively. Andrea turned right, then left. The obvious *Exit* sign was above the door they'd come through—the one that led straight to the parking lot where all the parents were. But then, as she turned to her right, away from the offices, she noticed another glowing red *Exit* sign down the long hall.

"There," she said, pivoting. "Let's go."

But at that moment, the door they'd come through flung open again. Light streamed in. A man in a security uniform stepped into the hallway, unassumingly twirling his whistle. When he turned and laid eyes on them, his face registered a look of terror. His gaze dropped to Piper on the floor.

"What the fuck?" he bellowed, reaching for something in his pocket. A phone. "Stay where you are! No one *move*!"

Andrea glanced at the second exit. Maybe, if she were a different person, she would have run for it. But as it was, the security guard was already barreling for them, cell phone to his ear, simultaneously yelling that they needed an ambulance and a police car and telling the women to absolutely, *positively*, stay where they were.

PART TWO

Piper

February

Here's the thing: your life wasn't always this beautiful. These days, you have the big house on the ocean, the pretty clothes, the flawless figure. You have enough money to send your son to private school and maybe enough capital to set up a second Silver Swans up the coast. You have sway over so many parents in this community—and they all want their kids to come to this place, learn from the teachers you've chosen, participate in the activities you've curated.

That feels good. Of course it does. And for a while now, you've felt untouchable, like nothing can knock you from your pedestal, like nothing bad will ever happen again. Something will, of course. The something looms close, coming in only a few weeks . . . but you don't know that yet. No one knows it yet. But today, you are letting the sunlight bathe you, listening to the kids' happy cries, and you are happy. Really, really happy.

You've nearly forgotten that it wasn't always this way.

Like your time with the Asshole. The relationship began sweetly enough. The two of you lived in a tiny apartment together in a good part of town. In the fresh, early days together, he promised to take care of you, financially and emotionally. He said he was going to make it big someday, and you believed him. He was so damn smart, and he made you laugh until tears rolled down your cheeks. You'd grown up in a household where laughter was scarce. Money troubles hung over your family; levity never punctured through.

But he swooped in and made everything light and sweet. He gave you permission to smile.

Then North happened. Things were okay for the first few months, but you could tell the baby's crying and constant need for attention got to the Asshole. Oh, he said he loved your child, but as time went by, you weren't so sure.

About a year after North was born, the Asshole barely came home anymore. You started to form a case against him. All the reasons you should leave. Then you found some emails between him and another woman on his computer: banal innuendo, cheesy banter, a few sexts. You were pretty sure he wasn't in love with this woman, but it was the final straw. Now it wouldn't be your fault if you left him. You could at last walk away.

When he decided to come home that night, he was surly and quiet. He passed by you in the kitchen without saying hello. He passed by North's room and gave it only an exhausted glance.

It was over fast. He barely cared that you were leaving. But when you went to take out your half of what was in the bank account, imagine your surprise when you discovered there was nothing left. All your years of careful spending and saving—how could this have happened? Turns out the Asshole had a few more credit cards in both your names you had no idea about, and when he sensed things were taking a turn, he used your joint savings to pay them off. He did it to spite you, it seemed, because you were always the frugal one, the careful one, the person who eschewed buying a bigger car or renting a nicer apartment because it was better to live within your means.

You and North took off even though you had next to nothing. Moved down the coast, ended up in a pretty town with a quaint name: Raisin Beach. You rented the first apartment you were able to afford, a terrible little place that was loud and cheaply built and had bugs. It was like you were in your childhood bedroom again, burrowed under threadbare sheets, watching the lights above you flicker because your family didn't have enough to pay the electric bill that month. No, *you thought.* I can't go back to that. *You looked at North.* We'll get through this, won't we, buddy? *North smiled brightly at you, but you could tell he was scared, too.*

The town was wealthy. You wondered if you made a wrong move, but at the same time, you wanted to belong here. You studied the people on the streets, in the shops, in the grocery stores, the polished mothers, the effortlessness of it all. You wanted to be one of them, the kind of mother people envied, the kind of woman for whom no one felt sorry.

The first few years were brutal. You struggled. You cursed the universe. And then, about four years after you moved, you took a walk. You brought North along with you, but he was angry about it. He'd already started pulling away from you. On one of your outings, when you were feeling particularly alone, you passed a statue of an angel, her wings outstretched. Her eyes searched you out and drew you in.

Only after you stared at the angel for what felt like hours did you look around. You were sitting not on the steps of a church but at a daycare. And there was a sign in the window: Director Wanted. Inquire Within.

You heard children squealing from somewhere inside. You watched the vehicles pull in for pickup time. Well-dressed little kids spilled out to greet their better-dressed mothers. It was only mothers in the cars, holding lattes, offering a thank-you to the school helpers.

One of the mothers turned her head and looked straight at you. You could only imagine how you looked that day: greasy, unwashed hair, tear-streaked face.

Her lips pursed. You lowered your eyes, only partly understanding her admonition. You'd never felt so ashamed. So low. So judged.

You felt called to Glory Be, but it wasn't out of benevolence, not totally. It was ambition. You were going to show that mother who you really were. You were going to show everyone.

Which you did. You made this place fucking perfect.

And you aim to keep it that way.

From *The Raisin Beach Chronicle*

INCIDENT AT PRESCHOOL
ACADEMY LEAVES ONE INJURED

Midmorning on September 26, EMTs and police were summoned to the Silver Swans Nursery Academy on Reyes Avenue in Raisin Beach in response to a 911 call of a potential assault in the facility's lower floor. Authorities found four women, three parents and a staff member, in a staff hallway unconnected to the school. All three witnesses seemed confused and very disturbed by the fourth individual in the basement, who was unconscious, struggling to breathe, and bleeding from a suspected head injury. This fourth individual has been identified as PIPER JOVAN, the school's director.

The parents found on the scene insisted they didn't hurt Jovan, but they could not offer any explanation of why they were in the hallway, which was only accessible by keycode security. All three were brought in for more questioning. Ms. Jovan was taken by ambulance to Ventura Memorial, condition pending.

This is a developing story.

Fourteen

"Watch your head, Ms. Vaughan." Andrea felt a hand on the small of her back as a police officer guided her into a squad car. "There you go."

Andrea was on her way home. She was being released from this mess—for now. As they drove down the clean, quaint streets of Raisin Beach, she slumped down as far as she could go, afraid someone might recognize her.

The vibe at the police station had been mostly calm, but there were undercurrents of panic—officers hurrying out of the station in groups, whispers, the phone ringing off the hook. Andrea and the others were terrified and confused at what had gone down, and who might have hurt them and Piper, and—the scariest thing of all—why they couldn't go to their children. The police assured them they'd get through their questions as quickly as possible and that their kids would be taken care of . . . but how did *they* know?

The twenty or so minutes Andrea waited in an interrogation room felt like days. She hadn't been asked to turn in her phone, so she used the tense, scary time of waiting to call Jerry. "This . . . thing happened," she'd said. "I'm okay, and I think Arthur's okay, but . . . but I don't *know*."

Jerry asked her to slow down, start over. When she told him she'd stumbled into some sort of "attack" in the office hallway of

Arthur's new school, Silver Swans, Jerry interrupted, in his barking, old-man voice, "Silver *Swans*? He's going to school *there*?"

"Yes . . . ," Andrea said. "I told you that." In fact, Jerry had been the one, indirectly, to tell her about Silver Swans.

Jerry couldn't make it to the station right then—he was with Susan at a chemo appointment. "Don't say anything to the police," he advised her.

"But I didn't do anything wrong."

"I know. But still, don't say anything. I'll make some calls. I'll make sure Arthur is okay. Don't worry."

Five minutes later, Jerry called her back to say that the kids at Silver Swans were fine. How he cut through the red tape and found this out, she didn't know. "Parents are allowed to pick them up," he told her. "So if you've got someone who can run over . . ."

"Great," Andrea gushed. "Thank you." She hung up immediately and called Martina, the babysitter who sometimes watched Arthur. Thankfully, she was free. The sooner Martina could get Arthur out of that place, the better.

Moments after that, Andrea's officer, named Detective Allegra, a young man with scraped-raw cheeks and a cowlick, walked into the room and shut the door. He'd looked her up and down suspiciously, and Andrea felt a sinking feeling. *Please just let this be civil*, she prayed. She was grateful when Allegra wrenched his gaze away.

He asked her what she'd been doing in that hallway, and she'd told the committee story that they'd planned. It was uncomfortable to lie, but she didn't know any other way. Allegra had looked at something on his notes and then said, "Says here you had a meeting with Ms. Jovan yesterday."

"What?" Andrea blurted. "H-How do you know that?"

Shit. Did this qualify as *saying something*? But Andrea's meeting wasn't official. She was also caught so off guard—it was the *attacker* they needed to worry about. "Is there security at the school?" she asked. "Are we sure the kids are safe?"

"The kids are safe," Allegra repeated. "How about we focus on you for a second, okay? Because you might know something that'll help us catch this person. Make sure this doesn't happen again."

So Andrea told the officer she'd gone to see Piper just for a check-in the day before—she was new to the area. She didn't get into it beyond that. Then he asked her to walk through the attack today. Why was she back at the school? Why was she in that hallway? Andrea muddled through those questions, saying she and the other moms were early to pickup and had some administrative questions. Did she see anyone in the hall? No, Andrea said. Especially not someone who hurt Piper. "And then I fainted," she explained. "Sometimes that happens, because of low blood sugar."

"Or out of fear," Allegra said, meeting her gaze. "*Sure* you didn't see anything?"

Andrea tipped her head toward the ceiling, staring at a water stain on the tiles. "I *wish* I did."

"You know anyone who might be motivated to hurt Ms. Jovan?"

Bringing up the notes crossed Andrea's mind—it felt wrong to leave them out, and yet she still didn't know what to make of them. Was Lauren right in that Piper was intimidating all of them so they wouldn't be part of her documentary? Was there a chance that by not talking about the messages, Andrea was obstructing justice somehow? After all, it could have been another parent who'd snuck in after Piper and hurt her, pushed to the brink even more than they were. But how would they ever know who it was? *Did* Piper keep a list?

It made her uncomfortable to have to make such a critical decision on the spot. It reminded her of the last time she was in an interrogation room: after Roger's dad dragged him out of the hotel room. He'd called the police, of course. Said Andrea coerced his underage child into going upstate. The officer who met Andrea said that considering who she was, it might be easier to bring her down to the station and question her in private, away from the reporters. Once at the station, they'd asked Andrea what she was doing in a hotel room with a girl so young.

"It's not what you think," Andrea said. "We were . . . helping each other."

But when they asked her to expound on that, she didn't know what to say. Roger's family didn't have a clue about the secrets he was keeping, and it felt cruel to reveal them just to save herself. So she'd chosen to throw herself under the bus instead. It felt easier to say they'd been a couple, that she was just a rich, older predator, taking advantage of a high school kid. A liar. A sneak. A deviant.

Now, in this police station, Andrea chose to stay quiet about the drawing in Arthur's bag. A lot had changed in her life, and she'd put a lot of measures in place to cleave her past from who she was now—Jerry had helped with a lot of it. But if someone wanted to figure it out, maybe they could. The less she was in the spotlight, the better.

Back in the present, the squad vehicle hit a pothole, jostling Andrea from her seat. After a few more turns, they were at the school, which looked beautiful in the low light and with all the waving palms. The parking lot was surprisingly empty. Andrea's car was parked all alone on one end, and she spied Ronnie's and Lauren's, too. But there were no swarming cops, no nosy reporters. The wind swished quietly. Wind chimes banged together. Finally, the cop deigned to lower the music and glanced at her in the rearview.

"Mighty nice for a nursery school," he said.

Andrea shifted her weight. What was she supposed to say, *thank you*?

The cop's posture seemed rigid, tense. She found herself stiffening, too, afraid he might lash out, but he didn't. The moment the car was in park, and the officer opened the back door for her, Andrea ducked her head, and hurried to her own car as if she was fleeing the paparazzi. She barely recalled the drive home, and when she hurried up her house's front path, her fingers shook as she tried to unlock the front door. Mercifully, her door swung wide that very instant. Martina, the babysitter, held the knob, her face sheet-white.

"Where's Arthur? What's wrong?" Andrea asked.

There was something unreadable about Martina's expression. But before Andrea could ask, there was a small sniffle down the hall. Arthur stepped out from around the corner. He looked at Andrea curiously, almost as though he wasn't sure what to say to her.

"Where were you?" he asked in a tiny voice.

"It's okay, baby," she said. "I'm okay." She wrapped him in her arms. But she could feel the babysitter still fidgeting on the periphery, and she turned back to her. "What is it?"

"It's someone named Cynthia Vandermeer?" Martina whispered, her gaze sliding toward the kitchen.

Andrea's heart stopped. Her mother. *Here?* But then the babysitter added, "She's on your landline. She said she wasn't hanging up."

"Oh. Okay." It had to be something unrelated—something about her father, maybe, or her brother. She sped through the kitchen and grabbed the cordless phone, which was sitting on its back on the kitchen island, the green power light glowing. "Mom?"

"Jesus Christ, Eric," Cynthia's voice growled down the receiver. "I can't believe you."

"W-What?" Andrea glanced in the doorway. Her mind thrummed at the name her mother just called her. "W-What are you talking about?" But as soon as the words came out of her mouth, she knew.

"I just got a call from some reporter saying a version of you dressed like a woman was called into questioning for assaulting the director of your preschool. *What the hell have you done?*"

Fifteen

Miss Stuckey." An older officer walked briskly into Ronnie's room and shut the door. It had taken him two hours to get here; rumor had it they had to call in backup from the next town over because the Raisin Beach PD was too small to interview three people at once. His badge read *Connelly*, and he seemed annoyed to be here. "How's your head?"

"It's . . . okay." Ronnie touched it gently. There was a goose egg above her temple, proof that *something* had happened. "I really want to get home to my daughter. I didn't see anything with Piper. Sorry." She needed to get out of here.

"I want to get home, too." The chair made a groaning, surrendering sound as Connelly slumped into it. "Why don't you just go through what you did see and help the both of us?"

Ronnie was so nervous she could barely get the words out. "I was walking down the hall. I didn't see anything or anyone—but I heard something. Thuds. And a scream. And then . . . something happened. I felt something sharp—an elbow?—at my throat. It hit me just right, and I went . . . down . . . and I must have hit my head because I lost consciousness." She swallowed hard. She hadn't quite allowed herself to fully grasp the terror of being assaulted.

"Next thing I know, I woke up and saw Piper. That's it. Is she okay, by the way? No one's told us anything." A lump formed in her throat.

"An elbow to your throat," the officer repeated. "You didn't get a look at *whose* elbow?"

Ronnie recalled a face, all right—Jerrod's. But she couldn't tell the officer that. *Who is Jerrod?* he would ask. *Oh, just the father of a little girl I stole. Who I've been hiding from for two years. Who I fear is lurking around every corner, about to kill me.*

"Miss Stuckey?"

Ronnie jumped. "I don't know anything else. I'm sorry." She looked at the officer. "There wasn't, like, a security camera on that hallway?" She hoped there wasn't. She thought of the piece of paper she'd found in the filing cabinet and shoved into her pocket. She wriggled uncomfortably, feeling its folded edges at her side.

Connelly shook his head. "There were cameras at other locations on campus, but not that particular hallway. I was told by her office manager that they'd planned to put a camera in there, but they hadn't done so yet. Budget cuts or something."

"Oh."

He sat back in his chair, giving her a devilish little smile. "So where are you from, anyway?"

Her blood went cold. "*Excuse* me?"

"I have a record that you and your daughter moved here a few years ago."

It astonished Ronnie that he could have dug up that information so quickly. "What kind of record?"

"An apartment rental." He smiled pleasantly. "So where'd you come from?"

Lie, a voice told her. *Say Montana. Nevada.* But somehow, her mouth couldn't form the words.

"Pennsylvania!" the officer crowed. "That's a long way. What made you make such a shift?"

He knows, Ronnie thought. He was baiting her. He knew the whole sordid story about Jerrod and Vanessa. She very well might have blurted it out when she was unconscious. And even worse—this was only occurring to her—he thought that because of that story, she was a person who could be guilty of things.

"Though I guess," the cop suddenly said, "I guess you don't necessarily need a license to exotic dance in a different state, do you?"

Ronnie's head shot up. "Excuse me?"

"It's a profession you can do anywhere. There's always a need." He winked. "No judgments or anything. I've heard Topless Maids is quite a swanky organization."

Ronnie was so stunned she couldn't form a thought. "What did you say?"

The door opened, sending a shard of light into the room. Ronnie's detective turned sharply, annoyed at the interruption. Ronnie shaded her eyes and stared at the figure in the doorway. A portly man walked in. "Ms. Stuckey? Come on. Let's go."

"What?" New panic seized her. They'd found out about Esme. She was going immediately to jail.

The second man pivoted to the detective. "Archer Cromwell. I'm her lawyer."

"My . . . *what*?" Ronnie laughed nervously. "I think there's some mistake. I can't *afford* you."

"It's covered," Archer Cromwell said, taking her arm. "All paid for. I'm at your service."

"Paid for—by *whom*?"

The lawyer's smile was wan and neutral. "Lane Wilder." And then he opened the door and pointed to a perfectly normal sedan in the parking lot. "And until we talk, you're saying nothing to anyone." As he hit the key fob, he winked at her. "Don't worry. Everything will be fine."

⁂

Thirty minutes later, Ronnie was sitting in Mr. Cromwell's office, a small storefront in a strip mall only a few blocks away. The room had fake wood paneling, a bunch of law books on shelves, and two bronze bookends shaped like frogs.

Lane sat next to her, his hands cupped over his knees. Ronnie couldn't look at him, she was so burning with shame. "How did this news get out?" she asked the lawyer. "How do people know that I . . . you know?" She glanced sheepishly at Lane again. She couldn't say *Topless Maids* out loud.

"Well, we aren't sure about that," Cromwell said. "Cops get information from all over, though." He had kind eyes that disappeared into the folds of his skin when he smiled, a round belly over khaki trousers, and strangely large feet. "Not that it has anything to do with anything. Chances are it was just some asshole wanting to share some gossip."

Ronnie could only peek at Lane peripherally. "I'm so sorry. About all of this."

Lane shrugged and looked away. "There's no point in getting into it right now."

"But I should have told you from the start. I just thought you'd leave me, and . . ." She trailed off. Lane was right. This probably wasn't the time or place.

"I didn't hurt Piper, Lane," Ronnie said slowly, regrouping. She was very aware of the conversation that she and Lane had had just a few days earlier, while they were sitting on the balcony. "I mean, when we had that talk about me not liking her—I didn't mean anything by that. You know that, right?"

"I do." Lane's gaze nervously cut to Cromwell. "Ronnie thought Piper—the moms in general—were judging her. Because she's not from here."

"And because I'm a dancer," Ronnie mumbled.

"Yes, but no one knew that, did they?" Lane asked. Though then he added, to himself, "Oh. That's why you brought that up the other day, isn't it? That's why you were worried. Because you thought someone did know."

"No one else heard the conversation," Ronnie told Cromwell. "It was just between us. But I'd never hurt anyone."

Although as soon as the words came out of her mouth, she felt like a fraud.

"Does someone have something against you?" Mr. Cromwell asked Ronnie. "Perhaps a client? Maybe *they* released the information? Found out somehow you were there?"

"No," Ronnie said, surprised. "Not a client—no way. What I do . . . it's all friendly. In good fun, really. All the work I do is up the coast, nowhere local. And all the people are screened beforehand, and we go in pairs." She was looking at Lane now. "Two girls, always."

"Well, good," Lane said, his voice stilted. "So this is where you've been, when you go to work? *Not* the nonprofit?"

Ronnie stared at her shoes. "No."

"And is there sex, in these visits?" Cromwell asked.

"No!" Ronnie's cheeks blazed. She wanted to curl up in a ball. "It isn't a client who told on me. I've done a good job. Never upset anybody. The clients understand my need for discretion as much as I understand theirs." She stared down at her fingers. They were shaking. "I actually wondered if it was another mom. Like maybe someone's husband uses the service, and she figured it out. That's why I was in Piper's hallway, actually."

Lane crossed his arms. Taking a breath, Ronnie explained the strange, crayon-printed message she'd found on Esme's device . . . and the various ways she'd tried to interpret it. "Ronnie!" Lane interrupted. "It said *hate*? Esme would never write that!"

"I know, but . . ." Then she explained how paranoid she'd felt in the school hallway, enough so that she'd hid in a supply closet to spy. Lane looked scandalized. When she said she saw Piper slipping the note into Lauren's kid's bag, Lane shut his eyes slowly.

"It just kind of snowballed," she said in a small voice as she finished up the story. "I didn't mean to go to the offices. I was just following Lauren to convince her to leave. We were all in the same boat. So I ran after her. And on my way down the hall, someone hit me. I fell. When I woke up, Piper was on the ground near me."

It was best, she thought, to leave out the part about opening drawers in Piper's office. That random spreadsheet she'd found was still balled up in her pocket; it was divine intervention that the cops hadn't searched her.

Lane was gawking at her with dismay. "I can't believe Piper was doing this to families."

"She isn't as perfect as you think," Ronnie said sharply, then glanced guiltily at Cromwell.

"Where were you when all this happened?" Cromwell asked.

"Me?" Lane looked surprised. "Well, depending on the time, we were either outside or I was in my office, and my assistant was getting the kids packed up." He looked at Ronnie. "I have an appointment to speak with the police tomorrow—they didn't have enough staff to talk to everyone on site. Thank God I was tipped off that you were one of the people who'd been found on the scene—otherwise I wouldn't have gotten Esme. *Or* called Cromwell here." He sighed. "I wish I would have seen something. *Anything.* And I wish . . ." He swallowed hard. "I wish you'd told me about this. The note, I mean. I could have helped."

"I . . . blamed myself." It felt like there was a brick in Ronnie's throat. "And then you'd find out about Topless. I was afraid you'd leave us."

"Ronnie." Lane looked devastated. "You can always tell me anything. I swear. I'm not leaving."

Her stomach soured. *Oh, but you might, if you knew everything*, she thought. It was disingenuous of her to make this all about her dancing career when there were darker things he didn't know. A man might stay with a topless dancer. That same man wouldn't abide a child abductor.

"Did you tell the police about this note?" Cromwell asked.

Ronnie shook her head. "I didn't know if it was a good idea. I was afraid it made me look like I had . . . motive."

"How about the other people who received notes? Was Piper targeting them, too?"

"Sort of." Ronnie bit her lip nervously, remembering that the others had had reasons to keep their identities private, too. Lauren and her rage. And Andrea: as soon as she said her family's last name, Ronnie remembered reading about Eric Vandermeer in a trashy magazine in the back room of Kittens. How he'd been caught with a young woman at a hotel upstate. The police were called. It was all over the news. Eric denied having relations with the girl, but the court of public opinion was against him. Ronnie was pretty sure the girl's family filed a restraining order.

"Well, I'm not sure what to do about the note." The lawyer tapped the tip of his pen to his lips. "My gut would be to mention it, but we don't want to give anyone extra ammunition. Unless we could *prove* who was sending them, of course. You said you saw Piper deliver one. But that doesn't mean she delivered yours." Cromwell turned a page on his legal pad. "Did you hear of other people not being happy with Ms. Jovan?"

Ronnie looked at Lane for this one. "Well, no," he admitted. "Everyone loved her."

There was a long pause, and then Cromwell raised his head as though he'd had a new thought. "You know," the lawyer said, shifting in his chair, "you look a lot like her."

Ronnie frowned. "Who?"

"Piper." His smile was dubious. "No one has mentioned that?"

Ronnie cast a startled look at Lane, who didn't look surprised. "Well, yeah," he said quietly. "Kind of."

"You *think* so?" Ronnie touched her hair. Piper dressed much more expensively than Ronnie, and her haircut was better, as were her makeup and jewelry.

But their features were similar. Their coloring, their height, their bodies, even. Ronnie felt flattered. But then she noticed the lawyer looking at her curiously, like he wanted to say something but wasn't sure it was appropriate. "What?" she asked.

"Look, I'm no detective." Cromwell showed her his palms in apology. "I could be way off base. But I suppose it's worth asking. Is it possible that whoever was also in that hallway . . . I mean, it was dark, the two of you looked the same. Could it have been someone out to hurt *you*?"

Ronnie stared at him in horror, and once again, Jerrod's presence washed over her like a dust storm. It was impossible—or was it?

But somehow she was able to tell Cromwell no. She didn't trust this guy. She didn't trust anyone yet.

They shook hands, and Ronnie was free to go. She and Lane walked out of the little office with their heads bent. When Lane pointed out his Honda in the parking lot, Ronnie started to cry.

"I can stay somewhere else," she offered. "If you need some space."

"Don't be ridiculous," Lane said, his voice heartbreakingly gentle. "We'll get through this."

He held the car door open for her. They drove home in relative silence, Ronnie's body vibrating with fear. Ronnie asked what they were going to do about her car, which was still at Silver Swans, and Lane said he'd jog over there and pick it up later. But she could sense that maybe Lane wasn't furious with her. And as their apartment complex crested into view, Lane sighed.

"The dancing stuff I can get over," he said. "But that *note*, Ronnie. I wish you'd told me. We're in this together."

"I know." When she looked at Lane, his face was haggard with sadness. It was because she'd betrayed him, surely. Her whole body throbbed with regret. She hated seeing him in pain.

At the front door, Lane opened their little mailbox and pulled out a few bills. "Can you hold these for a sec?"

Ronnie opened her arms. There was a magazine, circulars, a coupon book for services she'd never use. As she was walking to the recycling bin, a flyer fluttered loose. It was a bulletin announcing missing children, the kind that used to be on milk cartons. The images showed dated pictures of cheerful youngsters and used facial recognition software to age the child ahead the number of years from when he or she had disappeared. A boy named Juan had gone missing when he was six—over ten years ago—and the projected teenage version of him looked nothing like that pudgy-faced little boy. Would Juan's parents even recognize him if they saw him on the street?

Ronnie flipped the flyer over. On the other side was a little girl's projected appearance—a baby-toothed smile, crinkly eyes, fat cheeks. Then she glanced at the picture of the girl when she'd gone missing—more than two years before. She was about two years old, with the cutest dimples, and big eyes . . .

Wait a minute.

Ronnie froze, registering the face staring back at her. Instinctively, she slapped her hand over the picture. *No.* Why was this here? Why had it shown up at her door . . . *now*?

Lane had gotten the door unlocked and was stepping over the threshold, murmuring his thanks to Mrs. Lombardo. "Daddy Lane!" Esme cried, rushing forward to greet him. "Did you hear there was a whoo-whoo at school today?" Esme had trouble pronouncing *ambulance*, so she said *whoo-whoo* instead.

Ronnie couldn't go in yet. She peeled back her fingers to take one more look. The software that projected the girl's looks two years into the future hadn't gotten it right—her face was too round, her eyes set too far apart. It wasn't like anyone would see Esme on the street and *know*. But there was something right about her lips. And also her . . . *essence*.

Ronnie's gaze flicked to the details below. *Taylor*, read the top line. Ronnie had never liked the name. Esme wasn't a Taylor Johnson. *Last seen: Cobalt, Pennsylvania. Parents: Michael "Jerrod" Johnson, Father; Vanessa Johnson, Mother.*

Sixteen

When Lauren first opened her eyes on Friday morning, things felt almost normal. She was in her bed. The same sound machine they'd had since before the baby was born played soothing ocean sounds. She smelled coffee brewing. The sun shone through the blinds.

Then it flashed back: *Breaking into Piper's office. Piper's body on the ground. Blood everywhere. Everyone staring at one another in horror. And then that awful guard happening upon them. The way it must have looked, the three of them huddled over Piper's body.*

She grabbed her phone from the nightstand. No one had texted her except a joke from a college friend and, randomly, a text from her sister Gwen: *Just thinking about you!* Weird; had she gotten wind of the Piper thing? The police had promised that their names wouldn't be released since they weren't official suspects—*yet*, they added ominously—so she hadn't gotten, say, text messages from her mother in an uproar about why her daughter was involved in the assault of a preschool director.

There was an update about Piper, though, on the local news. The details were thin—all it said was that the police were "putting together evidence." But when she clicked on the Silver Swans Facebook group, there was already a dedicated thread called *Poor Piper!*

You'd have thought Piper was the Dalai Lama mixed with an Instagram model. People mourned her beauty, the "life and light she radiated"—whatever the fuck that meant—how smart, how resourceful, how *giving.* Comment after comment offered words and prayers for Piper. A mom named Kelly Mackenzie, who had a kid in the threes, piped in with an essential oil diffuser blend people might want to try if they were super-stressed—she sold them over on her website! More comments were filled with kids' artwork—sad faces, storm clouds, and, strangely, a picture of a dead bunny with an *X* over each eye. *We should restructure the documentary so that it's all about HER*, Jane Russell wrote. Lauren was pretty sure Jane Russell was the woman with the four-year-old kid named King and whose big-ass Tesla X took up two parking spaces at the breakfast. And then, below that, was another post about where everyone was when it happened. Everyone wanted to chime in on that one. Most of the accounts were the same: a parent (usually a mom) pulled into the parking lot at Silver Swans to see Frank the security guard's body half out the loft door. He was screaming something on his cell phone. Telling someone inside the hall to stay where they were. *I freaked, of course*, one mom wrote. *I thought: active shooter.*

Apparently, that was what had spread like wildfire: Piper had been shot. It seemed as though Carson perpetuated this rumor—one person saw him running heroically toward the hallway only to be barred from entry by the cops. Later, the cops shut down the parking lot, pushing the parents to exit with their kids as quickly as possible. *They wouldn't answer any questions*, another mom posted. *They were kind of jerks about it. I mean, this is our school, our life! We have a right to know!*

Only after the parents left did they bring Piper out on a stretcher. Lauren and the others had already gone by then, snuck out a back way to the side street, but a few intrepidly nosy parents had parked around the corner from Silver Swans and peered at the stretcher situation from their cars, texting all their contacts it was indeed Piper. A few nosy parents even followed the ambulance to the hospital and grilled one of the cops supervising the ambulance transfer about what had happened inside the hall. *All he said was there'd been an accident*, read a post. *But now Piper's in critical condition. Who could have done this?*

I heard it was one person, the theories began. Others said five. Then some quoted the news report that had come out, correctly identifying that it was three. *I saw a blond head in one of the squad car windows. She was quite tall.* And then another comment: *Oh, I think I know who she is. We've all seen that mother around, I believe.* Andrea? Lauren's blood curdled.

And then there was that pretty one, another anonymous poster wrote next. *But like, a trashy pretty.* Did they mean Ronnie?

The speculation about Lauren was disproportionately bland. *Don't know about the third parent. Someone from the infant program?* Though maybe it was good to fly under the radar. At least they weren't saying she was a violent bitch who'd probably done it.

Because . . . *had* she?

The moments she couldn't remember needled at her. If only she had a few details to hang on to. If only she could retrace her steps from the office to that alcove in that other hallway, as the time frame was a little fuzzy. Once she truly came back to herself, she was trembling. Sweating. Chattering. If only she could be sure who had also been in that hallway besides the three of them—the *real* person who'd hurt Piper. A presence of . . . *someone* lingered in her consciousness. A voice. Heavy steps. She worried it might just be her mind making up explanations, though. Scrambling for answers. Turning away to the ugly truth about herself.

From down the hall came the sound of a baby's coo, which made Lauren's nipples tingle. Crazy that after the day she'd had, her breasts still produced milk as usual. She hurried out of bed and slid her feet into slippers. In the living room, Graham sat on the couch, laptop perched on his knees; Matthew fiddled with a stacking ring on the carpet. Lauren felt a tug in her chest, which only intensified when Graham didn't glance her way. He'd already made coffee—a mug sat on the table next to him. Normally, he brought her a cup in bed.

Oh, how angry he must be. Yesterday, upon leaving the police station, she'd found Graham's car idling in the parking lot. "B-But your shoot," she stammered when she hurried to his window. "It's your episode."

"Just get in the car, please," Graham said stonily, staring straight ahead.

On the drive from the station, Graham didn't say a word, gnawing on his bottom lip like he wanted to chew it off. "It's all a misunderstanding," she'd pleaded. "You can go back to work. I'll be all right."

"That ship has sailed," Graham had said emptily.

"I didn't do anything," Lauren said. "Please go back to work. I hate that you had to leave. Is Gracie upset?"

"Lauren, *leave* it."

"We just wanted to talk to Piper." Should she have been offering up that information? "About . . . volunteering. It wasn't a big deal. I certainly didn't plan on appearing at a crime scene."

Something about her voice must have tipped him off, because when they halted at a stoplight, he gave her a strange, devastated look. "What?" she asked.

"Is that really what happened?"

"Of course it is."

"Are you sure?"

"*Yes.*"

The light changed; Graham rolled through it slowly. Lauren's cheeks burned. She knew what he wanted to ask her, really: *Is this like that night in the kitchen?*

She hovered in the doorway now, full of shame and confusion.

But then Matthew looked up. "Ma!" he exclaimed, his smile a gummy triangle.

"Hey, baby." Lauren rushed forward and slid to her knees so she could be next to him. "My baby," she whispered, pulling him onto her lap, holding him close. She never meant to hurt *anyone*.

Daringly, she touched Graham's bare knee as he tapped on the laptop. "Good morning to you, too."

Graham moved his knee away. Lauren felt a sting. "Graham," she said softly. He didn't look at her. "Graham?"

One of the plastic ring toys clattered against the other, and Matthew let out a bleat. "Graham," she said again, feeling defensive. "Okay, I'm going to assume that you not talking to me means you think I've done something. Even though I told you I didn't."

Graham shut the laptop with a snap. There were puffy circles beneath his eyes. His lips were cracked and dry. "You went behind my *back*. You wrote to Piper about the thing you said you wouldn't—in no uncertain terms, either." He shook his head. "Why would you tell her about your . . . *issues*?"

It took a moment for Lauren to find her words. She'd forgotten all about her email to Piper. "H-How do you know about that?"

"The police called."

Lauren blinked. It hadn't occurred to her that the police would get Piper's emails so quickly. ". . . When?"

"This morning. Why would you tell a total stranger about a personal thing we're going through?"

"Because . . ." Lauren peered again at her sweet baby on her lap. The bruise was still visible on his thigh, a fainter purple now. She and the others hadn't said anything about not talking about the notes to people they trusted. "Look, I got this strange note in Matthew's backpack after the first day. Saying we should enroll him somewhere else."

"*What?*" Graham was on his feet now. "Are you serious?"

"I'm sorry I didn't say anything. I-I thought you'd blame me. I figured it was my fault—that someone saw me freak out in public and took it the wrong way. So I got it in my head to write to Piper. Explain myself. Explain that I was getting help, that sort of thing. Except . . ."

She stopped. She couldn't say the part about Piper forwarding an email that said she thought Lauren was a crazy bitch. It was just the sort of thing to set her off, and Graham knew it. Then again, wouldn't the police have that email of Piper's as well?

"Where is this note?" Graham asked. "Do you still have it?"

Lauren bit down hard on her lip. "I threw it away. I didn't want you to see it."

And there it was on his face: the doubt. "Graham, no, I really got one. Ronnie and Andrea did, too. *That's* why we were in the hallway, we just wanted to *talk* to her." His hand fluttered to his mouth. "Honestly! Nothing else happened! None of us hurt her! We were in the wrong place at the wrong time!"

Graham sank to a kitchen chair and stared blankly at the top of the table. "So you were in cahoots with those other two."

"Cahoots?" Lauren cried. "They're nice people."

"How do you know they were telling the truth about getting notes?" Graham asked. "Maybe they were riling you up. People lie all the time. People like to stir up shit."

"Not them," Lauren said. Then she remembered something. Something she couldn't believe she'd forgotten. "Hold on."

She ran from the room and located Matthew's backpack, which was sitting on the floor near the front door. She hurried back into the kitchen with it, her hands shaking. "I can't believe I forgot. Yesterday, when we were talking outside the offices, Ronnie said she *saw* Piper go to Matthew's bag. With *another note*." She unzipped the bag and rooted around at the bottom. Her heart lifted when her fingers clamped on a folded-up slip of paper. "Here!" she cried, drawing it out and thrusting it at Graham.

He started to open it. Lauren rushed to be next to him so she could read the words, too. The typed message was in the same font as the note that had come before it, but it didn't make sense.

```
Dear Mrs. Smith—Can you call my office to make a
one-on-one appointment? I like doing it with
all my new parents. Thanks, Piper Jovan
```

Unceremoniously, Graham folded the paper. "But," Lauren whimpered, "the other note was *nothing* like this one. I *swear*!"

"Are you sure?"

"It said, *You are not wanted!*"

"Maybe you read it wrong. Maybe it said, *You* are *wanted*. Maybe it was one of those stupid-ass *affirmations* that are so trendy right now."

Lauren's vision was starting to tunnel. She placed her hand on the back of her neck, trying to cool her blazing skin. No. *Could* she have read it wrong? But how did that explain Ronnie's note, Andrea's drawing? But maybe those had been misconstrued, too?

A knot welled in Lauren's throat. "You really think I'd hurt someone?" she asked in a small voice. "You think *I* did this to Piper?"

"I . . ." Graham put his head in his hands. *Oh my God*, Lauren thought. But then he said, "I wonder if you should go into treatment."

". . . Treatment?"

"A . . . facility. Gracie knows a few. Just . . . you know. To get your memories back on track. To figure out what's going on."

Lauren shot to her feet. "You want me to go into a psych ward? *Gracie* wants me to go into a psych ward?" So he'd spoken to Gracie about it, then. She pictured them conspiring together in soft murmurs, Gracie saying it was for the best, Graham agreeing, and then Gracie giving him a long, consoling hug, and then . . .

Graham squeezed his eyes shut. "Lauren, no. Not like that. It's more like a spa, but I think it would be good—you could have some time away, work out what you're going through, get better."

"Who would take care of Matthew?" Lauren gasped, looking down at the baby, so cute in his jungle-print onesie.

"Clarissa could, for a little while. And me. I could take a few weeks off work. We're coming up to a hiatus anyway. Just until this blows over."

She pressed her fingertips against the sides of her face just to feel something. So that was it, then. She was crazy; she was replaceable. Something else Graham said hit her: *Just until this blows over.* He *was* ashamed of her.

On that awful night in the kitchen, after the police had gone, Lauren had turned to her husband, drained, scared, and humiliated. Her whole sense of reality felt impugned. She also felt very unworthy of her good fortune.

"I understand," she said flatly to her husband, "if you want to leave me."

"Come on," Graham said. "Stop."

"No. Really." Tears blurred her vision. "If I can do that—if I could *hurt* him . . ." She broke off and glanced over at Matthew. There was a boulder in her throat. She'd never hated herself so much.

"It'll be okay," Graham assured her. "We'll work through this together. But you have to promise to do the work, too. Will you promise?"

"Of course I promise," Lauren said.

Now, the smell of coffee turned putrid in Lauren's nostrils. She was a failure. She'd made a promise to Graham in the summer, and she hadn't followed through, and now this had happened. Leave her *son*? No. There had to be another way.

"I need an aspirin," she said miserably. And then she stood and walked back to the bedroom to retrieve one from the bedside drawer. The bed looked inviting, the sheets still in a jumble. Maybe she'd lie down again. Maybe she'd sleep forever.

As she bent to open the bedside drawer, her phone was lit up in the darkness, a bright rectangle on the nightstand. Lauren picked it up, half expecting it to be something damning about her—a call from the police, maybe, ready with questions about that email she'd sent to Piper, ready to arrest her. Maybe they *should* arrest her.

But it was a text from Ronnie. *I need to meet. Something's happened. Something bad.*

Seventeen

It took Andrea thirty minutes to leave her house, and that was only after making Martina *promise* not to open the door for anyone, after two outfit changes to ensure her face was fully covered, and after checking the security cameras to see that a surveillance car wasn't staked out past the trees. When she finally reversed out of her driveway, there wasn't a single long-lensed camera in sight that she could see. But that was even more unnerving than if there'd been a pack of paparazzi at the curb. *Bizarre*, she thought.

Her mother had been inconsolable on the phone last night. Cynthia said that "everyone was going to know soon" and that this was going to probably give Andrea's father a coronary. She also said Andrea's father would most likely take this out on Cynthia because Cynthia *knew all along* and didn't tell him.

Andrea understood the burden of her mom keeping this secret to herself, and she appreciated it. Who knew what he might do once he learned the truth? He might try to cut off her and Arthur's trusts. He'd try to take Arthur away, possibly putting his whole legal team on the matter, saying it was for the moral health of his only grandson.

But strangely, Andrea had received no phone calls from her father, or her brother, or any reporters. Not even any hang-ups. She called a few friends back in New York who knew about her transition, but no one seemed to have heard any brewing stories about her. She even tried her brother, Max, thinking maybe the family had been informed first. She and Max were on speaking terms, but they were more like distant cousins who only caught up once every few years. Max certainly didn't know anything personal about Andrea, including her transition, but she hoped he would be cooler than Cynthia. But all she got was his voicemail.

So once again, she'd turned to Jerry. He promised to look into it and, if needed, pay off the journalist who'd gotten the tip and called her mom. (Andrea had a hunch Jerry became used to paying off journalists when he worked for her father.) Jerry also assured her that she wouldn't be charged for doing anything to Piper—there wasn't enough evidence, at present, that Andrea had hurt her. It wasn't great that Andrea was inside a locked school building, he added—Andrea would have to beef up her story about that.

Now, Andrea turned onto a busier road that led to the business district and checked her rearview. No one was tailing her. Was it possible the reporters *didn't* know? But then who had called her mom? Cynthia knew specific details about what had happened—Piper's name, that she'd been found on the floor outside her office, even the name of the police precinct Andrea had been taken to.

Someone knew. And usually, that meant the press—all the press—probably wasn't far behind.

This morning, Ronnie had sent up her own flare. They chose to convene at a secluded walking trail at the edge of town. The trail was too out of the way for the mom set, who preferred to stroller-cize on the beach paths or the walking trail closer to the play-ground. It was also drizzly this morning, which would drive even more people away. When Andrea pulled the car into the lot, Ron-nie's and Lauren's cars were the only others there.

She stepped out, pulled up the hood of her raincoat, and lis-tened. The only sounds were the swishes of the trees and the spatter of rain. An airplane groaned high overhead.

Ronnie and Andrea were waiting behind a big sign that listed all the path's rules. When Andrea rounded the corner, Lauren quickly stubbed out a cigarette. "Sorry," she blurted guiltily. "I haven't smoked in years. But I'm kind of losing my mind."

"It's okay," Andrea said quietly. "We all are."

Ronnie started to walk, her hands thrust in pockets, her hood obscuring her face. Andrea and Lauren hurried to catch up. Once they passed a big green garbage can that looked like it had been freshly emptied, Ronnie said in a whisper, *"Someone knows the Topless Maids thing."*

"*What?*" Andrea said. "Who?"

"I don't know. But they tipped Lane off. And the cops."

Lauren blew air out of her cheeks. "If it makes you feel any better, the police know I wrote an email to Piper about having anger problems. They told Graham, not me. He's pissed I told strangers about it."

"It's your issue, though," Ronnie said petulantly. "Not his."

"My mom got a call saying someone from the press contacted her about me," Andrea chimed in. "She was on the phone literally the moment I stepped through the door from the police station, ready to read me the riot act. Also, this thing happened to me in New York that doesn't paint me in the best light."

"What do you mean?" Lauren asked.

Andrea paused for a moment. "Maybe you'd heard about it. Me and a young person? I was dressed in a suit—I looked like a man. People thought I'd been having an affair with this person. That I'd lured the kid."

The women nodded, not seeming that surprised. So they'd read about it after she told them who she was, then. What a strange, vulnerable thing it was to have such a public life. It was certainly nothing Andrea had ever asked for.

"Anyway, the real story isn't what was reported." And then she hurriedly told them the truth—including that she thought Roger would want her to keep his struggles secret, and that he'd never told his parents that he was trans. "I was acquitted of any formal charges, and the restraining order was technically dropped, but the story follows me," Andrea said. "Certain people linking me to that might think differently of me. See me as a liar. Someone slippery and suspicious, capable of deviant things."

"Same with my email to Piper," Lauren admitted. "When a detective sees *rage disorder*, of course they'll think I lashed out." Then she paused. "Though, you know what's weird? It sounds like they knew about my email to Piper, but not Piper's email back to me that I was a nutcase."

Everyone thought about this. "Whoever turned it over to them only sent your email and not Piper's reply?" Andrea wondered aloud. "That's weird."

"Who has access to Piper's email?" Ronnie asked.

"It wasn't *that* hard to hack into." Lauren shook water off her umbrella. "Maybe some other wronged parent figured out her password just like I did and found it."

"You guys," Ronnie blurted, her voice so doleful they both looked over in alarm. "I think the person who attacked Piper—they meant to hurt me, not her."

Andrea and Lauren stopped and stared. "Why would someone want to hurt you?" Lauren cried.

Ronnie raised her hood a little, and rain dripped on her face. "Esme isn't my daughter. She's my sister's. I took her out of a bad situation—but I didn't ask permission. She's technically a missing child." She took a breath. "I did what was right. Esme doesn't know. It's why I didn't want to be in the documentary—not because of the Topless Maids thing, not really. I didn't want Esme's father to spot me. He was . . ."

Andrea's gut clenched. Ronnie didn't have to explain what Esme's father was. There were various possibilities, but none of them were good.

". . . I've been living in fear that he's going to find me," Ronnie said. "So the last thing I would do would be hurt someone and get arrested and attract attention."

No one spoke. Andrea snuck a peek at Lauren only to see that she looked shattered, too. "So you just . . . *took* her?" Lauren asked.

Ronnie nodded. "I hit Jerrod. Knocked him out."

"But you had to," Andrea urged. "Of course you had to."

Ronnie put her head in her hands. "But I left my sister. I shouldn't have done that."

Lauren took a breath. "And you think that guy followed us into that hallway? Like, he found you . . . and came after you . . . and got Piper by mistake? No offense, Ronnie, but that seems kind of . . . I don't know. Unlikely?"

"I thought so, too, except this lawyer I spoke to reminded me how I resemble Piper, especially in the dark. And said that maybe Piper's attack was meant for me. I didn't want to believe him, but then, when I came home, I got this."

She turned over what she was holding, a piece of paper that was now half-soaked from the rain. Still, Andrea was able to make out that it was a *Missing* flyer for a little girl named Taylor Johnson. It took Andrea a moment to make the connection.

"I just got this yesterday, also when I came home from the police. I feel like it's Jerrod, saying, *I know where you are. I'll find you.*"

"Wait a minute," Lauren said. "If this guy is such a scary dude—and I don't doubt he is—why would he go to all the trouble? Why follow you to the school and then threaten you with the *Missing* flyer? I'd think he'd just grab you in a parking lot somewhere, and that would be that." She noted the horror on Ronnie's face. "Sorry."

Andrea agreed. "Not that you don't need to protect yourself from this guy. And I totally believe you that this *Missing* poster was timed to send a message. But I wonder if you're wrong about the message it's sending."

"What other message would it be?" Ronnie asked.

"Maybe . . . *keep quiet. Or else.*"

"Keep quiet about . . . *what*?" Ronnie whispered. "The attack?" Her eyes widened. "Who might have really done it?"

"Maybe? I mean, maybe someone's worried we saw something. And this same someone has leverage on us. They know things we don't want public. Things that tarnish who we are as people—make us look more culpable, maybe more unhinged. And it seems they're trying to use those things to make us look guilty . . . *and* to ensure we don't talk."

"Who could that be?" Lauren asked. "Who could have found out these things?"

"I don't know. But it's who we need to track down. We can't let whoever it is ruin us."

Everyone walked a bit. Andrea's ankles were starting to ache, but she didn't want to complain. Ronnie said, "You think it connects to the messages in the backpacks . . . or that's just a coincidence?"

"I don't even know if mine was so nasty anymore," Lauren mumbled. "I told Graham about it, and he said it didn't sound so bad. And then when I went to grab the *other* note—that one you saw Piper stick in my backpack yesterday, Ronnie—you know what it said?" She looked wrecked. "She just wanted to set up a 'new mom' meeting."

Andrea thought of the drawing Arthur had received. The *X* through her body. How someone had pressed so hard with the crayon to write *no* it had creased the page. Had she misinterpreted that, too? But no. *No.* There was no way that message was a joke.

"Maybe that was to confuse you. To second-guess yourself," Ronnie said.

Lauren just peered at her hopelessly. "What if it *was* Piper we saw in the hallway?" she asked. "Like, what if she was coming after us? She knew we were in her office. Doing things we shouldn't have been doing. And if she's keeping some kind of secret . . . if there's something in there we're not supposed to see . . ."

They thought about this for a moment. A plane zoomed overhead. Andrea got a faint whiff of cigarette smoke and suddenly felt uneasy. There was no one on the trail. Was someone lurking in the woods? *Listening?*

"What do we know about Piper?" Ronnie asked. "Like, could someone *else* have had an issue with her? Another parent, maybe. Someone else who got a note warning them away?"

Andrea remembered something. "I heard her speaking on the phone. I was in her office, waiting to meet, and she was in the parking lot. At one point, she told someone to fuck off, or to go fuck themselves. Then she hung up and just . . . *stood* there. But by the time she got to the office, it was like nothing was wrong."

Ronnie raised her eyebrows. "Maybe that's something? Your meeting was the day before the attack."

"Oh, and also," Lauren added, "when I was in her email, this draft to Carson popped up—*we need to figure out what to do about Jean.* Anyone know a Jean at school?"

"I could ask Lane," Ronnie said. "He has a directory listing all the parents."

Andrea turned to Ronnie. "Did you find anything in that locked drawer?"

"Just some paperwork. A spreadsheet of numbers. I, um, grabbed it, actually. I didn't have time to shove it back in the drawer." She peeked at them guiltily. "That's bad, right?"

"Who's going to realize it's missing?" Andrea asked. "It was Piper's office. *And* it was a locked drawer. Although . . ." She considered something. "Carson kept looking at that drawer suspiciously when I was waiting to meet with Piper. He even tugged on it. Maybe to make sure it was still locked."

"So maybe he knew Piper had something bad in there, something we might snoop for?" Lauren suggested. She looked at Ronnie. "Are you *sure* that paper is just numbers?"

"There were definitely no names. I can look at it when I get home."

They passed a small picnic table, and then a stream. A jogger came at them from the left and gave the group a nod. "We didn't do this," Andrea insisted after he passed. "We didn't hurt Piper. But we have to figure out who did . . . and who's trying to blame us."

Ronnie gave a weak nod. Lauren shrugged.

"We'll be our own advocates. And we'll find whoever's fucking with our lives—and get them to stop."

That got a little smile. Andrea stood a little straighter. They would prove someone else had been in that hall. They *had* to. Her story wouldn't break. She wouldn't lose her privacy. She and Arthur would get over this. She'd send him back to Silver Swans—or maybe she wouldn't. But she wouldn't lose everything. She'd still have control.

"Let's turn around," Lauren said.

And they did, heading back the way they came, sharing a comfortable silence that was more appropriate for lifelong friends, not for women who'd only known one another for a matter of days. There were times, Andrea supposed, when even if the details didn't match up, you had to go on intuition. To some, Andrea probably didn't seem so believable, either. Maybe everyone was capable of criminal acts if they were pushed hard enough. But in this case, they all had to trust one another. And maybe it was easier to bond together than try to wade through this alone.

But the feeling of goodwill lasted only a minute; on the walk back, there was that scent of cigarette smoke again. Andrea's gaze darted into the woods once more . . . but again, nothing. A chill wriggled down her back. There were so many unknowns. So many people they couldn't trust. And she couldn't shake the feeling that someone was close, *watching*.

Piper

May

The same sun is out, but you are chilled to the bone. You sit on the back of your beautiful car and stare at your empty school building. It's a Saturday. You're going through the ledgers. Admissions are down for next year. Way down—some parents have even pulled their kids out of school for the final month of this *year, demanding some of their fees back, saying that in this economy, no one should be expected to pay what you're asking. And for next year, people seem to be looking elsewhere, too.*

Who could have predicted an economic crash? And there you were only months ago, thinking that a school was something that could weather any storm—people always need to educate their children, after all. Parents go all out when it comes to schooling, especially if it's touted as the best.

How foolish you'd been to think life would never change. How careless you'd been not to put certain protective measures in place. But now, here you are, looking at your balance sheets. What had looked so promising months ago now downright terrifies you. It's amazing how you thought you had enough cushion to start a second school up the coast. Now, your worries are more pressing . . . and much more down-to-earth.

"We could look for angel investors," Carson suggests.

You sigh. "We've exhausted those options. They don't get it. We're a preschool. We shouldn't have to need additional funding."

"And I'm assuming you've already applied for the small-business loan?"

You give him a withering look. Of course you've applied for the small-business loan. And you received the small-business loan. And you've already blown through *the small-business loan.*

"Okay." Carson brushes his hands together. "We're going to think of something. Really."

If only you had some of Carson's optimism. And to think you almost hadn't hired him. You'd thought it strange when he applied to the position—a young, possibly gay man in his twenties, no children, with a bachelor's in art history? Then he'd said that he wasn't really interested in the kids, but he totally "got" moms. "I think I'm a mommy blogger in a pudgy twentysomething guy's body," he admitted. "Is that weird? I just know what gets them going. I think I could inspire everyone. Get everyone inspired in us." Then he'd waved his hand. "But you probably want someone more qualified. I get it."

You were intrigued, though. So you gave Carson an assignment you'd given none of the others applying for the assistant position: write a Silver Swans newsletter and some sample Instagram posts that would get parents' attention. "I want it to say, 'We are all in for your children, and you should respect us and tell all your friends about us,'" you told him. "I want it to say, 'If you aren't sending your kids here, and if your friends aren't sending their kids here, then you're losers.' But subtly. You got it?"

And he'd nailed it. Boy, had he nailed it! His voice was "cool mom who's up to her elbows in kids . . . but also makes time for her Peloton." He threw subtle shade at all the other schools in town. He low-key shamed those who didn't value education over everything else. He knew all the tricks that made mothers weak—you knew firsthand. After reading his sample work, even you started to feel that familiar guilt.

So you hired him. These days, he writes all the newsletters. Handles the fundraising. Pressures parents into volunteering. What his goal is in all this, you really aren't sure. Maybe he just likes being good at something. Maybe he's happy he's found his niche. Sometimes you wonder if he has a platonic crush on you. Sometimes you get the little-boy-wanting-to-please-his-mother vibe. But mostly, you're just glad you have someone on your side, an almost-friend.

You try to take care of Carson. You tell him that he's valued, and you pay him more than any other assistant doing his job is paid. But it's getting harder. His newsletters aren't working anymore. Parents, so recently robbed of their savings, are saying he's insensitive, even bullying. The money for Carson's salary could be better served elsewhere.

It's all going to shit.

You might have spent the past five years growing your kingdom, turning Silver Swans into a school every parent wants their kid to attend because of its cache, its guests, its resources. In the past five years, you've been on the covers of magazines and the subject of blog posts and have been on Happy Morning OC *six times to talk about mommies and kids. In the past five years, you've been able to give North everything he wants, anticipating his needs ahead of time, intuiting what a boy his age wants and adores. Last year—this very month—you had parents clamoring at your sides, begging to be put on the waiting list, practically throwing their money at you.*

This place is your identity. It's who you are, as a person. And now it's been stripped away. It's like you're walking around without a face. It's like your anthill has been smashed.

You stare up at the sun, a hazy ball behind a cloud. It's just the normal sun, obliviously shining, even though the world has gone to shit. The last time you felt like this, you realize, was when you were with the Asshole.

"So I have a few other ideas," Carson says. "But they're a little . . . outside the box."

His voice is so earnest and helpful that you want to hug him. Carson tries so hard to make you happy. "Okay," you say. "Shoot."

"Well, there's this," he says, and turns the notepad he's holding around so you can see. On it are two items. The first: Documentary.

"A documentary?" you ask.

"I've heard some rumblings about one in the works. About parenting, kids—and schools—during this time. If we were featured, maybe, it could bring us a lot of visibility. And they're going for something super highbrow."

You pause. You think of your glorious little school. And the beautiful children. Hell, the beautiful parents. Oh, there are a few rogue apples, some squeaky wheels . . . but you can deal with those. You always have.

"Interesting," you admit. "You know the person to contact?"

"I do." Carson nods, grinning. "He's going to love you."

This is a tiny glimmer of hope. You've always thought you had a face for TV. And if Silver Swans were the topic of an esteemed program, maybe you could charge even more when everyone returns. To balance things out.

Then you notice the second item on Carson's list. You read it over several times, making sure you understand what Carson is getting at. This, too, has potential. A lot of potential.

"This." You point at it, your heart picking up speed. With fear. With desire. With curiosity. And with admiration. Carson is more slippery than you'd ever imagined. "Tell me more about this one, too."

Eighteen

Isn't he the *nicest* baby?" Clarissa cooed to Matthew. She and Lauren sat on the carpet, Clarissa cross-legged, Lauren's spine pressed against the couch, Matthew balancing expertly on his diapered butt. He was so proud of his ability to sit. Clarissa tossed a soft block, and when it landed in Matthew's lap, she squealed with pleasure. "Good catch!" She pulled him close in a squeeze. "My good boy!"

Lauren tried to muster a smile, but it was more like a grimace. *My* good boy? She wasn't sure how much more of Clarissa she could take. "Um, I'm taking off now," she said.

"No prob!" Clarissa beamed. "Enjoy!"

This morning, when Lauren's eyes had popped open and she realized it was nearly 10:00 a.m., she'd run into the living room, panicked because she knew Graham had to drive up to LA for some meetings. Normally, she balked at him working on a Saturday, but she didn't feel she had the right to complain. Clarissa had been here, making the coffee, plopping a puree in a BPA-free bowl for the baby. "Oh," Lauren had said dazedly, rubbing her eyes. "Did *I* call you?" Maybe she'd done it earlier, half-asleep. She'd had one of those nights where her dreams were banal, blurring with her waking routine. She wasn't sure what was real.

"Oh, your husband did," Clarissa had said, shooting her a conciliatory smile. "It's no trouble!"

Lauren wondered how that had gone. Graham poked his head

into the room, sighing at Lauren's lassitude, maybe. But perhaps this was their new normal: they simply wouldn't talk to each other, and Graham's default would be that Lauren wasn't up to the job as Mom. She thought of their *old* normal, for a moment. Their short-lived normal, before the baby was born—how Graham would look at her with such reverence, and how they'd be all over each other at all times, and how they'd always respect what the other was saying. Now, Lauren wasn't even sure if Graham wanted her around anymore. Maybe he found her a burden.

Their conversation from the other night played in her head. *Did* she need to check in somewhere? She glanced at Matthew and felt a woeful ache. The idea of leaving him for a long period of time scared her. What if he forgot her? What if Gracie slipped into her place—*would* she?

But then those jagged, blank moments in Piper's hallway flashed in her mind. If only her memory would come back. If only there was an explanation for the blood she'd found on her palm. She needed there to be more to that story.

Her thoughts clicked to what she and the others had talked about on the walking trail yesterday—looking into Piper's life. Lauren was going to start with Jean, whomever she was. If only she'd had a better look at that email before she'd lost her nerve. And *that* still scared her, too—the fact that she'd been in Piper's office, and now the police were searching for evidence. What if they found some of Lauren's DNA on Piper's keyboard? A fingerprint? An eyelash? A hair?

She trolled the Silver Swans Facebook page. The Piper news was the same—the story hadn't been updated, though a woman named Hillary Tustin, who had a kid in the threes, said that she'd heard from a good source that Piper was still in a medicated coma. Lauren clicked on the link that listed every member of the group, searching for anyone named Jean. No one matched that name.

Next, she clicked over to the Silver Swans website portal, which, after she logged in, included a list of families in each grade and the email addresses they'd provided. No Jean there, either. The problem was, the list wasn't complete—you didn't have to provide your information if you didn't want to. If Jean was so *problematic*, maybe she hadn't.

Lauren climbed into her car. There were a few key places around Raisin Beach that moms frequented, and she wanted to look around. The park at the city center was one—when Lauren first moved to Raisin Beach, she took Matthew for walks down there, thinking it would be an easy place to make friends. But there was such an established squad of moms there already, and no one seemed interested in expanding their group. It also seemed like you had to sign up on some sort of reservation app if you wanted to score a decent park bench.

There was also Brytley, the yoga studio, where Lauren had gone a few times before having Matthew. This, too, was fraught with pregnant mothers aggressively comparing bodies, bellies, yoga abilities, birth plans, and where they were sending their little ones to preschool in many years' time. A Brytley prenatal yoga class was, admittedly, where Lauren first heard about Silver Swans. She remembered packing up her mat and trudging out of class, having spoken to no one, with at least a plan: *she* might not be accepted in Raisin Beach, but her kid would be. And yet when she drove past the studio in her car, she didn't stop. What was her plan, to barge into the studio and ask if they knew someone named Jean? That wasn't exactly keeping a low profile.

Still, it felt good to be out of the house and alone with her thoughts. It reminded her of the times before she'd had Matthew—before she'd been with Graham, even—when she used to drive around a lot, as it helped her think clearly. Her thought process in general had been so much clearer back then, a crystal stream instead of a muddy pond. Her brain had felt so freed up; she'd been able to work on multiple projects at once, juggle relationships, remember to buy her brother a birthday present, mentally compose a grocery list.

The light turned green, and she jerked forward across the intersection. Only then did she realize where she was—across from Silver Swans.

She slowed. Since it was the weekend, the parking lot was nearly empty. She glanced at the doorway to the offices and the loft; she'd expected to see police tape across it, but there was none. Maybe the cops had already gathered all their clues. Then something else caught her eye. Parked in the back of the lot was a large white van. Lauren squinted to get a closer look. The side of the van read *Raisinette Productions.*

The documentary?

Lauren wrenched the wheel and veered into the property before she lost her nerve. There was a woman leaning against the van, her head down, tapping on her cell phone. She had thick blond bangs and wore high-waisted pants and hipster sneakers. Lauren turned off the engine, got out, and started toward her.

"Hello?" Lauren said, and the woman looked up. She took a few steps closer. "I'm sorry, is this documentary still . . . happening?" It seemed like they'd put it on hold, all things considered.

The woman lowered her phone. "Hi, yeah, we're just getting started. I'm just taking some shots around the campus today."

"But . . . Piper." It felt strange to say Piper's name aloud.

"They wouldn't let us into the hospital to see her." The woman offered her hand. "I'm Kelsey. I don't think we've met."

"I'm . . . a mom," Lauren said, shaking. Maybe it was better not to give her name. "My son is in the nursery. Why wouldn't they let you see Piper?"

"HIPAA rules. Visitation for someone in her condition is family only. Or something."

"She has a son." Lauren felt a twinge of regret. She'd thought about Piper's son over the past two days. The kid was twelve, thirteen? Were there people in Piper's world looking after him? "Do you know if he's okay?"

"I haven't met him yet, but I am sure he is in good hands. Piper always seemed really organized." Then a conflicted expression crossed Kelsey's face. It seemed like she wanted to say more but thought better of it.

"The parents haven't been told anything. There's a lot of confusion," Lauren tried.

"Yeah, I'm sure it's really scary." Kelsey smiled benignly. "Now, if you'll excuse me, I—"

"I like your hat," Lauren interrupted, suddenly noticing the logo on the brim of the ball cap Kelsey was wearing. It was a familiar logo from Lauren's game-design days. "Taco Builder, right?"

Kelsey touched her hat, then smiled. "Oh God, yeah. I wear this just to shade my face from the sun. That used to be my favorite game. I won a contest, actually in college—highest score. I was paid five hundred bucks."

Lauren crossed her arms. "What if I told you I helped develop that game?"

"No shit!" Kelsey grinned and appraised Lauren closer. "You design any others?"

Lauren named a few more, and when she got to Huzzah!, Kelsey really lit up. "I was crazy about that game for a while," she said. "You should totally make more." Then she added, "A woman in tech. I like it. Though I bet you stick out in *this* place."

"Oh, you mean with the moms?" Lauren could tell she was getting somewhere. "I do. Most of the time. Especially at this school in particular. Everyone is so *competitive.*"

Kelsey's eyes lit up. She looked back and forth conspiratorially, then leaned in closer. "The parents we've recorded so far? They're so high-strung. I mean, come *on*, people. A lot of them are freaking out that their toddlers aren't bilingual yet. Or that their kid's going to eat a nonorganic yogurt squeezie at a friend's house. There's a major recession going on. I thought that would put things in perspective."

"I know it," Lauren murmured. "I see a lot of babies in Gucci around here. For some people—not all—it's like the economic crisis doesn't exist." And then, casually, she added, "Did you tell the police that some of the parents seem . . . tricky? I mean, stressed moms and dads make for some crazy shit going down."

Kelsey shrugged, becoming a little closed off again. "There isn't really anything specific. And anyway, these are my opinions. I'm probably overexaggerating."

"You're not, believe me. Though . . . I'm surprised to hear you've begun recording. I thought you were just in the early stages."

"We've started, a little," Kelsey answered. "We sent an email around about it—parents who wanted to participate signed up."

Lauren sank into one hip. She hadn't gotten an email, though that certainly fit her theory that Piper thought she was nuts and didn't want her to be part of the documentary. Perhaps Piper had deliberately left her name off the email chain.

She decided to share this theory with Kelsey, casting herself as the techie outsider who didn't fit the Silver Swans mold. Kelsey looked annoyed. "That seems really unfair and discriminatory. But then, it is her project."

"Did you get a sense Piper was doing that?" Lauren asked.

"Not really, no. But if she was deliberately leaving people off my list, I guess I wouldn't know."

"Did she ever bring up anyone named Jean?"

Kelsey thought for a moment. "Doesn't ring a bell. Why?"

"Oh, just wondering," Lauren said airily, though she was disappointed. This lead was going nowhere.

Kelsey picked at an invisible string on her jacket. "Before the incident, we kept scheduling an interview with Piper, but she's brushed us off. Sure, we've had general meetings, but I know very little about her personal life, what she's about, her parenting philosophy—I thought she'd be more involved. It's so strange, considering . . ."

"Huh," Lauren murmured. She recalled the way Piper had described the documentary at the breakfast earlier in the week. She'd made it sound like she'd hounded Hulu for weeks. Why would she do that if she didn't want to be featured? Then Lauren rewound her thoughts, thinking over what Kelsey had just said. "Considering what?"

"Well, considering that, like I said, it's Piper's project."

Lauren crossed her arms. "What do you mean by that?"

"I mean she's the executive producer." The corners of Kelsey's mouth tugged into a sneaky smile. "She became the executive producer after Hulu pulled out."

"*What?*" Lauren blinked hard. "That is news to me! What happened?"

"I guess she rubbed the guy at Hulu the wrong way for some reason. But then Piper called us up and said, 'Change of plans, we're no longer working with them.' She made it sound like a good thing, like there would be less cooks in the kitchen."

Lauren's mind was spinning. She glanced behind her at the empty parking spaces that would be filled with minivans and SUVs come Monday, feeling weirdly superior. "But no one has brought up someone named *Jean* to you?" she repeated. "Spelled J-E-A-N?"

"Not *Jean*," Kelsey said, and then she paused. "But there is *Jean*." She said it the French way, the male way.

"Who is he?" It had never occurred to Lauren that Jean might be a man.

"The exec with Hulu. The one who broke it off with her."

Lauren's eyes widened. *We need to figure out what to do about Jean.* Why? What did he know?

Then she realized something, and she looked at Kelsey in confusion. "Wait. How is the documentary moving forward without Hulu? I mean, doesn't it cost a ton of money to make a movie?"

"It does," Kelsey said. "But I guess Piper's getting money from somewhere."

Piper

September

It's a joy to see your loft filled again. When you sent out the email to put this event in everyone's calendars, you felt a tiny niggle of worry. Would they still come?

But they came. Cars fill the parking lot. Many you recognize: Teslas, BMWs, a gorgeous black Porsche 911 Carrera S. It doesn't seem like the downturn hurt everyone.

And what you did, between the last time you saw them and now? They'll never know. Or maybe, if they do know, they'll let it slide.

You spin around the breakfast, shaking hands, stroking egos, letting people admire you. They comment on how put together you look, how thrilled they are to be back at Silver Swans, how their children missed you so. They ask about North, which is sweet of them. You tell them he's doing well. You name a video game you bought for him and add that if you could do it all over again, you'd keep video games out of the house because they're all kids want to do. They ask if he's still in private school, and you say he is, and things are going well.

But the meeting isn't about North. It's about their children. Actually, more specifically, it's about them. *You're watching each and every one of them, looking for inconsistencies, looking for cracks in your perfect façade. And then, you notice something. A few somethings. And a shiver runs through you.*

You nudge Carson, and he slides over, standing just behind you so you can speak quietly without raising any alarm. "Look," you say quietly. One is your kindergarten teacher's way-too-sexy girlfriend. The other is the tall blonde with the enviable cheekbones.

Carson is dubious, even after you explain your case. "You think they know?" he asks.

"Did you vet them?"

"I didn't think I had to."

But maybe their newness is preferable, you think. At least they aren't as ingrained in the community, with tons of friends and connections.

Carson is shifting behind you. "You want them out?"

You nod. You'll let Carson handle this. He's always gotten his hands dirty for you.

But you continue to watch them as the tall one passes the coffee mug back to Lane's girlfriend. They're standing with that third woman, too, the blowsy one who made you uneasy in a way you didn't quite understand. Something irked you about her as soon as you met. The way she thought North was Carson. There is something else about her you can't put your finger on.

You tip back to Carson, who no doubt is already laying out the chess moves to execute a plan. "Actually, her, too," you murmur, gesturing to Lauren as she knocks back her coffee.

"Because she's talking to them?" Carson is dubious.

It's warm in the loft. The air smells pleasantly of coffee and powdered sugar. You can smell Carson's soap, too, a sporty blend you gifted him from Kiehl's. "We can't be too careful," you tell him.

Carson nods. "Whatever you say, boss."

You shoot him a smile, and he slips from the loft, and then you feel better. Plans are in place. Weeds are going to be pulled. You're this close to coming out of the woods, to reclaiming your kingdom. And you're not about to let it slip between your fingers.

Nineteen

"One, two, three . . ." Andrea looked at Arthur. "What comes after three?"

"Shoe?" Arthur asked.

"Ha-ha, very funny." She wrote the number three on the piece of construction paper. "What's after three?"

"Four!" Arthur cried triumphantly.

"Yes! Good!" Andrea pulled her little boy in close. He smelled like sunshine and shampoo. This was lovely. Maybe she could just teach him full-time. She thought of how her mother said homeschooling was a selfish travesty and that children grew up socially deranged and ill-equipped for the real world, but what the hell did Cynthia know?

But as though reading her mind, Arthur whined, "Why didn't I go to school today?"

"Well, because it's Saturday," Andrea said, deflecting. She capped the marker and popped it back into the pencil box. "Are you sure school is a happy place for you?"

"My room has cool diggers. I want to play with the car carrier."

"Yes, but . . ." How to talk to a child this small? What could she say? What should she leave out? "What would happen if the kids started making fun of you because Mommy's . . . you know?

Different?" She took a breath. "We've talked about how we've—*I've*—gone through some changes. How I'm not like other moms."

That drawing was burned in her brain. That *X* through her body. She'd described it to Jerry. He'd been quiet about it—the same kind of dazed quiet as he'd been the other day, which made her wonder if his mind was starting to jumble. He'd repeated that the drawing Andrea had found was horrible and insidious and perhaps indicative of something very, very wrong happening within the school . . . but it also gave her great motive to hurt Piper. He promised to dig in more. He'd also mentioned that he hadn't yet found a reporter who'd figured out Andrea's identity. "Is it possible someone *else* told your mom?" he asked. "Maybe someone *posing* as a reporter?"

But who would *that* be?

Arthur shrugged. "All people are different. Miss Piper says that. Everyone is *neek*."

"*Neek*?" Andrea frowned. Then she got it. "Oh. Unique. Piper said that?"

"*Miss* Piper. Mr. Carson, too."

Andrea hadn't been aware that Piper visited classrooms and gave talks about acceptance. Carson was even more surprising. Wasn't he just an administrative assistant?

"Do Mr. Carson and Miss Piper seem like they're friends?" she asked Arthur. "Like really good buddies, like you are with some of your buddies at school, or Reginald?"

Arthur thought about this for a beat, then said, "Uh-huh."

Andrea thought about how Carson kept popping into Piper's office when she was meeting with her. And how he seemed invested in the documentary—proud of it, even. Maybe he was more involved in the school than she thought. Maybe he was closer with Piper, too. She thought of the empty office they'd passed on the way to Piper's that day. On the Facebook group, it had been reported that Carson, along with the rest of the staff eventually, had been interviewed about their whereabouts when the attack went down. Carson had been near the playground, tending to the new garden the kids had planted. He only came running when he heard the bellowing security guard.

But had anyone seen him? Could *he* have something against Piper? Only, what would his motive be?

"Baby, I'll be right back," she said, ruffling Arthur's hair and walking to her laptop, which was open at the kitchen bar.

She clicked to the Silver Swans website. *Carson Dillard, office manager*, read his name in the directory. Below his name was a headshot of Carson giving a slightly snooty half-smile. Andrea had typed his name into Google; up came a few social media profiles. On Facebook, Carson posted pictures of himself with two small, fluffy white dogs; all the likes came from other members of his family and people who, through more clicking, had gone to high school with Carson in a very tiny town in Idaho. Andrea dug deeper. Carson's parents were lumpy, badly aging people with troubling dental hygiene. His father wore a lot of camo. His mother sold Young Living essential oils. Some of their posts were political. They seemed . . . *poor*, actually.

But the image Carson was trying to present of himself in Raisin Beach was far from that. There were posts of a groomed Carson next to Piper at school functions, dinners, conferences. Sometimes, in his captions, he described himself as a "deputy director" of the school, or the "marketing director," or once, simply "VP." He was inflating his duties there, Andrea thought. Trying to make his life out to be even better than it was. Distancing himself from his roots.

More recently, there were other photos of Carson posing in front of an Audi S-class, sleek with fresh wax. *How does one pay for an Audi S-class on an office manager salary?* Andrea wondered—but maybe he was heavily in debt, again to reinvent himself into someone from a different class. He was also really into mirror selfies and posting how many reps he'd done in a newly acquired boot camp routine. Andrea clicked on the groups he belonged to: Louis Vuitton Fan Club, Audi Enthusiasts of America, and Triple-L Farms, which, Andrea learned upon clicking, sold cuts of Wagyu beef for $99 a steak.

She texted the other women. *Carson Dillard's family are bow-hunting Trump supporters.* Then she included a picture of Carson posing next to his Audi.

If that was my family, I'd want to escape them, too, Lauren wrote back.

And Ronnie said, *How does an office assistant afford an Audi?*

Exactly! Andrea replied.

Andrea wished there was someone else in the office to call for questions, but as far as she knew, Carson and Piper ran Silver Swans as a two-person team. There was a parent-heavy board of directors, but they seemed to only step in for audits and approvals—half of the people didn't even live in Raisin Beach. Could she call another teacher, maybe? But what teacher would even *tell* her anything at this point, especially if they had an inkling she'd been one of the moms found in that hallway?

She looked up Piper's social media, but Piper's Facebook and Instagram—she didn't have a Twitter account—were carefully curated to the Silver Swans brand. On Instagram, Piper posed with teachers, parents, students, and quasi-famous people who popped in to give lectures. She ran parenting groups on Facebook. Andrea scrolled back through her account, curious if Piper had always been so polished and together, but both her accounts had been created five years before, right around the time she started at Silver Swans.

Who was Piper before that? There were a few posts of her son, but they were mostly school pictures, nothing candid.

Her phone beeped, and her heart jumped as it had done regularly since she'd been at the police station. Lauren had sent another text to both Andrea and Ronnie. *So get this. I think the Jean from Piper's email is a dude. Jean, like Les Miz's Jean Valjean.*

Interesting, Andrea wrote back. *Did you find out anything else?*

He's an exec at Hulu. The documentary is still happening. But Hulu etc. dropped out.

A text from Ronnie appeared. *Wow. Because of Piper being attacked?*

Nope. It happened before the attack. This producer I talked to says Hulu etc. left because of some sort of issue with Piper.

Like what? Andrea typed.

I don't know what. Also, when I asked how the doc was being funded, the producer said that Piper was paying for it herself. But don't documentaries cost a lot?

Andrea popped her head back into the living room to check on Arthur—he was looking at something in a heavy Richard Scarry picture book. It wasn't unthinkable to produce a documentary yourself. People in her father's circle put up cash to make films all the time. One had gone on to become a quasi-important producer, handing over tons of money until he finally got a film that did modestly well at the box office. Perhaps Piper was just drawing from private savings. What *was* weird, though, was that she hadn't been honest with the parents about Hulu dropping out. You'd think they would have gotten an email, something.

Had she pretended that Hulu was still involved because there was more cache? Maybe. Yet if they'd dropped out because of something simple—funding problems, a change higher up, scheduling conflicts—you'd think Piper would explain that away.

Her phone pinged. Ronnie had asked Lauren, *Have you found a way to contact Jean? Do you think he has something to do with this?*

Lauren wrote back: *Not sure, but the producer did say Jean spoke with the cops. You'd think they'd have interviewed him about his alibi.*

Yes, Andrea thought, but did that police station have the bandwidth to follow up? The three of them seemed to have gathered more clues at this point.

"Mommy?" Arthur called out.

When she turned, Arthur was behind her. Andrea tousled his hair. "What's up?"

"*Door*," Arthur said.

"Door?" She cast her mind back to what they were thinking about. "No, *four* comes after three, honey. Remember?"

"No, someone *at* the door." Arthur's face brightened. "Reginald!"

"Wha—?" Andrea murmured, rising to her feet. And then—oh. The date they'd arranged in the bookstore. It felt like a million years ago. Reginald shifted behind the glass.

"I'm sorry," Andrea blurted when she pulled the door open. "There's been some crazy stuff going on, and I completely forgot."

"Reginald!" Arthur said at the same time, running for him.

"Hey, buddy!" Reginald opened his arms, and Arthur ran straight in. "How've you been?"

"I cut my finger today, and I got a *Star Wars* Band-Aid," Arthur said with great importance.

Andrea looked at Reginald. "I'm such a flake. I'm not dressed, I didn't get a sitter . . ."

"It's not a big deal," Reginald said. "Arthur can always come with us."

It was a beautiful evening. The sunset would probably draw the community to restaurants with patios. Andrea imagined walking into a restaurant and having all those heads turn. Raisin Beach wasn't that big.

Reginald seemed to sense her hesitation. "Or . . . we could eat in. Hang out with Arthur here. There's always Postmates."

"Postmates! Postmates!" Arthur whooped, even though Andrea was pretty sure he had no idea what Postmates was.

The unbridled glee on his face made her burst out laughing, and so she said, "Okay. Sure. Let's do it."

⁂

Forty-five minutes later, they were surrounded by cartons and bowls of half-eaten Thai and a half-finished bottle of rosé. Andrea leaned back in her chair and shut her eyes. "That was delicious."

Arthur wiped his hands on a napkin and looked longingly at his iPad, which was docked on a charger. "It's okay," Andrea said. "Go ahead." Arthur had bravely tried a spring roll—probably for Reginald's benefit—and he'd been so good through dinner, not leaping up after every bite and racing around the room. Plus, she was nervous. The conversation with Reginald was flowing so naturally, ranging from games they'd liked to play as children to podcasts they'd recently gotten into to funny anecdotes about Arthur when they'd first moved to California. "I brought him to LA, and he was obsessed with the seediest parts of Hollywood," Andrea had said. "I tried to tell him that there were far nicer spots in the city, but how does the Chateau Marmont compare to Hollywood and Highland?"

"All those stars on the sidewalk," Reginald added. "And all those junk shops."

"And the *sex* shops," Andrea blurted, and then felt heat in her cheeks. "Sorry," she added quickly.

Reginald had given her a sly, almost grateful look, like he was pleased that she'd welcomed sex talk into the room.

Andrea shifted positions. "Anyway," she went on, "this has been a nice little adventure for us, I have to say."

Reginald placed his chopsticks back into the foil container. "Adventure," he repeated. "Does that mean this"—he waved his hands around the large room—"is a temporary thing?"

"It's working for now," Andrea said with a shrug. "We needed a change."

"Change is good," Reginald said. He looked at her carefully. "Hey, what about that stuff at school? With the teacher?"

Andrea crossed one leg over the other. It was amazing how much could transpire in a matter of days.

"Did you confront her?" Reginald went on.

It was amazing he didn't know. Andrea was so used to living in her bubble she'd forgotten there were worlds outside it. "Um, sort of," she said. "I've pretty much ruled out that Arthur didn't draw that picture, that's for sure."

"See? I told you." He hugged his knees. "Who did?"

She couldn't tell him. The story was too insane. Maybe too scary. Also, she didn't want to drag him in further, make him some sort of accessory. "I don't know for sure, but I'm trusting my gut."

"Well, good for you." He poured more wine into her glass. "Here's to instinct. And to making big changes." After they toasted, he added, "I've made changes in my life, too. Not quite so recently, but still."

"Oh? How?"

He sipped again. "Well, for about ten years, I didn't speak to my mom. I traveled, stayed as far away from her as I could, didn't leave forwarding numbers, probably worried her sick." Then he frowned. "Well, maybe I didn't worry her sick, actually, because she's not really the type to worry."

"You just . . . traveled around?"

"Camped. Made friends, stayed on couches. Picked up random jobs in random cities. I saw a lot of the country. It wasn't so bad."

"All to stay away from your mom?"

"And to calm the noise in my head." He wiped his mouth. "She's . . . difficult. My father was a good guy, but he passed away when I was seventeen. But my mom . . ." He sighed. "I just never felt like she really liked me. It was always about her struggles, her pain. I always felt like a disappointment."

"I'm sorry," Andrea said softly.

When Reginald looked up again, his eyes had a sheen. Not with tears, exactly, but of contemplation. "God. Sorry. I didn't mean to bring the conversation down."

"It's okay." Andrea had no idea when someone had last opened up to her—besides Lauren and Ronnie. Was this a date? Well, of course it was a date—she was a woman, he was a man. Andrea had firsthand knowledge; men didn't usually hang out with women and their four-year-old sons and start talking about their mothers unless they had more intimate motives, no matter how nice they were.

But where did *she* play in all this?

Teenage Andrea had had sex with girls because it was expected. It had been easy to say yes, and she'd been fascinated with their bodies—but also bereft, in a way, because theirs were bodies she wanted. Once Andrea had begun taking hormones, though, she looked at men differently. Men passing on the street, men gliding into restaurants, men on TV—they all enticed her, and she began to form fantasies. She'd read about how sexuality could flip-flop after transitioning; it was more common than one thought. But still, it felt miraculous, like she'd discovered a new room in her house that she'd never walked into before, complete with furniture and books and wonder and surprises for her to discover.

And Reginald? Here he was, tall and angular and stubbly, with big chapped hands and in a dark blue polo that brought out the color of his eyes, sitting in her living room, listening to her stories, looking at her as she ate her food.

With Arthur nestled in the chair across the room, Andrea rose and opened a second bottle of wine. The alcohol from the first bottle had gone straight to her head, and she had to remember to be careful with her walk, her voice, the way she sat. Because that was the truth of the matter: though it now came more naturally than before, she still had to watch herself.

"I was a disappointment to my mother, too," she said in a quiet voice.

"You sure?" Reginald cocked his head. "Actually, here's the thing—turns out I wasn't a disappointment at all. It was just in how I was perceiving it. This was something that came to me while I traveled. Yeah, my mom complained. Everything was a pain in the ass for her, even before my father died—*including* my father, who was probably the most decent, tolerant guy I'd ever met. But even if I'd been valedictorian, even if I'd won the lottery, even if I was the model son of her dreams, it wouldn't have mattered." He stared thoughtfully into the distance. "I don't think she would have treated me any differently. It was just the way she was, you know?"

"That's awfully big of you to let all of that go," Andrea said.

"People don't usually change. Once we understand that, life gets easier." He sat back and smiled. "I knocked on her door about a year ago. She doesn't live that far. I thought she was going to lecture me, give me hell because I hadn't come around, but instead she threw her arms around me and said she missed me, all that stuff I'd given up hoping for."

"How nice!"

"Well, I mean, she woke up the next day the same cranky bitch as ever." Reginald started chuckling. "But I do talk to her again. I spent ten years blaming her, being angry. I felt cheated, like if I'd had a nice mom, I'd know what I wanted to do with my life." He shrugged. "But maybe I'll never know. And at this point, I like what I'm doing. I'm content. I've found my path."

"That's good." Andrea's voice was merely a whisper. Hadn't she always thought about this, too, with her own family? She'd had every privilege, but people rarely looked past the Vandermeer money to see that they weren't actually a functioning family. What she'd give for a real connection with one of them, but it was probably too late.

But even as Andrea thought this, she began to doubt its validity. Was it possible Reginald was right? Was this just her perception of things? There probably wasn't any hope in forging a bond with her father, but if she spoke to, say, Cynthia differently, if she *thought* of Cynthia differently, if she just tried to put herself in Cynthia's shoes, could she perhaps see where Cynthia was coming from, and maybe they could work to heal?

And also, hadn't *she* found her path, too? She found gratitude in that. She understood the journey was so much harder for others than it had been for her. Maybe she had to come to terms with the fact that she wasn't going to have everything in life, and that was okay.

The wine made a *glug-glug-glug* sound as Reginald poured more into each of their glasses. "But I think being a good mother outweighs everything." And then he looked at her so kindly, Andrea ducked her head bashfully. "Arthur's lucky to have you."

"Oh," was all Andrea could say. And then, to her horror, she felt her eyes fill with tears. It was really all she wanted: to be a good parent. Not to screw him up. Cynthia was a mother, and so was she. They had that between them. How would she react if Arthur took a different path than the one she wanted? She'd like to think she'd take it in stride, as long as he was happy. But maybe she wouldn't know until it happened.

"Hey," Reginald said, ducking his head so he could look her in the eyes. "You okay?"

Andrea laughed and then waved her arm in a gesture that she hoped said, *Oh, don't mind me.* "Sometimes I get a little weepy," she lied. And then she smiled at him. It was a smile tinged with sadness—both because of her doubts and because she worried that this moment, warm and lovely and ordinary and precious, was fleeting.

Nothing stayed buried forever.

Twenty

On Monday, four days after Piper's attack, Ronnie awoke to Lane's hand on her shoulder. "Ronnie," he said. "Ronnie. *Veronica.*"

Her eyes snapped open. "What?" Lane wasn't the type to use her full name. She felt in trouble. Instantly, the *Missing* flyer popped in her mind. Someone knew what she'd done. Maybe whoever it was had told Lane.

"An officer's out there who wants to speak with you," Lane said. His face was gray. Grave. "I'm sorry. I tried to keep him away. And I called Cromwell, but he didn't pick up."

Ronnie shot out of bed. She pulled on jeans, a bra, a T-shirt. Then she changed her T-shirt because the first T-shirt was too tight.

On her way out of the bedroom, Lane caught her arm. "Honey, I'm so, so sorry."

"Stop saying that. It's not your fault."

"I know, I just . . ." He placed his hands on her shoulders and looked into her eyes. "I should have listened to you. You were trying to tell me something on the balcony that night—about the note you got. And I didn't hear you. I let my admiration for Piper get in the way. I should have stood by you."

Ronnie pressed her head into his chest, and they hugged. "You *are* standing by me."

A tall, gangly officer waited in the living room, his torso bent over his knees. He was examining some of Esme's drawings on the coffee table—Ronnie hadn't tidied the art supplies from the night before. He looked up when she walked in. "Cute pictures."

Ronnie wanted to tell him to stop touching Esme's things, but she knew better than to say so. "I'm Ronnie," she said.

"Detective Allegra," he replied, offering his hand.

Then they just stood there. Ronnie was dying for a cup of coffee but didn't know the protocol on hosting police officers. The *Missing* flyer swam in her mind. Andrea and Lauren had tried to convince her that Jerrod most likely wasn't in Raisin Beach, but it was hard for Ronnie to let that go. She'd felt so followed lately. So *watched.*

And there were other things about the flyer, questions Ronnie desperately wanted to ask but was too afraid to go searching. For one thing: Vanessa. Her name had been listed as a parent. Could she still be alive?

Her heart swelled at the idea. She pictured calling Vanessa up while *Jeopardy!* was on, like she used to. They would call out the answers they knew; surprisingly, Vanessa was a whiz with trivia. She pictured hugging her sister again, and making Thanksgiving apple pies together, and maybe inviting her out here for Christmas.

But then her emotions took a dive, because holy shit, she'd *stolen Vanessa's child* and of *course* she wouldn't be inviting her out here for Christmas. Vanessa had been a neglectful parent a lot of the time, but she still loved her kid. Did she know Ronnie had been the one to take Esme? But if *both* of them were alive and searching, why hadn't they made headway yet?

Unless, of course, Jerrod had.

She heard Lane and Esme rustling in the kitchen—Lane was getting ready for work, but Ronnie had argued that maybe Esme should stay home from Silver Swans another few days, until the dust settled. The last thing she wanted was for Esme to pick up things she heard at school.

Esme's high little voice peppered Lane with questions: *Is Mommy in trouble?* Ronnie could only hear Lane's murmuring baritone, not his answers.

She looked at the officer again. "Can I help you with anything?"

Allegra nodded. "Just have a few follow-up questions."

"Any news about Piper?"

"Uh . . ." He flipped through his notes. "The same. She's being kept in a medically induced coma for brain swelling. I don't know much else."

"Is her son okay?" she asked. "Is he being taken care of?"

He shrugged. "I'm sure he's fine."

"What do you mean you're *sure*? You don't know for certain?"

He sniffed with exasperation. "Look, Ms. Stuckey, I'm trying to figure out where we should go next with all this. These sorts of things don't usually happen in our community."

"Yes." Ronnie felt her stomach draw in. "I know. Of course I know."

"First"—he kept his face very neutral—"we tried to contact your boss yesterday to get some details about your client list, but he was uncooperative."

Ronnie gave a mental high-five to Bill for being discreet, though she was still annoyed with him for the reaming-out he'd given her because she'd missed an appointment the day of the Piper mess. "They like to keep the list private, so . . ."

She heard a *clink* on the other side of the wall and froze. Lane was still here. Was he *picturing* a client list? She hated that this was out in the open. Yesterday, she'd called Bill, telling him she needed some time off. Maybe indefinitely. Lane hadn't asked her to quit . . . but there was no way she could keep doing what she was doing, now that he knew.

"Anyway," the cop went on, "the reason I ask about your clients is because—well, is it possible any of them were upset with you?"

"Upset?" Ronnie shook her head. "No. Absolutely not."

"Okay, did you recognize any of them as parents at Silver Swans?" His eyes were bright and gossipy. "Dads? Granddads?"

"I'm careful not to take clients who live close by. But also, what does this have to do with Piper?"

The officer crossed his arms and gave her a level look. It scared her, too, that he was digging around Topless Maids, asking for client lists. This guy was too interested in her past. Next, he might dig into where she'd lived before, that she'd abruptly moved away.

She cursed herself for telling the police that she'd lived in Pennsylvania. It was like she'd drawn him a road map straight back to her nightmare—maybe they'd inquire into strip clubs there. Maybe they'd start connecting the dots. Even changing one's name didn't make the problems go away.

"Okay, moving on," the cop said, slapping his hands to his thighs. "Can you tell me about the women who were also on the scene? Ms. Smith and Ms. Vaughan. Do you know them well?"

"Somewhat."

"Have you spent time with them socially?"

"A few times, yes."

"And what about their significant others?"

Ronnie shook her head. "I've never met Lauren's husband. And Andrea is single, I believe."

"You believe, or you know?"

"I know." Was this guy trying to trap her into saying that Andrea had once been married—and to whom? Ronnie sure as hell wasn't going to let Andrea's past out of the bag.

But then her brain caught. Andrea had said her mom called her in a panic, saying a reporter had contacted her about the attack. If that was true, then wouldn't this guy already *know* who Andrea was?

The *Missing* flyer popped in her mind again. It was so confounding. Why wouldn't this person go to the police with what they knew? What was their angle?

"Okay. Third thing. Apparently, Ms. Jovan's office door was

wide-open when we went down to check out the scene, but her assistant swore that it was only ajar before he headed out. Know anything about that?"

Ronnie blinked. "I don't—" She frowned. "Wait, her *assistant* said that? Carson?"

"Uh-huh. Any chance you stepped into Piper's office to take a peek at something? Maybe one of your friends did?"

Ronnie's heart started to pound. She made a strange squeaking sound from the back of her throat. The cop took this as an opportunity. His eyebrows shot up like she'd just given a confession.

"Her assistant mentioned there was sensitive information in that office," the cop continued. "Financial documents, that kind of thing. Perhaps you knew this beforehand, though. Wanted to take a look? Steal your file?"

"I had no idea. I swear."

"Maybe you went in for another reason?" His smile was sneaky, confident. "Maybe you were hoping you'd find a petty cash box?"

"Now wait just a second." And here was Lane, his face red, jaw clenched, in the doorway. "What are you getting at?"

"Lane?" Ronnie shot to her feet. "Why are you still here?"

And the officer raised his eyebrows. "Pardon?"

"Would you presume another parent was riffling through the school office looking for money? A father?"

The cop waved his arm. "The office door was open, sir. Ms. Stuckey was in that hallway. I'm just trying to work through what might have happened, why she might have gone into Ms. Jovan's office."

"Ronnie wasn't *in* Piper's office," Lane insisted. "She doesn't need money."

"Lane," Ronnie said nervously, swinging her head around. It felt like she'd just slipped ten feet deeper into the hole.

Then she noticed Esme peek around Lane's legs. Ronnie motioned her into the room, and the little girl ran into her arms.

"This your daughter?" the cop asked.

"Of course," Ronnie said, hearing her voice crack. Esme had lifted her head from Ronnie's chest and was staring at him curiously, her eyes roaming from his badge to his belt and holster to his shiny black shoes.

"I'm calling our lawyer." Lane pulled out his phone. "No more questions without him."

"Lane," Ronnie repeated, "it's okay." She looked back at the cop, daring herself to say something—because maybe it seemed safer to speak up?

The cop's phone beeped, and after he studied it, he was on his feet. "I have to go," he said grumpily. "I'm just asking questions. But let me leave you with this." He turned to her, narrowing his eyes. "If you were in that office, Ms. Stuckey, you're better off telling us."

Lane walked the officer out. As the door closed, he turned back to Ronnie, his mouth twisted. "What a jerk," he muttered.

"Lane." Ronnie swallowed hard. *Here goes.* She had to tell him. "It's true. I *was* in her office."

Lane blinked at her. She rushed on. "Only for a minute. I just . . . I didn't *touch* anything, not really." *Liar!* a voice screamed in her head. "It was so, so wrong, but we just felt picked on, you know? And frustrated and small and . . ."

Lane held up his hand. "It's okay. I get it." He sighed. "I wish you'd told Cromwell this to start, but it is what it is." But then he looked at her strangely. "You *didn't* know there was a file on you in there, did you?"

"No!" Ronnie cried. "I swear!"

Lane nodded slowly, but he didn't look like he quite believed her. "Because, I mean, if you *did* know, and if there's something in that file you didn't want people to know about, then it makes logical sense you'd want to steal it back."

"What would be in my file I wouldn't want people to know?" Ronnie blurted.

Lane cocked his head. "That you work as a topless dancer? Unless there's something *else* . . ."

"No," Ronnie said quickly—maybe *too* quickly. "No, of course there isn't anything else."

Her heart was pounding. It felt like she'd dug herself into a hole. She didn't even know if the evidence about stealing Esme was in that file at the school. Most likely it wasn't, because wouldn't the school feel obligated to report her?

But then there was someone who knew. She looked at Lane in horror, something new coming to mind. "Did *you* know they kept files on people?"

"Of *course* not." Lane's eyes flashed. "No way." Now he looked really concerned. "Ronnie, what's going on? You're acting strange."

Ronnie licked her dry lips. She had to get a hold of herself. She had to try to breathe.

There was a scruff of beard on Lane's cheeks. His eyes were bloodshot, too, as though he'd tossed and turned last night. *I'm acting strange because there's so much I haven't told you*, Ronnie almost wanted to scream. She wasn't sure she deserved to have someone so squarely in her corner.

But instead she shook her head. "I'm fine," she said. "I . . . I just don't like the police being here. I want this to end."

"I know," Lane said, holding her tight. "But don't worry. It will."

⁂

After Lane left, Ronnie parked Esme in front of a My Little Pony app on the iPad—she could only imagine what the women in the Silver Swans Facebook group would say about that—and called Andrea. Andrea's voice was cagey when she picked up. "A cop was just here," Ronnie said.

"What? Why?"

"They know we were in Piper's office."

"*How?*"

"Carson. He saw that the door was different from how he left it. I didn't confirm we were there." She paused, considering telling Andrea that she'd told Lane. She decided to hold off for now. "The cop also said Carson mentioned there being a lot of sensitive files in the office. I wonder if that's how they knew I worked for Topless Maids, actually."

There was a long pause. "Silver Swans has a file about you working for Topless Maids?"

"I don't know how. I certainly didn't offer that up on my application."

Andrea took a breath. "That *Missing* flyer. Do you think *that* was in the file, too?"

"That's what I was thinking," Ronnie said nervously, shaken that Andrea had drawn the same conclusion. "So who has access to those files?"

"*Carson.*"

Ronnie shivered. Carson was the person closest to Piper. Ronnie couldn't picture the teachers being involved. "But why would he threaten us?" she whispered.

"He loves Piper. Maybe he thinks we're going to tarnish her reputation by spilling the beans about the notes our kids got."

"But why wouldn't he just turn me in for Esme?" Ronnie went on, her mind reeling. "Then I'd just be in jail."

"Good point," Andrea said. "Unless he *can't* turn you in. I mean, how did he get that information on you in the first place? Maybe he hacked something. Maybe he did something illegal. Or maybe he thinks we know something else Piper's done wrong? Or . . . or maybe something *he's* done wrong?"

Ronnie racked her brain of what that could be. "The cop implied I might have been looking for money."

"You didn't find money in the office, did you? I mean—I know you didn't take it. But was there any in there?"

"Not that I saw. The only thing I found was that spreadsheet." She took a hiccup of a breath. "I haven't looked at it, though. I've been too afraid."

"It's okay," Andrea said thoughtfully. "Let's look at it together. Maybe we can figure out what it is."

Ronnie really, *really* didn't want to. But eventually she stood, then walked down the hall to the coat closet, trying to remember the jacket she'd had on the day everything went down with Piper. Her black one, she was pretty sure. When she reached into the pocket, the paper was still there, crumpled on one side, but intact. She smoothed it out and stared at the information.

"It's just random numbers," she told Andrea. "There are no dollar amounts. No names." But then she thought about student IDs—maybe that was what these were? "Hold on," she said to Andrea. "Let me confirm something."

She went to a drawer in Lane's desk, which housed office supplies, a curious array of keys, canceled credit cards, and a small handbook of all the students and parents who had attended Silver Swans last year. Most parents only had their child's class list, but the teachers got a more comprehensive picture of everyone attending the school.

Ronnie opened it; the first page were the children in the baby class. But her theory was short-lived: Silver Swans kids were assigned student IDs, but they were six-digit numbers, not the long strings on the spreadsheet. She sighed, closed it up again, and tossed it back in the drawer.

"Even if this is nothing, I still don't like having this in my house," she told Andrea as she padded back to the kitchen. "It proves I went into her office."

"Don't get rid of it just yet," Andrea said. "Take a picture of it for me first."

Ronnie recoiled. "I don't want evidence of it on my phone!"

"Okay, okay, mail it to me, then."

"Why do you want it so badly?"

"We can't rule anything out. Just pop it in an envelope. I'll text you my address. It'll be in my possession—and you'll be blameless."

Ronnie reluctantly agreed. Before she hung up, she said, "So how are you doing, anyway?"

Andrea sighed. "I don't know."

"Tell me you aren't reading that shit online," Ronnie said. "That Facebook group."

"Are *you*?"

"Trying not to. But I'm so afraid my face is going to appear somewhere."

"It hasn't yet, right?"

"No." Ronnie sighed. "It's why I'm not leaving the house, for the most part. I'm worried about sending Esme to school. I don't want her to be judged."

"I know. I'm worried about that with Arthur, too. But you'll be okay. Your lawyer said he'd keep your image from showing up online, and that's all you need to worry about. As for what people are saying . . . well, you can't stop that."

"Did Arthur go to school today?"

"Oh God, no." Andrea sounded sheepish. "Sorry. I don't practice what I preach."

Ronnie sighed. As much as she didn't want to admit it, she felt the same way. "I was wondering something else," she said, hoping Andrea wouldn't mind that she asked. "That young person? The one they caught you upstate with? What was his name again?"

Andrea took a breath. "Roger."

"Do you hear from him ever?"

"We lost touch," Andrea admitted. "I mean, after the hotel thing, and the police, and it came out in all the papers, I wanted to reach out to him—but I knew I shouldn't. It would have just made things worse—for him, not me. Before I left to come here, I looked him up on social media, typing in a bunch of names I thought might work . . . but he wasn't anywhere." She sighed. "I think about him a lot."

"I get it," Ronnie said.

"What about you? You don't think of . . . of that awful guy, do you?"

"No," Ronnie said quickly. "Or, well, I *do* . . . but not fondly." She shut the door to their bedroom. "I hope I never see him again. But I worry—"

"*Don't* worry," Andrea interrupted. "It doesn't seem possible."

After she hung up, she placed the spreadsheet in an envelope and wrote out Andrea's address. She thought about leaving Esme alone for the few minutes she'd be outside, but it made her nervous. As luck would have it, Mrs. Lombardo was watering her flowers right below Ronnie's balcony. Ronnie smiled down at her. "Do you mind coming up for a sec?"

"Don't have anything else to do," Mrs. Lombardo said, amicably enough.

Once the babysitter was in the apartment, Ronnie headed to the mailbox at the corner. The metal door made a dissonant squeal as she pulled it open and dropped the letter inside.

There was a shortcut back to the apartment through the parking garage, which was sparse at this time of day. Her hard flats echoed loudly against the concrete. Something dripped in a corner near a parked minivan, and there was a noxious smell of oil coming from one of the bays. Something metallic sounded from the other side of the garage—like someone had dropped a set of car keys. Ronnie turned around slowly, suddenly alert. Someone was moving stealthily through the shadows, like they didn't want to be seen.

"Hello?" she called out.

She crept around a bulky black SUV so it would form a barrier between her and whomever it was. "Hello?" she called out again.

Another footstep. Ronnie squinted into the darkness, only able to make out the shape of a person coming toward her. Her mouth went dry. *This is how it ends*, she thought. Her mind flashed to Vanessa lying unconscious on the carpet where Jerrod had left her.

"Please," she said, a sob rising in her throat. "Who's there?" She almost said his name. *Jerrod?*

The figure stepped forward. Ronnie began to bargain. *Please keep me safe*, she willed. *I'll be a better person. I'll always tell the truth.*

An overhead spotlight shone down on the advancing figures, sharpening their features. Ronnie was so surprised that she straightened against the wall abruptly and banged her head on the concrete pillar. "Oh!" she cried out.

"Hi, Ronnie," Vanessa said. Her sister stepped forward with a sad smile. "I've been looking for you."

Twenty-One

"Here we go." Graham gripped a serving platter with two oven-mitted hands, waltzed to the table, and set down a plate of cacio e pepe. The rich, buttery scent wafted into Lauren's nostrils.

"Oh my God." She sighed. "Smells heavenly."

Graham broke off a piece of garlic bread and smiled. He'd come home early from work, Whole Foods bags in hands, announcing that he was going to make his signature meal. He'd wooed Lauren with cacio e pepe on one of their first dates, proclaiming he'd learned to make it in a cooking class in Italy. Lauren had been so charmed by the meal that she'd told him, woozily, that she wanted to marry him and have his babies. Later, she'd found out that he'd taken the trip with an ex-girlfriend, which marred the gesture slightly, but it certainly didn't deter her from eating the meal whenever he made it.

But today, Lauren stared down at her plate, dubious. What was the occasion? Granted, it wasn't like *she'd* prepared anything—she'd slept through most of the morning and had been in such a daze all afternoon that it hadn't occurred to her to go to the store. But that happened often.

There was a distinct possibility that Graham had found out about her sleuthing at Silver Swans. Perhaps someone had seen Lauren and reported it back to Graham. But why should Lauren feel guilty about what she'd done? She hadn't set out to go to Silver Swans. She'd had an innocent conversation with a producer. And hell, maybe she'd found out something that could exonerate her.

"Piper kept us on as producers after she and Hulu parted ways," Kelsey had admitted after dropping the bomb. "She only told us this week. Wednesday, I think."

Lauren thought about that. Wednesday was the day before Piper's attack. The day Andrea had met with Piper. Was this what she heard Piper arguing about over the phone in the parking lot? "But why would Piper continue on without a network?" Lauren asked. "Why was it so important?"

"Because she has faith in it," Kelsey said. "She wants to make it into something all her own—and honestly, it was going in a more reality show direction—in hopes of selling to a network down the line."

"*Really!*" Lauren cried, recalling how Piper had recoiled when someone had asked at the breakfast if the program was going to have a reality show vibe. How quickly she'd changed her tune.

"Yeah." Kelsey shrugged. "But it's not my place to criticize."

"If she's turning it into some sort of *Real Housewives: Preschool*, I'm surprised Piper hasn't done a zillion interviews with you for the program," Lauren said. This was starting to make her feel better about Piper's nasty email—naturally Piper didn't want a whole chunk of a program being taken up by a mother going through postpartum rage. It seemed too tragic for reality TV.

"Yeah, I don't know," Kelsey said. "Maybe she's a private person. She slashed out a bunch of preliminary questions we asked her to approve. She didn't want to talk about anything personal. Not even her son."

"So the show isn't about motherhood anymore?"

"Well *technically*, it's about this school. But who knows?" Kelsey sighed. "Anyway, it's why we haven't pivoted to investigating what happened. Piper wouldn't want an attack—especially on her—to be in a show she's financing. You know?"

"Do you think I could see your footage?" Lauren had asked. "Like . . . with the parents?"

Kelsey shook her head. "Sorry. Those interviews were done in confidence."

Later, Kelsey emailed Lauren with Jean's contact information at Hulu. *Can you not mention I gave you this?* Kelsey wrote. *I think it's okay you talk to him, but I don't want to get in the middle—especially if it's weird.*

Naturally, she called Jean right away. She needed to know why someone would drop Piper. The information might save her—save all of them. But the call had gone to voicemail. Jean hadn't yet called back.

"Parmesan?" Graham asked.

"Uh, sure." Lauren reached for the canister and sprinkled the cheese. Graham was eating heartily. She tried to recall the last time Graham cooked this dish. The day he'd gotten the job at *Ketchup*—that was it. Lauren had been eight months pregnant, swollen to the point of bursting and anxious as hell. Sometime in the second trimester, the baby thing had become all too real. She was having a child with a man she'd only just met! Did they actually love each other, or were they just playing house down the coast? Graham hadn't even gotten around to painting the nursery, so she was considering hiring a company to do it.

"I just don't know what to do with myself," he told her. "I feel so stuck here."

"We didn't *have* to move," Lauren answered. "I thought we both wanted this."

"It's easy for you. You've made something of yourself."

She'd felt confused. Was he going to back out? Ditch her one day, turn her into a single mother, stuck in some random beach town? She also hadn't realized he'd felt so adrift, and that made her feel bad, too. Maybe she wasn't so attuned to him; maybe they didn't know each other that well. Maybe the baby was a mistake.

But then, just days later, he'd gotten the call from Gracie. It was a whirlwind, and his whole personality brightened practically overnight. All at once, Graham became more excited about the baby—and about her, too. Lauren's doubts vanished.

Now, she put down her fork and dared to ask what was on her mind. "So . . . I hope this isn't a last meal. Before, you know, I go off to the funny farm."

Graham cocked his head. "You shouldn't call it that, Lauren."

"The funny *spa*?" This didn't crack a smile, either. She stabbed at a noodle.

He glanced at her with concern. "I just want you to be your best self. And get the help you need."

"But I'd rather do that at *home*. Around my child. I'd miss him too much, Graham. It would kill me."

Graham nodded thoughtfully, then spooned another bite into his mouth. After he swallowed, he said, "Well, *you* know yourself best."

"I do. I really think this is the right decision." She had her hands clasped in prayer. The relief she felt was palpable. Graham was on her side. Vigorously, she pushed a bigger bite into her mouth. She was all of a sudden hungry again.

"Oh," Graham said a little while later, after he'd served himself seconds. "I forgot to mention. I had a visit with the police today."

Lauren lay down her fork. "You *what*?"

Graham looked surprised. "I thought you knew. They said they were going to call you."

Lauren searched through the day. She hadn't received a call from the police. Nor had she missed one. "What happened?"

"They had a lot of questions about you. But don't worry. I didn't . . . *say* anything."

The scent of Parmesan grew sharp in Lauren's nostrils. "Okay . . ."

"And now, it seems that they're focusing on a few others. I'm pretty sure you're no longer a person of interest."

"Wait, a few others are?" Lauren blinked. "*Who?*"

"Those women who were with you in that hallway." Graham raised an eyebrow. "I mean, from what you told me, they were the ones who had the compelling reasons to shut Piper up—way more than Piper just accidentally forwarding you a mean email." He pointed his fork at her and smiled. "I pitched that in a story meeting, by the way. Well, a funnier version. The Jimmy character receives a nasty email about him that's not meant for him. It's about his dick. And then things go badly."

"About his . . ." Lauren's mind stepped backward a few paces. "What do you mean, *from what I told you*? What did I say about Ronnie and Andrea?"

"You told me they'd also received notes. And then later, you added that they would go to extreme means to stop it from happening again. Because they have things to hide." He grabbed another piece of garlic bread. "I thought it would be useful for the cops to know that."

Lauren could only stare at the rising steam coming from the breadstick as Graham tore it in two. She couldn't quite grab on to the memory of *telling* Graham this. She hadn't said anything about Andrea being a Vandermeer, had she? And what Ronnie confessed about Esme flashed in her mind, too. Ronnie absolutely had a reason to keep Piper quiet, but if Graham knew that—if Graham had told the cops—Ronnie could lose that child.

"I shouldn't have said anything about them," she whispered. "Um, *when* did I tell you? That other stuff, I mean. The stuff I said about Ronnie and Andrea having things to hide. I know I mentioned the notes Friday. But . . ."

"You . . ." Graham was looking at her strangely. "Saturday

night. You don't remember?" He set down his fork. "I thought this was a good thing. Had I known you didn't want me to share, I would have kept quiet."

"I just . . . I said I wouldn't. I *promised* them." *Saturday night?* She scrambled to remember. Saturday, she'd talked to Kelsey. She'd come home, then, and tried to play with the baby, but she'd felt so nervous, so she'd had an illicit, breastfeeding-taboo glass of wine, which made her woozy. Graham worked late, and she'd fallen asleep on the couch. She'd awakened to the lights snapping off and Clarissa shutting the door, but she'd been disoriented—kind of drunk. Graham had stood over her, and she'd felt a little sheepish, afraid he could smell the alcohol on her breath.

Was *that* when she'd betrayed Ronnie's and Andrea's trust? They'd confided in her. Look what she'd done.

Graham reached across the table and touched Lauren's hand. "I just want you to be safe, babe. I want us all to be totally, totally safe."

Lauren nodded shakily. "I know, but . . ."

She didn't feel safe. How was this her mind? If she'd confessed things to Graham, who else had she told? How could she do this to Ronnie and Andrea?

She dropped the fork into her uneaten food. Nothing felt real or solid. Lauren glanced at her baby, her throat closing up with sadness. "Graham," she said in a choked voice. "Graham. Maybe I was wrong. Maybe I do need help."

Graham's expression wilted, and he stood up and moved around the table and gathered her crumpled form in his arms. "It's okay," he whispered. "We'll get you help. We'll get you all the help you need."

Twenty-Two

Ronnie's fingers trembled as they held a paper cup of coffee. Across the wooden bench outside the café, her sister calmly stirred mint tea. Ronnie couldn't recall her sister ever drinking mint tea before—not unless it was spiked with vodka. The innocence of it felt incongruous and wrong. In fact, all her feelings felt wrong. On the one hand, she was overjoyed to see her sister. She'd cried for a year, numb with grief, because she thought Vanessa was dead.

On the other hand, she was scared shitless. Because here was the end of the road. If Vanessa was here, surely Jerrod must be close behind.

"This sandwich is good," Vanessa mused. "Yours?"

"Um," Ronnie squeaked, "sure."

She was too jacked up to try the sandwiches she'd bought for both of them for an early dinner—blessedly, Mrs. Lombardo said she could stay on with Esme back at the apartment. And anyway, they weren't supposed to be talking about sandwiches. They weren't supposed to be sitting outside a sandwich shop in the late afternoon California sunshine like everything was fine.

Finally, she couldn't stand the silence. "You're looking . . . okay," she told Vanessa.

"Thanks," Vanessa said, almost proudly.

Her sister's hair was greasy. She'd lost at least thirty pounds since Ronnie had seen her last. She had broken capillaries around her eyes, and her clothes were oversize and threadbare, not that she'd ever dressed well. And she'd doused herself in cologne, which Ronnie feared was to cover up the smell of something else, like weed. There was also something wrong with her teeth, and she had a sore on the inside of her wrist that looked infected.

But her eyes were cunning and determined. She had Ronnie cornered, and they both knew it.

"When did you get here?" Ronnie asked next.

"Oh, last night. Drove in."

"Are you working? Are you . . . you know, *healthy*?"

"Would I be here if I were using?" Vanessa's voice was sharp. "I've been clean for years."

Ronnie didn't trust that. "Did you do a program? NA?"

"I found Jesus." Vanessa's voice was mocking, sarcastic. "Praise the Lord."

Ronnie believed that Vanessa was born-again as much as she would have believed Vanessa if she told her she'd enrolled in law school. There were some things about people that didn't change; when she and Vanessa were young, they lived across the street from a clapboard Baptist church, and when the parishioners dutifully filed in on Sunday mornings, Vanessa stood at the window in devil horns, snickering at their piousness. It made Ronnie sad to think about that; it was an affectionate memory, all things considered.

"This is quite the place," Vanessa went on, looking up the boulevard, which was lined in palm trees. "Sunny Cal-i-forn-i-a." She said the last part like *eye-ay.* Was there a slur to her voice? Had she always talked like this? "I drove around a little bit this morning before finding you. That beach is gorgeous! Must be nice, living near the ocean."

Ronnie licked her lips. "It's okay."

Vanessa snorted. "So's the fact that you're two thousand miles away from me, I bet."

When Ronnie shut her eyes, she felt hot tears. "Nessie. I wanted you to come. I didn't mean for it to be like this."

"Yeah, right." Vanessa's voice was brisk. When Ronnie opened her eyes, her sister was calmly unwrapping the rest of her sandwich. "Then you would have called me from the road. You would have checked what happened to me instead of just grabbing my kid and getting the fuck out of town without another word. You changed your *name*, Ronnie. Who the hell is Ronnie *Stuckey*? And what's this I hear about changing my girl's name to *Esme*?" She made a face. "What kind of name is that?"

The hate was so seething it practically radiated off Vanessa in concentric circles. Ronnie wanted to grab Vanessa across the table and say, *Hey. Remember me? Remember playing tag in the backyard, and elaborate stories featuring our dolls, and you squeezing my hand after you gave birth to your girl?*

The two women were nothing alike, and they never claimed to be friends. They had fought a lot as kids and adults, and there was a lot of shit that was unsaid. But they'd come from the same family. They had the same memories, up to a certain point. They shared a bed as kids, and helped their mother make pies at Christmas, and sledded down their backyard hill on cardboard boxes. They fought like wild animals, but they always made up. Back then, Ronnie liked to think she had her sister's best interests at heart, and vice versa, but that was before the bitterness, and her parents' death, and the drugs, and Jerrod, and finally Esme.

It had been easier imagining Vanessa was dead, Ronnie realized, because then she didn't have to fully confront what she'd done.

"I'm sorry," she admitted. It felt like there was a big rubber band around her chest. "I was scared. And . . . well, *Jerrod*." She dared to look at Vanessa. "Taylor would have died there, you know." It felt strange to use Esme's original name. "And you would have, too, eventually."

"You're being dramatic. And also, it's not up to you."

"So I was supposed to just stand there and watch it happen?" Bile rose in Ronnie's throat.

"You always did think you could handle things better. Always got the good grades, had the better boyfriends, made the better money."

Ronnie shut her eyes. "I love that kid, Nessie. I was just thinking of her."

"Oh, Ronnie." Her sister's voice was almost gentle. She felt Vanessa's cool, small hand on top of hers, and Ronnie's heart lifted. "It took a lot to track you down. I almost gave up."

"How long have you been following me?" Ronnie thought of all the shadows she feared, all the bodies darting into corners. That had all been Vanessa?

"I hired a PI. It cost a ton of money. Said I was looking for my long-lost sister. That we had a *lot* to talk about." She smirked. "He looked and looked. It wasn't easy to find you."

"Has he been watching me all this time?" If only that could explain her paranoia. "Did he send me the *Missing* flyer?"

"No!" Vanessa looked intrigued. "*You* got one? How about that? I put that flyer together years ago—I had no idea they were still printing them."

"Nessie, I-I've felt terrible," Ronnie stammered. "Terrible that I got her out of there, terrible that I didn't have enough time to get you." Her eyes filled with tears, thinking of Vanessa on the ground, unconscious. "I should have," she decided. "Even if it meant Jerrod coming after us. But I . . . I thought you were gone already." She lowered her head. "I was just thinking of Taylor. I was afraid Jerrod was going to kill us."

"He wouldn't have killed you."

"How can you be so sure?" Ronnie cleared her throat. "He was about to rape me."

Vanessa rolled her eyes. "Funny. He told me you came on to

him. Told me you came on to him a lot. Wanted to be his wife, wanted me out of the picture. It's why you took off with Taylor. If you couldn't have him, then at least you'd have his little girl."

Ronnie gaped. How could Vanessa say that after all that Jerrod had put her through? She wanted to shake her. "If you knew I was the one who took her, why did it take you so long to find us?"

"Yeah, well. *I* wanted to." Vanessa's eyes lowered. Something dark and heavy passed across her features.

"But Jerrod didn't?"

Vanessa shrugged. But maybe that made sense. If the police came, they'd see the squalor and Vanessa's bruises. They'd suspect that *they* had done something to the baby. So why now, then? Had Vanessa had to save up the money? Was she doing this without Jerrod knowing? Maybe this was her first opportunity to get away? It was all so puzzling.

Desperation roiled up inside Ronnie, along with regret. This was still her sister, and she still loved her. "I wanted you to come with me," she repeated. "I begged for you to wake up. But then you didn't, and I heard Jerrod moving around in the bedroom. I was afraid Jerrod was going to come out, and . . . I didn't know what to do."

"You should've had your own damn kids, if you wanted them so badly." Vanessa's eyes blazed. "But it was easier to just take mine, wasn't it?"

"Oh, so you'd rather I left her there? Where she was unsupervised half the time? Where neither of you were sober, and you barely held down jobs—"

"*That's* what it's about." Vanessa crossed her arms triumphantly. "Since we didn't make the same money as you, you thought we were beneath you."

"That's not what I'm saying. *Any* job would have done."

"You realize"—Vanessa raised a wavering finger—"that you're nothing more than a slut, right? All you have is your tits and your ass. It's not like you're using your big brain. You're sticking your cunt in men's faces—*that's* how you're making money."

Ronnie recoiled. She could sense that the street had quieted down, like the whole world was listening in. Then she felt the tears come. Vanessa was right. Of course she was right. Yet she wished some karmic spirit would realize that she'd only tried to do the right thing and just . . . make a ruling in her favor, maybe.

"Oh, stop crying," Vanessa snapped. "Now, where is she?"

Ronnie looked up at her in terror. "No."

Vanessa scoffed. "I've come for Taylor. I want my baby."

Here it was. *Please*, Ronnie wanted to beg. *Please, don't you see?* She knew it wasn't fair to ask to keep Esme, but the idea of letting her go felt like walking off a cliff. "We could all stay here," she tried. "We could have a good life here."

"She'll have a good life with her mother, too. Back east."

"Are you going to take her back to . . . *him*?"

Vanessa looked away. "Jerrod doesn't know I'm here. Not yet."

"You mean you're still married?" Her heart was hammering now. She couldn't let this happen. Maybe she could grab Esme and run. Disappear again. She hated to think of leaving Lane behind, but she would do it. She would do anything.

"Taylor's coming with me. And if you're going to make trouble, well . . ." She puffed out her cheeks. "Don't test me. 'Kay?"

"Please," Ronnie whispered, suddenly feeling like she was going to start hyperventilating. There was so much rushing in her ears. "What about a mediator?"

Vanessa squinted. "Huh?"

"It's like . . . a therapist. Someone to help us navigate this. Figure out a plan."

"I don't need a shrink."

"Your daughter doesn't know you. She was two when we left. She thinks of *me* as her mother. Babies aren't dogs. They don't know your smell." Ronnie couldn't quite meet Vanessa's gaze. "We have to ease her into it, get her prepared. You can't just take her—she'd be traumatized." Ronnie started crying. "Think of *her.* Not just yourself."

Vanessa chewed on the inside of her lip, then lifted up the mug of tea and drained it as though it were a shot of tequila. "Fine. Get your fancy mediator. Schedule it for tomorrow."

Tomorrow? "B-But I need to find someone first. And I don't know if someone will have an opening for to—"

"I'm coming to your place at noon," Vanessa said, her eyes turning dark. "I know where you live. I'm gonna gather up my stuff, pay off my guy, get gas, and then I'll be by." Then she hefted herself up and grabbed the canvas Safeway bag it appeared she was using as a tote and gave her a final glare. "You'd *better* be there."

Ronnie scrambled up, full of both relief and doubt, not sure what she needed to do next. As Vanessa turned, Ronnie felt a strong, protective sensation rush over her. "W-Where are you staying tonight?"

Vanessa didn't answer; she rolled her eyes and started for the curb. She glanced at Ronnie one more time, then shook her head with disgust. "You always were too fucking *pretty*, Ronnie."

And then she was gone. Ronnie sat back down, running her palms against the rough surface of the bench. Then, shakily, she gathered up their trash and walked back into the café to throw it away. The barista glanced at her, but her smile dimmed when she saw Ronnie's blotchy cheeks and wet eyes. Wordlessly, Ronnie shut herself inside the bathroom, safe from everyone's gaze.

No one saw her twist the lock. No one saw her bang the mirror with her fist until it created a small hairline crack. No one saw her sink to the filthy floor—still cleaner than anything in Vanessa's old house—and break into sobs, wondering what the hell she was going to do.

Twenty-Three

"Mommy?" On Tuesday morning—*five days after Piper's attack*—Arthur had climbed into Andrea's bed and was lying next to her, stroking her hair. "Can I please, please, *please* go to school today?"

"No school today," Andrea said, grateful that this was true. "Remember? You go Mondays, Thursdays, and Fridays."

Arthur went boneless, flopping over the side of the bed. "But why didn't I get to go yesterday?" He stuck out his lip. "I miss Johnny and King. Can I have them over at least?"

"Maybe . . ."

It hurt to tell her child no, but any interaction right now felt dangerous. There was the buzz online, for one. The comments the other parents posted weren't pure vitriol—some of them were more like backhanded compliments: *I have to say, she's much prettier than most women* and *Ugh if I didn't have ovaries I'd have skin like that too*—but she wasn't ready for the stares, or for Arthur to feel uncomfortable in any way. Also, after she talked with Ronnie yesterday afternoon, she'd received a voicemail from Detective Allegra. In his message, he asked if she could "check in" with him, as he had a few more questions. About *what*, Andrea wasn't sure.

According to the Facebook group, Piper was still unconscious in her hospital room. It rocked Andrea's core. *Unconscious.* That meant a coma. That meant something had shaken up her brain. *And she'd been right there.*

Even worse, the Piper news had spread to the state level; also yesterday, someone from an ABC news affiliate had sent her an email request for an interview. *This is Joanna from Channel 10 in San Diego*, the message read. *Apologies if I'm overstepping here, but I've been informed you might have something to say about the director who was attacked at the preschool in your town. Can you please reach out at your earliest convenience? Would love to hear your side of things.*

And yet—*and yet*—this reporter hadn't made a reference to Andrea being a Vandermeer. Surely, if a reporter had contacted Andrea's mother, all the press would know by now—meaning it was certainly the blackmailer who'd called Cynthia. *Carson?*

Arthur slid off the bed and headed for the master bath, and the sound of his urine stream hitting the toilet reflected off the hard surfaces. He was probably peeing all over the bowl and the floor, but Andrea didn't care. She grabbed her phone and pulled up the Instagram page she'd found for Carson. Up came glamour shots of a vegan meal he'd had the night before, along with a bunch of kissing-face emojis. Then, Andrea noticed he'd posted something on his Instagram Stories. She tapped it, and up came a photo of the same vegan dinner. This disappeared, and next Carson's face appeared—he was smooshed next to another man at a fancy restaurant. With his shit-eating smile, Carson certainly didn't look *that* destroyed that his boss was clinging to life in intensive care.

A final image appeared in the story: Carson and the same guy were standing outside the restaurant, but this was more of a body shot. Andrea was about to click past it, but she noticed that Carson's messenger bag was printed with a familiar herringbone pattern. She looked closer. Was that Goyard? Her mother had a tote with the same print, except hers was navy. Cynthia didn't own a handbag that cost less than a normal person's monthly mortgage. After a quick Internet search, she found the messenger style's price: $2,100.

This guy had an Audi and an expensive bag, and yet he worked as an assistant at a preschool? Did Carson have some sort of lucrative side hustle? Maybe his family was wealthy after all?

She sat up straighter and typed in Silver Swans' web address. The school had an audit board, though most of the people on it were parents. If she called and checked, would she find out that Carson was the one managing the accounting? The paper Ronnie took from Piper's office. Maybe it was a balance sheet. Some sort of cash record after all. She'd heard about schools doctoring invoices. Last year, there were nuns who'd done it at a Catholic school in Iowa.

She slid off the bed. "Honey?" she called to Arthur, who was still in the bathroom. "I'm running to the mailbox, okay?"

The grass was wet with dew, chilling her bare feet as she ran across the lawn. The mailbox hinges creaked as she pulled open the door. The box was stuffed with letters; she'd kind of forgotten mail existed in the past few days. She grabbed the stack between her palms and hurried back to the house, then spilled all the mail onto the couch.

"Whoa!" Arthur exclaimed, mixing up the junk mail, magazines, bills, like the pile was a stew. At first, Andrea didn't see anything out of the ordinary, but then there it was—an unmarked white envelope, thin with only a single sheet of paper. USPS was on the ball. Andrea tore it open and stared at the swarm of numbers on the page. They marched across six Excel columns and down at least twenty rows—more than a hundred numbers in all. But they didn't look like expenses—the numbers were too big, and there were no decimal points or dollar signs. They were too long to be social security numbers.

Credit card numbers, maybe? Some of them started with the same four digits. Then, Andrea spotted the beginning numbers for the bank account at First National she'd set up when she moved here. The more she looked, the more she noticed other numbers with the same beginning digits. Were these bank accounts?

Actually, wait a minute.

She stared hard at the numbers in one particular Excel square. Unless she was losing her mind, that *was* her bank account number. Exactly.

She hurried to the desk in her office and pulled open a drawer. A checkbook sat under a pile of tax forms; the routing number matched what was in the spreadsheet, as did the account number.

What did that mean? Andrea grabbed her phone and called the only person she could think of. "Jerry?" she said when he answered. "It's Andrea. Sorry to bother you again."

"You're not bothering me." A bird sang in the background. He must have been outside. "But I'm afraid I don't have any updates. You haven't been charged with anything. Your mother still doesn't know the name of that journalist—"

"Is there a reason a nursery school would have my bank account number?" she interrupted.

There was a pause. "Huh?"

Jerry sounded old. Tired. He was retired, more or less. Andrea felt terrible dragging him into this. He'd left New York to *escape* trouble, not wade back into it. And also, admitting what she was looking at, right now, meant admitting she'd been in Piper's office.

"I can't say how I know this," she said. "But does the school have a right to have our bank information?"

"Did you give it to them? Maybe for an ACH withdrawal? How are your payments structured?"

"Oh." Andrea felt like a dummy. After Arthur was accepted into the program last spring, Silver Swans sent out forms about automatic withdrawals. Of course Andrea filled them out—the more automated the bills, the better. "Right. Sorry. That's totally it."

But then Jerry said, "That doesn't mean they haven't abused their power."

Andrea frowned. "I'm sorry?"

"We're talking about Silver Swans, right?"

"Of course we are. That's where Arthur goes to school."

Silence followed. Out the window, several birds flew to her feeder. Jerry had given her that bird feeder, actually; he and Susan, avid bird watchers, had the same one at their house. Andrea could picture Jerry sitting on the glider on the front porch, watching the birds fight for seed. She could also picture him in her family's town house twenty years ago, smoking cigars with her father, slipping into a back room to talk and not coming out for hours.

"Jerry?" she croaked. "What are you saying?"

"I should go," he said. He sounded hurried. More lucid, too. "Susan needs me. I'll be in touch, okay? I'm still trying to figure out who called your mother."

He disconnected. What on earth did Jerry know about Silver Swans?

Andrea peeked back in on Arthur and was pleased to see he'd fallen back to sleep. It gave her extra time. She drifted to her computer again, waving the mouse to wake up the screen, then navigated to her banking portal.

Admittedly, she didn't track her bank account very carefully. She had never been taught to be fiscally responsible on her own. By the time she was seven or eight, she'd known there'd been a man in a tall office building who managed her money—not even her family's money but *her* money, her trust. Back then, she'd pictured her money in a giant piggy bank. She'd never held a paying job in high school. In college, money just appeared in a bank account; she was always one of those people who could take unpaid internships, if she so chose, because she didn't have to worry about paying rent. It was only after she was married that she learned to write a check, and when she bought this home, she'd been able to pay cash—she didn't even have to juggle a mortgage. And she *wouldn't* have to, unless her father decided to disown her.

Now, it occurred to her how unrealistic her life was. Did she want Arthur being so cavalier about finances? She made a mental note to think more about how to talk to Arthur about money, and then figured out the correct password and was into her bank details. As she started to scroll through the transactions, everything looked pretty normal: there were charges for bills, purchases, and transfers to investments that had been automatically put in place by that same financial guy who guarded her piggy bank. There was also a sizable sum of money to Silver Swans on the second of September. This was the payment for the first month of school, presumably; the ACH withdrawals would happen monthly. Tomorrow was October 2, when the next withdrawal was due.

But when Andrea scrolled back, she noticed a charge for $540 on August 15 that she couldn't place. She clicked on the details, figuring it was probably clothes or a day trip she and Arthur had taken, but only a jumble of numbers came up. She frowned and then, thinking about what Jerry had just said, clicked on the September Silver Swans charge once more.

The money in that charge had gone to a bank account in Silver Swans' name. The money in the $540 charge had gone into a different account number . . . but only *slightly* different, she noticed. The routing number was the same. The account number was only different by a few digits, as though the two accounts might have been set up within days or even hours of each other.

Two weeks earlier in August, there was a charge for $680—this also went to the mysterious account. Andrea found three more charges dating back to June. Then they stopped. Together, it totaled nearly $3,000.

She sat back, making the chair creak. First, she was disgusted with herself that she hadn't noticed $3,000 missing. And then a different kind of anger followed.

Andrea dialed Ronnie. No answer. Then she dialed Lauren. No answer there, either. Frustrated, she pulled out Miss Barnes's class list, which she'd stashed next to the computer, and scanned the names. Most of these people she hadn't even spoken to, but there was one name that stuck out: Jane Russell, King's mom. Aka the owner of the huge house at the top of the Raisin Beach cliffs. If there was one person who maybe didn't notice if some money was missing in her account, it was Jane.

The phone rang once, then twice, then a silvery voice answered. "Uh, Jane?" Andrea said, and introduced herself, laying it on thick that she was Arthur's mom from the fours class.

"Oh, yes, Arthur!" Jane said. "King liked playing with him!" But then: "Wait, you're *Arthur's* mom?"

"Yes," Andrea said, hurriedly. "So . . . I need you to do me a favor. I need you to look at your bank account."

"My . . . what?" Now Jane was more guarded. "Why?"

"Please tell me if you see a charge, and then I'll explain."

Andrea waited, holding her breath. And then Jane told her to hold on.

⁂

Midday on Tuesday at Silver Swans was quiet; the only sounds were the joyful shrieks from kids playing on the jungle gym in the back. Andrea's heart hammered as she parked, pocketed her keys, and got out of the car. Her ankles wobbled in the high heels she'd chosen to wear, and she almost considered kicking them off, but she glanced at her reflection in the car window. She'd always felt powerful in these shoes. She needed them now.

There was a buzzer to get into the offices. Andrea pressed it; she had a speech prepared in case Carson wanted an explanation for why she was here, but to her surprise, he buzzed her in right away. *That* was strange.

The office hallway was dark. Sun streamed down from the

stairwell to the loft just as it had five days before, when she'd last been in here. For a moment, Andrea felt woozy with the memory. The neurons in her brain rearranged, and she could *smell* that day: that rose candle, dust, blood. She shut her eyes, putting herself in the moment, trying to figure out who was in the hallway with them.

She turned toward the end of the hall. The big camera brought in for the documentary was no longer there. She wondered where it had gone.

Carson's door was ajar. Andrea gathered her courage and walked into the doorway where he could see her. Carson was on the phone, talking quietly, but when he noticed her, he got a strange smile on his face, murmured something into the receiver, and hung up.

"Oh!" he said—so he *was* expecting someone else. "Ms. Vaughan, right?" He gestured her inside. "What can I do for you?"

Andrea could barely breathe. A huge part of her wanted to turn and bolt. But instead, she said quietly, "What you did to the parents isn't right."

Carson tipped back in his chair. His blink was as slow as a turtle's, and that strange smile was still on his face. "What did I do?"

She flashed the list Ronnie swiped. "How many of these parents had little increments removed from their bank accounts? Ten? Twenty? Everyone?" This was a tiny bit of a bluff: she wasn't 100 percent *sure* that second account was Silver Swans'. Jane had read out the account number on her illicit transactions, though, and they'd matched Andrea's exactly. What else could it be?

A bloom of red was creeping up Carson's neck. "Where did you get that?"

"Did Piper know? Or was this your little endeavor?"

Now Carson was getting up and walking around his desk. "That's property of the school. I could have you arrested."

As if on cue, a police siren rang out down the street, and

Carson froze. Andrea straightened. "I called them. You can't steal, Carson. A lot of these people lost their jobs this past year. A lot of people are making serious sacrifices to send their kids to this place. Do you realize how up in arms the parents are going to be when they find out?"

Carson burst out laughing. "Oh, come on. You didn't even know that money was missing." Andrea looked away. "And for the record, we didn't take from people who were hurting. Only those who could afford it."

"And you think *that* gives you the right?" Andrea said carefully. "You don't know people's financial situations. It might seem like they're doing okay, but maybe they aren't."

Carson sighed. "Do you know what we do for your kids? Do you know how hard we work?"

"Everyone struggled." She pushed the list of account numbers into her back pocket and listened. The sirens didn't sound much closer. "So, did Piper find out about what you were doing? And, what, she asked you to stop it? But you didn't want it to end, did you? I've seen your Facebook posts—your fancy car, your messenger bag, your dinners out. It's nice to have money, isn't it, when you grew up with nothing?"

Carson crossed his arms. "You don't know me."

"So you had to take matters into your own hands? But then *we* come along, and it's so convenient! But what's going to happen when Piper wakes up?"

Carson's eyes popped wide. "You think *I* hurt her?" He let out an incredulous laugh. "You sound like you're on fucking *Law & Order*. Piper was in on the scam. She approved the idea."

Carson strolled around his desk, opened a drawer, and riffled through some file folders. He located what he was looking for and thrust it in her direction. "It's her name on the account. She knows *everything*. See?"

He handed her a sign-up sheet for a local bank. The account's digits looked familiar—perhaps the second account where the money was being siphoned. Andrea didn't trust it, though. "You could have Photoshopped these, after the fact."

"I didn't. This was all her idea. Besides, Nancy Drew, the police already questioned me about an alibi. I was out back, behind the school, planting a fucking garden when it happened." Then he cocked his head. "Okay, yes, I *did* leak that information about you guys to the press, the police, your mother. But it was only so you would keep your mouths shut."

Andrea frowned. "How did you know we'd figure this out? Because we were in her office?"

Carson looked at her like she was nuts. "You already knew. You and that . . . that stripper girl. *She* told both of you."

"Who's *she*?"

He put his hands on his hips, looking flustered. "Flora. The . . . the bracelets. She told you to wear them, didn't she?"

"The . . . bracelets? Flora?" Andrea looked down at her wrist. The only bracelet she was wearing was the stretchy yellow one Jerry had given her. "This?" She held up her wrist.

"Yes!" Carson said, exasperated.

Andrea laughed. "I haven't spoken to Flora about anything." But as she said this, the back of her neck began to prickle. Jerry had told her—without telling her—that something strange was going on in this office.

"Come on. Flora's kid went here last year." Carson was saying this like she should know. "She was the only one who noticed the increments of money missing. She confronted Piper. We had to pay her off, but I always worried she'd tell people anyway." He slapped his sides. "We got rid of all the parents who knew her. Came up with bullshit excuses of why we couldn't welcome them back after Silver Swans reopened its doors. Made this school even more exclusive. But then you and Veronica whatever-her-name-is came along wearing her stupid bracelets." He stared at her. "She *didn't* talk to you?"

"I know Flora's father," Andrea said slowly. "I don't know Flora." She was so dazed she took a step back, bumping into a low credenza on the far wall. "Wait, so you sent those notes then, too. The ones to our kids. You pretended to draw like a kindergartener to . . . to mess with our heads. To make us withdraw. Do you realize how sick that is?"

"Wasn't my idea." Carson sighed. "Look, Piper was paranoid. She didn't want anyone to find out what we'd done. This school is her life. She figured, *Even if Flora didn't tell them, she might. We need to nip it in the bud.*" He raised his palms. "I'm just her errand boy. And look, I'm sorry, especially if you didn't know. Hell, I guess this makes you look a little less guilty—though, I mean, I could still see you wanting to bust open Piper's head after getting those notes."

"And how do I know *you're* telling the truth? Maybe Piper had regrets at scamming the parents. Maybe she has a heart—unlike yourself."

"I have an alibi, remember?" Carson sighed heavily, as though this were all so tiresome.

"Well, you've still done something wrong. And I didn't hurt Piper, either. So stop threatening me. Stop threatening my friends."

Carson's brow was furrowed. He seemed just as blindsided by this as Andrea was. "Huh," he said. "So you weren't lurking around her house, either?"

"What?" Andrea put a hand to her chest. "Why would I lurk around her house?"

"Because you wanted to scare her." Carson searched her face like he didn't believe her. Andrea shook her head vehemently. "Well, someone was! She was really freaked out about it!"

"Someone was stalking her?" Andrea repeated. "Another parent who found out?" she volunteered.

Carson gave her an exasperated look. "I don't *know*. If she told me *that*, we would have already solved this, wouldn't we?"

Andrea pressed her fingers to her temples. This all sounded too convenient. Carson was sending her off in a crazy direction to deflect guilt. He was trying to minimize the fact that he'd committed a huge crime. Andrea straightened, regaining her focus.

The sirens finally grew closer. Andrea grabbed the folder Carson had handed over—stupid, stupid man!—and pressed it to her chest. "You really think parents—even wealthy ones—are going to allow this? I have evidence now."

"You're not going to say anything." That eerie smile on his face again. "Or else I'll tell them about *you*." Carson put his hands on his hips. "Who you really are. And then your father will know."

His pupils were huge. A tiny *ping* sounded on Carson's computer, but they both ignored it. Andrea could feel the heat rising up her neck, the abject embarrassment and humiliation of being so, *so* wrong about this situation. Of course Carson knew who she really was. He'd been the one who called her mother, posing as a reporter.

Carson shrugged. "Your family history has been in your file this whole time. I just chose not to share that with the cops. It felt . . . *cruel*, I guess? But don't point fingers at *me* for stealing. You're stealing, too—in a way. Stealing from your bigot of a father. Lying about who you really are. What do you think that guy will do when he learns the truth about you?"

The way the light hit his face, he looked almost angelic. He had chubby cheeks and dimples and wore a nice dress shirt in a delicate check pattern. The more Andrea stared, the more she realized *she* had owned a very similar shirt, back in the day. Christine had bought it for her.

"And that's not all I'll talk about," Carson added. "Your old lawyer friend? Jerry? I have a list a mile long of shit he's done. Bribery. Insider trading. There's even a hint he put a hit out on a guy."

"Wait, what?" Andrea's throat was almost too dry to speak.

"It's why we got Flora for so cheap. We found out a lot of it shortly after she came to us."

Andrea shut her eyes. "Jerry's a good person, all said and done. His wife is sick. Don't do that to him."

Carson shrugged. "*I'm* not the one making that choice."

Andrea considered taking the folder and running with it, waving it to the cops like a white flag. But then she thought about the retaliation. How fast the press would swarm in. And Jerry. *Oh, Jerry*, she thought. If he'd just *said* something to her earlier. Maybe this could all have been avoided.

The sirens were in the parking lot now. Carson tipped his chin toward the window, as if to say, *Well, what's it going to be?* Reluctantly, hating herself, Andrea placed the folder of information back on his desk and walked away.

Piper

September

Carson calls when you are in your kitchen, packing up things to head off to work. "I'd have to think they've seen the messages by now."

"And?" you ask.

"They'll be out of here soon."

You pace the house. North has already gone off to school; a spare hoodie hangs on a hook by the door, unworn. You focus on it a moment, noting how new it still looks. North keeps his things so nice.

You want to feel calm. You want to feel like this is under control. But something feels off. You feel followed. Watched. You want to think you're just paranoid—you've been paranoid for months, ever since Flora Haines came to you, having figured it all out and expecting some sort of medal for her efforts.

You think of Flora and her pinched little face when she rang your doorbell in late spring, not long after you'd begun the withdrawals. "What the fuck do you think you're doing, Piper?" she'd demanded. "Why am I getting charged random amounts from you people when my kid isn't even in school?"

You smiled in mock surprise. Told her you had no idea what she was talking about. It was a shame, really—you'd considered Flora a friend. She was one of those mothers who took it upon herself to make the school better, looping in special guests to visit and donating art supplies and even hooking you up with a playground equipment supplier that was eco-friendly and BPA-free.

Not so deep down, you seethed with annoyance that she was being so self-righteous. Flora came from vast amounts of money; her father was some hotshot corporate lawyer back in New York. She didn't even have a regular job; she was starting some bullshit sportswear line, clearly a vanity project, the pieces made in China and shipped here and stamped with her holistic seal of approval. You even wore her stupid rubber bracelet for a while, supporting her cause. You went to her stupid launch party. You bought her leggings and a headband you'd never wear and a pair of socks that were no better than the ones you used to buy in big packs at Walmart. And this is what she throws back in your face? A few dollars siphoned from her account?

Flora didn't need the money. Silver Swans did. You *did. Not that you could have told her that. Flora was furious when she came to you. She said she'd figured it all out and was going to blow the whistle. "Everyone else might love you," she said, "but I think you're full of shit. Exploiting parents, especially during this time? Do you realize how wrong that is?"*

You had to act quickly. It was so easy, in the end—all you had to do was pinpoint what really mattered to her. You'd never met a girl who didn't want to protect her father. Hell, that even included you, not that your dad had any secrets worth keeping.

She took your money and shut up. She knew what bombs you could detonate, and she stayed away. Her capitulation was a relief at the time, but now you wonder if you'd been naïve. You'd noticed her bracelets on not one wrist but two. *New mothers at that. It's more than a coincidence. Flora knows these women; she must. Maybe she said the things she wasn't supposed to.*

This paranoia seeps into your every thought. Every door slam you hear at the curb you think is an angry parent coming for you—or worse, the police. Every phone call you worry is someone who's turned over another rock. You wonder if North is starting to notice how jumpy you've become. You wonder, even, if North knows what you've done—but no. That's impossible. You keep telling yourself that only Flora knows, and perhaps these three new women don't know a thing, but you curse that you've let them slip through the cracks. Now they're in your community, and it's not so easy to kick them out. You have to be careful.

"But we can turn up the heat, if we need to," Carson adds, after you've been silent for too long. "I . . . found some more things."

"What things?"

"On them. Well—two of them, anyway. Veronica and Andrea. Stuff they probably don't want broadcast, if they can help it." He sighs. "It's amazing, what people hide."

"That's good," you say. "There's also an email I got from Lauren. About her anger." You feel better now. This will all go away. Carson has it under control.

"Are you still noticing strange things about your house?" Carson asks then.

You swallow. "Sort of."

It's only little things. You swear you locked the back shed before leaving, but when you get home, it's open. At night, you'll bolt awake, certain someone is standing in your yard, though when you peek out the windows, no one is there.

"Can't you turn on your alarm?" Carson asks.

You pause. Your home's previous owners installed a system, and a sign for said system remained on a stake in the lawn to deter potential burglars, but you never actually had it reactivated. It was a corner you'd cut, a nonnecessity you thought you could forgo so you could afford the place's mortgage. You never thought it would matter. Wasn't Raisin Beach supposed to be ridiculously safe?

For most people, maybe. But perhaps not for you.

"And what about North? Has he noticed anything?"

"I already asked him. I'll ask again."

You notice another call coming in, then. "I need to go," you tell Carson. You try to put your imaginary stalker out of your mind. No one has snuck into your house. You left a window open yourself. You left a book in a spot you didn't remember. "I'll see you in the office. I'm about to get into the car."

You click over to the other line as you grab your bag and head out the door. "Piper?" says a crisp woman's voice. "Please hold for Jean Gillout."

You break into a grin. The Hulu guy. The documentary. You cannot wait to get started.

"Jean!" you cry when he comes on the line. "How are you? I was just asking my assistant to set up some more interviews! We're so excited."

There's a long pause. You think the connection has been lost. Finally, the exec clears his throat. "Listen, I know we haven't known each other very long, Piper." He sounds strange. "But . . . something's come to my attention."

Your veins go icy. Twice this summer, you met with Jean in swanky LA eateries to pitch your case. And both those times, you feared Flora was lurking somewhere, somehow knowing you were there, ready to spill your secrets. But it never happened. You always told yourself it was because she'd been taken care of—her hands were dirty, too. But now you wonder.

Only, you can't let on you're scared. So you say in a bright voice, "Is everything all right, Jean?"

He sighs. "I've been informed about something that is kind of . . . well, concerning."

"Concerning?" you repeat. You're suddenly shaking. You need to call Carson. You need to mobilize.

And then Jean says it.

And you're so startled you drop the phone.

Jean keeps talking, but you don't really hear him. Because it's worse than what Flora knows. Worse than what you've done to the parents. It's a bad dream. Impossible. You want to leap through the phone and shake him and say, No, you're wrong.

Instead, all you ask is who told him. You blurt it out furiously, angrily. You don't mean to. Jean says he doesn't know; the tip was anonymous. But he made some calls, he says, and he was able to confirm everything.

What's the point in denying it, then? You are on the road, you realize, driving to work. You don't even remember starting the engine.

After another awkward pause he suggests perhaps you *could be the focus of the documentary—what you're going through. "But it would be a very different documentary," he admits. "And I doubt you could keep your position at Silver Swans."*

"No." You step out of the car. You feel numb. "I-I can't do that."

"Are you sure? Because it's certainly intriguing. Juicy, even."

"Fuck you, then," you hiss. "Fuck you and fuck juicy.*"*

But then you feel terrible for lashing out, and you whisper a whole bunch of things you'd promised yourself you'd never say. You are standing in the parking lot now. Thank God no one is around. You make him swear not to tell anyone. You feel you might start to cry. "Fuck you," you whisper

"Piper," Jean says, "I'll keep this to myself. I promise. We can say we parted ways because of creative differences. That okay with you?"

You tell him yes. What else can you do? If you kick up a fuss, he might go to the press. The parents. Your world will crumble.

You quickly get off the phone after that. Doesn't he realize what good subjects these parents are, how invested they've become? But he's already made up his mind. With another puzzled, uncomfortable look, your chance is gone. And all it's done is open up new, terrible possibilities. Who told him? Your paranoia may have been right all along.

And then a thought comes to you, there in the middle of the parking lot. A dark, ugly, festering thought. You push it away, certain it can't be right, but then you realize, maybe it can.

You can't confirm your fears right away. One of the moms who got a note wants to meet. You have to play it cool, play your cards, and then get her the fuck out. After that, you have a staff meeting with Carson, who notices something's off with you but can't guess what it is. Finally, right before you work the drop-off, you have a few moments to yourself. You lock yourself in your office. You click on the folder on your computer where you keep digitally scanned files on your parents' applications. You find the one you're looking for and leaf through it. Now you know why you feel like there's been something niggling at the back of your brain. You curse yourself for not being more careful, but you'd just thought—there's no way.

His name is the same. It's a common name . . . but not that common. You start to google him, connecting his address. Google comes up with an image. A face. You draw in a breath, because you've been so stupid. When you see this face staring back at you, you know how badly you've fucked up.

Maybe he's been watching you all along.

Twenty-Four

The North Ridge Wellness Facility, according to the website, didn't require a patient to bring much. Clothes were provided. Toiletries. Reading materials, appropriate footwear—all of it was there and waiting. Yet Lauren dropped a large suitcase on the bed regardless. She couldn't pack *nothing*.

Lauren turned to her breast pump, which was sitting on the floor. As much as she wanted to give up breastfeeding—and this was a great excuse—it felt like the only tie to Matthew she had left. She stuffed it and its clean parts into the carrying case and put it into the suitcase. She added a photo of Matthew she kept on the bedside table; she'd need it to look at if she wanted to produce any milk.

Just looking at the picture made her chest seize. She was leaving her baby. She didn't even know for how long. Was she nuts? She imagined how her mother would take this, her sisters. Mel's high-achieving children, Gwen's Instagram-perfect life, and here she was, unable to handle herself, unable to handle a single child.

She'd sold out her friends, and she didn't even remember doing so. She was losing the plot. Whole chunks of her life were gone—and maybe she'd even hurt Piper. Being in an environment where she could concentrate on herself was the only way to fix things. This was the rational thing to do. She needed to be well for the baby and Graham. Matthew would be okay—he was so young he wouldn't even notice Lauren was gone.

Her phone rang. *Andrea*, read the caller ID. Lauren froze. She'd been afraid of Andrea and Ronnie calling ever since Graham had dropped the bomb that she'd ratted them out. Early this morning, the police had even come to the door—to corroborate what Graham told them about Andrea and Ronnie in the station, no doubt. Lauren had been so traumatized and ashamed, she told Clarissa to tell the cops that she was sick in the bathroom and couldn't see them. Later, Clarissa had brought Lauren a cup of digestive tea and the officer's card. *Please call*, Detective Allegra had scrawled under his name.

The phone kept ringing. Maybe the cops had hauled in Andrea and Ronnie without Lauren's verification. Was Andrea calling from the police station? Oh God. She let the call go to voicemail, but moments later, Andrea called again. Lauren let out a silent scream. Was Andrea going to call and call until Lauren picked up?

Her fingers had a mind of their own; they pressed the green *answer* button. "Lauren." Andrea's words were rushed. "We need to talk."

Oh God. Oh God! "I'm sorry," Lauren blurted. Her voice was an octave higher than normal. "Andrea, I'm so sorry."

"You're . . ." Andrea sounded confused. "Why?"

"I didn't mean to say anything. Not about you, or Ronnie—I'm sick. Really sick. I don't know what I'm doing half the time. But I'm going away. To deal with it."

"Going . . . away?" Andrea sounded flabbergasted. "*Now?* But we need you!"

Lauren could feel warmth through the line. Even after all Lauren had done, Andrea was still being nice.

"I can't get a handle on this anger thing," Lauren said. She stared down at the breast pump in her suitcase, the picture of a smiling baby Matthew in its silver frame. "I black out. I've been saying things that I don't remember—and doing things, too." Her heart was pounding so fast. "That day with Piper—I don't remember. I mean, I remember being in her office, and then running out, but after that . . . I don't know what happened. I'm scared I did something."

There was a long silence. Andrea cleared her throat. "You think you hurt Piper?"

"I don't *want* to think it. But it wasn't the first time it happened. I've . . . I've even hurt my baby." She felt tears blur her eyes. "I need to get a hold of what I'm doing." Something else occurred to her, too, and she took a breath. "As far as Piper goes, I'll call and confess. I don't want anyone blaming you or Ronnie. I'm sorry if they've already reached out to you. I'm sorry if they know more about you—it's my fault. I'm sorry for everything."

The line was silent for a long, long beat. "The police *know*?" Andrea whispered. "What did you tell them?"

Lauren moved her tongue into her cheek. "Nothing. But I must have told Graham . . . and *he* did. That Allegra guy came to the house earlier, presumably to talk to me personally."

"But I just saw them, at Silver Swans." Andrea sounded puzzled. "I even talked to that Allegra guy. I mean, unless he's *withholding* it for some reason, but I think he'd enjoy taunting me with it, asking if my father knows." Then she paused, took in a breath. "Why did you tell your husband?"

"I don't remember. I guess I was desperate."

"And you're *sure* he told the police?"

What *had* Graham said? Just that he'd spoken to the police about what she'd said about Andrea's and Ronnie's motives . . . but not specifics. Had she misinterpreted this, somehow?

"Lauren," Andrea said. "First off, I don't think the cops know. I could check with Ronnie—you're worried you told your husband about Esme and he repeated it, right? Well, I don't think that happened. We would have heard from her by now."

Lauren sat down on the bed. Her head swam. "But Graham made it out like he told them something . . . vital."

"Maybe he only thought he did—or maybe they made him think that for some reason. But also? You didn't do this to Piper."

Lauren wiped a tear. "But what if I *did*?"

"No, I've figured something out. With Carson. With the *parents*."

Andrea told her everything about how Piper and Carson were systematically withdrawing small amounts from people's accounts all summer. "Who *knows* how much money we're talking about," she said, "but surely enough to fund a documentary and a nice life while other people were suffering."

Lauren felt breathless. Had she and Graham lost money, too? "Do you believe Carson's telling the truth that Piper was involved?"

"He showed me the bank information."

"And do you believe Carson when he says he didn't hurt her?"

"No, not totally. But he has an alibi. He seemed pretty confident, and he's already been questioned."

"But this doesn't rule it out that it's me," Lauren said. "It just opens up the possibilities."

"Someone else knew," Andrea said. "Her name is Flora Haines—I actually know her father. I guess Carson paid her off and, as he put it, systematically blocked other parents in her circle from attending the school. But he was still afraid she was talking." Andrea explained that the bracelets were what tipped off Carson. Flora made those bracelets for a sportswear clothing line she was starting, but he and Piper thought they were some sort of symbol of solidarity.

"Okay, but *I* didn't know this Flora person," Lauren said. "Why did *I* get a note?"

"I guess because you were talking to us," Andrea suggested. "Carson also said Piper was really freaked out before her attack—she was afraid she was being stalked. Someone was trying to get to her."

"Flora?" Lauren guessed.

"That was my thought, too, but why? What would she be coming for? She looks just as bad for taking the bribe. It's someone else. And *that* person is who hurt Piper."

Outside, a dog barked. Someone started up a leaf blower down the block.

"I really don't think you did this, Lauren. Please don't leave and go into some . . . *rest cure*. I mean, unless you want to—but don't do it because you think you're responsible or that you told on me. The police don't know anything. And I need you to help us. I feel like we're close . . . to something."

Lauren ran her hands down the length of her face. "But what about other memories I've lost? I've said things, done things—and it's gone."

"That could be something serious, but it could also be you being an overwhelmed new parent. You think I remembered everything when Arthur was a baby? Whole weeks went by that I lost. And back then, I wasn't even the mother!"

Lauren let out a halfhearted laugh that morphed into a sob. Tears ran down her face, partly from relief and partly from grief she couldn't quite pin down. Maybe it was the picture of Matthew staring back at her from the bottom of the suitcase. It had been taken this summer, only a few days before her argument with Graham in the kitchen, her blackout, her . . . *violence*. So she hadn't hurt Piper, but she'd still unintentionally hurt her baby. She still wasn't absolved.

After she hung up, Lauren sat on the bed, listening to Clarissa and the baby in the living room playing with an electronic toy drum. Lauren suspected Clarissa knew Lauren was checking herself in somewhere—she was treating Lauren extra gingerly, as though she were made of tissue paper. *Did* Lauren want to go? The time alone would be nice. The reflection. And Graham certainly thought it was a good idea. And yet . . .

Experimentally, she removed the picture of Matthew and put it back on the bedside table. Then she unloaded the breast pump and placed it back on the floor. As for the suitcase, she set it back in the closet—for now. If she changed her mind, she could always pack it again and still be ready for when she and Graham had planned to leave tonight. But until then she needed to think some more.

Something bumped against the closet door as she went to close it. Lauren bent down to move the offending items out of the way, a bunch of books that had fallen a while ago but she'd been too lazy to put back in their proper places. Her fingers closed around one of them, a small hardcover. *Italian Cooking Class, Puglia, 2007*, it read.

She smiled. This was the book Graham used to make the cacio e pepe; he'd gotten it at that Italian cooking course he'd taken before they'd met. She'd looked through it when they first started dating, but their kitchen didn't have any shelves for cookbooks, so they kept a lot of books in here.

Maybe she and Graham could take another class together right here in Raisin Beach—Williams Sonoma always held courses. Lauren pictured the two of them standing over a stove at a classroom oven and felt buoyed. In fact, why not start now? If you could read, you could cook. She needed something new to do, something new to be proud of. It would be good to be excited about something again.

She cracked the book open, smiling at Graham's crabbed notes on the lined pages. Besides cacio e pepe, there were recipes for cappelletti in brodo and ricotta tortelli. She turned the pages, trying to see which dish looked easy.

A few of the pages were stuck together, and she fought to pry them apart. When she did, a Polaroid photograph fluttered out and slid under the bureau. Lauren dropped to her knees to fish it out. She had to shake dust off the photo, too, and watched as motes drifted through the air toward the floor. Then she turned it over.

She'd looked at this photo when they first started dating, but today, it looked entirely new. Graham was in his twenties. He had a beard, which didn't suit him. He stood against a bright white stucco wall in a sunlit lane. It was a quintessentially Italian scene—cobblestoned streets, leaning bicycles, tiny, thrown-open windows. The same red book of Italian recipes that sat on the bed was tucked under Graham's arm, and he was smiling. There was a woman with him, too. It was the ex-girlfriend, a woman Lauren knew little about but who had accompanied Graham on this trip. When they'd first started dating, she'd glanced at this photo briefly but then put it away, feeling intimidated. But now, she looked closer.

The woman was tall, with long, silky dark hair and the kind of body that could pull off wearing a strappy sundress with no bra. She had her arm draped casually around Graham's shoulders, but there was something fake about her smile that Lauren didn't like. Her eyes were an aqua blue. She had long lashes, a pointed chin, and high cheekbones. But what really did it was the Marilyn Monroe–style beauty mark above her lip. Lauren recalled staring at that beauty mark the first time she'd laid eyes on this person, and watching the mouth beside it move so beautifully as she spoke to all the parents, telling them their children would be safe and sound.

The ground beneath her seemed to shift, then give way. She was staring at Piper Jovan.

Twenty-Five

It was a good thing Clarissa was here all day. And it was a good thing Graham was at work . . . because Lauren didn't trust herself. If someone were to disturb her in this bedroom right then, flames might shoot from her mouth. This felt like waking up on another planet with a completely unknowable landscape. The lakes were lava. The air was sludge. The sky was purple. The world was unrecognizable, and no life could be sustained.

She stared down at Graham's smiling face in the faded photo. His smirk made her stomach twist. Was her memory acting up—*had* he mentioned he'd dated Piper? But no. She would have remembered *that*.

She looked at Piper's face. It was definitely, *definitely* Piper. She looked happy but slightly uncomfortable. How long were they together? How was she just finding out about this now? Lauren's mind flipped back to the Welcome Breakfast; Graham had come with her willingly . . . and he'd said nothing about the director of their school being an ex. But Graham had remained in the car during the breakfast. Claimed he had a work meeting. Had he hid out to avoid seeing Piper?

It hit her like a punch to the throat. Lauren had made him read the school literature. She'd leaned over him as he perused it on his laptop, scrolling through all the pictures of the staff. Piper's name, her picture—she was everywhere on the site. And yet Graham hadn't let on. *This place looks great*, he'd told Lauren. *I'm in.*

Then something else hit her, something more sickening. She thought of the impassioned speech Piper gave at the breakfast. The story of how she'd come to Silver Swans after a *bad breakup with her son's father*. And the principles she'd instilled and how she wished that her own child could have attended the school when he was young.

Her brain was muddy. She wasn't sure she was thinking straight. She grabbed a notepad from the bedside drawer and scrawled the dates on a piece of paper. If the kid was thirteen, he'd been born in 2008. Piper and Graham had gone to Italy in 2007.

Her stomach heaved. She rose quickly and made it to the bathroom just in time to vomit in the toilet. She felt her stomach empty, tears springing to her eyes. When she stood, her head whirled. She grabbed the edge of the sink and took a deep breath. The lie felt like a physical wound.

She stared at her bloodshot eyes in the mirror. Her mouth was a slant. Beads of sweat dotted her forehead. Her husband had a secret ex-girlfriend and a secret son. Too many thoughts came at once. Why hadn't the police dug into this? Did Piper know that Graham was here? Why did the relationship end badly? And had she been in touch with Graham all this time?

Lauren took deep breaths. Graham couldn't have another son. It was one thing to hide an ex, but a thirteen-year-old boy? Lots of people had children from other relationships. Lauren wouldn't have lost her shit had she known Graham had a family before her. There was nothing to be ashamed of.

And yet there *was* shame. Lauren could feel it oozing out of her pores. And then another pinprick blinked in her brain—weak at first, but then stronger. Shame came with a whole lot of complicated, heavy feelings. Shame could make you do irrational things.

Shame could make you hide things. Shame could make you want someone gone.

No, she told herself. She was overreacting. She was having an episode.

She stood and walked back to the bedroom. She found her phone on the nightstand, all at once determined to know for sure.

She dialed the number for Jenny, one of the PAs on *Ketchup*. Jenny had been Lauren's point of contact the few times she'd visited the set and was friendly but distant, seemingly without any personal ties to Graham. "Uh, I think Graham's in the writers' room right now," Jenny said when she answered and Lauren identified herself. "But I can see when they're going to break."

"Oh, don't bother him," Lauren said quickly, surprised at how calm she sounded. "I was just wondering—there's this Uber transaction on my credit card, and it *could* be from Graham—I know he Ubers around LA sometimes, for lunches and things. But I have such mom brain, and I can't figure out this day from the last. I just want to make sure it's not fraud, you know?"

"Ohhh," Jenny breathed in. Nothing like the threat of credit card fraud to lower a person's guard. "I can look at the schedule, sure."

"Thank you!" Lauren cooed sweetly, astonished at how easy this was.

Jenny asked Lauren the date, and she was careful to keep her voice modulated as she told her that it was last Thursday, the date of Piper's attack. Graham was supposed to be on location for his episode, but he'd come back to get her at the police station.

"The charge is for midafternoon," Lauren added. "It *could* be a lunch, something like that?"

Lauren heard typing on the other end. Jenny let out a breath. "Uh-oh, Lauren. You'd better call your card company. We didn't need Graham that day."

"*What?*" Even though Lauren had been the one to make the call, even though it had been her intuition that had been pinging, this announcement still startled her so much that she had to sit down. She remembered Graham that morning. He'd been excited to go to work. It had been *his* episode they were working on.

"What do you mean?" she said in a near whisper.

"I mean we were off that day. We didn't need any of the writers. Graham definitely wasn't here."

Piper

September

You can't believe your stupidity. There he is, the Asshole, the man you'd left, now a parent in your inner circle. You've been so careful, and yet this has slipped by you.

You pore over the paperwork; it's hard to believe this is the same guy. Married. Working. *And a new baby? What happened to his disdain for children? You think of North, how Graham backed away from parenting, washed his hands. The memories fill you with searing fury. Then it occurs to you that if he had any interest at all where his child was going to daycare, he already knew you were here.*

You feel sick. In all likelihood, he has been closing in for weeks. Stalking your moves. Driving by your house. Breaking into *your house. And, surely, calling up Jean at Hulu. Wrecking your dreams. That's how it works with him. He doesn't want you to be happy.*

Next to his name on the application, he listed a separate cell phone number from Lauren's, and that's what you dial. He picks up right away, as if he already knew you'd be calling—and maybe that's why he listed the cell phone, a cheeky little come and get me *that he alone will answer, not his wife.*

It's painful to hear his voice—not in a nostalgic way but more with a knee-jerk shudder of revulsion. You tell him you have some things to discuss. You keep your voice controlled. He says he's able to meet. You try not to sound too grateful. You give him a few time windows, most of them quite early in the morning, before the other parents—and Carson—arrive. He needs to work with your schedule, not the other way around.

The day comes. There's a buzz at the office's main door, but you don't get it right away. A shiver runs up your spine. This hall is so desolate, the walls so thick. Your security guy hasn't even shown up for the day yet. All of a sudden, meeting early sounds like a terrible idea.

Finally, though, you hit the buzzer. You hear the latch click and the heavy thump of the door as it swishes closed. Then come footsteps. And as he rounds the corner, you realize he's not alone.

He's brought his baby.

"Piper," he says. He waits hesitantly in the hallway as though he's as nervous as you are. But you can't look at him, not really. All you can look at is the child, who is tucked into a little stroller, a blanket over his belly. Your insides go liquid. The kid's eyes are the same as North's. His fat little fingers. His socked little feet.

"This is Matthew," he says, pointing. "Sorry I had to bring him. My wife . . . she was still sleeping. I didn't want to bother her. We share the responsibilities."

You want to throw your computer monitor at Graham's head. There are so many things wrong with what he's just said. He brought his son here as a tactic.

"Well, come in." As much as you want to interact with the baby, you resist. "Listen," you say, once he wheels the stroller through the door and awkwardly sits in a chair. "I believe we need to clear some things up." You have a script. You aren't going to let the baby derail you. You are going to plow forward.

"Oh yeah?" Graham asks. "What's that?"

The baby makes a little coo, and Graham turns to him and grins. That gesture is what does it. Why did Graham get a second chance? Why did things work out for him? You know about his fancy credit on that television show.

*"I need you to stop," you say, losing your tempered tone. It's not just that he's smiled at the baby. It's that he isn't taking this meeting seriously. He's distracted, relaxed. "I know you talked to Hulu. You told them. About . . ." You can't say the words. "*You *know."*

Graham's eyes are full of concern. "You can't keep lying, Piper."

"What do you care?" You dig your nails into your palm. "It's my life. So stop, okay? Otherwise, I'll tell your wife about us. *About* you."

A muscle in his jaw tightens. So he never told her. You were right. "You wouldn't do that."

"Yes, I would."

"My life means a lot to me. I have . . ." He trails off and looks at his kid, who now has his whole fist in his mouth. North used to do that, too. "Look, things have changed. I'm different now. And my wife . . . she's going through something hard."

"You expect me to believe that?"

"She is." *Now his eyes are pleading. "You and me—it was a long time ago. Can't we just leave the past in the past?"*

You cross your arms. "I would have. But you already made the first move."

"I thought they should know."

"Well, maybe I think your wife should know."

Suddenly, he rises over you. You slide backward in your chair and feel your body curl into itself. You hate that this is your response, but it's an old reaction, etched in your wiring. He seems to understand this, and it fuels his fire. One corner of his mouth curls into a satisfied smile. He rubs his hands together. The sound is like sandpaper on wood.

"Let's make a deal," he says. "I'll stop talking about you, and you won't talk about me."

And then he's out of the room without another word, taking his beautiful baby with him.

You're so riled up you kick a filing cabinet, hurting your toe. And then the tears come, salty and thick. You want to say it's because of the pain in your foot, or even because of the anguish you're feeling from dredging up old memories, all that was lost. But it's neither of those things. It's fear.

You don't think this is over. Not by a long shot.

Twenty-Six

Ronnie had no idea how to tell Esme about Vanessa, and so she didn't say anything. Instead, they went to the park. They ate ice cream—*real* ice cream, not the almond milk crap Lane tried to pass off as real.

Then they spent the evening with Lane, watching a movie. It was awful, saying nothing to either of them, counting down the hours until their lives were blown apart. She kept looking around the peaceful living room and thinking, *Tomorrow, I won't have this. In a few hours, all this will be gone.* And she didn't just mean Esme would be gone. She meant Lane, too. She'd hid too much. Lied too many times. He would want nothing to do with her.

In a few hours, she'd have no one, nothing.

That night, when Ronnie slipped out of her own bed and curled into Esme's, taking her into her arms, her fear was so overwhelming that she couldn't even cry.

On Tuesday morning, Lane asked Ronnie if he could come home early and take them out to lunch. Ronnie made an excuse to Lane that Esme had coughed a lot through the night and that they should take a rain check. Lane's gaze lingered on Ronnie a few seconds too long, like he thought something was up, but he didn't argue. Ronnie's heart broke. She almost said to him, *Please make your goodbye meaningful. You're never going to see us again. I'm so sorry.*

But she couldn't form the words. Maybe she was more terrible for keeping even this from him, denying him a last moment—but actually saying what was about to happen made it so *real.*

It made her ache to see Lane kiss Esme's forehead and tell her to feel better. Then Lane kissed Ronnie on the lips and said to call him right away if she got any calls from the police. "We are not going to let them mess with us," Lane said.

She almost laughed. The cops were the least of her worries—they weren't the ones wrecking her life. Funny enough, the cops *had* called that morning—Ronnie saw their number show up on the caller ID. She hadn't answered. Her brain couldn't concentrate on two nightmares at once.

Ronnie followed Lane as he headed to the door. Walked him all the way to the hall. He turned and looked at her quizzically, a worried smile on his face. "You sure you're okay?"

She licked her lips. She could tell him. He loved her. Maybe they could figure this out.

He leaned against the door. "Should I stay? What is it?"

But then the fear took hold. Ronnie turned away so he wouldn't see her expression. "I'm fine. Go to work."

At about 10:45, Andrea called. "We all need to talk."

"Um." Ronnie felt so damn exhausted. What was the point of talking? What was the point of anything? "I'm kind of in the middle of something."

"Ronnie," Andrea said. "There is fraud going on at Silver Swans. Piper and Carson are in on it." Her voice lowered. "*Embezzlement.*"

Ronnie frowned. "They're stealing from the parents?" Certainly this hadn't happened to her. Ronnie maintained a tight control over her finances. She knew exactly how much money went in and out—nothing had gone missing.

Andrea said she didn't want to talk about it over the phone. "But I think this will get us off the hook as far as being suspects. When can you meet?"

"I'm not sure." Ronnie couldn't look past this afternoon. "I'm kind of busy."

"Are you all right?" Andrea asked suddenly. "What's going on?"

More tears filled Ronnie's eyes. She let out a little squeak. "It's nothing," she said. She wished she could ask for help. Andrea wouldn't judge. But Ronnie had been so self-reliant for so long, she didn't have the vocabulary.

As the morning ticked by, she hemmed and hawed and stressed over telling Esme something, anything. She didn't want to just drop it on the poor kid. And more than that, she had absolutely no idea what to say, and most of all, she feared Esme's reaction. This was going to traumatize her. She saw Vanessa's arrival coming, as inevitable as a sunset. And so they sat in the living room, the television on, Esme blissfully unaware, Ronnie in a state of panic. Forty more minutes. Thirty.

And then it hit her. She could leave. She could throw some things in a bag and leave with Esme, *now*. It was the only answer. She hated leaving her friends, and Raisin Beach, and her heart shattered at the idea of leaving Lane—but she would always choose Esme over him. She had to.

She jumped up from the couch, annoyed she hadn't planned this sooner. "Baby. Let's go."

"Wha?" Esme blinked sleepily; she was in a TV coma.

"Come on, come on. We're taking a little trip. Let's pack your bag." She hurried to the back bedroom and tried to think. Some clothes. Overnight pull-ups. Her favorite stuffed animals. Her ponies. She threw things randomly into a backpack, then fled into her room and started doing the same. In a drawer was some cash she'd saved from Topless Maids—it would hold them over for a while, anyway. She tossed it in. Zipped up the bag.

"Esme?" she called into the living room. "You ready?"

But when she walked down the hall, Esme's eyes were wide. Vanessa had burst through the door and was standing over her.

"Well hello," Vanessa said, her eyes flitting from Ronnie's face to the two bags in her hands. "Going somewhere?"

"I . . ." Ronnie felt a swoop of danger through her gut. "Um, no."

"Good thing I came early."

Then she turned back to Esme. "My God," she whispered. She pressed her hands to her heart. "Oh, my darling girl."

Esme pulled back. "Who are you?"

"Didn't Ronnie tell you?"

Esme turned to Ronnie curiously.

Ronnie cleared her throat. There was so much acid in her mouth. "I couldn't find a mediator. No one could come."

The truth was, Ronnie had been too afraid to call a mediator. How could she admit to a stranger that she'd bludgeoned a man and left her sister for dead and kidnapped their child? Who'd want to mediate that situation, especially with Vanessa here, twisting the story, making it sound like Ronnie had been gunning for Esme all along?

Vanessa was sitting next to Esme now, openly weeping. She reached to pet Esme's My Little Pony, but Esme wrinkled her nose and arched away. "This is mine."

"No, baby, it's okay," Vanessa said softly. "I'm your mama. I'm *here.*"

"Uh, *that's* my mama," Esme said, with attitude. "*Her.*"

"Actually, she's your aunt, baby. *I'm* your mama. And I've come to take you back with me."

Esme cast a nervous look over to Ronnie. "I thought we were going on a trip."

Ronnie cringed. She looked at Vanessa. "This is too soon for her. Too much." How could Vanessa think a four-year-old child could comprehend such a life-altering declaration? How could a mother think this was a good idea?

"You and me," Vanessa was saying to the little girl. "We're

going to live on a farm! With doggies, and kitties, and some chickens! What do you think?"

"A farm?" Ronnie stared. "What farm?"

"Farms are stinky," Esme declared.

"Well, this farm smells good. And one of the cats is having kittens! You could have your own kitten and name her whatever you want!"

Ronnie felt so dizzy she had to hold the wall. "What farm?" She had a vague recollection of someone in Jerrod's family having something to do with farming.

"Are there horses on the farm?" Esme asked.

"Uh, there are some horses close by." Vanessa touched her arm. "Baby, we have a long ride ahead of us." Then she eyed the suitcase on the floor, her mouth in a twist. "Lucky for you, you're already packed. Or is this *mommy's*?"

"Wait." Ronnie had never felt so desperate. "Stay a few days. Esme can go with you to a hotel or something. You can get to know each other. But just stay in town—to smooth the transition." Her gaze slid across the room to her purse. "I'll pay. *Please*."

Vanessa twisted her mouth. "I don't really *like* it here."

What about Esme? Ronnie wanted to scream. *Have you asked* her *what she likes?* "There's a motel nearby. It's clean, nice—I'll call them now. It . . . it has a pool." She looked at Esme and smiled. "You can go swimming!"

Esme squinted at Vanessa, then back at Ronnie. She held one of her ponies by its long, flossy tail. "You'll come too, Mommy?"

"I . . . could." Ronnie smiled hopefully at Vanessa. "I could get a separate room. So you two could be together. But I would still be close, just in case."

"Just in case *what*?" Vanessa took Esme's forearm. "I don't think Auntie Ronnie can come, honey. You're with me now."

Something about this seemed to penetrate Esme's brain. She

glanced at Ronnie with increased trepidation—it was the same look she'd given Ronnie last year at a local swimming pool when she'd stepped beyond a spot her feet could touch and was suddenly foundering. "No," she said. She was doing that rabbit-nose-twitch thing when she was about to cry. "No, I don't wanna go."

"Baby," was all Ronnie could say. How could she explain? "Baby, I did something bad. A long time ago."

Esme's eyes filled with tears. "No!" she shrieked. "I don't wanna go! I wanna stay here!"

Ronnie's eyes filled, too. She glanced at Vanessa; didn't she see what she was doing? But Vanessa was standing tall, one of her hands on the crown of Esme's head. "Ronnie did a bad thing," she repeated. "And she doesn't want to make it any worse by making a scene, does she?" Then she smiled down at Esme. "Let's take more things. Let's find all your favorite toys. How's that?"

"I'm not going!" Esme shrieked. Now she was in full tantrum mode, throwing herself on the ground. Screams heaved from her body.

There had to be an answer. There had to be a better way. Ronnie didn't know what it was except to plunge her hand in her purse and practically throw all the money in her wallet in her sister's direction. "The motel. Just a night or two. Just to see how it goes. And I'll be standing by, if you need anything. *Please.*" She licked her lips. "Kids are *hard*, Vanessa."

Vanessa's eyes flashed. "You don't think I know?"

"No, I'm just saying—she's four. It's hard to reason with her, but at the same time, she understands a lot. And it's hard to get her to sleep."

"Not going!" Esme screamed again. "No!"

Vanessa's features were scrunched in the middle of her face, which made her look like a prune. But after a moment, she blew air upward, sending her stringy bangs aloft. She grabbed the bills and stuffed them in her pocket. "Jesus, fine," she said. "Two days. Make the arrangements. But we won't need you. We'll be okay on our own. You'll see."

"Okay," Ronnie gushed. "Good." It amazed her how grateful she felt for just this, how low the bar had become. "Okay, I'll call them now."

She dropped to her knees next to Esme. "Baby," she said. "You're going to spend time with . . . your auntie . . . mommy." She didn't know what to call Vanessa. "It's only for a few days. And I'll be close!"

"She smells!" Esme pointed at Vanessa. "That mean lady smells!"

Vanessa reached for Esme's hand. "That's not nice. Now c'mon. We're getting the rest of your toys."

She dragged Esme to her feet and walked her down the hall. Well, *lugged* her down the hall was more like it. It took every ounce of strength in Ronnie's body not to tackle Vanessa. Esme bellowed for a little longer, but once she got into her room, she quieted down. In moments, Ronnie could hear her talking to Vanessa in a normal tone, probably pointing out her favorite things.

Esme's sudden placidness hurt the most of all.

⁜

It was over fast: Esme's things packed up, Esme loaded into the car, Esme breaking down again and crying for Ronnie, and Ronnie trying to muscle her way into the back seat with the little girl but Vanessa saying, calmly, that if Ronnie did that, she'd regret it. People were already giving them curious glances on the street. If Ronnie called more attention to this situation, it would make things worse.

It's okay, Ronnie told herself. She knew where Vanessa and Esme were going. She had tabs on them for the next few days. She pressed her hands to the window and told Esme she would see her soon. She had to pry Esme's fingers from her own and give her a few extra hugs just to get her to calm down. "It's okay, honey," she said. "Spend time with Vanessa. It's just a little trip. I'll see you soon."

Esme kept her gaze on Ronnie as Vanessa's junky car drove off. It was almost too much to take. Ronnie was gripped with such sickness she felt like she couldn't form a rational thought. Her whole life was gone. How on earth could Vanessa care for Esme? What was Ronnie supposed to do? What was she going to tell Lane?

Taking her phone in her trembling fingers, she dashed off a text to him, saying that she and Esme were taking a little trip up the coast for a few days for a breather. There. He'd be baffled, but that would buy her time, at least.

But time for *what*? To storm into the motel Vanessa was staying in and steal Esme back to her safe, calm life? Could she *kill* Vanessa? Ronnie gasped, horrified that the thought entered her mind. What was happening to her?

As if reading her mind, her phone rang. It was the police—*again*. Ronnie let the call go to voicemail. She was in no mood to give answers. She had to figure this out on her own.

Her heart started to pound. Her chest tightened in a way she'd never experienced, and her vision narrowed. She tried to breathe but found it impossible. Something was happening to her.

"Help," she said weakly. Through blurred vision, she could see a sand-colored monstrosity two blocks away: Ventura Memorial Hospital. It had always comforted her that the hospital was close, in case Esme ever took a fall or got a high fever. Could she make it there? Ronnie took one step, then another, picturing her heart straining against its scaffolding inside her chest, overtaxed or maybe just broken.

She made it across an intersection. The sun beat down on her center part. A sharp pain in her side made her gasp, and then she fell sideways into a fence. "Miss?" A man's face swam in front of her, his brow crinkled with concern. "Are you all right?"

Wheezing, Ronnie pointed at the hospital's ER entrance. "I just need to . . . there."

"Do you have anyone we could call?" the man asked. Ronnie shook her head. She wanted to call Vanessa. *Bring Esme back*. But she said nothing.

The double doors to the ER opened, and the cool air conditioning was a relief. She tried to breathe. The man leaned toward her. "Do you want me to get a nurse?"

Ronnie shook her head. Whatever was going on with her was beginning to subside. The cool air, perhaps. The act of sitting and breathing. Her heart wasn't pounding so rapidly in her ears anymore. "I just want to take a minute," she said. "I'll be okay."

The man didn't seem convinced. He offered to get her water, food, something. He was older, Ronnie noticed. She looked down at herself and realized that the shirt she was wearing was tight, revealing the outline of her bra. Once more, she said she was okay. "Thank you," she told him again and again. "Really." Finally, he left.

The ER waiting room was nearly empty save for a woman at the front desk, who barely looked up as Ronnie wrote down her name for triage. Since she was calmer now, she was told to wait. Ronnie took a seat in the plastic chair, trying to calm her heart and collect her thoughts. Eventually, shakily, she lifted her phone and dialed the motel she'd arranged for Vanessa. "I booked my sister and her daughter to check in," she told the receptionist once he answered. Her tongue felt strange forming the words *her daughter*. "Under Johnson. Have they arrived?"

The man told her to hang on, setting the receiver down with a *clunk*. A few seconds later, he returned. "Yep, they're settled in. Want me to get them?"

Ronnie was stunned. Vanessa had followed her advice! It gave her a rush of euphoria. She told the man no, she just wanted to check. When she hung up, her spirits were buoyed. Okay then. Ronnie had two days. She would figure this out—and get Esme back.

She moved toward the triage nurse and told her that she didn't need to be seen after all. The double doors to the ER, emblazoned with the hospital logo, slid open as she walked past them to leave. She stopped. Ventura Memorial Hospital. This is where Piper was.

She didn't move for a whole minute.

Through a directory, she learned that neurological intensive care, which was where they kept patients with potential brain injuries, was on the fourth floor. The elevator doors swung open on a quiet unit. To the right was a waiting room; a few people sat scattered in chairs, reading or sleeping or staring numbly at a television. Down the hall were a few open doors; Ronnie could see a line of beds and machines. A nurse bustled past without looking Ronnie's way.

If she dared ask for Piper's room number, she'd be prohibited from visiting—surely it was family only. Instead, Ronnie walked the perimeter of the floor like she belonged here, avoiding nurses and peeking into each room as she passed. Most of the doors were ajar; only half the rooms were full. There was a sleeping man in the first room, and then an old lady with bandages on her head, and then a youngish man who was speaking angrily into a cell phone. She passed a hallway filled with tanks and machines and then squashed against the wall to let two nurses wheel an unconscious patient on a gurney.

She hesitated in front of the next room, 410, and couldn't believe her luck. *P. Jovan* had been written in marker beside the door. A nurse turned the corner and headed in her direction. Taking a breath, Ronnie twisted the knob and slipped inside before anyone spied her.

Piper's bed was against the wall and next to a bank of windows. The only sounds were the rhythmic beeping of monitors and a funny little *grrrr* of a blood pressure cuff tightening on an arm.

Piper lay beneath white sheets, flat on her back. Her black hair was fanned around her, and her eyes were closed. She had a lot of tubes in her arms and one in her nose, but she looked peaceful.

Someone had attacked her, put her here. That hit Ronnie sideways: It *hadn't* been Jerrod. Vanessa might be a liar, but there was no way Jerrod was in Raisin Beach—he'd have already found Ronnie and finished her off. The notion made her shaky with relief, and she fell softly against the side of Piper's bed, bumping her ankle against the metal bedpost.

"Ow!" Ronnie said, moving away. To her surprise, when she turned back to Piper, the woman's eyes were open. Piper stared at the ceiling, then peered slowly around the room and finally settled on Ronnie. Ronnie froze. Should she alert someone about this?

The tiny wrinkles around Piper's eyes deepened as she squinted at Ronnie. Ronnie raised her hand in an embarrassed little wave. "Um, hi. I'm . . . from the school. A mom? We met at the Welcome Breakfast? I . . . just wanted to see how you were doing."

Piper blinked at her, long and slow. And then she rose up, pointed at Ronnie. What she said next would haunt Ronnie for a long, long time.

Twenty-Seven

Clarissa seemed surprised when Lauren announced she was going out. "Are you sure you're okay to drive?" She looked her up and down. "You look a little . . ."

"I'm fine." Lauren knew how she looked: red-eyed, wild-haired, frantic. But she had to do this. She felt a lump in her throat as she gazed at Matthew; she felt like she'd barely spent any time with him lately. But also, she feared for his future. Who would care for him? Lauren was unstable—but so, potentially, was his father.

Before heading to LA, she swung by Andrea's house. Andrea hurried out, looking pale and worried; Lauren had only told her glossed-over details about what she'd found out about Graham. She'd asked Andrea to come along as backup, so Lauren wouldn't get too scared of confronting Graham.

"I've barely heard from Ronnie," Andrea murmured worriedly as they pulled onto the highway.

"Maybe she's just lying low until this all blows over?" Lauren suggested.

"It's something else. But she won't tell me what."

Lauren was so hyped-up during the two-hour drive she couldn't listen to music. Graham clouded Lauren's mind. His lies. His deception. *Piper.* Andrea asked Lauren to expand on what she'd found out, exactly, but it wasn't like there was much to tell. Just a photograph. Just a hunch that Graham had been lying for a long time.

"They were together," Lauren said. "But I think it ended badly—remember how Piper mentioned that, in her talk at the breakfast?"

Was that why Graham had hidden the relationship? Because it was toxic? Because he didn't want Piper and Lauren talking? And was this why Piper placed that note in Lauren's backpack—to push her away from Silver Swans because she wanted nothing to do with Graham?

What bothered Lauren more, she said, was that Graham potentially had a son he never spoke about, never saw.

"I saw a picture of North once," Andrea said. "Piper showed me at the meeting. Out of the blue, *Want to see my son?* He had dark hair, dark eyes."

"So does Graham," Lauren said miserably.

Every time she thought about North, her chest sizzled. All this time, she'd feared Graham was keeping secrets, maybe sleeping with Gracie. She would have never guessed *this.*

She'd only been to the *Ketchup* set a few times and had to drive around the streets of Culver City searching for the studio gates. As they pulled into visitor parking, Andrea put a hand on her arm. "You sure you want to do this?"

"I *have* to," Lauren said through gritted teeth. "I'm going to make him tell me the truth."

She had to wait for the snaking line of a tour group to pass on the walk to the *Ketchup* offices. One of the tourists, a plump, friendly-looking woman with a black vinyl backpack, smiled at Lauren eagerly, her smile telegraphing, *Isn't it so wonderful we're all here?*

"I need to see Graham," she said to Antoinette when she finally reached the office floor. Antoinette was the long-suffering office manager/production assistant Lauren had met a few times before—rumor had it she'd worked on every season of this show and never smiled. She gave Lauren and Andrea a strange look but didn't rise from her desk.

"They're working," she said flatly.

"I don't care," Lauren said, and grabbed Andrea's hand to continue down the hall.

"Uh, hey!" Antoinette sounded shocked. "I said *they're working*!"

The writers' room was the last door on the left—Lauren had come once, on a tour with Matthew when he was a few weeks old. The door was shut, but the knob turned, and Lauren pushed it open with force. Inside, a table of sloppily dressed people looked up. Lauren half-expected Graham not to be there—this whole scenario felt Hitchcockian, suddenly. It seemed very plausible that Graham didn't even have a *job* here. But there he was, seated at one of the table's long ends, twiddling a pen. She recognized a few others—a writer named Matt whom Graham said was a jackass, a writer named Rami who'd low-key hit on Lauren at the Christmas party, and of course Gracie Lord at the head of the table.

Everyone blinked in surprise, as though Lauren were wearing a clown suit and Andrea was carrying a bomb.

Graham leapt to his feet. "Lauren. What are you doing here?" His eyes flicked to Andrea with confusion. "And . . . hi?"

"I need to talk to you," Lauren asserted.

"But . . ." Graham glanced nervously at his fellow writers.

"It's okay," Gracie said gently. There was a look of understanding on her face—of *pity*. For Graham. To Gracie, Lauren was the unstable one, the wife who needed handholding. Lauren seethed with the idea that Gracie was so cavalier about sending her away. Separating her from her child. She had it so wrong.

Graham gave the room an apologetic smile and hurried out, but when he closed the door, the corners of his mouth turned down disapprovingly. "Lauren, what are you doing here?"

She took a deep breath. "Did you hurt Piper Jovan?"

Graham's eyes went wide. "Why would I—"

"I know you weren't working that afternoon she was attacked. And . . ." *Say it*, she told herself. "Why didn't you tell me you dated her?"

The color drained from Graham's face. But instead of answering, he whirled around and darted through the fire door.

"Hey!" Lauren cried, and she and Andrea started after him, catching the door just before it swung closed. Graham clambered down the stairwell; both women followed. Lauren could see the top of Graham's head on the first-floor landing. "Graham, what the hell? Just talk to me, damn it!"

Graham stopped, breathing hard. His hand was on the doorknob to the outside, but he glanced up at her rather than leaving. He looked no different than he had that morning, she thought sadly. Maybe a little paler, but the same guy. The sick feeling Lauren had dealt with all morning rose in her throat again, but she pushed it down.

"Go," she said to him, pointing to the door. "Out there. I'll meet you." Then she glanced at Andrea. "I'll talk to him alone, okay?"

"Okay." Andrea didn't look pleased. "But I'll be close."

Graham obeyed. They stepped into the blinding sunlight, and Lauren led Graham to a shady area near one of the other sound stages. The curb was littered with cast-off bicycles, empty cardboard boxes, cigarette butts. It was desolate, but at least there were people zipping by in golf carts every so often—and Andrea wasn't very far away. For a while, there were only the sounds of Graham's heavy breathing. The longer he didn't look at her, the more she was convinced that all her suspicions were true.

"I called your office, and you weren't here the afternoon Piper got hurt," Lauren said. "And now I don't know what to think. Who *are* you?"

Graham looked up, his eyes full of defeat. "I didn't do anything to her. I promise."

"But where were you, *really*? Because you weren't shooting."

Graham pressed his lips together and looked down. "Somewhere else. It's complicated."

"Try me!"

Graham's eyes flashed, and he backed away from her a step. "Keep your voice down, Lauren. Okay?"

It was the look he got when she became worked up. The same look he'd had in the car after the breakfast—or, for that matter, from the night in the kitchen. Lauren could feel the rage coming on, but of all the times to feel enraged, now was a pretty justifiable one—and he wasn't going to make her feel bad about it. Besides, if Lauren lost her shit, Andrea was close.

"How do I know you're telling the truth?" she asked.

"Because . . . I want nothing to do with her. She's crazy, Lauren."

Lauren felt a sharp prickle of fury. "Oh, *she's* crazy now, too?"

Graham shut his eyes. "Lauren. Come on. It's me. I love you. Think about what you're saying."

"But why hide that you dated? Tell me. *Please*."

On the thoroughfare, a few people passed, happily chatting. Graham glanced over at them longingly, probably wishing that he could go back to this morning, when he had his life—and wife—under control. "I should have told you about Piper. But it was such a mess . . . and I didn't come out of the relationship looking great. I fucked up, okay? I'm *so* sorry."

"Did you know she was here when we moved to Raisin Beach? Is she the *reason* we came?"

"No!" Graham shook his head vehemently. "*You* were the one who chose this place. Nice community, safe, all that. And *you* wanted Matthew to go to that school . . . I had no idea Piper was working there. We lost touch after we split up. I didn't know what happened to her, and I didn't care. It was the shock of my life when you showed me the website and I saw she was the director."

"Nice of you to tell me this *before* we enrolled Matthew." Lauren didn't know whether to believe Graham. She hadn't seen any shock in him when he'd studied the Silver Swans website. He'd been relaxed, easygoing. *Hadn't* he?

"I should have," he repeated. "But the longer I waited, the bigger of a deal it seemed, the bigger a lie."

"So have you seen her?"

"I . . . saw her, yeah," Graham admitted, and this, too, felt like a slap.

"*When?*"

"The other day. I . . . I went to her office." He sighed. "She called me. We . . . had a talk. It was weird."

"And you decided, even after that, that you both would pretend you were strangers?"

"Well, yeah. But, I mean, it wasn't like we had any chance to be around each other. She was attacked later that same day." There was something accusing in his voice, something that almost said, *You attacked her.*

"Why would you keep this from me?"

Graham looked away. "It's complicated, but it's in the past. I didn't love her or anything."

"You went to *Italy* with her," Lauren spat. "You looked in love *then*." Graham winced, but that just made Lauren want to press more. "All this time, you were telling me how badly I should feel about my email to Piper, how I shouldn't have written to her, but you dated her! The police are going to figure that out, Graham. They're going to ask why you didn't come forward with this to your own wife."

"Look, the police *know*." Graham sighed heavily. "They're not idiots."

Lauren stopped. "They do?"

"Yeah. They found a shared lease agreement from back in the day. They asked me about it that day I went into the station."

"That day you . . ." Lauren remembered the cacio e pepe dinner. "The day you told stories about all my friends?"

He avoided her gaze. "Uh-huh. They asked me about Piper. I said she and I were on okay terms but pretty much ignored each other."

Lauren blinked. "And then what?"

Graham shrugged. "They asked why we ignored each other, and I told them Piper and I were both really surprised we lived in the same town. And that she asked me not to bring up the past," Graham said in a small voice. "So I did. To protect her reputation."

"Why did you need to protect her reputation?"

"Because I didn't want to complicate *our* marriage—believe it or not, she was looking out for you, too. People around here talk. The cops got that. I don't know why you don't."

Lauren pressed her hands over her eyes. Was Graham right? Parents would gossip about a random dad dating the director back in the day. They'd speculate. People in Raisin Beach had little else to focus on. She cleared her throat, remembering the other detail. "And what about Piper's son?"

Graham's face fell. "Lauren . . ."

Lauren could feel her pulse at her throat. It was incredible that people could hold so many secrets inside them.

"Is he yours?" she squeaked out. "Do you ever see him?" Part of her hoped he'd say yes. A big part of her was even willing to make space for this kid—especially if Piper was gravely sick.

But Graham lowered his eyes. His expression was conflicted. "Well, *no*. I don't."

Bile rose in Lauren's chest. Her knees weakened, and then she could no longer stand. Graham's eyes widened in alarm. He reached out to catch her, but it was Andrea who grabbed her instead. "Hey," Andrea was saying, leaning over Lauren, supporting her so she didn't crumple to the ground and hit her head. "Hey, it's okay."

Lauren's breaths came faster. This, too, was new—not the prickly rage but instead a falling feeling, a depthless, dark despair. She looked at Graham again. He stood over her uselessly, blinking hard, his hands halfheartedly reaching toward her. "Lauren," he said. "Lauren, I'm *sorry*. I'm so sorry this is such a mess. I shouldn't have hidden this from you. I just . . . you weren't in a good way, you know? I was worried about you. I worried another complication would just make you worse."

"Get away from me," Lauren mustered. She couldn't believe a word out of his mouth anymore—even about herself. "Don't come home. I mean it."

"Lauren," Graham pleaded. "You don't know what you're saying. I love you. I love our life together."

"Do you, though?" Lauren took another step away. "Don't come home. I can't deal with you right now."

"But what about Matthew? You're not fit to be alone with him right now."

Lauren tried to laugh, but before she could answer, her field of vision grew fuzzy, and she had to shut her eyes. And when she opened them again, Graham was gone.

Twenty-Eight

It took a long time to track down Ronnie. When she finally answered her phone, Andrea could immediately tell something was very wrong. She kicked herself—she'd sensed this *before* they drove to LA, too, but she'd given Ronnie her privacy. "Lauren and I are coming to get you," she said promptly.

"Well, I'm not home," Ronnie said. And then she gave the name of a motel complex inland. It was a hike to get there, and when they did, Ronnie trudged out of a dark upstairs room all alone. Andrea felt a chill. Ronnie hadn't told them anything yet, but Andrea got a terrible feeling that something dreadful had gone down when she saw that Esme wasn't with her.

Ronnie climbed into Andrea's car with them so they could talk. Then again, there was so much to say, they didn't know where to start. Finally, Ronnie spoke. It took a while for the shock of what had happened with Esme to sink in with all of them. Ronnie seemed like a shell of herself, brittle and broken.

"What did Lane say about it?" Andrea finally asked. "Maybe he can help."

Ronnie ducked her head. "Lane can't know. I just said Esme and I took a little trip to clear our minds. It was to buy time so I could figure things out, but I don't know. It's possible I'll never see Lane again."

"Never see Lane?" Lauren cried.

"How can I tell him? It's impossible. *Shameful*." She rubbed her eyes. "Maybe I *do* get the police involved. I'm just not sure how."

"And you're really going to stay at that motel in the meantime?" Lauren asked. "You can come to my house. Graham won't be there."

"The only reason I'm there is because that place has a view of the motel where Esme's staying." Ronnie felt her chin start to wobble. "My sister's car is still there. It hasn't moved. I haven't seen them walking to the pool, though." She looked up fearfully. "Is that weird? Should I be worried?"

Of course you should be worried, Andrea wanted to say. But instead, she said, "We can help you spy on her, if you want."

Ronnie gave them a small, hopeless smile. "Also, the police are calling me nonstop," she added. "Are they calling you guys?"

"They came to my door," Lauren said. "I thought it was about you guys—but now, I wonder if it was about Graham."

"I've gotten some calls," Andrea admitted, and then cleared her throat. "And *I* called *them* this morning." She launched into the story about Carson extorting the parents, everything he said in his office, and how he threatened to spill *her* secrets if she told.

"So he's the one threatening us," Ronnie said, her eyes wide. "He's the one who knows about Esme."

"Are we sure Carson didn't hurt Piper?" Lauren asked. "There's something really off about him."

"I don't think he did," Ronnie said.

Andrea shot her a look. "What makes you think that for sure?"

Ronnie shifted awkwardly. "I mean, didn't you just say he had an alibi? People saw him?"

"People can lie."

Across the street, a police car was parking in a McDonald's lot. Andrea could see an officer through the tinted windows chowing on a burger. She slid down in her seat a little, then chastised herself. *You've done nothing wrong*, she thought.

"Maybe Graham did it," Lauren said after a beat. "He swore he wasn't at the school, but he didn't say where he was instead. And what sort of person keeps quiet about an old relationship? It's just so *odd*. He gave me all these excuses . . ."

Now it was everyone's turn to look at Lauren with pity. No one knew where Graham had gone. Andrea had been so busy tending to Lauren that she hadn't seen where he slipped off to.

Ronnie cleared her throat. "I . . . saw Piper, actually."

"What?" Andrea whipped her head around to look at her. "In the *hospital*?"

"Uh-huh. Just before I called you. I . . . went to the hospital." She tucked a lock of hair behind her ear. "I snuck into her room."

"How did she look?" Lauren whispered, aghast.

"She . . . woke up while I was there."

"What?" Andrea felt her spine straighten. "Why didn't you *lead* with this, Ronnie? Does she *remember*?"

Ronnie twisted a small silver ring around her thumb. "If she does, it's not good." She licked her lips. "She looked straight at me and said, *Get away from me*."

A chill went through Andrea's veins. "She knew who you were?"

"I'm not sure. Because then she said, *You were both there. I said I'm sorry, okay? Get away! I'm sorry, all right? I'm sorry I'm not the person you need me to be*." Ronnie shrugged. "I was so confused. I have no idea what she meant."

"Shit," Lauren whispered, the color draining from her face.

"And *then*," Ronnie added, "her machines started beeping. And a nurse ran in, but Piper was still screaming to the nurse. She goes, *Get him out of here!* And pointed at me."

"Him?" Lauren repeated.

"Yep," Ronnie said.

Andrea thought about this for a moment. "She mistook you for a guy?"

"I think she was seeing someone else entirely."

"So it's a guy who hurt her," Andrea said slowly. A car swished past them, pulling into a spot closer to the motel's lobby. "Maybe you look like him?" Andrea asked. "Could it be?"

"It's why I said it couldn't be Carson," Ronnie admitted. "We don't look alike at all."

Lauren leaned back in the seat, her arms crossed. "Graham has dark hair like Ronnie, but he's much taller."

Then Andrea remembered something. "Carson said Piper worried she was being stalked."

Ronnie chewed on her bottom lip. "He has no idea who it was?"

"He thought it was me," Andrea said. There was a groan in the sky: somewhere above the clouds, a jet was passing through. Andrea tipped her head upward but couldn't see it. Then her gaze drifted to Lauren, who had a strange, haunted expression on her face. "What?"

"I was thinking about one of the things Graham said. One of the reasons he said he didn't tell anyone he dated Piper was that she asked him not to. And he obliged because he wanted to protect her reputation. Then he gave me some bullshit about how people around here talk and how Piper had a certain brand. But you know what I think? I think it's about their son. *His* son. Graham never sees that North kid. I can't . . . *That's* what people would talk about. The deadbeat dad who left his wife to care for a kid all on her own. Living in the same town, not even seeing his son." Her voice broke. "It's more for *his* reputation, not hers."

A gust of wind kicked up, blowing an empty plastic bag through the air. Andrea thought back to going to Piper's office for that meeting about the drawing, how the woman had lurched forward to show her a picture of North even though she hadn't asked to see one. There had been something forced about her actions, something Andrea couldn't put her finger on. Why wouldn't a man see his own son? Was he like how her wife, Christine, had been, someone who didn't want kids in the first place? Except Graham had a new baby now . . .

"How old is Piper's son, anyway?" Ronnie asked, breaking the silence.

"Thirteen." Lauren laughed bitterly. "Graham would have been, Jesus, twenty-seven. No wonder he didn't want the responsibility."

"You know, I remember asking the police if they'd spoken to the kid, how he was doing," Ronnie said. "And he sort of deflected my question. He was like, 'I'm sure he's fine.' But when I pressed—why didn't they *know* he was fine—he brushed me off."

Andrea's head whipped up. "What are you thinking?"

"I got this weird sense they didn't know where he was," Ronnie said. "Or maybe that he wasn't cooperating."

"Maybe he saw something," Lauren said quietly. "Or *knows* something." Then her eyes widened. "Or *did* something?"

Everyone was silent. Thoughtful.

Andrea considered Piper's impassioned speech about how she wished Silver Swans had been there when her child was in preschool; how it might have helped him. But helped him from *what*? Even what Ronnie said she'd been mumbling about—*I'm not the perfect person you think I am*—that seemed like something a mother who'd tried her best but hadn't been able to make things right might say to a vengeful, irrationally aggressive teenager. The idea of North skulking around the house, *stalking* her—well, maybe that even made sense, too. Teenage boys were unpredictable. Andrea had known tons of them. She'd been one.

When she looked up, everyone else had haunted looks on their faces, too. Ronnie curled her fingers around the car door. "I have an idea."

"Me too," Andrea said. "Maybe we should talk to that kid."

Twenty-Nine

Piper's house was a two-story beauty of stucco and glass. Not as big as the modern masterpiece on the cliffs, but also not the kind of house a poverty-stricken woman could afford after fleeing from a bad breakup in Los Angeles, either. It was on about an acre, surrounded by trees, and then sloping downward to sharp cliffs that led straight to a gorgeous slice of Pacific Ocean. Ronnie could hear the breakers crashing from up here, and the air smelled like sea and sand. Esme would love it out here, so close to the water.

Esme. She was nuts to be here instead of staking out that motel, making sure Vanessa didn't leave. She'd come in her own car, she'd only stay a few minutes. Ten at most. Then she'd drive back and resume her post at her window.

She looked at the house again. What was it like to live in a house like this? To walk through such a grand front door? It was the type of house that probably had a grand foyer. A backyard pool—*and* that stunning beach. What child could be miserable, living here?

Yet every day, Ronnie saw dysfunction, loneliness, unhappiness. So many of her clients, still practically boys themselves, watched her with wide, hungry eyes. That was what shook her the most: the difficulty men faced when it came to controlling giant swings in emotion. Men could explode with inappropriate ecstasy;

they could burst with unconscionable anger. They could have an orgasm and beat the shit out of you in nearly the same breath—like Jerrod. Like others, too.

"What do we do now?" Andrea whispered, shaking Ronnie out of her thoughts. Andrea and Lauren were sitting in Andrea's car, parked in front of Ronnie's; they were speaking on the phone, too afraid to get out of their vehicles yet. The hope was that something obvious would reveal itself: Piper's son shooting hoops in the front drive, some vital piece of evidence scattered across the front lawn. But the property was quiet. Almost impersonal.

"What about that light in the top window?" Lauren's voice crackled through the speakerphone. "At the back there. See? On the left?"

Ronnie peered upward. A single light blazed. It looked like it could be a bedroom. North's?

"Piper's . . . son?" Miss Barnes from Silver Swans had repeated, when they'd called her a few minutes before. She was the only person they could think of who might know something and might be willing to talk. Andrea hadn't wanted to call her, and neither had Ronnie—it felt sensitive, as their kids were still technically part of Miss Barnes's class. So Lauren made the call, and both of them had listened in.

Lauren asked Miss Barnes what she knew about the boy and if he was okay after Piper's attack. "I'm assuming he's fine," Miss Barnes said. "But . . . I haven't heard much. Piper and I don't really run in the same circles. I'm sorry, who is this again?" Miss Barnes didn't sound so friendly anymore. When Lauren explained she was a concerned mother, Miss Barnes said, "Well, look, if Piper wanted everyone to know where her son could be found, that's her information to share."

"Please, if you could just—" Lauren started. But already Miss Barnes had said her goodbyes.

Now, Andrea bit her lip in frustration. "I think Piper mentioned the name of the school to me, in the meeting. But I can't remember."

Ronnie looked around the property to see if something would jog her memory. There was a car in Piper's driveway. It was the same tricked-out white Range Rover she'd noticed in the Silver Swans parking lot—Vanessa had always had a thing for Range Rovers, so she always noticed them. Ronnie hadn't realized it was Piper's car. Who had driven it home after she was attacked?

She got out of the car on a hunch. Lauren poked her head out Andrea's passenger window. "Where are you going?" she hissed.

"I want to check something," she called over her shoulder. It wasn't a big deal that she was walking up Piper's driveway, she told herself. She could just be a concerned mother dropping off a baked good for Piper's kid. Of course, if a nosy someone from the Facebook group caught her, that was one thing . . . but the street was empty, the only sound the ocean breeze.

The vehicle was unremarkable. There were no boastful bumper stickers—the 26.2 one was popular around here—and after a cursory peek inside, the seats were spotless. Piper was likely the kind of person who cleaned her car (or had someone clean her car) on a regular basis. Ronnie was about to turn back when she noticed a white folder lying on the passenger seat. She moved closer to get a look. *St. Sebastian School*, read a crest across the front. *Welcome materials.*

By the time she was back at Andrea's car, she'd already pulled up St. Sebastian's website. The school featured oceanfront views and a diverse mix of boys in blue jackets and red ties. *A 9–12 school with three clear tenets: hard work, a solid foundation, and a stable family life for behavioral modification so boys can grow up to lead a productive, meaningful adulthood.*

"So . . . reform school?" Lauren said aloud after Ronnie showed them the welcome slogan. "She wasn't kidding when she said she wished North had had the Silver Swans opportunities."

They tried to call St. Sebastian's offices and inquire about North, but an automated voice said all the lines were busy and that they could leave a message. Lauren babbled something about being a friend of Piper Jovan's and having some concerns for North Jovan, a student there. She left her phone number and hung up.

Ronnie checked her watch again. Ten minutes had passed. "I need to get back," she said. Every second away felt dangerous. What if Vanessa was getting restless? What if she'd decided to start the cross-country journey early?

"No, wait," Lauren said. "Someone's home. I think we should ring the bell."

"Hang on, then." Ronnie lifted her phone and redialed the first number on her recent calls. On the second ring, a chipper voice announced that she'd reached the Golden Palm Motel. Heart pounding, she asked about Vanessa and Esme, praying they hadn't unexpectedly checked out. The girl at the front desk clacked on her computer, then said, "Nope, the room's still in use. You want me to ring them?"

"Oh, that's okay, thank you," Ronnie said, breathing out. Of course, there was a chance Vanessa had taken off without officially checking out, but she wanted to think Vanessa had stayed put. This bought her a few more minutes, anyway.

Once she was off the phone, everyone peered once again at the light in the upstairs window. "Let's claim we're here for a book group," Lauren decided. "And we've gotten lost, the wrong house."

"A book club before dinner?" Ronnie gave her a strange look. "Even a teenage boy would call bullshit on that."

But Lauren was already stepping out of the car and starting up the front walk. Ronnie exchanged an uneasy glance with Andrea, then scrambled after her. This felt like the hallway all over again, and perhaps Lauren sensed this, because she stopped and looked at them.

"We don't have to," she said.

The air had grown chilly, suddenly. The sun was starting to set, turning the clouds above them a candy pink. Ronnie took a breath. This might be their only chance.

"Okay," she said. "Let's do it."

"Yeah, but if anything's weird, we're leaving," Andrea said.

At the door, Andrea rang the bell. Lauren stood at the front, jiggling on her heels, her lips moving softly to themselves. She was nervous, Ronnie realized.

They waited, but there was no answer. Andrea rang again. Ronnie cocked her head, listening, but heard no footsteps. "False alarm?"

Lauren's brow was knitted. She pointed through the glass sidelight, which offered a translucent view into the foyer. "I see another light back there."

"Maybe Piper's just the kind of person who doesn't care about wasting electricity," Ronnie guessed. "Or maybe the lights are on a timer."

Lauren put her hand on the knob and twisted. The latch on the door released, and the door swung open. Lauren smiled.

"What are you doing?" Ronnie hissed, planting her feet.

"Someone's home." Lauren angled her body to step inside, then looked at them. "I just . . . I have to see him, okay? I just want to see him for a second."

"Lauren," Andrea warned, but it was too late—Lauren was already through the door. They couldn't let her go in alone.

The foyer was grand, with a double-height ceiling. The wall colors were gray. To Ronnie's right was a sitting room, but to her surprise, it was devoid of furniture. Not a chair, nothing—an empty shell.

"Huh," Andrea murmured. "*How* long has Piper lived here again?"

Ronnie wanted to snoop around the first floor, but Lauren was already heading up the curving staircase. "Lauren!" she called. Did Lauren think it was a good idea to ambush a teenage boy they now worried was dangerous? Lauren seemed to rethink this and froze. The only sound, for a moment, was the ticking of a far-off clock.

"North?" Lauren whispered. "Hello?"

So much for the lost book clubbers excuse, Ronnie thought.

"We should go," she whispered. "I don't like this vibe." The idea of being knocked out and not being able to check on Esme—*rescue* Esme—was unthinkable.

But Lauren started up the stairs again. Ronnie groaned and followed her, if only to drag her down by her hair.

The landing opened onto a long hallway. Doors lined either side; one opened into a pretty tiled bathroom—though, strangely, with no shower curtain, no bath mat, no towels on the rack. The other opened into a bare square. Did they have the wrong house? Lauren padded down the carpeted hallway toward a closed door with a strip of light shining underneath. "Hello?" she whispered, knocking. Ronnie couldn't believe this.

Still no answer. Lauren glanced at Ronnie and Andrea, who both vehemently shook their heads—they needed to *go*. But there was determination in Lauren's face. She turned back to the door and pushed it open wide. Ronnie held her breath, terrified.

"Oh," Lauren said.

Ronnie peeked inside. There was furniture: a queen-size bed with a generic white bedspread and a small dresser. The overhead light blazed and a ceiling fan whirred, but there wasn't anyone in the room.

"Okay," Ronnie said shakily. "Okay, he's not here. Now can we go?"

"I guess." Lauren sounded disappointed. She turned on her heel and started down the hall back for the stairs. But when she got to the first door on the right, she stopped cold. Her eyes popped wide. Her mouth fell open. "*Oh.*"

Ronnie and Andrea rushed to her side. The walls of this room were painted a soft blue. A navy sleigh bed was pushed into one corner. There were bookshelves full of paperbacks—*Harry Potter*, a bunch of graphic novels—and an Apple laptop sitting on a bare desk. There were Dallas Cowboys pennants and a Cowboys helmet and a Cowboys jersey from a player Ronnie didn't know, but then also a flag in the corner for the Philadelphia Eagles. There were vacuum swirls on the rug. Not a speck of dirty clothes on the floor. The bedspread was astonishingly free of wrinkles.

Ronnie shifted her weight. Something bothered her, something she couldn't put her finger on. She looked again at the football stuff. Maybe it was different out here, but where she came from, Eagles country, no self-respecting person would be a fan of both the Eagles *and* the Cowboys.

Snap.

Everyone looked up, freezing in the darkness.

The sound came again: another snap, and then a *shush*. Of fabric, maybe. A hand rubbing against a cushion or the back of a couch. And then the squeak of door hinges, somewhere downstairs. Ronnie glanced at the others, her mouth an *O*. Someone was here.

Andrea bolted out of the room and started down the stairs. Ronnie followed, but when she heard another slam of what sounded like a drawer, she froze. The noise sounded petulant. They shouldn't have come here.

She reached the foyer. All they had to do was get to the front door and let themselves out. But another slam came. A rustle of papers. And . . . footsteps. Someone was at the back of the house. If they were lucky, North wouldn't notice them before they slipped out.

Then Lauren's phone rang, a loud bleat echoing through all the emptiness.

Ronnie whipped around and glared at Lauren, who was fumbling in her bag to turn the thing off. "Sorry!" she mouthed. Everything went still again. The rustling and slamming had stopped, but Ronnie wasn't sure if that was a good thing or a bad thing.

Then Lauren sucked in a breath. Her gaze was on her phone screen. She looked up at them with the kind of expression one would make if they'd just gotten word that half of California had been wiped out in an earthquake.

"What?" Ronnie whispered. "What is it?"

Lauren looked at her screen again. "That school called me back. Left a message. I'm just looking at the transcription. They're saying North Jovan isn't a student at St. Sebastian. They've never heard of him."

"Okay." Ronnie felt a pinch of annoyance. *This* was what was slowing them down? She needed to get out of here. She needed to get to Esme. "They must have chosen another school, then. Somewhere else."

"But I swear Piper mentioned *that school*," Andrea said. "In the meeting. I swear she did." She gave both of them an uneasy look. "Why would she lie about that?"

"Piper lies about a lot of things."

Everyone whipped around. A man stood in the hallway, one hand carrying a sheaf of papers, the other holding a gun. Ronnie had no idea who he was, but he was smiling at the group like they were old friends. "She lies about a lot of things," he repeated. "There is no North anymore. North is dead."

Lauren drew in a breath, her whole body shrinking. "Graham," she whispered, her voice small and doomed.

Thirty

Lauren's husband stood five feet away. He wore a T-shirt she'd bought for him at a fancy boutique when they first got together. It cost over a hundred dollars, which Graham said seemed excessive, but she'd liked the way it hung on him. It still fit him nicely. The shirt was so achingly familiar that it made everything else about him right now—his frantic expression, his gnashed teeth, and that *gun*—even more incongruous.

"Graham," Lauren whispered. "W-Where did you get that gun?"

"What are you doing here?" Graham shot back.

Lauren opened her mouth, but no words came. Ronnie stepped forward. "What do you mean, North is dead?"

Graham's throat bobbed as he swallowed. "He died when he was a baby."

Fury rose in Lauren. Lies upon fucking lies. "What are you talking about? Why would Piper keep saying he is alive?"

"I don't know!" Graham said. "But . . . she couldn't bear it after he passed. She kept talking to him like he was still there; she would walk around the block with an empty stroller. It's why we broke up. She couldn't move on. It just got . . . too much. I was hurting, too. We had to part ways."

This was all just too strange. "So you pretended not to know her to protect that lie?" she said, trying to work out his reasoning.

Graham shrugged. "I had no idea she was still doing it until a few weeks ago. I only started to put it together when I looked at the preschool website and after you came out of the breakfast. After all this time . . ." He shook his head. "I can't believe she still thinks he's alive." Then he looked at Lauren. "I *told* you she's crazy."

Everyone's heads bobbed. Lauren didn't know what to believe. There *were* signs of North's existence: The perfect bedroom upstairs. The welcome packet from the school. And who was that picture Andrea had seen in Piper's office? Some *other* little boy? But it made Lauren feel light-headed, the wrongness of it, the sort of disturbance that had to be taking place in Piper's mind to carry out such a thing.

"I'm really sorry, Graham," she said quietly, because she couldn't quite fathom the devastation of losing a child. But on the heels of it, she felt hideously betrayed. He should have told her that he'd gone through that. Also, it didn't explain why Graham was here. Her gaze fell to the papers in his hands. "What are those?"

Graham shifted them behind his back. "Just old stuff Piper never gave back."

"*Now* you've come for it?" Lauren scrambled to understand. "After all these years?"

"I didn't know she was *here* until a few weeks ago."

When Lauren breathed in, she could smell the sharp, tangy, sweaty scent Graham always emitted when he was under stress. She used to like it in the same way she liked the smell of her family dog's paws. But now it made her sick. She breathed in sharply. "Were you the one stalking her, Graham?"

Graham scoffed. "*Stalker* is a little intense."

"Have you been lurking around this house? Scaring her?" She put her hands on her hips. "Were you the one who attacked her?"

"*No*," Graham growled. "I'm not."

"Yes." Lauren's voice shook. "You knocked out Ronnie. You nearly killed Piper. You *slammed her head against the wall*."

"I. Wasn't. There." Little droplets of spittle flew from Graham's mouth. He stared at the gun in his hand like he didn't quite know what to do with it. "Can you go? Let's just pretend this didn't happen."

Lauren could feel Andrea and Ronnie backing away. Her gaze fell again to the papers in Graham's hand. It was a slim bundle, but she was able to make out that the top sheet was a series of printed pictures. In one of them, she could see half of Piper's face. Her eyes were cast down. She looked troubled. Her face was eerily pale.

"Why do you have photos of Piper?" she asked, pointing to them.

"Lauren." Graham stuffed them into the back pocket of his jeans. His voice was pleading, desperate. "It doesn't matter."

"Lauren," Ronnie warned. "Let's just go. *Please.*"

Lauren's legs were trembling, but she couldn't move. "Tell me, Graham. Tell me the truth."

Graham stared at the ground. The gun trembled in his hands, and then there was a little *click*ing sound, releasing the safety. "*Lauren!*" Andrea screamed. Ronnie whipped open the door and hurried to the porch. Andrea followed. But they didn't run across the lawn. They stood just beyond the doorway, watching.

"Please, Lauren," Andrea urged. "Just come with us. It's going to be okay."

But something was happening here. The police were probably going to search this place, if they hadn't already. They would find out that North had died, if they didn't already know. They probably *did* know, Lauren realized. If they knew Graham and Piper were together, of course they'd looked into the records about their child.

So what were these pictures, then? What was so damning and terrible Graham needed to break into a house and get rid of the evidence?

And then a crack opened in her brain. And here came the low

boil, too, lurching up to a simmer in mere seconds. "Give me those," Lauren roared, lurching forward. She grabbed a few of the papers, ripping one down the middle. A few bunched in her hands, and she took a big step back. "Hey!" Graham screamed, diving for her. In the split second before he landed on top of her, Lauren got a look at the images.

There were bruises on Piper's face. Marks on her arm. Scratches on her back. Her eyes cast down, her expression deeply ashamed. Picture after picture, documenting everything.

Time sped up. Graham's body was suddenly crushing her chest. One hand clamped on her neck, cutting off her airway. Lauren looked at him pleadingly, gasping for air that wouldn't come. Above her, Andrea and Ronnie were screaming, pleading. Lauren just stared into her husband's eyes . . . and there it was. *Snap*, a memory returned.

She saw herself standing in the kitchen. It was a summer night. *That* summer night. She was angry, screaming at Graham, holding the baby to her chest. And then she saw what came next, what her mind had previously wiped away. Graham had lunged at her. "Just stop," he'd growled. "You're acting insane. *As usual.*"

He pushed her against the sink and pressed his hand to her throat. Lauren let out a weak cry, still holding Matthew. Lauren clawed at Graham, trying to get him away from them, her fingers making contact with his face. Enraged and surprised, he shot out his fist. He'd intended it for Lauren's cheek, but he misjudged. His hand connected with Matthew's chubby thigh.

The baby was silent, and then his screams intensified. Graham froze in horror, and then guilt, and then deep regret. But after, a calm came over him. He lifted the baby from Lauren's arms. And then she went blank.

When she opened her eyes again, Graham stood opposite her in the kitchen. Matthew was still screaming, Lauren's hands were still trembling, but now, Graham looked at her with condemnation. He'd had time to prepare a story. He'd planned a way to twist the blame.

And Lauren had believed him.

"It was you," she hissed, her voice croaky under the weight of his hands. "You hurt Matthew that night. Not me."

Graham's eyes narrowed. "It could have been you, though. Sooner or later, it *would* have been."

"But I didn't. You wanted to hurt me, but you hurt him instead. Just like you hurt Piper."

"It's not like I meant to do it," Graham said. "You're making me out like I'm some kind of monster."

"Oh, like you've made *me* out to be a monster for the past months?" Lauren exploded. "Making me think I'm blacking out and forgetting things with my *mom brain*? You've been gaslighting me!"

"I was trying to keep everyone safe!" Graham roared.

"Safe?" Lauren whispered, shaking all over. And then she looked at the ripped photo in her hands. Piper looked so sad. And Lauren felt sad, too. This man she thought she loved was a whole other person. And soon, she wouldn't know him anymore.

When the blow came to the side of her head, she wasn't expecting it, and her teeth came down hard on her tongue. The pain was white-hot, exploding stars and a bouncing brain. Behind her, Andrea screamed. Lauren could feel the image of Piper being pulled from her hands; she tried to tug it back from Graham, but that just made it rip more. And then another sound: a *crack* of something. The gun? Lauren tried to roll onto her side, but she couldn't move. Andrea screamed again, and then Lauren felt Graham lift off her, maybe going for Andrea instead. Sound danced in and out in warped waves, but she heard footsteps, and then shouting and then . . . a voice.

"Up against the wall!" came a bellow.

Even years later, the image Lauren saw when she opened her eyes would remain crisp in her mind. It wasn't Ronnie and Andrea cowering against the wall of Piper's foyer but Graham. That baby-faced police officer aimed a gun at his chest. Graham had his hands curled at his sides, and his mouth was gummy and pleading, and then another cop swarmed in, and another. "Don't move!" they were all shouting—to *Graham.*

How? Lauren wondered. She glanced at Andrea and Ronnie, but they looked just as surprised that the police were here.

The police spun Graham around and placed handcuffs on his wrists. As they nudged him out the door, he shot Lauren an exasperated look, as if to say, *Why did you do this to me? Why did you overreact again?* The look he gave her, time and again, since she'd had Matthew.

She just stared steadily back at him. She wasn't overreacting. Maybe she never had been.

Thirty-One

Thirty minutes later, the sun had set, and the only lights on the street were the bright blue and red ones from the tops of the police cars and ambulances. Andrea sat on the tailgate of a police SUV. Ronnie was drinking from a big bottle of water the EMTs had brought. Lauren was sitting on the curb, a blanket slung over her—the emergency workers were afraid she might be in shock. Detective Allegra, the baby-faced police officer Andrea had completely written off initially, was taking her statement. They were softball questions—about what had happened, what she'd witnessed. Allegra had been interested in Graham for the past few days, he told her, ever since he found out that he was Piper's ex-boyfriend.

Apparently, the cops had been keeping tabs on Piper's property, too—turns out, Carson had mentioned the whole "Piper's afraid someone's stalking her" bit shortly after her assault—which may have been why they hadn't jumped to arrest Andrea and the others. The cops had arrived at the property for a routine check after Lauren, Andrea, and Ronnie had already gone inside, though when they saw Ronnie and Andrea scurry to the front porch—when they saw Graham in the foyer, aiming a gun at Lauren—they rushed in.

The images of Piper battered and bruised were scattered all

over the foyer floor for the cops to find. So was a USB stick, which contained several video files of Piper documenting the injuries she'd sustained from Graham back in the day. They were old, grainy files, recorded on an ancient digital camera, but they were good enough. Piper had been creating a narrative for what was happening so that when she went to the police, she'd have proof.

Except Piper never did go to the police. She just ran away.

Allegra closed his notebook and looked at Andrea curiously. "While I have you, Ms. Vaughan: you're quite the investigator. Anything else you figured out you want to tell me?"

Andrea opened her mouth, then shut it again. There was a whole piece of this the police didn't know; Carson was holding it hostage. It didn't seem fair that Carson was going to get off scot-free, yet there was no other reason for the police to search Piper's office or her home. Even though Graham insisted he hadn't hurt Piper, the cops had their guy.

And now, they'd never find evidence of the embezzlement.

She thought of the parents hurrying their kids into Silver Swans each morning. They'd worked hard to get where they were, and they only wanted the best for their kids. And, okay, the mothers were kind of ridiculous at times, but that didn't mean they should be robbed. And what about the kids? They certainly didn't deserve that.

If Andrea said nothing, what would happen? Piper would never get her job back at Silver Swans—the story of North would break shortly, and her mental health would be called into question. But Carson could continue on. Maybe *he'd* be made director. He'd keep charging an arm and a leg for tuition. Maybe he'd stop stealing, but he was still a dishonest person, not the sort of guy you wanted caring for your kids.

Allegra took Andrea's silence as affirmation that she had nothing more to tell. He'd moved over to the squad car to make a phone call. Andrea looked at Ronnie, still guzzling water, and Lauren, shaken and shivering under the blanket. They'd both lost so much in all this. Their lives were indelibly changed. What they were facing made Andrea's stakes look less severe. Was she really going to conceal massive fraud and cheating just to save her own truths from coming to light? So what if her father cut her off? So what if the tabloids wrote about her for a while? It would be painful, but it wouldn't ruin her.

Maybe that wasn't worth keeping quiet. Only, what would telling what she knew do to Jerry? Could she really ruin his family?

Andrea slid off the tailgate. She didn't doubt Carson would retaliate, but she could deal.

But there was something she needed to do first. Two things, actually. Scrolling through her phone, she located Jerry's number and dialed. He picked up quickly. "Are you all right?" he asked, as though knowing exactly where she was.

"Your daughter told you Silver Swans was stealing from the parents, didn't she?" Andrea started right in. "And she told you she tried to fight it?"

Jerry sighed. "I'm sorry you got mixed up in that."

"You should have told me! I was almost attacked! Almost arrested!" Was there anyone she'd be able to trust? Anyone who fully had her back, who wasn't just looking out for himself?

"I'm sorry," Jerry said helplessly. "Andrea, I'm sorry, but Flora made me promise not to say anything."

"Because they have something on you, right?" Andrea chewed hard on her bottom lip. "I don't want to push you into a corner. I know things are hard, with Susan. They'll release my past, too, if I tell the truth. But maybe I'm okay with that. And maybe you should be okay with it, too. What they did wasn't fair, and you know it."

There was a sharp intake of breath on the other end. Andrea waited, watching the swirling red and blue lights blink against the pavement. Jerry sighed. "You're a lot more forthright than your dad, you know," he said finally. "A better person."

"Thanks," she said stiffly, though she felt touched. She liked this notion of herself.

"Do what you think is right." Jerry sounded resigned.

And then he hung up. The phone was hot in her hands. It felt like the end of something. She probably wouldn't see Jerry after this if she decided to talk. She mourned that for a moment and wondered if there was some kind of middle ground. But then she thought of telling Arthur about this, years from now. She would want to tell him the version where she did the right thing, not that she'd kept her mouth shut.

Next, she located Reginald's name in the contacts. He was still under Blue Iguana Landscaping. Her heart thudded as she lifted the phone to her ear and listened to it ring. Reginald answered gleefully, sounding happy to hear from her. It occurred to her their date was only a few days before. It felt like years.

"Hey," Andrea said, unable to shake the jitteriness from her voice. She wasn't even sure what she said next. An amalgam of speeches she'd meant to say for months now—the whole truth about her family, her legacy, even Roger.

"I'm sorry," she blurted when she was finished. "I'm so, so sorry, but I wanted you to know."

Reginald paused before speaking. "What are you sorry for?"

"For not telling the truth." Then Andrea tried a joke: "But women can apologize way too much. A bad habit."

Reginald laughed. Andrea wanted to sink to the grass with gratitude—he could still *laugh* with her. "Well, I'm sorry, too," he said. "Because . . . I kind of already figured it out. You reminded me of someone. Your eyes. And my mom used to read the sorts of magazines your family was in. *Vanity Fair*, the tabloids, that sort of stuff. I hunted around. Maybe that makes me an asshole. But I put two and two together."

"Oh," Andrea said. Then she laughed. "I guess I'm not as stealthy as I thought."

She felt like a dolt, and also a little tricked, but on the heels of that: *Reginald doesn't care.* He knew what she was and where she was coming from, and it didn't matter. She tipped her head upward and looked at the clouds.

"So do you want to come over later?" she asked him. "Once the police let me go?"

"The police?" Reginald sounded worried. "What are you doing with the police?"

She hung up a few minutes later, saying she had another call to make. Andrea really wasn't looking forward to this next call, but she dialed her mother's number in New York all the same. It was 9:30 p.m. on the East Coast, and Cynthia was probably sitting in her bed with a cup of tea. As for Andrea's father, who knew where he was—probably out, eating a steak or drinking a whiskey or making some kind of complicated deal.

But to her surprise, a different voice answered when she picked up. "Max?" She was shocked. "Put Mom on, will you?"

Andrea realized too late she hadn't properly modulated her voice. Max was silent a long time. She sucked in her stomach. She hadn't wanted it to come out like *this.*

"Mom, um, told me." Max said quietly, "Andrea, right?"

Andrea blinked hard. Her blood was ice. She had no idea what to say. She couldn't gauge Max's tone.

"Is it weird that I knew even when we were little?" he then said. "I always had that sense. Not specifically or anything—just that you weren't happy. But hey, if this is your truth, then live it."

Andrea's hand fluttered to her mouth. When even more silence passed, Max said, "Are you still there?"

"Y-Yes," she stammered. "I . . . I'm just surprised."

"That I'm not the asshole you always thought?" Max chuckled. "I'm not *Dad.*" Then he added, "You want me to put Mom on?"

Their mother. Andrea's heart sank. "I don't know. I'm going to tell her that everything's going to come out. All of it—about me. I'm going to make a preemptive statement. It's time."

The line fuzzed with static. The pause was so long that now Andrea was about to ask if Max was still there. Maybe he was having second thoughts, now that this would no longer be a secret. "She might have a heart attack," Max said carefully.

"I know. I get what that will mean for her—and for you. If you're done with me, I understand."

"*I* don't need to be done with you." Max cleared his throat. "I can't speak for Mom or Dad, but if you need someone, you can call me."

Andrea was so stunned she merely nodded instead of spoke. Then Max asked if she still wanted their mother on. "Maybe not," Andrea said. Because, suddenly, she knew how this would go. She wasn't going to get her happy ending with Cynthia. Her mother wasn't going to magically say everything was okay just because Andrea was ready to live open and free. She thought of what Reginald had said when they'd had takeout on her couch—people generally didn't change. It was usually your responsibility to just work around them . . . or cut them from your life. As much as she'd hoped that she would tell this to Cynthia and Cynthia would embrace her with open arms, that was about as far-fetched as Cynthia uprooting her Upper East Side life and going to live on the moon.

And also, maybe it was okay that Cynthia wouldn't accept her with open arms. Because look at what just happened. *Max* had.

The officer was off his phone now, striding back to Lauren and her group. Andrea dropped her phone back in her pocket and started through the grass, feeling wet blades prickle her bare ankles. "Excuse me, Detective Allegra?" she called out to him, and he looked up. And then it began.

Thirty-Two

Ronnie sped down the highway. Lane kept calling—he probably suspected something was up, maybe had even heard there were police cars at Piper's property—but she'd ignored him. She needed to get back to Vanessa's motel.

It was only ten minutes to the motel. When Ronnie looked at the odometer, she realized she was going fifteen miles over the speed limit.

Finally she was at the turnoff to the shell-pink motel where she'd put up Vanessa and Esme. Ronnie rounded the corner to the motel, her heart pounding hard. *Please be there, please be there*, she prayed silently.

The parking lot came into view. A few cars were scattered here and there, but Ronnie didn't see Vanessa's battered Mercury. A lump formed in her throat. Her brain stalled. She pulled into the parking lot and drove around the whole thing, even circling to the dumpsters in the back.

She pulled into a space, so distraught she couldn't think straight. Ask the desk? She darted to a trash can by the automatic doors of the entrance, spying an empty McDonald's Happy Meal container stuffed into the bin. Had that been Esme's Happy Meal?

She tried the cell number Vanessa had begrudgingly given her. No answer.

Ronnie placed her hands over her face and felt her legs give out from under her again. This was her fault. All her fault. What kind of mother turned a child over to a stranger? Why hadn't she stalked this place more carefully? *Please*, she prayed. *I'll do better. I'll never leave her out of my sight. I'll only give her the best. I'll be a better person, too. I'll try my hardest. Just bring her back*.

And then her phone rang.

She stared at it. The call was from a number she didn't recognize. She considered just sending it to voicemail—maybe it was a reporter, something about Piper, or maybe a cop following up—but something made her answer. "H-Hello?" she said uncertainly.

"Mommy?"

Ronnie's heart leapt. "*Esme?*"

"Mommy!" Esme sounded chipper. "Mommy Mommy Mommy!"

"Oh my God, Esme." Tears were running down Ronnie's cheeks. "Honey, where are you? Whose number is this?"

"I'm eating donuts!" Esme said, then giggled. "Don't tell Daddy Lane."

"Donuts? That's fine, honey!" At least Vanessa was feeding her. "Are you on a big highway?" Ronnie tried to keep her voice calm.

"No," Esme scolded, like Ronnie should know better. "I'm eating our *favorite* donuts. You know, the ones with the sprinkles?"

Sprinkles? Ronnie thought of the red sugar around Esme's mouth just days before when they'd gone to the donut shop around the corner. "Where's Vanessa?" she asked. "Your . . . auntie?"

"She told me to sit here and be good and eat my donut. I'm on a really big phone that makes a lot of beeps!"

Ronnie had no idea what she was talking about. "Can I talk to her?"

"Umm . . ." There was a *clunk* and some shuffling, but then Esme was back on the line again. "When are you going to be here, Mommy?"

It was all the permission Ronnie needed. She'd never run so fast to get back to her car. She sped through a red light and a yellow light and then another red light, certain that the gods of motherhood were watching over her and diverting all traffic cops to other intersections. She parked in front of a fire hydrant at the curb and burst through the front door of the donut shop and there was Esme, oh my God, Esme, her hair tangled, her eyes bright, red sugar all over her mouth.

"Mommy!" Esme cried, grinning wide.

She jumped from the booth, and Ronnie ran across the floor, and they met in the middle in a giant hug. Ronnie was crying, but Esme was smiling wide. "I missed you, Mommy! When can we go home?"

"Um, hang on, honey." Ronnie looked around. The shop was empty save for Esme and a worker at the counter Ronnie had never seen before. "Where's Auntie Vanessa?" she asked. Esme just blinked big cow eyes back. She turned to the woman at the counter. "Excuse me? Which way to the bathroom?"

The counter woman scowled with exasperation. "We don't have one for customers. Sorry."

"Oh." Ronnie checked behind the counter, even stood on tiptoes to see into a back room. "Where's the person this little girl came in with?"

"My rate's twenty bucks an hour, you know. She said you'd pay."

She held out her hand, expectant. Ronnie frowned, but when she fished in her wallet and handed the woman a twenty, the woman seemed satisfied. "What did . . . ?" Ronnie asked, then stopped. She looked out the window. Out on the street, there was no sign of Vanessa's car. She looked back at Esme, too afraid to ask what had happened.

She sank into the booth, shaken and buzzed. The suitcase they'd packed for Esme that morning was sitting against the window, though when she opened it up to check the contents, all the clothes were rumpled. They looked hurriedly stuffed in, not carefully folded, as they'd been when Ronnie packed. She bent down to sniff the clothes; they smelled sour, the way Vanessa did. Esme's bathing suit smelled like chlorine. There were a few drawings crumpled up—bright suns, houses, smiling stick figures. And then she saw a folded note, her own name scrawled across the front.

She pulled it out. "What's this?"

Esme glanced at it and shrugged quizzically. "We made cards. I made one for you!"

As the little girl reached for her bag to find the drawing, Ronnie opened the paper. Vanessa had written what she had to say lengthwise across the page in small, cramped letters.

I can't. You win.

Ronnie's eyes bulged. To her surprise, the sudden image she had of Vanessa driving home alone—feeling sad? bereft? unequipped?—made her heart crack. Who knew what Vanessa's breaking point was, but she'd paid so much money and put forth so much effort, all for nothing.

But then came the elation. She pressed the note to her chest and felt another sob rise up, this one pure joy.

Another piece of paper had been tucked inside the message; it had fluttered to Ronnie's lap when she'd opened it. She picked it up and unfolded this one, too. At first, she didn't understand Vanessa's message. The words swam before her eyes.

You killed him, years ago. But don't worry. Nobody knows except me.

Ronnie folded the note quickly, sucking in a breath. Was that true? Vanessa had become a stranger to her; Ronnie didn't know whether this knowledge was a gift or a trick. She wanted to believe that Vanessa was telling the truth. Jerrod was gone. Jerrod was *dead.* So that was the reality she chose. Vanessa was still her sister. And Vanessa was giving her a gift—*two* gifts, actually. She turned to Esme and, in a burst of elation, plucked Esme's half-eaten donut and took a huge bite.

"Hey!" Esme said, grabbing it back. "That's mine!"

"We'll get you another," Ronnie decided, shooing her daughter out of the booth. "We'll get a whole dozen to take home."

Thirty-Three

"Come on," Lauren coaxed, her arms outstretched. "Come to me. You can do it."

Matthew stood five feet away, teetering on two stout legs, holding fast to the edge of the coffee table and looking at Lauren with a mix of uncertainty and determination. His big blue eyes went wide with fascination at his own abilities; he kept breaking into a smile, showing off a new bottom tooth.

"Go on," Clarissa, who was sitting on the couch, goaded. "You got this!"

Matthew had started flirting with walking a few days ago, not long after Piper's attack. But Lauren had been so out of it—and so had Graham, apparently—that only Clarissa had witnessed and acknowledged the feat. But Lauren wasn't going to miss the baby's first steps. She held her breath as Matthew dared to remove one hand and then the other from the table, suddenly standing alone without support. He lifted his foot as if to take a step, and then toppled down on his butt.

"Oh!" Lauren cried, rushing to help him back up. Her hands were sure on his back now, not tentative as they'd been before. She didn't have to worry about herself. She would never harm her baby, and she could trust all her instincts. In fact, she scooped him up and held him tightly, probably more tightly than Graham would have liked, just to give him an extra squeeze. And you know what? Matthew squealed with delight.

"Some kids cruise for months before walking," Clarissa said when Lauren put him back down. "He'll get there."

It was Lauren's first instinct to snap, *I know he will.* But Clarissa cared about babies and was trying her best. It wasn't like she'd asked to get mixed up in the family's dysfunction. Lauren wondered if she'd been too quick to judge her before, because when Clarissa came to work that morning and Lauren told her that Graham was no longer living at the house and had been in jail for assault, Clarissa sucked in a breath and said, "Oh my, Lauren, I'm here for whatever you need."

There was no suspicion in her voice. No malice, nor any disappointment that it was Graham who was gone and not Lauren. If Clarissa was curious about what happened—surely she *had* to be—she didn't press Lauren for details, as Lauren worried she had done with Graham about her postpartum rage.

A story had been released that Graham had been arrested for breaking and entering and aggravated assault—*and* that he was Piper's ex—*and* that he was the lead suspect in Piper's attack, despite the fact that Graham was still vehemently denying having anything to do with it. What the public didn't know, however, was the depth of Graham's cruelty and how Lauren and Piper had both been victims.

Graham had been a suspect from the start—once the police got their ducks in a row and couldn't get a confession out of Lauren or the others or even get any real answers, they started looking elsewhere. And then, Graham landed in their lap. They'd actually called Graham into the station *earlier*—the day after Piper's attack, in fact, when Graham was supposedly at work. That day, they got out of Graham that their child died when he was a baby and that Graham had promised Piper not to expose her lie. It baffled the police why he'd do that; Graham simply said it was out of loyalty: *She* was *my girlfriend, and that was my son.*

The police told Lauren that he'd then said—and this was the part that turned Lauren's stomach the most—"The person you really should be looking at is my wife. She's violent. She's capable of hurting someone." Officer Allegra told her all this in a clinical tone, though when he got to this part and noticed the tears rolling down Lauren's cheeks, he pushed a box of Kleenex across his desk. Had Graham *ever* loved her? Was he even *capable* of love? She thought of his face when Matthew was an infant—the joy, the wonder. He'd been hiding so many lies. It baffled her that a person could do such a thing.

There was something sticky about Graham, Allegra said. Something not quite right. The detective had followed up on Graham's alibi—he'd told the police he was not at the *Ketchup* set, as he'd told Lauren, but in LA having a drink with a friend. But they couldn't track that friend down; Graham was evasive about losing his number. Then, they started to drill into what exactly happened to his child who'd died. SIDS, is what the medical report said; maybe that was all it was. But it was strange that one child died and now there was a new wife with a violent personality . . . *and* an ex-girlfriend had been attacked. It didn't add up.

They'd called Graham in again to ask him some more questions—this was the visit Graham told Lauren about on the cacio e pepe night, the one where he purportedly deflected the blame to Andrea and Ronnie.

"He didn't bring up Andrea or Ronnie," Allegra said. Lauren was baffled, but only for a minute. *Of course he didn't*, she realized. *Because I never told him anything.* He'd been toying with her memory like it was a ball of yarn. Inventing a slip in her memory that would seal the deal for her to check into the mental facility. Making her think it was *her* idea after he'd said that she should be the one to decide. And she'd fallen for it.

"We said we didn't buy his alibi," Allegra went on. "Said he'd better start telling the truth. Asked if maybe he'd found his ex's presence a bit of a nuisance and wanted her gone. Asked if he'd specifically chosen Silver Swans to get close to her. Graham denied that, said he had no idea Piper was living here when your family moved in. And then he said that he was pretty sure *you* had figured out Piper was his ex."

"That's not true!" Lauren said. "I had no idea they were together!" She explained how she'd found the recipe book, the picture. Allegra said they didn't believe anything Graham was saying at that point. He was grasping at straws. They just needed to figure out what he'd done.

Lauren took a careful look at the day Graham made her the pasta. He'd been so calm and collected at that meal—and meanwhile, the cops were closing in. It was another reason why he made up a memory that didn't exist. He made Lauren doubt her loyalty, her sense of time and truth—going to the rest cure wasn't just to fuck with her; it was to prove her instability to the police. To exonerate *him*. If Lauren had gone to the wellness place, it would have only proven Graham's theory that she was crazy. The police might have even bought it. How close she'd come to doing exactly what he wanted!

After Graham left the police station the morning before he made her pasta, the cops had come to Lauren's door to corroborate his story—they wanted to know if she'd found out he'd once dated Piper, and so on. But Lauren had hidden in the bedroom; she'd been afraid they were calling about Ronnie and Andrea. Allegra even cruised by Lauren's house, intending to pay a visit—but caught her just as she was pulling out of the driveway to go to LA to confront Graham. "I followed you," Allegra said. "All the way to his workplace. Gained access to the premises with my badge."

Lauren had stared at him. Allegra had been *there*? She hadn't known.

Allegra and his partner listened in as Lauren questioned Graham. Her accusations were those not of a woman who'd known for a while that Graham had been with Piper but of someone who was blindsided. Then, Lauren fainted; Graham took off. The team tailing him was so discombobulated that Graham was running that he managed to lose them on the highway. They figured he'd gone back to Raisin Beach, and after trying other likely spots, they went to Piper's house on a routine check. Imagine their surprise when they found Lauren there as well. And Andrea, and Ronnie.

While in custody, Graham had admitted to "fighting" with Piper back in the day. He'd also admitted that Lauren's anger didn't result in harm to anyone but herself and that he'd *maybe* used it to his advantage to control her—"though she's blowing it all out of proportion." They got him to own up to being too rough with Matthew, causing minor bruises and blaming Lauren. But he would not take the blame for North's death. Again and again, too, he swore he hadn't been the one to hurt Piper—when pushed, he'd admitted that he'd snuck to her house shortly after making the connection about who she was. He'd tried to break in, desperate to get the photos he suspected she had so that she could never use them against him with Lauren. He hadn't been successful, though, because he was pretty sure a neighbor down the street saw him lurking around—the guy turned on his porch lights, leashed up his dog, called out "Hey!" a few times. Graham got cold feet, left. A few days later, Piper called him to meet. Hours after that, she was lying bleeding in the hallway of her school.

Did Lauren think Graham had been the one to hurt Piper? So much had been revealed about Graham's true nature that she could believe anything at this point. Here was a man so deceptive that he threw his own wife under the bus to escape blame.

She kept trying to wrap her mind around who Graham truly was. He hadn't been manipulative when they'd met—he hadn't tried to convince her of memories that weren't there. Only after she had the baby did it start to change. It was a trigger, maybe, from the memory of the baby he and Piper had together? Maybe something changed in his brain chemistry, same as how women's brains changed after giving birth, and something about parenting made him violently irrational. But unlike Piper, who documented what Graham did, Lauren's mental state was shakier. Graham was able to use her angry bouts and selective memory to his advantage. He would do anything to cover up that he was the bad guy—including making her think she was the one to blame. Lauren hated what had happened to Piper, but it had opened a door that might have otherwise remained shut tight. She shivered at the idea of living next to him still, believing so little in herself, trusting him implicitly with the baby . . .

Though as it turned out, Lauren and Piper weren't the only ones Graham tricked. The day after his arrest, Lauren bit the bullet and called her mom. She was going to find out at some point. "*There* you are," Joanne said as soon as Lauren answered. "Why haven't you called me back?"

"What do you mean?" Lauren had asked.

Her mother told her she'd called often. On the house phone, she said, because she figured Lauren was always home because of the baby. *The house phone.* Joanne was from the generation who didn't realize that even though some people still had landlines, few of them actually *used* them. "Graham kept answering," she said. "He kept telling me you were busy. Mel called, too, and Gwen—he assured us you guys were great. But it was weird that we didn't hear from you. We thought you were upset, but Mel started to worry something was wrong."

On the heels of that, she also got a call from Gracie Lord. "Oh honey, I would have never come to you about this, because I thought you were going through enough," Gracie started out, her voice heavy with regret. "But I was starting to wonder about Graham."

"What do you mean?" Lauren asked, still suspicious about Gracie's relationship with Graham.

"He just started to get . . . *strange.* We would be in meetings together, and he would bring up things I said, promises I'd made to him. I swore I hadn't said any such thing, but he had a way of making you doubt your reality. He did it with the writers, too. He'd take credit for ideas that were for sure someone else's, twisting things so the other writers wouldn't know which end was up. I was starting to see a pattern in it. Starting to see it was toxic. It's why we canceled his episode. He wasn't happy about that."

"You canceled his episode?" Lauren repeated. She thought of how mopey Graham had been when he'd had to come collect her from the police station when he was supposed to be shooting his episode. Meanwhile, it had been canceled.

"I think he's just one of those people who wants what he wants, and when things get out of hand, he . . . snaps," Gracie said. "I should have seen through it, Lauren. I should have talked to you more. I feel terrible I believed what he said about you."

"It's okay," Lauren said softly. She'd seen Gracie and Graham on one side, her on the other, and hell, even *herself* on one side, and the rest of the family on the other. But it wasn't that way at all. Incredible that Graham could dupe so many strong, successful women into questioning their sanity. Or maybe, in Piper's case, losing their sanity altogether.

She thought a lot about Piper pretending North was still alive for thirteen years. Neighbors were baffled when they found out North had passed away as a baby, as there was always evidence of kid things strewn around the property—bicycles, Rollerblades, balls. They swore they heard high-pitched kid squeals coming from the backyard pool.

As for an actual child, though? Collectively, no one could say for sure say they'd ever seen North, but they were the sorts of neighbors that didn't meddle in others' business. Piper kept to herself; her son kept to himself. Back when Piper first moved to Raisin Beach, she'd lived in a dumpy apartment on the outskirts of town—and must have perpetuated the North lie at least to herself back then. But the press, who was hungry for more of this story, couldn't find anyone from that time in Piper's life to verify that.

But how hard that must have been to keep up living a lie! All the maneuvering, all the pretense! Yet Lauren understood what might drive Piper to have done it. If something happened to Matthew—something *could* have, the night in the kitchen, if Graham's fist had been a few inches higher—Lauren would have fallen apart, too. She could see the comfort in imagining a child growing and changing, achieving milestones. She could see how it could be a coping mechanism to buy new toys for him appropriate to the age he'd be if he'd continued to grow. She could see making a room for him in a new house, placing the books he might have read on the shelves, the posters of sports stars he might have liked on the walls. Lauren *got* it. She did. Maybe anyone was capable of doing such a thing, if the circumstances were just right.

She pushed to her feet, squeezing one of Matthew's chunky arms. "You're doing so good, buddy." She cast Clarissa a departing smile and fetched her bag. "I won't be too long."

"Take your time!" Clarissa said, almost too quickly.

Lauren turned without saying anything else. For the first time since Clarissa had come to work for her, Lauren left without feeling ashamed, or guilty, or judged. Clarissa was no longer here as a buffer against Lauren's instability; she was here to simply lend a hand.

And that reframing made all the difference.

⁂

There was a guard at Piper's room. Not because the staff feared someone might attack her—although, with the news of the embezzlement scheme, that wasn't so far-fetched—but because now that she was awake and growing stronger, she was a flight risk. Once the doctors cleared Piper to go, she would be thrown into county jail alongside Carson to await her trial and sentencing. The public, who'd so recently praised Piper and damned Lauren and the others, had quickly changed their tune. Lauren's, Andrea's, and Ronnie's struggles were set aside—even Andrea, who'd been so worried Carson was going to expose her in retaliation, hadn't had to deal with that yet.

But the public outrage at a school director stealing from hard-working, trusting parents was powerful. People were appalled that a *nursery school* had screwed them. The story was splashy—there were spreadsheets of the embezzlement operation, how brazenly they'd extracted small amounts from more than one hundred parents' accounts. Piper's and Carson's finances had been subpoenaed; the amounts transferred into their accounts correlated to what had been stolen. In a time when so many people were laid off, they were making money—*and*, ironically, collecting state unemployment payments. It kept them more than afloat during that time—$500 times one hundred parents, after all, was a big chunk of change coming in monthly. It was enough for Carson to buy an Audi. Enough for Piper to assemble a very large closet of designer clothes.

But Lauren tried to put this aside as she stood outside Piper's room. She had to think of Piper as a person who'd been broken and manipulated by the same man who had broken and manipulated her. Ironic that Piper had pushed Lauren away with that snarky email; had she let Lauren in, maybe they would have figured out the Graham piece much sooner.

The door squeaked open. Inside, a single bouquet of red roses rested on a side table. A tray held an untouched lunch. And there was Piper, sitting halfway up in her hospital cot, staring blankly at her cell phone. She looked pale, and her hair was stringy, and her lips were cracked. She peered up at Lauren with a defeated, expectant look that seemed to say, *Oh. It's you.*

"Hello," Lauren said quietly.

Piper just stared at her emptily.

Lauren pushed her hands in her pockets. She pulled a plastic chair over to the bed and sat down. She focused, as the first time she'd met Piper, on her beauty mark. Had Graham focused on it, too? Had Graham found it sexy? What had Piper *seen* in him? What had Lauren?

When it was clear Piper wasn't going to say anything, Lauren cleared her throat. "He had me so mixed up, I was about to check into a mental retreat."

This got a small eyebrow raise from Piper, so Lauren continued. "I thought Graham was protecting me. I thought he wanted the best for us." She uncrossed her legs and leaned forward a little. "Was it that way for you, too?" Piper's situation was a little different. Graham had been abusing her openly. He was stealthier about it with Lauren, using her untrustworthy memory to cover his tracks.

Piper concentrated straight down the bed at her toes. "When we first got together, I thought he knew better about everything," she said in a small voice.

"Right?" Lauren felt a rush of deep despair. "Same. And with . . . with the baby," Lauren stuttered. "Did he make you think that you were doing things wrong?" And then she swallowed raggedly, something new occurring to her: Did Piper *still* think North was alive, after all of this?

"I know about North," Piper said, as if reading her mind. There was defeat in her voice. "I know he's not . . . you know. But I just . . . couldn't . . ." She waved her hands around, searching for the words.

"It's okay," Lauren said gently. "You don't have to explain."

Piper laughed bitterly. "But I *do*. To lawyers. To the reporters who keep calling." She sounded a little unhinged. "Oh, and by the way, it was your husband who called my contact at Hulu. My producer said she slipped up and told you they'd pulled out. Graham did it as insurance, I guess. So I wouldn't warn you about him."

Lauren pushed her spine against the back of the chair. She hadn't put this piece together, and she didn't know what to do with it. Did this mean Graham *did* love her, in some twisted way? He didn't want to lose her? Or maybe he just wanted to keep her close so he could control her.

"I'm sorry," she said quietly.

Piper shrugged. "He really didn't want you to know what kind of monster he was. That was his main concern. He kept talking about how he loves his baby, how he doesn't want to lose what he has. Although, I'd keep him away from that kid, if I were you."

Lauren nodded. And then she said, "Do you think Graham . . . Do you think . . . what happened, it was his fault?" She hated to even think of Graham accidentally hurting a baby—but she needed to know.

"I don't know." Piper sounded empty. "I always thought it was my fault. I put too many blankets in the crib. It was hot in the room. I second-guessed everything I did that day. But . . . I guess we'll never know." She shut her eyes as though she hadn't slept in years. "I just . . . I just always wanted to be a mother. I couldn't bear *not* being a mother."

"You still *are*," Lauren said sadly. It was such a secret society, motherhood. It defined you in ways a career couldn't, not entirely. It gave you a center, it gave you a drive, it gave you an excuse to push forward every day. For Piper, it gave her a story—which launched Silver Swans. To have that ripped from you—it would be like losing a vital organ.

"Why did Carson write that note to me?" she asked. "That I wasn't wanted at Silver Swans? Because of Graham?"

Piper shut her eyes. "I thought you knew something about the money. You were hanging around with those other women, so . . ."

"But then you left me a second note," Lauren went on. "You wanted to see me in your office."

"I did. I wanted to warn you. About Graham."

Lauren's mouth dropped open. "You did?"

"Well, sure. He would have been pissed if he knew. He said he'd tell everyone everything. But I thought you needed to know."

Lauren felt touched. "I wish you would have told me. I wish . . ."

But she wasn't sure what she wanted to say next. Even if Lauren had never run into Ronnie and Andrea and they'd never shared that they'd all received notes and drawings, Graham would have still come for Piper. Maybe he sensed Piper was going to tell Lauren about him.

"And . . . that day in the hall." Lauren's heart thudded fast. "When you were attacked. Do you . . . *remember* Graham there?"

Piper smiled serenely. "Oh, yes. I remember Graham."

Lauren widened her eyes, surprised by Piper's certainty. The police hadn't specifically said they'd gotten a statement out of her. Graham, her *husband*. So he really was a monster, then. He was so far from the person she knew it was hard to even mourn his loss. Sitting in the hard plastic chair, Lauren began to think about what her life would look like going forward. She couldn't picture visiting Graham in prison. What would she tell Matthew?

"I remember Graham in the hall," Piper said again, her voice taking on a dreamy tone. "I remember a red sweater . . ."

Lauren mentally searched Graham's closet; she'd bought so many of his clothes. "He has a good Burberry red sweater."

"Uh-huh," Piper answered. She stared at Lauren intensely. "That's the one."

"God." Lauren sat back. Piper sounded dazed and maybe suffering from a touch of PTSD. "I'm . . . really sorry." She felt herself welling up. "For *both* of us. What a fucking mess."

"Oh, *please*. I did you a favor."

Something light and strange had invaded Piper's voice, and

Lauren looked up. There was a twist to Piper's mouth. Did she think something was *funny*? Piper's mouth went slack, then puckered once more, like she was fighting not to snicker.

Lauren pulled back, suddenly uneasy. "What?"

A smirk slipped through, though Piper was quick to make her expression neutral again. "I'm sorry, I'm really tired. Maybe you should go."

"Okay . . ." The world seemed to tilt as Lauren stood.

"Okay," Lauren said again, lingering behind the chair, hoping that Piper would say more. Weren't they compatriots at least, having endured the same enemy? But maybe that was foolish. Piper was still the same person as before—the same woman, in fact, who said Lauren was nuts.

Have your stupid secrets, Lauren thought bitterly, shoving the chair back against the wall. *Pretend you're better than me. I was just trying to help.*

She mumbled a goodbye and then was in the hall. A nurse at the computer station looked up at Lauren curiously as she passed, but Lauren didn't even look at her. *Good luck in prison, Piper*, she thought, not feeling particularly broken up.

Through the double doors, into the parking lot. Lauren peeled off the badge with her ID picture and tossed it into the trash can. Something about the way it pinged against the metal—or maybe the oily smell in the parking lot—knocked something loose in her brain. She stopped short, staring down the line of cars.

Graham didn't have that red sweater anymore.

He'd *loved* that Burberry sweater—but it was so damn old and worn. Graham wanted to keep it, but Lauren insisted on throwing it away. Into the bin it went, the lid making the same *clang* as the sound that had just echoed in her ears. Unless Graham had a secret closet Lauren didn't know about, she could think of no other red item of clothing.

Lauren swung around and considered the entrance to the hospital. Should she go back in and confront Piper? Only, why? Didn't she *want* Graham to be convicted? He deserved it—more than Carson, more than anyone. But what if it wasn't true? *I did you a favor.* Did Piper remember something involving *Lauren*?

Overhead, a jet cut through the clouds, leaving a trail of exhaust. Lauren studied it until her eyes blurred. *No*, she decided, shaking out her shoulders. No, that was Graham's influence rearing its head. She hadn't done anything. She was sure of that now.

Piper

Last Thursday

You are alone in your office. The Asshole has just left. You close your eyes, hold the edge of your desk, and take a centering breath. You can do this. You aren't going to let him ruin you. But he scares you all the same. He knows where you live. He's been poking around your house when you aren't there—you're sure of it. Looking for those photos, probably. He knows you took them all those years ago. When you left, he was relieved. He thought he'd never see you again, that your lives would never intersect. But now, they do. Those photos are dangerous again.

His baby's eyes sear into your brain. His happy smile, his gurgling laugh. It broke your heart to see that baby today, and Graham knows it. That was how old North had been when it happened.

Finding North unresponsive. Pulling him from the crib, trying to get him to breathe again. Calling an ambulance, screaming to Graham, rushing to the hospital. It had been too late already. You'd known that the moment you'd found him. But you didn't know what else to do. You wanted to be in the hands of kind nurses, knowledgeable professionals, someone to explain to you what the fuck had happened. You wanted someone to hold you close and tell you how sorry they were. You knew, deep down, that Graham would do no such thing.

You'd gone through the days after North's death in a fog. There was the small, brutal funeral you barely recall. How, on your drive home—your fucking drive home from the cemetery!—Graham said that maybe he should sell the crib, and he knew some parents who might want some of the baby toys. You wanted to rip his head off. "We aren't selling anything," you roared. "North is still with us. He's still here."

How could someone be so present, so loud, so all-encompassing, and then . . . gone? Even worse, maybe gone because of something you could have prevented?

And it just sort of started there.

Part of you understood that there was no baby in your arms as you slowly moved around the nursery, rocking and cooing. Part of you knew that you should take the car seat out of your car, and fold up the stroller, and stop the monthly diaper delivery. Part of you understood that you could revert to a more adult sleep schedule instead of waking in the night and padding down the hallway to check if your nonexistent baby was still sleeping. But another big part of you really couldn't bear North being gone, so you decided it wasn't true. Your mind conjured him growing, changing, thriving. You bought him new baby toys, then toddler toys; you played nursery rhyme songs in the car and sang the ABCs and talked about plants and animals. You didn't talk about him to your co-workers—they knew what had happened—but you mentioned him to strangers all the time. "My baby just turned one," you'd say to people in the grocery store a few neighborhoods away as you plunked a jug of whole milk on the counter. "We're going to see how he likes full-fat milk!" Or, "My baby just turned two and a half," you'd say to a new massage therapist you were trying out, one who lived in a different part of town and didn't cross paths with anyone you knew. "And ooh am I sore from chasing him around!"

It was a salve to keep North alive in these moments. You cherished the pleasant, ordinary interactions you had with strangers who fully believed you were just another mother muddling through. It was the only thing that kept you going. Graham was already checked out—he was done with you just months after North died, unable to live with your coping mechanism, and it was only a matter of time until you would find those affair emails on his computer. And once that happened, once you headed off to Raisin Beach, you couldn't go alone. So you brought North with you.

North grew from a toddler to a young child. You cuddled with him in bed. You played dump trucks with him on the carpet. It strikes you what this must have looked like to outsiders, had they been looking in on you: a woman playing alone on the floor, talking to thin air. Though, to be fair, you aren't sure anymore if you actually played or if it all took place inside your brain. The strangeness of what you were doing didn't even seem so strange anymore. It had become a habit, a crutch, maybe even a second personality. You couldn't just excise North. You couldn't just ditch him. And when you went for the position at Glory Be and blurted out North's name in one of your first speeches, making him part of your narrative . . . well. You were in it for the long haul. You wanted to be a single mother of an eight-year-old, not a grieving mother of a child who'd died when he was a baby for reasons that were possibly your fault.

And so, on you went.

"Ms. Jovan, we've been informed about your child," Jean from Hulu had said on the phone the day before. "And first of all, I'm very sorry for your loss."

He'd paused for a long time, then, as though checking your level of sanity. Did you even know that your child was gone? You did, intellectually. But what most shocked you was that after all these years, someone else knew. Your neighbors, your co-workers, parents at the school—no one had ever asked point-blank. Oh, sure, they'd wondered where North was, but you always had an excuse. How lonely that had been! How removed your life was from anyone else's.

"I'm not equipped to help you with what you're going through, though I do think you are *going through something," Jean went on. "But I think . . . I think that perhaps we should step away from focusing on your school and let you sort all that out internally."*

He had been diplomatic, at least. He probably didn't deserve you telling him to go fuck himself. But what more was there to say? Hulu was out. If you were going to do the documentary, it would have to be on your dime. Which—fine. It was a small price to pay.

But things don't feel fine. Now that Graham has been here, you feel stirred up and more unsettled than you have in years. The walls are cracking. Soon, they will crumble. Graham isn't going to keep his word. He's going to tell everyone about you simply because he can. It's his only defense against those pictures—if he can get to everyone first, if he can convince all of Raisin Beach that you have serious delusions, then it will throw those images into question. He might suggest that you were self-harming and that he had nothing to do with it. He might paint himself as the concerned and caring but helpless husband.

It's going to happen. You can feel it. But you can't let it.

You think of his wife. You remember the email she sent you before you knew who she was, talking about how she suffered from postpartum rage. At first, you'd figured it was just a reaction to the note you'd slipped in her child's backpack. But you hadn't known she was married to Graham then. And now you wonder: How bad are this woman's postpartum issues, actually? Is Graham just twisting it into something bigger than it is?

Your body feels prickly. Jesus. This woman needs your help. If she's with him for much longer, she might lose too much. Her confidence. Her sanity. Maybe even her child.

And then you stand. You need to talk to her. You need to warn her. North's death was an accident—at least you thought so. Now, suddenly, you aren't sure. Now, suddenly, everything feels turned upside down.

You could try calling, but you worry about Graham seeing the number and picking up. Instead, you dash off a note on a piece of stationery. You don't want to indicate what you want to talk about in the message—you just need to get her into your office, alone. You fold up the note and stride down the hall and push out the heavy front door that leads to the parking lot. It's nearly empty now—all the parents' cars that were here for drop-off are now gone.

You push through the red door to the classrooms. Inside, there's the pleasant hum of classes in session. The air smells like paste and nontoxic paint; the music teacher is playing melody bells several doors down. You turn to the line of nursery cubbies, inspecting the tiny baby jackets and sweaters hung on the hooks outside the room. Each child's name has been painted above their hook; there's also a cubby above for larger items, like toys or diapers. After a few moments, you find her child—Matthew Smith. His backpack is in the shape of a cheerful raccoon. You touch its edges, feeling that awful ache again. Through the years, you've become more desensitized to being around little kids, especially babies, focusing only on what you need to do for them as their school's director. But it's the kind of backpack you would have gotten for North, had he lived.

After the note has been delivered, you feel restless, antsy. So you poke your head into the other classrooms. In the twos, the teachers are helping toddlers pretend-play with fake wooden food. You bite your lip, remembering how you imagined that you and North did the same thing. In the threes, the kids are making a craft with glue, glitter, and feathers. How many crafts did you make "for" North and hang on your refrigerator?

The fours are listening to the music teacher playing the melody bells; you spy Andrea's and Ronnie's children sitting politely and suddenly feel a pang of regret for what you'd asked Carson to do. Not that those parents aren't a liability, but the kids look so innocent and vulnerable—and also rapturous. You picture their small faces when their mothers tell them they're no longer attending this place. They'll be okay, you know—it's amazing how resilient kids are. But at the same time, you hate that you see this heartbreak up ahead for them. You hate that you know it's coming and you are the cause.

Unless there is something you could do to stop it. Somehow, Graham's presence is putting everything in perspective. It's not about being the best here—it's about doing what's right and good.

All at once, you want to get back to your office again and make a plan. How much do *those women know? Where* is *Flora, exactly? Is there a way to dig yourself out of this without ruining anyone else's life?*

You pass through the courtyard and around the playground. The other threes class is out there, and you spy Carson in the garden, inspecting some of the vegetable patches. You don't wave. You're too distracted to talk to him right now. You reach the loft building from the back entrance and stand for a moment in the cool shade of the stoop. The first time you key in the code on the security panel, you get it wrong—your fingers are slick, suddenly. Perhaps with guilt. The door clicks *as it opens, and you push into the cool darkness of the hall.*

The back door's latch closes slowly, barely making a sound. You blink in the darkness, suddenly having a strange feeling that you aren't alone. A rustle comes from around the corner. A tiny click of movement. You pause. Carson is outside. You'd seen the security guy in the parking lot. Everyone else who has access to this building was in their classrooms.

"Hello?" you call out.

You swear you can hear someone breathing, and you can feel your stomach sucking in. Someone is *here. Graham flashes through your mind again. Maybe he hadn't left at all.*

"Who's there?" you whisper.

The air feels fraught. If you reached out, would you be able to touch an arm, a shoulder? You take another step forward. And then another. "Graham," you say, though you can't see anyone.

And then there's a tap on your back. Disoriented, you swing around and see a shape standing on the riser behind you. Then, features materialize. It isn't Graham, though. You squint in confusion, your brain a few steps behind your eyes.

"Piper." The voice is not much more than a whisper . . . and then a sob. "How could you?"

You don't understand what's going on. You don't have time for whatever they want. You're ready to say that, too, but then you feel hands against your chest, and in those moments, you want to take it all back. I was just trying my best, *you want to say.* I know that *sometimes* wasn't good enough. But I was going to undo all of it. Let me do my best to make amends.

But then the darkness falls over you. And for a long time, you don't know whether you're alive or dead.

Thirty-Four

Sign here," the flower delivery woman said, pushing an iPad-type object toward Ronnie. After Ronnie scrawled her name on the electronic screen, she grabbed the giant bouquet of peonies with both hands and stepped back into the apartment.

"Whoa!" Lane said as Ronnie placed the flowers down on the kitchen counter. "Those are gorgeous!"

"They're from Andrea," Ronnie said as she opened the card.

Lane spied the inscription before Ronnie could hide it. "'So happy for you'? Why, because you weren't killed?" His voice had an edge.

"Um, yeah, I guess," Ronnie said shakily, dropping the card into a drawer. "Basically." Really, Andrea had sent the flowers when Ronnie texted over the news that Esme was back with her . . . and Vanessa was gone.

It was astonishing, what Ronnie had narrowly avoided. She and Esme had come back from the donut shop like it had been a normal day. It hadn't been, obviously—during dinner with his parents, Lane had heard the news about Ronnie breaking into Piper's house and being held at gunpoint by Lauren's husband, and naturally he'd wondered where Esme was, because hadn't Ronnie said something about she and Esme getting away for a bit?

But Ronnie had glossed over that part. She'd felt sort of

invincible. Her sister turning Esme back over to Ronnie's care was the kindest, most motherly thing Vanessa had ever done. Ronnie had tried to call and thank her with the number Vanessa had given, but the call didn't even go to voicemail. Maybe it wasn't even Vanessa's number.

She positioned the flowers next to the bouquet Lauren had sent, admiring how nicely they paired. "I guess you should send them flowers, too," Lane said. "Since you all went through everything together."

"True," Ronnie said, lowering her eyes.

Lane wrapped his arm around her shoulders. "I don't know what I'd do if something happened to you," he said. "You know that, right? You or Esme."

"I know," Ronnie said, and she did.

She felt so . . . *relieved.* This was all over. Esme was safe. Vanessa wasn't coming back—and though that gave her a specific sort of ache, maybe it was for the best. And Jerrod was gone. Well, hopefully. She looked at Vanessa's note again and again—*you killed him*—as well as searched for Jerrod's name online. Facebook. Google. Anything. He wasn't there. He didn't seem to be among the living. Maybe she could really believe that.

But that she'd killed him? Well, that unnerved her a little. But she was trying to bury it. That was her past, and it was gone. She'd put it in a box. Lost the key. Lane never needed to know about it. Maybe in time, the memory would fade for her, too. Sometimes she wondered if this was a big flaw in their relationship . . . but how could it be a flaw if one person didn't even know the secret existed? And would never *have* to know?

"Anyway." Lane bent down to kiss Ronnie's cheek. "Wish me luck!"

"You'll be amazing."

Ronnie squeezed his hand. Lane had an interview with the Raisin Beach public school system; a kindergarten teacher was retiring, and they needed to fill her spot. A lot of Silver Swans teachers were jumping ship; it wasn't even certain if the school would be able to continue past this year. There was no leadership. The dwindling board of directors—who were in hot water for overlooking the fact that Piper and Carson had set up a separate account to siphon cash from the parents—scrambled to find a replacement for Piper, but no one qualified had applied. And since Piper and Carson had spent all the money they'd stolen on things for themselves, the school was in a mountain of debt. An inspector had been called in; the place needed new windows, stairways brought up to code, and a mural contained lead paint.

Ronnie was sad that this was the end of an era, but maybe Esme didn't need a Grammy-winning songwriter to teach music class, and an occupational therapist on staff, and a guy who came in weekly to show them how to write Japanese characters with long-tipped brushes. Those seemed like such privileged, trivial things; she was focused on the big picture. Esme was going to turn out fine.

She kissed Lane again, standing on her tiptoes to reach his high forehead. She thought, too, of the box in her dresser drawer with the ring Lane had bought for her. She could say yes now. They could start planning something. She smiled to herself, forming a plan. Later today, when Lane came home and announced he'd gotten the job—because surely he'd get it—she would tell him the good news.

After Lane was gone, Ronnie went to sit next to Esme, who was on the couch paging through a book that listed all the My Little Pony characters in the world of Equestria. "How you doing, baby?"

"Good." Esme pointed to a blue pony with multicolored hair called Rainbow Dash. "I love her."

"I know," Ronnie said. She cleared her throat. "Did you and, um, your auntie Vanessa play ponies, too?"

Esme gave her a side eye, like she couldn't quite remember who *Auntie Vanessa* was. "Not really," she said. "But she did give me a Popsicle."

Then she turned a page. The next spread was dedicated to an orange pony called Applejack. The pony was standing on a farm; behind her were apple trees, pigs, and more horses. Ronnie touched one, remembering how Esme had asked Vanessa if the farm they would be living at had horses. Was her daughter just really resilient, or had she suppressed the memories of the time she'd spent with Vanessa? She didn't want Esme in therapy years from now, talking about that weird, mysterious, harrowing time this random woman took care of her in a motel up the street—trying to piece together what it all meant. Someday, Ronnie would tell her the truth. Maybe. But not now.

"I'm sorry I couldn't be there with you two in that motel," she said. "You know that, right?"

Esme didn't answer, just turned a page.

"And . . . maybe don't mention any of that to Daddy Lane," Ronnie continued. She was stroking her daughter's back now. "We should just keep it a little secret between you and me."

"Ooh, secrets." Esme's eyes gleamed. "Me and Daddy Lane have a secret, too."

"Oh?" Ronnie cocked her head. "Did he make you listen to that awful protest music?" The sixties folk Lane loved was like nails on a chalkboard; Ronnie had made Lane promise never to play it in her or Esme's presence again.

Esme shook her head, her pigtails swinging and smacking the sides of her face. "It's a secret about school."

"School?" Ronnie frowned. "What do you mean?"

"It's a secret that I had to stay in Miss Barnes's room for a while. But it was fun! I got to play with Miss Barnes's dress-up box without all the kids around, meaning I got to try on *all* the costumes."

Ronnie blinked. The last time Esme was in Miss Barnes's class was the day Piper was attacked. The cops had come, Ronnie had been taken away, but Ronnie had called Miss Barnes from the police car, saying she was caught up somewhere and to tell Lane to bring Esme home. "Why did you have to stay in Miss Barnes's room for that long? Was Daddy Lane doing some stuff in his room?"

Esme's eyes were wide. "He told Miss Barnes he was talking to the police."

"With the officers," Ronnie repeated. "Because of the attack." But that didn't make sense. Lane talked to the police the following day. There weren't enough Raisin Beach officers to get to the staff the day of the attack.

Ronnie's skin was prickling. Why had Lane lied?

All Ronnie could see, suddenly, was Piper flailing like a wild animal in her hospital bed, pointing at Ronnie and saying, *I'm sorry I'm not the person you need me to be.* And thinking Ronnie was a guy. She pushed it out of her mind, but it bounced right back in. It's possible Piper *didn't* think Ronnie was a guy—she was speaking to Ronnie *about* a guy, giving her a warning Ronnie could convey to this guy because she knew this guy best?

Then she thought of something else, something that had been jabbing at her for a few days now. "Be right back, honey," she told Esme, and headed down the hallway.

She yanked open the same desk drawer where she'd found the lists Lane kept of all the parents at Silver Swans. The book was still there, and so was the curious silver key Ronnie had noticed but dismissed.

She lifted it to the light. The tiny key had an unusual square head and a tiny, slender shaft, just the type that would slide into a file drawer. Ronnie had held a similar key only one other time—in Piper's office, when she'd unlocked the drawer containing the school's doctored financial documents. She'd never seen the same sort of key before, and certainly *they* didn't have any furniture that would fit it. Theoretically, this *could* be to some old piece of furniture Lane had now parted with. But something told Ronnie that if she used this on that drawer to Piper's desk, the lock would turn, and the drawer would slide open.

She sat back on her haunches. What did this mean? Probably nothing. But maybe something?

Lane and his scruples. Lane and his admiration of Piper. *Had* Lane figured Piper out? Had he left his classroom that day to tell her what he knew? He wouldn't have wanted anything from her. It was for the principle of the thing. His idol had fallen. But then . . . but then *what*? Had she pushed back? Had they . . . *fought*?

She dared to imagine it. Had things gotten out of hand? And then, afterward, what? Surely he hadn't gone straight back to his classroom—he would have never been able to collect himself in time.

Ronnie closed the key in her palm. But if that was true, did that mean Lane had been the one to hurt *her*? She pictured the tears in his eyes in the aftermath. *I'm so sorry*, Lane had whispered. Because he hadn't been able to shield her from the police, because this was happening to her, because it seemed unfair. But what if *I'm so sorry* was an admission of guilt?

Ronnie didn't know what to do with this blender of thoughts. Was she living with a violent man?

Footsteps padded down the hall. Ronnie glanced up, expecting Esme, but then Lane himself appeared in the doorway. "Sorry, I just forgot my . . ." He stopped. His gaze drifted to the open drawer, and then to the key in Ronnie's palm. The color drained quickly from his face. "Ronnie," Lane whispered, his eyes darting again to the key. "Oh."

It was all Ronnie needed to know. She held up the key. "Is this to Piper's desk?"

Lane's mouth opened and closed, like a goldfish. He took a step toward her, but Ronnie stood and moved to the other side of the bed to form a barrier. "Did you hurt her? Should I be afraid of you? Do Esme and I need to leave?"

"Oh God, oh God *no*," Lane blurted. He was crying now, the tears spilling out of him. "Ronnie, the day after we talked on the balcony, do you remember? I went into her office. Something you said bothered me—I wanted to make sure she wasn't judging you for some reason, like maybe because we weren't married. And . . . okay, there was this file on her desk. It was about . . . *you*."

Ronnie blinked hard. "So you *did* know there was a file."

"Yes, but only for a day." Lane looked wrecked. "I swear, only for a day."

"You knew about Topless Maids before I told you." It explained, then, why Lane had seemed shaken but not nearly as wrecked as she'd predicted—he'd had time to wrap his head around it.

But then she realized what else he might have known. A hand fluttered to her mouth. She took another step immediately. "Oh," she whispered.

Lane knew right away what she was thinking. "Honey, I was going to talk to you about all of it. Really." He ran his shaking fingers down the length of his face. "But I wanted to talk to Piper first. Get an explanation for why she had this big dossier on your past. I stewed over it for a while, but then I couldn't wait another minute. I found her in her hallway that next day."

"The same day I was there."

"Yes, but I mean . . . I didn't *know*. I tried to talk to Piper, but . . . but she wasn't listening. She tried to push past me. She didn't want me there."

"So you *attacked* her?"

"I didn't!" Lane backed away. "I-It was Lauren. She saw Piper blowing me off and got in her face and then Piper took her shoulders and tried to say something and Lauren just pushed her away and Piper . . . she *tripped* or something, I'm not sure, but suddenly she'd smacked her head against the wall. Then she was on the ground and there was blood and she was *unconscious*. And then *you* came around the corner, and I was so freaked out that I sort of banged into you, I didn't want you to see anything, and then you fell . . ." He put his face in his hands. "Ronnie, you can leave me. You can turn me in. I deserve it. I'm sorry. I just didn't want her to get away with it anymore. And I didn't want her to hurt you. I didn't want you to lose Esme." He took her hands. "Whatever happened in your past—I trust you. I'm not going to pry. Maybe it's better I don't know. But I know you. You're a good person. You wouldn't do anything unless you had a good reason. But I was afraid Piper didn't know that. I was afraid she would hurt you. Hurt *us*."

Ronnie sank to the bed. Too much had been thrust on her at once. Too many stories. And now Lane was sobbing so hard that he was crumpled against the doorframe. Esme had come up behind them, her eyes wide with concern. "Come on, come on," Ronnie said, gesturing for Esme to climb up on the bed. Esme crawled over to her, and Ronnie held her close while Lane continued to cry.

"I'm sorry," he said. "I'm so, so sorry."

"Is Daddy Lane okay?" Esme whispered.

Ronnie hugged her daughter tighter. Not because she was afraid. Her mind had sharpened. For whatever reason, she thought of a time when she was very young and had fallen on the sidewalk outside her house, getting a scrape on her knee. Back inside, her father had poured hydrogen peroxide on the wound, and once Ronnie got over the sting, she marveled at how it bubbled. "That's the medicine working," her father said. "It's flushing out all the bad stuff with the scrape, and it's going to help you heal."

Maybe that was what had happened here. Bad stuff had been flushed out. A school's sins were exposed. A woman was finally facing that her baby had died. Lauren was given her mind back. Andrea had found the strength to be more open with who she was, no matter the consequences. And Ronnie—well, Ronnie still had Esme, and she wasn't scared anymore.

Lane swallowed another sob. "Seriously, though. Call the police on me. It's okay. I deserve it. I've lied."

Esme's eyes popped wide. "Daddy Lane in trouble?"

"No," Ronnie said gently, rubbing Esme's back. "No, he's not."

Lane sniffed. A wrinkle formed on his brow. Ronnie walked over to him and put her hand on his shoulder. There was no point in opening up a closed case, was there?

Was this the same as being a good parent? Overlooking certain things, highlighting others, picking and choosing your battles? Maybe it was. Maybe Ronnie would always question what she decided. Whether she went back to dancing or pursued something more legitimate, whether she let her daughter eat real sugar-laden ice cream and sent her to a preschool without expensive murals in the hallways, the choices she made when she was a teenager and beyond—it would never end.

But this choice, this choice she could make.

She dropped the silver key back into the drawer and shut it. "I never saw this," she decided. "It was never here."

Lane blinked at her in surprise. "*Really?*"

"Don't look so shocked."

Too many bad things had happened to her already. If karma was a real thing, then it stood to reason that this could be swept under the rug. Ronnie needed Lane. She *wanted* Lane, *deserved* him. And he was a good person—for her, for Esme, for the world. Besides, even if Piper remembered Lane being there, she'd already accused Graham. This, too, felt like a gift. Ronnie said a silent prayer to Piper, which felt ironic but also totally right. And then, turning, she smiled at her family and led them out into the sun-filled, messy living room, where they would continue their day.

Epilogue

The party took place in Andrea's backyard. Before Andrea issued the invites, there had been some discussion among the three of them about who should come. They thought about all those pointed Facebook posts around the time Piper was attacked; how the mothers danced around confirming their identities, how they condemned them before really knowing the full story. But they decided to give everyone the benefit of the doubt. These were Raisin Beach parents, for better or for worse, and they were all in this together.

Ronnie and Lauren came early to help Andrea get ready. Andrea insisted that they didn't have to—she'd hired someone to help clean, ironically a young woman Ronnie knew from Topless Maids. And she'd hired caterers, who brought in trays of finger food and kid snacks and fizzy beverages. But Lauren and Ronnie came anyway. They gathered around Andrea's kitchen island to catch up.

Lauren bobbled Matthew, now a year old, in her arms. "You're getting heavy," she said to the kid, who kicked his feet in delight. There were dark circles under Lauren's eyes, and she seemed a bit ragged—she'd gone back to work remotely for her old gaming company and was managing Matthew on her own sometimes, though she still employed her nanny. But there was something brighter about her, too. She wasn't nearly as fragile, and she wasn't nearly as on edge—or, rather, she *was* still on edge, but now she was owning it.

Lauren had come into her own after everything unraveled with Graham. And now that Matthew was a year old, her hormones had begun to level out. Graham's absence probably helped. So did stopping breastfeeding—she'd switched to formula, "and let me tell you," she'd said to her friends, "it is a fucking *relief*."

Or maybe she felt more herself because she no longer felt as ashamed. She'd joined a support group of other women who'd experienced postpartum rage, too, and it seemed her experience wasn't that abnormal. Tons of women were hiding these terrible thoughts from their spouses, their friends, their families. As they all talked about it, they felt seen and heard and normalized. And with them, she didn't have to hide. It helped she was working again, too. Right now, she was working on a fantasy game involving dragons and gnomes . . . and loving it. So there was that. Another identity, finally, after all this time.

"Have you heard from . . . you know?" Andrea asked, lowering her voice as if Matthew might guess who they were talking about.

Lauren shook her head. "I can't bring myself to go yet."

Graham was serving a prison sentence for Piper's attack, though he was still trying to appeal it. But Piper had identified Graham at the scene, which pretty much doomed his chances. "Maybe when Matthew's bigger, I don't know. But not now." Then Lauren held up a finger. "Though my family visited last week from back east. It was really nice. Funny, I thought they all found me ridiculous, but they kept gawking at Raisin Beach, saying how fantastic my life was. My sister Mel even said she envied me because I didn't have to deal with a husband." She rolled her eyes. "Which, I mean, was probably too soon to joke about, but I was weirdly flattered. Oh! And guess who met us for lunch one of the days?" She paused dramatically. "Graham's old boss. Gracie."

The women widened their eyes—they'd heard about Gracie.

But Lauren and Gracie Lord had struck up a friendship, and these days, Lauren . . . well, she *liked* her. Gracie was quintessentially California and Hollywood and ridiculous, but she cut through the bullshit, and Lauren now saw that not as a threat but instead as something refreshing. Gracie had also paid for a lot of spa days for Lauren *and* offered to pay for Clarissa to help with the baby while Lauren went back to work, but Lauren hadn't been ready.

"I think she still feels guilty," Lauren admitted. "There was a lot she should have warned me about. But how do you know what line to cross with a couple? Graham was telling her his own version of the truth, and she believed that." She shrugged. "She's a lot of fun. And you know what? I'm kind of coming around to *Ketchup*. When I watched it with Graham to prepare for him working there, I thought it was kind of dumb, but now I'm into the characters. And there's this frazzled mother in the latest season—I think she based it on me." Her eyes sparkled.

There was a shout from the yard, and everyone's heads popped up. Arthur and Esme were playing on the swing set Andrea had installed a few months back. Lane stood a few paces away, watching them. Reginald was also there, nursing a beer. The two guys were having an impassioned conversation about something.

"What a bromance," Andrea murmured, chuckling. After Reginald became more of a fixture in Andrea's life, they'd had Ronnie, Lane, and Esme over for dinner a lot.

"It's a lot of *Lane this, Lane that*," Andrea went on. "But I'm never going to knock someone for volunteering. I doubt Reginald would ever give up his day job, though. His first loves are trees and shrubs." She grinned.

"And what about *your* good works?" Lauren asked Andrea. "That still going okay?"

Andrea nodded. "Better than okay." Carson hadn't made good on his promise to expose Andrea or Jerry, but when the Piper story hit, reporters had taken an interest in the women who'd solved the case. Andrea felt ready to live her truth. She hired a media trainer, and they'd come up with a strategy of how they were going to release her news and control the story. She did an interview for *People* with a tasteful photo shoot. She did a chat on Oprah's podcast. More interviews followed. Each time, Andrea reminded herself that she was doing this for trans visibility, that maybe this would help someone else struggling. It helped with her stage fright. Sort of.

Not surprisingly, her mother was furious, and she made Andrea's announcement all about herself. Andrea's father basically made a public statement disowning her, though he stopped short at trying to take her child away—probably because, deep down, he didn't want the responsibility. But Max remained steadfastly by her side. They even did a few interviews together. Andrea had never felt so grateful for her brother . . . and certainly never so surprised by a member of her family.

Not long after, Andrea received a phone call from a woman who introduced herself as the guidance director for the St. Sebastian School. It took Andrea a moment to recognize the name—St. Sebastian was the place Piper pretended North attended. The woman, Wendy Reed, said she'd followed Andrea's story and read her blog and message boards; she wondered if Andrea was interested in speaking with some of St. Sebastian's students.

At first Andrea said no. But Wendy explained that St. Sebastian was often a place parents sent their kids when they felt they didn't fit anywhere else. "A lot of our kids are struggling," she said. "With their identities, with their feelings. I can think of a few of them who'd benefit from your story. I'm thinking of just a luncheon or something like that. A small group of kids who might want to talk. We'd pay you, of course."

Andrea had been nervous. What did she have to say to a bunch of teenagers? By the time she was in the little room off the cafeteria where her "group" would take place, her stomach was in knots and she felt even more nauseated than she had speaking to Oprah. But then a few kids filed in. Boys slumped over, fidgety, quiet. When one of them looked up at her, his blue eyes round and yearning, her breath caught in her throat. The yearning in them reminded her of someone.

They talked about normal things—movies, video games, sports, their favorite flavors of ice cream. It felt like a win to get remarks out of them. When a few kids laughed, Andrea sensed it was the first time they'd done so in a while, at least on school grounds.

She met with the same group the next week, and then the next. At that point, they were her kids. They told her things she knew they didn't tell their parents. And then it clicked: she understood why she recognized the yearning. *Was* Roger somewhere out there? She hoped so.

Which then made her realize—Roger was old enough by then to make his own decisions. Find his own path. Now that she'd gone on the record about who she was, maybe it would serve as a beacon for him. If he wanted to reach out—which she hoped he would—now he knew where she was.

The back door slammed. Lane waved to the women as he passed to the fridge. "Just grabbing another water. Kids are thirsty." After he retrieved a bottle, he brushed past Ronnie and squeezed her hand. Ronnie blushed and ducked her head, and her gaze fell to the engagement ring she'd recently begun to wear.

"You guys are so cute," Andrea exclaimed. "Did you set a date yet?"

"Oh, I think we're just going to do something simple," Ronnie said absent-mindedly. "We don't really have the money to throw a big wedding. Lane's parents have offered . . . but I don't know. And anyway, it's not like *I* have any family."

She trailed off with a sad sigh. About a month after Vanessa left town, Ronnie received an envelope in the mail. Inside was paperwork entitled *Termination of Parental Rights*, intended to be filed in Cobalt County, Pennsylvania. Ronnie stared at Vanessa's name at the top of the page for a long time. This was Ronnie's chance to officially adopt Esme. But it still felt like a trick, like too great a gift. She'd tried to call Vanessa to say thank you, to say that she could be part of their lives, but Vanessa didn't answer.

Ronnie found a lawyer in Pennsylvania and got things moving with Vanessa's relinquishment hearing. Vanessa was being responsive, at least to the lawyers—the hearing was scheduled in a few weeks. Ronnie still felt on tenterhooks; she still waited for the other shoe to drop. But then again, she'd also allowed herself to dream. *Esme might get to stay with me. Always. She'll never have to leave. I'll get to worry about normal parenting things, like teenage drama. Texting while driving. Heartbreak.*

Esme was thriving, though. Lane had taught her to read over the holidays—simple sight words, mostly, but it was a start. And Ronnie and Lane were doing great, too. Ronnie said she'd told Lane about Esme and her past, and it had really opened a floodgate between them. They were so vulnerable with each other now, truly soul mates. It had been Lane who'd encouraged Ronnie to go back to work. After a lot of discussion, she'd decided to return to Topless Maids—not as a dancer, but in the office. She'd gone in with a proposal for Bill about how the group could be more of a community.

These days, the girls went out in pairs, same as before, but now they were always the *same* pair. They got to know each other. They didn't always become friends, necessarily, but they knew each other's routines, and they knew to look out for each other if anything got sticky. There was more thorough vetting of the clients now, and an increase in their fees, and the scheduling was all done online. Ronnie also organized regular happy hours for the dancers so they could bond with one another, as the girls at Kittens had done. Ronnie loved watching all of them at the bar as they compared their stories. A lot of them were in school, getting degrees. Some of them had kids, like Ronnie. Some of them were married. They *knew* one another now.

Ronnie knew better than to keep secrets anymore. Secrets ruined you. Though ironically, it was the secrets she and Lane were keeping that bound them together. Countless times she'd wanted to tell the other women what Lane had told her about that day in the hallway, with Piper—especially Lauren's role. But she didn't. It would open up a box that needed to stay closed. In the past. Did she ever glance at Lane across the room and think, *I can't believe it*? Sure. But anyone was capable of rash actions. Anyone was capable of lying. Especially if the lies protected someone else.

The doorbell rang, and they turned. Arthur was already bolting through the house and flinging it open. "King!" he exclaimed. "Mom! It's King!"

In ran King, a floppy-haired four-year-old. He'd also moved to the new preschool that Arthur and Esme attended, even though it was far less flashy than Silver Swans. Following him was his mother, Jane. She wore a whisper-soft cashmere sweater and jeans that accentuated her toothpick-thin legs, and she had cascading tendrils of honey-blond hair. Jane was the sort of woman who made you pause—sort of the way Piper used to. There was a perfection about her, something you were pretty sure you'd never live up to.

"Hello!" Jane called out to Andrea and the others, trilling her fingers. And then, "King! Take off your shoes!"

As though Jane had given some silent go-ahead, the rest of the mothers descended almost at once. It was practically all of them from Esme and Arthur's old Silver Swans class, and a lot of other Silver Swans parents, and some new classmates. They crowded in the doorway en masse; Andrea flitted around them, taking their coats. Ronnie recognized a few from Trader Joe's. Lauren was pretty sure she'd fire-breathed next to the mom in the corner at her awful prenatal yoga class. Andrea had even invited a few parents who sent their kids to St. Sebastian's. There were so *many* of them, filling the space.

"One minute," Andrea murmured to her friends when she returned to the kitchen island. "I win."

"Nah," Lauren said. "It was *three minutes*, not one."

"What? It was like *eight* seconds," Ronnie said. "*I* win."

They burst into laughter. Before the party, they'd taken bets on exactly how long it would take for Raisin Beach mothers to start talking about their children in that specific, competitive way they did best. But these days, it didn't irk them. It was almost endearing, actually. It wasn't like the moms were going to change.

Jane Russell breezed into the kitchen. When she saw the women laughing, she smiled, too. "What's funny?"

"Oh, nothing," Andrea said. "Can I get you something to drink? Sparkling water?"

Jane pursed her lips. "Got anything a little stiffer?"

"Seriously," another parent, Tricia, who also had a child in the Silver Swans fours, had appeared in the kitchen, too. "I had to endure *screaming* in the car on the way over here. I need *something* to take the edge off."

And then, suddenly, more mothers were in the kitchen, comparing all the reasons they needed a drink. One mom's toddler drew all over her brand-new leather couch with a Sharpie. One mom's five-year-old twins had endured back-to-back ER visits for falling off the same piece of playground equipment. Someone's kid shaved the family dog that morning. Someone's kid was keeping a squirrel in her bedroom as a pet.

Ronnie, Andrea, and Lauren all exchanged a glance, both delighted and smug. It was obvious they were all thinking the same thing: these moms were always going to compete, whether it was their kids at their best . . . or their kids at their worst.

"We have wine," Andrea said, the corners of her mouth stretching into a smile. "And beer. And liquor. We have anything, actually."

She turned to get the women their drinks, and when she turned back, the group wanting alcohol had multiplied. And when everyone had been served, it was Jane who raised her glass. "These ladies deserve a toast," she said.

"We do?" Lauren looked startled.

"You *know* why," Jane said meaningfully.

Her voice had an edge. Piper Jovan was a cautionary tale. Her desperation, and all the measures she took to cover it up—maybe it could happen to any of them. And North was just heartbreaking.

Piper was up north somewhere, not incarcerated, per se, but getting the help she needed. But no one had spoken to her. No one was sure they'd ever see her again.

After the holidays, Silver Swans closed its doors for good; so many teachers left, and the school was so in debt because of all the money the account had to return. Now, in winter, the school sat empty. Leaves clogged its gutters. Its lawn hadn't been mowed. The only people on the property, actually, were Kelsey and her documentary crew; they'd been able to pivot, pitch Hulu again, and start a project about Silver Swans and the spectacular way it went down in flames. Lauren spoke to Kelsey occasionally, and she hinted that she was *this close* to getting an interview with Piper, and if Lauren knew of any moms who wanted to go on the record, she knew where to find her.

But neither Lauren nor her friends wanted to go on the record. They were surprised that most of the other parents didn't, either. It all felt a little too personal . . . and after this year, maybe not the message she wanted to project. Sure, a lot of people would want to see perfect-seeming Piper's life collapse like a house of cards, but really, Piper wasn't that different than anyone else. It was so easy to trick yourself into believing the thing you needed to believe to get you through. That you were successful. That your actions were warranted. That the child you lost was still here.

If Piper's expectations were different—if the *world* was

different—would this have happened to her? Or maybe she would have cut herself some slack.

"Cheers," Jane said, holding up her glass. "To quite the trio of ladies."

The three of them looked at one another and held in a laugh—funny that these mothers, who strove for the same ideals Piper did, were toasting *them*. But maybe, in a funny way, Lauren, Andrea, and Ronnie had it figured out more than most. They weren't perfect. Their pasts weren't perfect. Sometimes they slept late. Sometimes they let their kids eat junk food. There was too much screen time and not enough vegetables, and Esme slept in the bed with Ronnie and Lane most of the time.

But they were becoming okay with it. Their whole lives, they'd been hit over the head with directives on how to be perfect—do this, don't do *that*, shame on you if you do. It had ruined Piper. It had almost ruined them. But it didn't have to—for anyone. Maybe there was something to be said for just doing their best. Life was messy and tangled and both long and achingly short. Parenting was tedious and precious and no one, *no one* was doing it right. But at least they had one another now. And together, they'd never let one another feel badly.

Lauren looked at her friends and held up her glass. "To us," she said. And they clinked, knowing they deserved it, and knowing that no matter how badly they messed up, they were *trying*. And that was what mattered.

Acknowledgments

The writing and revising of this novel occurred at a very strange time in history—COVID-19, so much social unrest, and everything else that 2020 threw at us. As I wrote this story, much of the world felt unstable, uncertain, and in flux, though as a result, I felt even more inspired to acknowledge the struggles of motherhood and how it's not always about being the "best" or "perfect" but accepting where you're at and cutting yourself some slack. And I can't thank my team at Dutton for following and supporting me through this journey. That includes my fantastic editor, Maya Ziv, her assistant and co-reader, Hannah Feeney, copy editor Andrea Monagle, production editor Alice Dalrymple, Caroline Payne and Rebecca Odell on the marketing/PR team, and my amazing book jacket designer, Dominique Jones.

Thanks also to Andy McNicol at WME for guiding me to tell this story, Laura Bonner for seeing it through in its end stages, and Richard Abate at 3 Arts for your continued support. Also, enormous thanks to Alice Gorelick for your careful read for Andrea. And thanks to the many moms I spoke with who shared their parenting ups and downs, whether it be close friends, social media connections, or wise words I listened to on the many, many fabulous parenting podcasts out there in the world. A big thanks to my own mother, Mindy, for providing an exemplary motherhood guide and endless love, and to my husband, Michael, for giving me space to write this during a very stressful time in all our lives. And thanks to my kids, Kristian and Henry, because without you, I wouldn't be as versed in this world. What on earth would I be writing about?

And also, a big hug to mothers far and wide. It's tough to be a parent these days—especially in the past year. But seriously, you're doing great.

About the Author

SARA SHEPARD is the number one *New York Times* bestselling author of the Pretty Little Liars series. She has also written other young adult series and novels, including *The Lying Game*, *The Heiresses*, and *The Perfectionists*.